BLOOD OF EMBER

THE CROWNS OF TALAM

LE VAN VEEN

storied stars

First edition November 2024

Published by Storied Stars Books

Cover Design by Story Wrappers

Interior Illustrations by Nathan Hansen

Copy and Developmental Editing by Becky Wallace

Proofreading by Noah Sky

Map by Alyssa Hurlbert

Author Photo by Marigold Visuals Photography

ISBN 979-8-9892243-3-3 (e-book)

ISBN 979-8-9892243-4-0 (paperback)

ISBN 979-8-9892243-5-7 (hardcover)

www.LEVanVeen.com

*To those with hopes and dreams that burn within their very blood,
may you breathe life to every last one.*

BOOKS IN THE CROWNS OF TALAM SERIES

Under Cold Moons
Blood of Ember

Fuar
GEIMHRIGH
Sruthar
FOMHAR
Tusnua Sea
BRIONGLOID
Caillte
EILEAN
Omra
N
W
E
S

World of Talam
Beannaithe Sea
Scamhog
BITU
Scamall
EARRACH
Blathriel
SAMHRADH

THE VOICES OF TALAM

AISLING (AISLA) TARKIS

ash • ling, (ash • la), ee • ark • iss
Mathair Apparent of Eilean | The Gheall Ceann | The Mallaithe

WEYLIN MYRKOR

way • lynn, mur • core
Udar Apparent of Iomlan | The Young Wolf

RANIA DORCAS

ruh • knee • uh, door • cass
The Gem of Dreams

RUAIRI VILULF

roor • ee, vil • ulf
Eilean's Scout and Sailor

EIRE TRYGG

air • uh, trig
Eilean's Joy and Believer

CALLUM RONAN

call • um, roan • in
The Captain of the Udar Apparent's Personal Guard

ESOS IN TALAM

ASHER
the esos of flames
begins with an itching of the palms

TSUNA
the esos of water
begins with the feeling of dry mouth

TERRAN
the esos of nature
begins with the chattering of teeth

ZEPHYS
the esos of winds
begins with a rush of wind in the ear

SHADOW
the dark esos
begins with a ringing in the ears

MENDER
the healing esos
begins with sounds feeling muted

SHIFTER
the esos of shifting
begins with transformation of body

PRYER
the esos of mind manipulation
begins with the eyes going white

SEER
the esos of future sight
begins with the hands growing cold

THE GODS

EABHA

ay • va

goddess of wisdom,
mother of the gods

CION

kee • on

god of beauty,
love, and fate

SIONNA

see • on • uh

goddess of mischief,
discord, and war

LEIGHIS

lay • hiss

goddess of healing
and harvest

IFREANN

if • run

god of death,
ruler of Hel

OF TALAM

TARAN

tear • in

goddess of thunder,
protector of mortals

MUIR

moor

god of the seas
and waterways

AIRDEALL

are • dell

goddess of the heavens,
protector of ancients

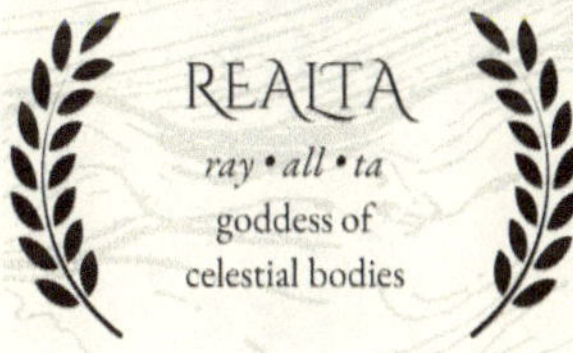

REALTA

ray • all • ta

goddess of
celestial bodies

THE NORNS

weavers of fate

THE GREAT

EILEAN

eye • lee • an

The Forgotten Realm

SAMHRADH

sour • rah

The Wolves' Den

EARRACH

are • rah

The Realm of Hope

GEIMHRIGH

gev • ree

The Frozen Realm

HOUSES OF TALAM

BRIONGLOID

[bring • loyd]

The Realm of Dreams

FOMHAR

[fove • err]

The Realm of Abundance

BITU

bite • oo

The Realm of Life

TAISTEALAI

The soft hums of a lullaby from the days the ancients walked Talam reached Taistealai's ears from where he crept along eerily silent hallways.

His chest was heavy as he listened to the song of the mother who grieved for the future of her daughter. Tensions had grown within Castle Farraige since the last time the squirrel that served as messenger to the gods found his way there.

Always in the dark. Always through the shadows. Never to be seen. Never to be heard.

As the norns willed it.

The door creaked shut and the mother's soft footsteps paused outside of the room, followed by a long, shaky exhale. Taistealai nestled into the hallway's corner behind long green curtains. Guilt gnawed at him. He should not be here, but he could not resist the urge to visit the young elf on the eve of her seventh naming day. The following sunrise, she would begin her schooling. It was yet to be known if she would train as a world teller, medic, harvester, laoch, sailor, scout, hunter, priestess, or choose another path entirely. She would have four years to make her choice.

The gods and goddesses had placed bets on her chosen path. Both of her parents had been world tellers, so many assumed that was the route she would take, but Taistealai had visited the halls enough to see the fire that burned in her eyes—a fire that did not exist within the eyes of her parents or her grandmother. A fire that could not be contained forever. A fire that he had only ever seen in the eyes of a god.

Taistealai expected Aisling Iarkis's demeanor to lead her down a path entirely different from either of her parents'. One that would serve better to protect her as the *Gheall Ceann*.

A second pair of footsteps approached. Taistealai's ears perked towards them. His nose twitched as he caught the scent of the grand-mother—the ruling Mathair of Talam.

"I was not expecting to see you tonight," Aine Iarkis's voice was strained as she sniffed away the sorrow she would not allow the matri-arch to see.

"I did not realize my presence need be announced within the walls of my own home," Cliona Iarkis's voice was laced with an iciness that sent a chill down Taistealai's back.

"That is not how I meant it," Aine replied, slowly, carefully. "Aisla is already asleep, if you were hoping to visit with her. She has a long day ahead of her. She needs the rest."

"It is not her I wished to see."

"Then it was me, I suppose?"

Anxiousness filled the air, which told Taistealai that Aine knew exactly why Cliona had sought her out. It would be a conversation she had been hoping to avoid. Taistealai's ears burned with the sensation of being a voyeur to moments not meant for his ears or eyes. Never-theless, he was always invested in keeping up with the state of the Iarkises, especially since Aisling's birth.

"I cannot let you continue to ignore the risk she poses as she begins training. It would be against my responsibilities as the Mathair —against my responsibilities to the people of Eilean."

"You cannot tell me you hope to hold her from scoil. How will she ever learn to control it if she doesn't begin now?" Aine hissed, fighting to keep her voice low as they had not strayed far from the door to the bedroom of her sleeping daughter. "She needs this. She needs the opportunity to live among her peers, if she is to find the right path."

"One thing about your child, Aine," Cliona's voice heightened with authority. "She will never be normal. You'd do yourself, my son, and her a favor by giving up such folly sooner rather than later. Her fate is in the hands of the norns, but it is up to us to guide it. We need to mentor her, yes, but we need to protect those around us, as well. We both know what the realms on the main continent think of her. Our island has been exiled in hopes of stifling her. We must prove them wrong, and that begins by showing them we can keep our own safe from her outbursts."

Taistealai's eyes widened, and his two tails twitched nervously. He had heard nothing of these outbursts from the norns or the gods. Most of the time, the esos of elves did not begin to show until age fifteen. It was considered rare if esos showed before then.

But this female would be able to wield all nine forms of esos. She would be the rarest of them all. And she was hardly seven.

"And what do you propose?" A deeper voice entered the conversation. Taistealai had not heard him approach.

It was the voice of the father.

"I will train her myself," Cliona stated with a decisiveness that said she would not be argued with.

Taistealai froze in place, and it seemed the rest of the world had, too. There was something sinister in the tone of the Mathair. Something chilling that was all too reminiscent of a being Taistealai knew far too well. He hadn't noticed it before, not until that moment. There was a scent of the viper that clung to the Mathair, like mildew on old cloth. He had long feared Sionna's interference in the prophecy and the lives it affected, but he could never know how far she would go.

How far she would go in disobedience of her mother, Eabha.

It was easy to manipulate a mind motivated by power. Taistealai had seen it happen far too many times.

His ears perked and his nose twitched as Taistealai leaned forward, listening closely, and wondering if it was his paranoia that had blinded him from sensing it sooner, or something beyond it. He could only hope it was the former.

"Absolutely not," Aine protested with a sneer, growing bolder in the presence of her mate. Something like pride filled Taistealai's chest at her defiance. "She needs others her age. She needs to see them learning—others with the same esos that runs through her veins. You only possess one of nine, as do we."

"You may train her," Feargal interrupted. "They do not teach esos in scoil this young, and I agree that her exposure in this area is necessary. But," the elf continued, and he could feel the two females tense, more than ready to argue with him, "she will begin scoil with her peers tomorrow, as she is meant to. She needs to integrate with her people. One day she will lead them, and how would it look for her to lead a people she spent her whole life locked away from? They will learn to fear her as Iomlan does, if we treat her the way they do. It would only be natural for them to wonder why we choose to keep her secluded."

"Others already speak of her seclusion," Cliona said through clenched teeth.

Feargal's compromise was evidently not enough for her.

"That is enough," Feargal's voice deepened with anger. "If Aine agrees, it will be so."

Hesitancy lingered in the air, and Taistealai itched with the need to move and break the stillness.

"That seems suitable, for now," Aine answered with carefully chosen words. "You may speak with Aisling after her first day to see when she would like to begin working with you."

"As you wish." The grandmother spoke in a way that said this would not be the end of the conversation.

"Good night, Mother," Feargal said dismissively.

Taistealai held his breath as he dared peer out at the trio. Aine elected silence, as her mate wrapped a protective arm around her shoulders. The couple made their way down the hallway towards their own rooms, completely unaware of the messenger of the gods.

Taistealai turned his attention to Cliona, where she stood. He watched her long, slender fingers curl into fists, and there was a gleam to her yellow-green eyes that made Taistealai want to run as far as he could from the castle of the forgotten realm. It was the gleam of someone willing to sacrifice selfishly for power; but to what end, he could not say.

He waited as his claws twitched with an urgency he could not explain. At last, she turned on her heel.

Once she was long gone and out of sight, and only when Taistealai was sure she was sound asleep, he took off on unsteady legs to Crann Na Beatha. He was eager to exchange words with the dragon who lingered at the base of his home, awaiting news of the *Gheall Ceann*.

PART ONE
RUINS OF FAMILIAR

I
AISLA

The ash tree splintered beneath the force of Aisla's blow. Blood coated her cracked knuckles.

Again. Again. Again.

She grit her teeth through the pain of it. Dark shadows crept into the corners of her vision, and a ringing sounded in her ears.

Again. Again. Again.

A flash of amber eyes. The snarls of a raging barghest. Folk tunes played in a village across the sea. A roaring river. A flash of amber eyes.

It wouldn't stop.

Again. Again. Again.

A hand grabbed her shoulders.

Aisla whirled around, teeth bared, prepared to meet the amber gaze that haunted her sleep. But those eyes were not his.

Her arms dropped to her sides as the shadows retreated to the depths of her mind and the ringing ceased. She met the wide hazel eyes of one of her students.

Embarrassment heated Aisla's cheeks as she tucked her battered hands behind her back and out of sight. But she could not conceal the blood that dripped to the forest floor.

"Are you okay?" Roisin asked in a voice both eager and wary. "Ruairi has been worried about you. We all have."

"I'm fine," Aisla snapped back, defensively.

She hadn't meant to speak to Roisin that way—to let the way Ruairi's name riled her and the ever-present guilt in her chest show. It was guilt she had only learned to cope with through anger, through a rage seated so deeply she feared it had become a permanent part of herself.

"You could come back," Roisin suggested, unfazed by Aisla's reaction. And for that, Aisla was grateful. She had always felt close with Roisin out of all her students. The female was smart, quick, and clever. "We would all be happy to see you home."

Home. The word alone made Aisla wince.

"That place is no longer a home for me."

Aisla could not call a place she had failed so miserably home. She could not give herself that honor. Aside from that, there was a selfish part of her that was not ready to face Eire again, or what was left of her. She could not find the words to speak to Ruairi. How could she ever apologize enough? How could she expect him to forgive her when she could not forgive herself? No words she could speak would undo what was done. No utterance from her lips would bring the spark of life back to his eyes, and she would miss it until her dying breath.

And then there was Cliona. Their last conversation that had shaken the walls of Aisla's baile. She was certain the entire city of Caillte had heard the bile spewed between the two females. The words they had speared each other's way were meant to maim and scar.

She did not have a home any longer. She had not since the sunrise that followed her return to Eilean.

"Just know, to us it's still your home," Roisin insisted, softly.

Aisla watched the young elf's face fall. Her hope was dampened by half a conversation, and Aisla hated herself for it, but she could not stop herself.

She took a deep breath and turned on her heel.

"Go home, Roisin. And tell Ruairi not to bother sending any more students my way."

Her heart fractured along familiar lines as his name left her lips for the first time since she'd last seen him.

Roisin did not reply, but Aisla did not expect her to. She made for her tent she had set up to the south of the wyvern caves. Shame turned her stomach that they knew where she was, and where she had run to. She had seen Gaotha flying through the skies on more than one occasion with her red-haired rider, and knew Ruairi had scouted out where she was living. She wasn't mad at him for it. Aisla knew he would not be able to rest if he did not know she was somewhere safe —somewhere he could reach her. And she found comfort in seeing him, too.

Aisla caught a glimpse of emerald-green scales reflecting in the light of the dawn sun between the trees of the Tus Forest. Muinin gathered himself to his feet and made to greet her as she approached. She knew he missed the wyvern caves, and the wyverns that were his own family. But greater than the longing to be among his own was his need to protect her. He had hardly left her side since the moment he rescued her from the home of the Udar.

Even now, the thought of the male made her fists clench and bile rose to the back of her throat. She could not think of the Udar without also thinking of his son—of the Young Wolf, and the moments shared between them. It was in the darkest hours of the night that their whispered secrets, their long days, and the way that their lips had met on the bank of the rushing river haunted her.

Sometimes, she even longed for the friendship they had built over their few sunrises spent together. That longing was often followed by a guilt so strong she would empty whatever was left in her stomach.

While she had been fraternizing with the enemy, Ruairi had been tortured at the hand of the Young Wolf's father. While she had been enjoying wine and a night beneath stars in a tribe far away, Eire had been fighting a losing battle with the lofa that ravaged their land and their people like no other illness ever had before. Eire had been one of its earliest victims. It was a plague her realm would not soon recover from—if it ever got the chance to.

It was unforgivable, what she had caused. And it made her question the interpretations of the prophecy she found herself at the center of.

There was no written translation in any record across the realms. Only whispers on the wind spoke of an elf born into the richest bloodline in the ninth generation, who would be given the source of all nine forms of esos and would end up with the power to save or end the nine realms of Talam. The norns had confirmed that Aisla was indeed that elf upon her birth nineteen years ago.

Every realm was quite opinionated on the matter one way or the other, but the great house of Samhradh believed Aisla would cause the demise of Talam as they knew it, and that was all that mattered. They held such power that no one would dare stand against them.

Not anymore.

Then, Aisla had begun the Inevitable War with a call to Muinin. It was never lost on her what that choice would mean. During a time when wyverns were banished along with the rest of Eilean, it had been declared an act of war to send one to the main continent, Iomlan, that housed the other six worldly realms, but Aisla had seen no other choice. Not when Ruairi's life would've been the price to pay.

Aisla could only hope her name would be enough to rally realms willing to put their belief in her.

But as the norns wove the golden thread of her fate faster than she could comprehend, she had to wonder which it was. Which version of the prophecy she had stumbled into.

Would she find a way to save the realms from destruction? Or was every move she made playing into a doom foretold?

A shudder travelled through her as she shook her head of tangled, mousy brown hair. She reached out and ran a hand along Muinin's familiar scales.

She let out a long breath at the comfort he radiated. She had taken enough supplies to last a while longer at their makeshift camp. Aisla would have a few more sunrises before she would decide between hunting for her next meal or stooping low enough to raid the kitchens of Caillte at night. She had also considered going to a nearby city when the time came.

Muinin curled up outside of Aisla's tent, and Aisla settled against his warm body, not ready to retreat into the tent yet. She matched her breathing to his and closed her eyes, allowing her head to fall back and the crisp air of new spring to envelop her. Her fingers absentmindedly toyed with the necklace made of twine and nine pieces of wyvern tooth that fit snug against her throat.

Her esos had gone cold since flames had erupted from her palms in Eire's infirmary room. The power had retreated from her, as she had from the rest of the world. It had sunk so deeply into her blood; she no longer felt a trace of the whispering rush that had once been as natural as breathing. She could not blame it. This power—she did not wish to be burdened with it—and it seemed it did not wish to be burdened with her.

She could feel it enough to know it was still there, that it was not fortunate enough to escape her altogether. She didn't know how or if she would ever be able to reach it again.

And Aisla did not know if she wanted to.

"You do not deserve a lick of that esos the gods have blessed you with," Cliona had shouted, the sunrise following her return to Eilean.

"Blessed?" Aisla had snarled with the force of a thousand barghests.

"Call it what it is. Call it a curse, just like the damned lofa. Call me your mallaithe. *Call me what you will, but don't you dare call me blessed."*

"You're right," Cliona snapped back. She had stepped forward then until they were a mere sword's length apart. Aisla's chest heaved with anger, and her hands itched with the urge to react. "You have led us further down the path of dusk than I would have imagined possible at your young age. You have proven to Iomlan that they were right to exile us here. And how should I fix this now? How do you expect me to stop a war that you have declared entirely on your own? Aisla, there are forces we could not even hope to stand against in our wildest dreams—"

"You think I don't know that?" Aisla roared, clenching her fists so tightly she could feel her knuckles pushing against her skin. Her esos had not riled with her emotions as it usually did. It was a lonely feeling. "I am fully aware of my own faults that led us here—painfully so—of each and every misstep. But what about you? How did you help me when you kept my esos for your own molding, until I hardly knew my own power? How did you expect any of your half-assed plan to turn out for Ruairi? Or did you even care?"

"One life would've been a fair price in exchange for the cure to save your people."

"Oh, the cure that never existed? And that one life—that one life was Ruairi Vilulf, and his one life is worth a thousand of yours."

Cliona struck her then.

Across her left cheek.

With such force that Aisla's shaking knees gave out, and she was sent sprawling to the floor, hot tears of anger streaming down her red cheeks. She hardly felt the pain that seared from the arrow wound just above her ankle. She glared up into the eyes of their Mathair and wondered how there could have ever been love there.

All that she saw was the rage that reflected her own.

"You will not speak to me that way, ever again. Whenever I next see your wretched face, it will be far too soon."

Cliona left her baile, and Aisla left Caillte.

She packed her bags like the coward she was.

There was a moment when she paused outside of Ruairi's door—a moment when she held her fist to it, prepared to knock and prepared to collapse into his open arms. She would have done anything for his comfort and that familiar scent of ash and mint.

There was a moment when she hesitated, waiting there, and praying to the gods that he would just happen to open his door and see her there, so she did not have to be selfish enough to knock and take what she did not deserve.

When the door did not open on its own, and her prayers went unanswered, she slid the small silver ring with an emerald gem under the door to his baile. She could not bear the way it called to her, and she knew his wariness of it was safer than her curiosity for it.

Once it left her hand, she turned on her heel, silent tears rushing down warm cheeks, and left.

She did not look back. Not one time.

Aisla had not cried since. She had not the energy to.

Her legs felt restless as those memories flooded her brain. She would give anything for even a moment of peace and quiet within her mind. All the same, her bones ached with the need to do something, but she had already done far too much. It seemed any action by her hands was cursed.

Her eyes blinked open, and she reached inside of her pack to retrieve the deep green book she had taken from the library before it all had gone awry. She opened it where she left off, near the very beginning. Her spot was held by the letter Cliona had demanded. Aisla had sworn up and down that she didn't have it. And when Cliona had torn through her things, wrecked her entire baile, she had not checked the sock Aisla wore, where she had tucked it away against her skin.

In just the few pages, Aisla had read in *The Dawn of Talam*, she had found a story she had never heard of in scoil.

The story of an empty Talam.

A Talam where only the norns and the gods existed. Taistealai, messenger of the gods, had not even yet come to be.

It told a tale of peace. A peace that could not last while the dark goddess dwelled among them.

Sionna, goddess of mischief. Goddess of discord. Goddess of war.

2
RUAIRI

Ruairi Vilulf looked up from the stale bread held in constantly shaking hands when he caught sight of Roisin returning. It was easy to spot her when hardly anyone was awake yet.

But no one trailed behind Roisin.

He had expected as much, if he was being honest with himself. All the same, he could not stop his heart from sinking. He gave Roisin a knowing nod, and she returned the gesture with a sad smile before carrying off towards her baile to get ready for the day ahead.

It had been her idea. She had approached him after class to ask if he had heard from Aisla, to which he had given the honest answer of "no." She asked if he knew where she was and if she could go to her and invite her back home.

Ruairi couldn't deny her, not when she was so hopeful. Aisla might not realize it amongst everything that had gone wrong, but there was a generation under them. And they were a generation of elves who believed in the good of her esos. They believed in a prophecy that promised a liberator. And his students—their students —believed Aisla to be that liberator. He was there to witness their shock when they heard of Aisla's retreat. It was not in line with the character they knew her to be. The laoch who had once trained at their sides would have never abandoned them in their time of need. He would never forget the sunrise after the word had spread by the whispers on the wind. It was that dawn that nearly every soul in Caillte ran to him, asking if it was true.

And they had been shocked again to learn that he knew nothing.

He still believed in Aisla. Nothing short of death would make him stop. He still hoped she would return of her own accord, and they could start working together again in the face of the Inevitable War, as they had come to call it. Eilean did not have allies—not a one. They did not have strength or a prepared force of laochs large enough to even think they stood a chance in the face of their enemies. Especially not without Aisla. With their *Gheall Ceann* among them, Ruairi felt they could at least hope for something more than inevitable destruction.

All that she had left behind for him was that haunting silver ring that warmed his pocket. She had slipped it under the crack of his door without so much as a note. He did not blame her. Not entirely. They had both experienced their own traumas and trials on Iomlan during their sunrises spent apart, but he had imagined they would get through them together. As they always had.

Now, when he needed her most, he was more alone than he had ever been.

His finger grazed along the icy edge of the metal. The ring held secrets, that much Ruairi was certain of. Secrets that would change more than just Aisla's life.

He intended to investigate it more. He needed to find out what made the ring feel so alive, as though it had a heart beating to its very own dark rhythm. It called to his esos in a way that made his blood turn uncomfortably beneath his skin. But there had hardly been time to do so.

Even more, he needed to know where it came from, and how it was made. And whatever it was, it held a power. Why would Cliona want to give this power to their enemy? They were all answers Ruairi needed, but he did not know where to begin.

With war on the horizon—a war that had been declared to save his life—he was training students from almost dawn until dusk every day. It was all he could do to prepare the people of Eilean for whatever was coming their way when the Udar decided to act on their declaration.

Everyone was on edge, and understandably so. No one knew exactly what Muinin's flight to Iomlan would mean for them. Only that it gave the Udar permission to begin the Inevitable War at his own leisure. Eilean would be foolish to act first. They had nothing benefiting them, and the best they could do would be to prepare their people and their home.

So that is what Ruairi did.

With a sigh, Ruairi stood from the table where he took his breakfast alone. He had some time before his first training class. He made his way to the infirmary, as he did each sunrise. It was a chilly walk. Ruairi inhaled deep, calming breaths, readying himself for the unfamiliar face that was becoming familiar.

It killed him that each visit to Eire solidified that new, mangled vision of her in his mind. Every time he saw her, the memories of her brilliant blue eyes and lively smile grew further and further away from the reality of what she'd become. Ruairi made an effort to see her, even though she still did not remember the full extent of their friendship from before the lofa. He couldn't bear for her to believe that her friends had abandoned her. Her parents still visited. They continued sending up prayers to silent gods each sunrise and each dusk. Ruairi would pass them in the halls, and they would thank him for coming each time. It made him uncomfortable—their gratitude. As if he visited her out of obligation, and not longing to reconnect to what they once shared.

They had stopped asking if Aisla would visit soon.

The plague victims, who could no longer be considered real, living souls, still haunted the long-forgotten shop-turned-holding area that Edi had showed him upon his return to Eilean. They had begun to call them husks. It was the only word they found fitting for their peculiar state of being. The medics had yet to decide what to do with them.

Ruairi had told no one yet of their existence in Samhradh. He had not found the words to, and didn't know who he would even tell. He would soon. He could no longer carry the burden of being the only one to know, even though he was not yet certain of what it all meant.

The menders had gotten used to seeing him enter their halls. They no longer escorted him through the building. They merely nodded whenever he crossed through the threshold.

Ruairi paused outside of the door to Eire's room. There was a rustle of sheets and a sharp gasp. He pushed the door open and stepped quickly into the room.

"You okay, Eir?" he asked, looking about the seemingly untouched room.

She was sitting upright, her eyes wide and her hair wild.

"What are you doing here?" She snapped, ignoring his questions as her head turned, and her glazed eyes locked onto his.

"Just stopping by, as usual," Ruairi replied, ignoring her attitude. He pulled up a chair and settled beside her bed. He never knew exactly what he would be walking into, but it was not uncommon for her to lash out upon his arrival.

"It is a waste of your breath and your time," she spoke through a mouth that had deteriorated until her teeth showed through a hole in her skin. Ruairi had grown used to the grotesque sight of her, and her new, distant voice no longer sent a chill through his blood. "It is far too late for me. Your time is better spent preparing for the conflict you founded."

"Who told you about that?" Ruairi asked, curiosity lacing his tone.

She had yet to bring up the war.

"You think I don't hear the whispers these walls carry? They can only hold them so long before the secrets seep through cracks and into my own ears. Nothing can remain hidden forever."

Ruairi paused to ponder the meaning of her words, parsing through their cryptic nature. He had to assume she overheard the menders speaking of it at some point or another.

"And how do you feel about it? The coming conflict?"

"Our lost realm will fall. I don't know how anyone could hope for anything other. It would be foolish," she spoke, and her eyes focused past him to a place on the wall that he did not bother turning around to see.

"Without hope, what do we have, Eire?"

"A view of what is to come. The ability to grasp a realistic future."

"I'll remain here in the land of the fools then, I think," Ruairi said, to which she did not reply.

He pressed his lips into a thin line. The lofa had really brought out the cynic in her. It seemed to have destroyed all the positivity and hope she had once radiated like rays of sun.

"And what of your gods?" Ruairi questioned, hoping to pull out that one thing Eire held on to despite it all.

"My gods," she hissed back. She tilted her head to the side and locked her eyes onto his. "They deal punishment as they see fit. What we have done to call upon their wrath, I do not know. But how could I when I remain here, away from the outside world—away from the games of mortals who wish to play as ancients?"

Ruairi remained silent when he sensed more words lingered on her tongue. He would wait for her to loose them.

"For all I know, the punishment is a consequence of your friend. The one who burned me."

Anger rushed to his chest at her indication and a familiar guilt entwined with it.

"She is *our* friend," was all he could reply. Eire said nothing. She only continued to gaze at him with eyes that looked through him.

Ruairi drew in a long, shaky breath. He allowed his emotional reaction to fall from his shoulders, and willed it to dissipate until he was left only with the placid calm he had taught himself to find.

"Shall we read now? I think it's time to start a new story."

Eire's pale eyes brightened, and she nodded ever so slightly. When he first began visiting, she did not speak at all. His initial visit with Aisla broke any trust there was between them. Aisla's flames had made Eire so fearful of not only Aisla, but him too. There was no logic to it, but he wouldn't dare tell her that.

So, when he knew he would need to rebuild the friendship that once lay between them, he read and she would listen. Then he would leave with an unanswered farewell. Each visit, he read to her from storybooks for the younger elves, and she seemed to enjoy it so he continued.

And with time came a greeting, no matter how snappy, and eventually small conversations as well. And he would keep coming back while there was still breath in her chest.

Ruairi pulled the storybook from his pack. He flipped through the parchment until he reached the page that began the story of the young elf who earned the title of Dragon in his conversation with Taistealai, the ever-evasive messenger of Eire's elusive gods with two tails and four bright green eyes.

"There once was a young elf who longed for an immortality like the gods' . . ." Ruairi began, and Eire leaned forward, clasping her hands in her lap.

3
AISLA

There was a chill in the air at sunrise when Aisla pulled Muinin's leathers out. She did not know where they were going, only that she needed to get away from her makeshift camp for a time. Her restless mind turned into a restless body, and she could no longer stand it.

She approached Muinin, and his golden eyes blinked open ever so slightly, but he did not lift his head.

"Morning, sleepyhead," Aisla teased. "Time to wake up."

Muinin let out a deep groan and nestled his head back into his wing. It wasn't like him to want to sleep in late.

"Come on," Aisla said as she laid a hand on his scaled neck. "What are you doing?"

After a pause, Muinin lifted his head and slowly, intentionally, turned it towards the west. He gave her a pointed look out of the corner of his eye without turning his head.

He looked towards Caillte. Towards Castle Farraige, Cliona, Ruairi, and Eire.

"And what of it?" Aisla snapped. Her arm that held his leathers fell limp to her side.

Muinin chuffed again before turning his head and then jerking it towards Caillte again. He made his message clear, then curled up on the ground where his body had left an impression on the soil.

"You can't be serious," Aisla grumbled. "I can't go back there."

Muinin ignored her, closing his eyes and feigning sleep. If she could ever master the esos of shifters, she would hear his voice, and she wished more than anything that she could. She wished she could tell him all the reasons she had to not return. She wished he was a friend she could speak with, not merely talk at.

"I'm just not ready yet," Aisla said, but even as she spoke the words, she knew they were not true. And she knew Muinin knew it as well.

She lowered herself to the ground and curled up against his side, and he only hesitated a brief, defiant moment before wrapping a massive wing around her, cocooning her in the comfort of his familiarity.

Not that she was not ready, but that she didn't know where to begin. There were so many conversations awaiting her—so many reparations to make—and she did not know where to start.

She did not know if she ever would.

"I know you're right," Aisla murmured to her wyvern. "I do. I just wish things had gone differently."

Muinin let out a low purr in his throat. A sound that said he understood her where words could not. Aisla's eyes fell shut, and she realized just how tired she was. In her body, her mind, her bones. She had not slept well since a night that smelled of red wine.

She turned on her side with a final decision weighing heavy on her heart. But first, she let sleep overcome her. She gave herself that favor, and soon she was enveloped by a darkness that felt nearly too good to be true.

When Aisla awoke, it did not take her long to realize she was not truly awake at all.

She was dreaming, but so very aware of herself that she could feel the stone beneath her bare feet as she padded down a hallway that was all too familiar.

She passed banners of maroon and marigold and statues of wolves. There were portraits of tyrants who had made an enemy of her family.

Her hand shook as she continued in the dim torchlight, but her heart was steel as rage thrummed in the blood of her veins.

She came across a door and a ringing started in her ears, and only because she knew this could not possibly be real, and she knew she was sleeping soundly against Muinin in a realm far away, she pushed it open.

The ringing was replaced by the thunder of her heart and a roar of emotions as she turned to find an enormous bed, with an all too familiar male asleep within it. She was so close; she could see the rise and fall of the Udar Apparent's chest. She bit her lip as her eyes catalogued all the familiar details of his face.

Her heart was torn somewhere between longing for the friend she'd thought she'd made and hatred for the enemy of everything she'd ever loved. She inhaled a deep breath and shook out her hands before she took one step forward.

He turned onto his side, facing her. She froze, but his eyes did not open.

There was something so real about it all, and she knew with every fiber of her being that if she closed the distance between them, and touched her hand to his cheek, she would feel real skin—his skin.

It was a dream, but not.

The possibilities flooded her already racing brain, and she wondered if she had been granted a gift from the gods. Could she end him here and now? She waited for the voice that had once spoken to her, and provided guidance when she needed it most, but just like her esos, it had abandoned her at her lowest moment.

Aisla swallowed around a knot in her throat, then scanned the room for any sort of weapon she could use. Her eyes locked on to a sword that she quickly recognized to be the same blade he had carried with him throughout their entire journey together.

She padded softly over to it, listening for any sound, and was relieved when the male remained asleep.

She laid her hand on the hilt of the blade and an overwhelming sense of power rushed through her. She sucked in a breath as she took the blade in both hands and toyed with the weight of it. A chill cooled her blood, and her mouth dried as she returned to the side of his bed, watching the rise and fall of his chest.

So peaceful and blissfully unaware.

She'd thought of him this way before, when they were in a puball together in Spiorad. He was as afraid as she was, and as comforting as that feeling was, it was also terrifying.

Terrifying, because it was that confession that had made her sympathetic to the male—a feeling she could hardly shake, no matter how badly she needed to.

Tears stung the corners of her eyes as she lifted his blade above her head.

She wondered if it was even possible to bring the male harm in this dreamlike trance. If this was her fate as the *Gheall Ceann* all along. It seemed an awful cowardly fate, and it did not sit right with her.

She closed her eyes, willing a sign from the gods to show itself, and when she opened her eyes, the male was staring back at her.

A gasp escaped her as her grip on the blade tightened, but she did not move. She stood there, waiting to see what he would do.

"What are you doing here, *banphrionsa*?" He spoke, and the very sound of his voice took the air from her lungs. And that nickname. It was all so familiar, so friendly. Her knees grew weak.

She felt as though she was drowning, but she could not let it show —would not let the male glimpse any sight of a weakness from her.

He knew she was not Ellora. And she knew he was not Fenian.

"That's my blade, you know," he said without taking his eyes from her.

"I know," she whispered, and her ears filled with the sound of metal clanging against stone as the blade fell from her hands and suddenly, she was back in Eilean, gasping for air as she jolted up from where she had fallen asleep, curled against Muinin.

Panicked breaths rushed in and out of her lips as she dug her fingers into the soft earth beneath her.

Muinin growled and pulled her in closer to his body with his wing.

She didn't know what it had meant. She didn't know if it was real. She didn't know if Weylin saw her. She didn't know if she should have acted faster.

But she did know that she could not have done it. She would not have been able to bring herself to drop the blade upon his throat, no matter how long she'd stood there.

She snarled a curse under her breath and leaned back against Muinin once again, pulling her knees into her chest.

"It's time," she said aloud, even though there was no one around to hear except for Muinin.

It did not take her long to pack her few belongings she had brought with her from home. She had been running short on supplies, anyway.

She hoisted her pack onto her shoulders, and felt pressure building in the pit of her stomach. The night had brought many emotions, ranging from fear to regret to relief, but most of all, it served as a reminder of all she had been running from.

And she could not run forever, only stall. And the time for stalling had passed.

Aisla walked to Muinin, bossy Muinin, and placed a gentle kiss on the tip of his long snout. He blinked slowly at her, and there was a look in his eyes that shone with pride. It was a look that gave her the courage to take the steps that would lead her back to Caillte and all that awaited her there.

"Thank you," she murmured.

He chuffed in response, before taking to the skies, back to the wyvern caves where he belonged.

And then she was alone once again.

It felt like a ghost of the past as it caressed her cheek with a taunting familiarity. It was a phantom of the last time she had been completely alone, looking for an ally, only to fall for the lies of an enemy.

Aisla shook her head, willing the feeling to release her—willing the ghost to remove its hand and return to the realm of the dead, where it belonged. But it did not. It only held on as she took that first step.

With a heavy heart, she began her journey to a house that felt less and less like a home the closer she got.

Aisla walked around the outskirts of Caillte to avoid running into anyone who would recognize her. She took a long route that wound around the city, so she could enter behind a cluster of bailes near hers.

It was dark. The sun had disappeared below the trees a little while after Caillte had first entered Aisla's field of vision.

Aisla pulled her cloak over her head, concealing herself in the dark of dusk as she took the two wooden stairs to the stoop of the baile.

She closed her eyes and drew in a breath that filled her chest with cool air, and lifted her hand to knock on the wooden door.

Her hand shook, but this time, she did it.

Her knuckles rapped against the wood and the sound filled her ears as her hand fell back to her side and she waited with held breath. When no answer came, she pressed her ear to the door, and heard nothing beyond it. She turned the knob, the metal almost warm to her stiff hands. She pushed into the familiar home.

She looked behind her once, peering beneath her hood, but no one was in view. Aisla pulled the door shut behind her and settled onto the bed to wait.

His familiar smell filled her with such relief she sobbed into her hands, cursing herself for every lost moment.

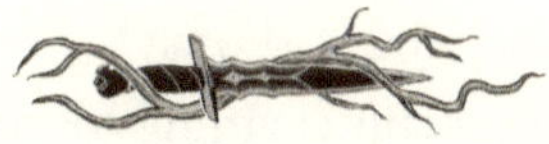

Aisla jolted up, shaking off the fog of sleep like a cloak at the click that meant someone had opened the door. She had fallen asleep waiting for Ruairi, and did not know how much time had passed since she'd let herself into his baile.

Her heart thrummed in her chest as she waited.

Ruairi stepped through the door, his eyes focused on the floor. The sight of his brilliant red hair and slumped shoulders sent Aisla rushing to him.

His head snapped up as shock filled his green eyes. The expression was quickly replaced with relief that again brought tears to Aisla's eyes. She threw herself into his embrace, and his arms wrapped around her, almost on instinct.

He pulled her into the warmth of his body and the smell of ash and mint. She clung to him, her throat too tight to find the words to say. His fingers curled into the fabric of her cloak as if to hold her there—as if to ensure she was really in his arms.

The door fell shut behind them and the sound reverberated through their heavy breaths.

"I'm so sorry," Aisla whispered as she nuzzled deeper into his chest.

They were the only words she could think to give him. How could she put every thought that had crossed her mind since they last saw each other into any other words?

Ruairi's hand travelled up her back and held the back of her head, his fingers tangling in her hair.

"I'm just glad you're back," he said, and she knew he meant it.

She was thankful that, of everyone she would have to face, Ruairi would not hold her disappearance against her.

"I can explain . . ." she began as she reluctantly pulled away from the warmth of his embrace. The absence of him immediately hit her like a wave crashing against the seashore.

"You don't have to explain anything to me that you aren't ready to, Ash," Ruairi replied.

"I-I know. But it's the least I can do."

Ruairi didn't say anything else.

He stepped away from her and sat down on his bed. Aisla sat next to him, folding her legs towards her body. A flood of memories crashed over her. How many nights had they sat just like this? How many more would they have like this?

She feared the former number would be far greater than the latter. Her breath caught around a knot in her throat, but she swallowed it, finding the courage to speak once more.

"I know you know where I've been staying. I saw you and Gaotha above the clouds on more than one occasion. And I don't blame you for looking," she added when his mouth opened in protest. "I didn't want you to worry about me. And if I'm being honest, I didn't really plan on coming back yet. Muinin told me I should come back. He refused to let me put on his riding leathers today, and I knew he was right. I've been hiding from things I should have already faced. I've been running from Eire and what I did to her. I've been running from you and the pain you endured because of my own naivete. I've been running from Cliona and the words neither of us can take back. I've been running from my home and all the people I have failed and continued to fail the longer I stayed away. I've been running from the war—the war that I started." Aisla stumbled over those last words that hardly felt real no matter how long she had to sit with them. The confession rushed from her trembling lips, and her chest felt a little lighter with each admission. "Ultimately, I've been a coward. And I still am. I waited for you to get to your baile, because I still don't know how I'll face the rest of it, but I know I'm not doing any favors by hiding out in solitude. Not when the one thing I would really like to hide from is myself, and not even in the deep of the woods will that be possible. So, this is me trying to be brave." She looked up and met his gaze. His green eyes softened with understanding and not a flicker of judgement.

She knew she didn't deserve the sort of friendship Ruairi gave her.

"You're no coward, Aisla Iarkis," he said. "We start here, and we'll figure out the rest. Like we always have."

Aisla merely nodded, longing for him to fill the space.

"I think, if you want to know the truth, Eire is more hurt by your disappearance than what happened before you left."

Ruairi did not have to remind Aisla that she'd lost control of her esos and burnt the flesh of Eire's shoulders. The memory of it was still so fresh, so new. She relived it every time it passed through her mind, as it often did.

"She still . . . lives, then?" Aisla did not know what to call the state she was in. It was not living, but she was surely not dead either. It was something in between—something they had never seen before.

"She is about the same as you last saw her. She's still Eire, but also not." Ruairi's lips pressed into a thin line, and she saw the thoughtfulness in his eyes when he talked about their friend.

"Do you see her often?"

"Every day," he replied with no hesitation. Guilt turned in the pit of Aisla's stomach, and her throat dried as she nodded. "I would love to take you there. Whenever you're ready, of course."

"Thank you," she said with a smile. She hesitated before asking her next question. "And what of my grandmother?"

"I see little of her," Ruairi replied, his entire demeanor changing as he adjusted himself to look down at the ground. "I was removed from her inner council the sunrise after you left. She's appointed a few new members, but no one speaks of anything to me. She explained that they would need me training, not politicking behind closed doors with them, but the unsaid words were still there. She doesn't want me involved anymore. So, I've been working extra in scoil to train anyone we can as laochs. We're working our best to prepare in whatever time we are given. No one knows what to expect—the Udar has not sent any word, as far as I know."

"I suppose no word is better than an attack on our people," Aisla murmured.

She had not expected war to break out immediately. No, the Udar was more calculated than that. He had all the advantages in his pocket now, and full right to act whenever he wished, and he would use the timing to his advantage as well. And in the meantime, Eilean would wait in fear of the unknown.

"Does Cliona still hope to negotiate peace terms?" Aisla asked, but already knew the answer given the enemies they had made across the Tusnua Sea.

"Not that I've heard," Ruairi replied. "Do you still have the letter?"

"Of course." Aisla reached down to pat her boot, where she kept the parchment tucked into her sock. "Always on me."

"I think you should burn it," Ruairi stated, with no hesitancy.

Aisla's eyes shot to his in surprise.

"And why would we do that?"

"So, she doesn't know we lied to her, Ash. Nothing good could come of that letter. We've both felt it. The Udar never got his hands on it—that's what we wanted. Now we need to get rid of it," he explained. "I've thought a lot about it."

"I need to know what it says," Aisla said, shaking her head. "We need to know."

"Why? What does it matter? It was never meant for our eyes, anyway."

"I finally started reading that book," Aisla said, nerves lacing her tone. "The one I found in the library before we ever left Eilean. *The Dawn of Talam*. Believe it or not, it gets quite boring in the middle of the forest with only Muinin as company. There's still nothing about the lofa, but I read about a society in the south. It's called the Silenced World Tellers. They have records that libraries around the world have burned and banned. There are secrets to discover there, and I don't know if they could help us, but at the very least there might be someone who reads the runic language—someone who could translate it for us."

Aisla had puzzled over the cryptic letter for many sunrises. Why her grandmother would translate a letter to the Udar of the worldly realms in a language so hard to decode, she could not say, but it gave her a foul feeling in her gut. Especially when that letter had been key in her plan for Ruairi to obtain a cure of the lofa that didn't exist—and had maybe never existed.

"Silenced World Tellers? Aisla, this sounds like a tale for young elves," Ruairi said, and Aisla's confidence deflated. "There's no telling if it's real. And if it was, who knows if they survived lofa? They might have migrated north like so many others did. And if they survived lofa, how could you trust a stranger to translate something so secretive? It's all far too risky."

"I'm not burning it, Ru."

"Then hold on to it, if you so desire, but don't go letting it fall into the hands of a stranger."

"I'm not dense," Aisla snapped before carrying on with a defensive edge to her voice. "And what of the ring? Did you burn that?"

"No," Ruairi answered, calmly. "I don't know what it was made for. There's still something off about it."

"Why are you so eager to destroy the letter then, but not the ring? We've lied about both," Aisla pointed out.

The ring and the letter had both been a part of Cliona's plea bargain with the Udar. Aisla needed to know what they were and how they carried such a weight that Cliona would think the Udar would listen to their reasoning and pleas for help.

Even though they had failed.

"I-I don't know."

"I'm sorry." Aisla reached out and rested her hand on his knee. He looked up to meet her gaze again. There was so much to decipher in the green of his irises. The brightness had faded within the walls of Castle Eagla, and had yet to return. Scars still marred his body but had grown fainter in her time away. A hollowness lingered still, and she wondered if he would ever shake it completely. He had endured trauma and torture that no living being deserved, least of all her Ruairi. Her good and honest and caring and brave Ruairi. "I'm sorry," she repeated, for so many reasons. "I don't want to argue."

"Me neither, Ash. I trust you. The letter is yours to do what you wish with it. Just please don't close me out. Allow me to help you."

"I will," she replied. "Thank you, Ru." He moved his hand to rest atop hers. His thumb stroked the back of her hand in mindless circles. It was a feeling that took her back to that clearing just sunrises before they left Eilean for the first time, and hopefully the last. "Tell me everything. I need to know, and I need you to know that I can handle it."

Ruairi swallowed once, then nodded his head. Then he began.

He told Aisla of the husks they kept on the outskirts of Caillte. They talked about his visits with Eire, how she had grown cold and distant, but was no longer deteriorating. The medics did not know what to do with her. It was all so unprecedented.

Ruairi spoke of his training with their classes, and the new classes he had picked up. He shared what little he knew of Cliona's new inner council members, and his fears of a regime growing stricter in the face of the Inevitable War.

Throughout it all, he let pieces of his story on Iomlan slip through. He would reference his time spent in the dungeon of their enemy briefly, and stoically, obviously not wanting her pity, and not wanting her asking more questions about it. She was thankful he opened up at all, no matter how badly it hurt her to hear.

She had far less to share, but she filled in her own gaps as she could. She spoke of the passages from *The Dawn of Talam* she had found most interesting, and a little of her own time on Iomlan with Weylin Myrkor. She kept it brief and vague and intentionally left out any mention of her vivid dream.

They talked until they were both lying on their sides across from each other in his bed. His voice filled the air until Aisla's eyes fell shut, and she had not realized how much she missed the comfort of a bed—and the comfort of his voice.

It was a welcome solace from her self-induced solitude.

When Aisla awoke, some time later, in the middle of the night, their bodies were pushed towards their own sides of the bed. Too much had changed, too much was still left to process to return to the tangle of limbs they had been the night before he had found himself in the company of the Udar's laochs.

She would have stayed there, finished the night by Ruairi's side, but her own baile was calling to her, and she had missed the feeling of her own place to call home. She slipped off the side of his bed, careful not to disturb the sleeping male. She tiptoed to the door and glanced once more over her shoulder.

There was a peace about him this way—a peace she wished he

could wear during the light of day. His red curls fell about his face and his hand was tucked beneath his head.

As quietly as she could, Aisla slipped into the dark hours before dawn and found comfort in the sheets of her own bed. It was cold and unmade from the last time she had been there.

She had not known the comfort she would feel beneath the heavy quilt she had brought with her from Castle Farraige. Or the way this glimpse of her life as it had once been would feel like a welcome she longed for.

4

EIRE

A chill filled the halls, sending a shiver down Eire's spine. She pulled her arms closer to her body. The thin fabric of her shirt hung loosely from her emaciated frame.

She was alone as she took her evening walk around the infirmary. They had come to trust her enough to allow her to wander the halls unattended. She didn't know what they would do with her, and it seemed as if they didn't know either.

The menders tried to ignore her questions, but she heard their murmurs—the way they spoke of her as though she were already gone.

And some days, she found herself wishing she was.

Eire shuffled one foot in front of the other. Her condition had not changed since before Ruairi and Aisla returned to Eilean. Every time Ruairi visited, memories of them would fade into her mind. But they were always held by a fog—a fog she was entirely incapable of lifting. She wanted to remember. She wanted to know why the red-haired male cared enough to continue to appear, despite the cold shoulder she had shoved his way in the hopes he would give up.

It was not romantic between them, and she was sure it had never been. She was sure she had never loved a male in that way, but there was another bond between them—a closeness like siblings would share, that kept him coming back, even more often than her own family. It hurt her to see him hurt himself over and over each sunrise. If he could forget her, or even give up on her at last, maybe he could stop tormenting himself with the hope she would ever recover.

She had already given up her own hopes of a normal life.

As Eire walked the halls that had become far too familiar, she wondered how many there were like her. How many souls had stopped changing when the lofa ended its rampage on her continent? How many others were stuck in this realm between life and death, with not the slightest idea how they should move forward?

She could only hope there were few.

Eire had a fear that she couldn't shake or explain. It was a fear that none of them had ever died at all. That all the others were like her in some form or another.

Not dead, but not alive.

That there were hundreds and hundreds of beings that were hardly a shadow of who they once were.

She once thought they were put out of their misery somewhere else, out of sight, but she had never seen anyone die. Not even Fiona as she convulsed before her very eyes. Eire was certain it was her nightmares playing to her own terrors. Surely, the families would want better for them than this life.

But she couldn't help but wonder where their bodies went. If their friends and families were permitted to grieve for them and pray over them one final time before they were laid into the ground.

She had not had that opportunity with Fiona.

Eire stopped outside of the room that had been turned into a makeshift chapel for the infirmary residents. She had not entered the place in many sunrises—finally believing that the gods had given up on her, as the others had.

But something called her there that evening, something deep in her rotten, black blood. It tugged her onwards until she fell to her knees before the altar of a faceless god—a god who could be whoever she needed them to be.

Eire's head hung low as her shoulders slumped forward. Desperation overcame her in a wave that dragged her body down into the core of Talam.

She thought of Leighis, the goddess of healing. She thought of her as she clutched her arms closer into her chest and sobs wracked her shaking body. It all poured out before she could stop it, and she was afraid it would never stop now that she had set it free.

"Please hear me. Please see me. Please take me. Take me or save me. Please."

The words tore from her lips in between violent sobs and fell into the empty air.

5
AISLA

There were hands all over her body.

Aisla's eyes shot open, and it took her no longer than a moment to realize she was not in a dream. It was real. Figures surrounded her in a dark she could scarcely see through.

She blinked rapidly as she fought to tear the hands away from her body. A yelp escaped her lips as fingernails pierced the flesh of her biceps.

"Stop! Get off me!" she shouted frantically, but her pleas were only greeted by a harsh, humorless chuckle.

They were masked figures—that much she could tell. Cowards hiding behind dark cloth. She couldn't pull herself from their grasps.

Hands grabbed at her chest. They yanked her arms. They dragged her up from the bed. Hands grabbed her legs. Snatched at her hair, ripping it in clumps. Nails marred her olive skin and burned on their way out.

"Stop!" Aisla cried again, desperation fogging her senses.

They shoved a cloth between her lips the moment her mouth opened. It stole the air from her lungs. She could hardly breathe.

She grew dizzy with panic.

They bound her wrists behind her back. Someone struck a blow to her gut that made her double over as she gagged on the cloth.

Fight back, Aisla. That voice from so many moons ago. It had returned. *Fight back.*

Rage flooded Aisla's veins as she kicked out as hard as she could and watched as a shadowed figure bent over from the impact, and a renewed sense of purpose cleared away the fog of Aisla's panic.

Get out of here, the voice said, as if Aisla wasn't already focused on an escape.

She kicked again, unable to use her arms that were now tied behind her back. They grabbed her ankle, and her moment of victory did not last.

Hands tore at her legs as they attempted to lift her and bind her ankles. She flailed madly, trying to scream around the cloth. She was so helpless. So out of control.

Someone grabbed her backside. Another hand yanked her hair back so hard she saw stars.

"Stupid *mallaithe*," a male voice taunted, and spit flecked her face as she continued to fight against the hands that held her. "Selfish *mallaithe*. You care for none save for yourself. Bringing war upon your people for the sake of two souls that matter to you and you alone? Stupid, selfish *mallaithe*."

A realization consumed her all at once.

She had been right to fear her return home, but not for the reasons she had thought. If anything, she had not feared her return enough. She feared the judgement, the disappointment, and her own guilt. She would have never thought her own people would be capable of such violence against her.

Her own people had turned against her. She was no longer safe in Caillte.

If she could ever make it out of Caillte.

If only she could call out, surely Ruairi would hear her just next door.

Aisla squinted her eyes in the dark as she continued to writhe and kick and throw her head around madly, praying to land a blow to someone somehow. She fought against the hands that meant to bind her ankles together, refusing to give them that. She worked to sort out how many of them there were.

There were only four that she could tell, and that gave her hope. Enough hope that an energy surged through her core, and she kicked one straight in the jaw. A sickening crack flooded the room, as he dropped his hold on her, and her legs fell to the floor. She quickly got to her feet and brought her knee up between another's legs. She heard the air leave his lungs as he fell to his knees. She whirled around and kicked at the third, knocking his knees out from under him, but he grabbed her on the way down. She tripped but did not fall. The third made to snatch her.

Behind you, that female voice snapped in her head.

Aisla dodged to her right, towards the door that would lead her outside. The final intruder met her there.

"You sure fight nasty for a pretty thing," he growled, and Aisla fought past the shudder that racked her body.

His fist flew at her, and she sidestepped the blow as if controlled by an external force, moving purely on instinct, having little time to do anything else as the three behind her regained their footing.

Her hands were still bound. She could not pull them apart.

She reared back and flung her head forward into the nearest masked being. A crack sounded through the air and reverberated through her skull. Aisla bit down on the cloth, fighting her own pain as the edges of her vision blurred red, and a ringing sounded in her ears.

The male went down with a grunt, and Aisla nearly did, too.

She did not have time to feel the pain, as she was all too aware of the others now rushing towards her. She backed up a step and her bound hands fumbled with the doorknob until she managed to twist it to the right and flung the door wide open.

Someone grabbed her arm, hard enough to bruise. Aisla willed that silent esos to respond to her call—to whisper to her once again. She was sure it could save her now, if only she could reach it. A silence answered her call. It was a silence that turned her stomach.

There's no time to waste, the voice reminded her. *You've never needed your esos before, and you don't need it now.*

Aisla grit her teeth as she kicked her foot out to keep the door open, and she swung her elbow to free herself from the female who had grabbed her arm. Her grip faltered but grabbed Aisla's shirt, curling the fabric in her fist.

Aisla yanked free, sprinting through the open doorway as the sound of ripping fabric tore through the silent night. The left side of her shirt hung, torn open, her bare torso exposed to the chill of night.

The thought did not linger long as Aisla's legs carried her forward. There was a challenge to running without the balance of her arms to push her onwards, and the steady swing of them to propel her.

She scanned the ground before her, careful not to trip over any loose rocks or branches. Any second lost was a second of advantage for her attackers, and she could hear their heavy footsteps mingling with the sound of the pounding of her heart in her ears.

Crisp ash wood flooded her nostrils despite the absence of her esos. Aisla made her way around the back of the bailes.

It was the same way she had returned home, trying to sneak into Ruairi's baile without being seen.

And apparently, she had failed at that.

At last, she broke through the tree line of the Tus Forest, and relief that ripped a sob from her throat flooded her entire being as emerald scales glinted in the light of Talam's dual moons.

Muinin had heard her and dove towards her. Black smoke that threatened the esos of flames emitted from his nostrils. Aisla did not look back as Muinin reached her.

Sharp claws wrapped around her shoulders as Muinin lifted Aisla from the ground. His wings beat around her, cocooning her in a nest of air that was safe from the four who sought to steal her from her bed.

Aisla squeezed her eyes shut as her body hung from Muinin's talons. It was uncomfortable, but far preferable to the situation she had found herself in just moments ago.

She had been helpless. Unable to protect herself from the wrath of her own people.

And if that was any indication of what awaited her come sunrise, Aisla knew she had to flee.

Ever the coward and ever helpless, Aisla only wished she had the chance to explain herself to Ruairi this time.

But she could not risk returning to her home.

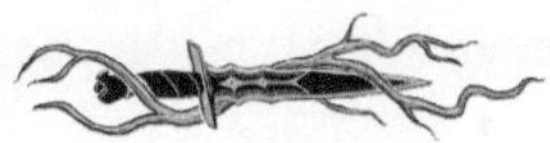

Muinin dropped Aisla in a clearing a safe distance from Caillte. They were nestled amongst tall pine trees whose tops reached into a star filled sky. There was a full moon in Sneachta, while Braon only showed a quarter of its light potential.

Her hands itched for freedom. Her body ached with the fight she had put up to escape as the adrenaline shed its energy like a second layer of skin. In its place was a deep-seated fear.

She burned with the need to shower and scrub away the memories of their hands on her.

Muinin landed beside her with a loud thud. Aisla lifted her wrists that had been bound behind her back to him, and Muinin slashed through them with a talon. Aisla immediately used her free hand to rip the gag from her mouth as cool air flooded her dry tongue. She shook her hands out, fighting the urge to fall to her knees and curl into herself and weep. There was no time for such things. She glimpsed the purple bruises lining her wrists and arms.

Her shirt was left in tatters, between the attacker that had ripped it and where Muinin's claws had held her.

Aisla pulled the shirt over her head and ripped it again, then knotted it in a way that would cover more of her chest and torso, as she had nothing else in her possession.

She had no pack, no food, and no weapons. The only thing she had were the clothes on her body, her wyvern tooth necklace against her throat, and most importantly, the letter still tucked into her sock —the letter that never left her skin.

"Thank you," Aisla spoke quietly, even though they were far enough from Caillte now and no one could hear them. "What would I do without you?"

Muinin shook his wings out in response and nuzzled his massive head against her side. It was rare when he showed affection like this, but Aisla could see the relief in his golden eyes. He had saved her yet again.

There lay an unspoken fear between them. What would happen if he wasn't fast enough next time?

Aisla wiped tears from the corner of her eye and pushed the thought away. She could only hope and pray that she would not live to see that time.

"Where to now?" Aisla murmured aloud as she slowly turned around the clearing, trying to orient herself.

She could not go back to Caillte, and she could not leave Eilean. Her options were limited, and her resources were even more so.

The conversation with Ruairi nagged at the back of her mind. Her desire to have the letter translated, and his to have it destroyed. She felt no satisfaction as she realized her desire might be the only way to find shelter away from her home.

She did not have her copy of *The Dawn of Talam*. She did not even have her dagger, *Oidhe,* to guide her through the woods. She had looked at the map of the marked location of the Silenced World Tellers long enough to know the general direction she would supposedly find them—if they existed at all.

"To the secret society, I suppose," Aisla quipped with a half-hearted smile to Muinin. "If not answers, may they at least grant us a place to stay until we figure out what to do next."

Muinin responded with a chuff that Aisla hoped to be approval. She eyed the wyvern cautiously, knowing what came next.

She had never ridden Muinin without his leathers. It wasn't really practiced.

Muinin looked back at her with a gleam of a challenge in his eyes. He took one step towards her, bent his neck, and lowered himself to the ground. She clambered ungracefully atop him, squeezing her legs tightly behind his shoulder blades as she worked to find her balance and clenched her core tight. She leaned forward and wrapped her arms around his neck as far as she could reach.

"Go easy now," she whispered to him.

Muinin roared in what Aisla wished was agreement, but sounded much more like a thrill, and took off into the skies.

He started slow and careful, and as soon as she got comfortable, he dropped rapidly, and Aisla's heart lurched into her stomach. It was a careful, planned maneuver, that he knew she could handle even bareback, but had her stomach turning just the same.

"Hilarious, you jerk," she muttered.

Muinin fell into a steady glide, interrupted by the occasional sharp turn to keep her on edge while she gave him directions towards where she recalled the Silenced World Tellers to be on the map from *The Dawn of Talam*.

As they glided above the tree line, Aisla wondered which wyvern she would have inherited had her parents still been alive. She might have gotten one recently hatched, or a different elder looking for a new elf. While she would give anything for her father to still be here, and knew that things would be so very different if he were, Aisla was thankful that Muinin was hers.

She could not imagine her life any other way.

6

WEYLIN

"Looks like someone's got some morning after Ifreann's Day rust to shake off," Callum Ronan teased the Udar Apparent, as he stabbed the wooden sparring sword into his friend's side.

The wind rushed from Weylin's chest on the impact.

He hadn't wanted a reminder of the holiday they celebrated the night previously. Weylin always found it ironic that they celebrated the Prince of Hel during the middle of spring, and not in the dead of winter. Maybe it was a reminder of what he could bring and what he could take away.

Not all the realms still honored the days of the gods, but Samhradh would never miss an opportunity to fill their halls with drinks and merriment.

"Something like that," Weylin grunted back and let his arm that held his practice weapon fall to his side.

Callum lowered his sword, and Weylin watched as victory lit his deep green eyes.

"It wasn't your finest Ifreann's Day, though, was it?" Callum teased. But Weylin would have none of it while his head still pounded.

"And was it yours?" He snapped back. "I recall you matched me mug for mug up until the very end. I can't imagine you enjoy that, being stuck by my side as I politick and parade when you could be out courting and drinking with far fewer worries."

Weylin did not hold his tongue. He never had with Callum, and for that level of comfort, he was thankful. Ifreann's Day had once been a time when they would spend the evening drinking until they forgot how much they detested dancing. They would savor the food as though it were the last meal they'd share. There was once an indescribable feeling of life that came with celebrating the peak of spring that filled Weylin with a longing for a future he often dreaded.

There was no such feeling this Ifreann's Day.

This holiday, Weylin found himself amid conversation after conversation of the Inevitable War.

There was so much to be done, Weylin could hardly bother himself to eat.

Everyone wanted to know how they were preparing. When and if war would reach their shores. How it would affect the economy. If their sons would be recruited as laochs against their will. And the most asked of all, would the *mallaithe* end it all before it could even begin?

It was all too much. And they were nearly all questions that Weylin did not have answers to. And that was a feeling he hated more than most.

He had taken full advantage of the opportunity to drink, though, and there was ample opportunity at that.

It was all he could do to stay in the great hall of Castle Omra while the smell of red wine lingered so heavily that Weylin thought he might never be free of it. It reminded him of a night he had spent his waking moments trying to forget. A night of vulnerabilities whispered between strangers, and a night he could only regret. Weylin had never shared such sentiments with anyone else, and if anyone was worthy of carrying them, surely it was not the damned *mallaithe*.

In lieu of the wine, Weylin had turned to a strong ale to clear his own senses and shade his worries, if only for a night. And the throbbing in his head was a reminder of just that. He drank until he passed out in his cold bed, and for one night, he was free of the yellow-green eyes that never seemed to leave him.

Or he had been, until the early hours of the morning.

He hadn't heard a thing, but there was a feeling in the room that woke him. A feeling that, even in his sleep, made the hair along his arms rise. He blinked his eyes open, and the *mallaithe* was standing above him, gripping his own blade as if she were born with it in her hands.

And despite it all, he had not been afraid. He did not know what he felt. He wasn't panicked or angry. It was almost amusing to think she would end it all before it could begin. As if their preparing and fears and worries were for nothing at all.

They shared a sentence or two, then she vanished into the air. He had been left to wonder if it had been merely a dream, but something about it felt so real. He knew that if he'd touched her skin, it would have been Ellora Morlee.

He knew he would not be sleeping well, knowing she had appeared and disappeared in his room as if by some otherly esos, but he could not bring himself to tell Callum about it.

It was his secret.

So much had changed since his journey alongside Ellora Morlee, who he refused to think of by any other name. It would feel like too much of a failure to think of her as Aisling Iarkis, when he had saved her life not once, but twice.

They had been so close to ending the *Gheall Ceann* in the throne room, but Weylin had the feeling if they had succeeded, her eyes would have haunted him in a very different way. And there was the smallest part of him—a part he had been consciously pushing to the very back of his mind since the moment she escaped with her male and her massive beast—that did not want to imagine a world without her in it.

He could not help but know her for the female he had come to care for, no matter how much of it had been a lie. He knew not all of it was.

"Believe it or not," Callum spoke up as he eyed Weylin curiously and called him from the depths of his thoughts. "I did. The conversations may have been a bore, but I feel we've both outgrown the antics of previous Ifreann's Days, anyway. Speaking of which, this was your final Ifreann's Day without a mate. The next one, it won't be me by your side, but her."

Weylin cleared his throat and turned to face Callum, not bothering to force a smile. He lifted his sparring weapon once again, and Callum did as well.

An uneasy feeling churned in his gut. He had left Castle Tromlui with high hopes for the union between himself and Rania Dorcas, but something about it no longer felt right. He could not explain it, and had no desire to pin it down for fear of what he might discover.

"Yes, *her*," Weylin said and brought his wooden sword down with a loud crash against Callum's, who responded to the movement with ease. "I suppose you'll have the pleasure of meeting Rania quite soon."

"I look forward to it," Callum grunted as he stepped back and thrust his sparring weapon forward. Weylin dodged with a sidestep to the right. "What is she like?"

"She's fine," Weylin said evenly. "She's elegant and charming, with a grace that typically takes centuries to master. She seems almost natural at it. It's unnerving as much as it is admirable. She's cunning, to be sure. She's the sort to play the game, to remain one step ahead. Even so, Rania seems genuine enough. You'll get along fine."

"Surely you can think of a better word than 'fine' for your mate," Callum said with a grin before slicing his blade above his head and bringing it down gently against the side of Weylin's neck. It happened so quickly, Weylin hadn't the time to react, or roll his eyes at Callum's remark. It was impressive the way Callum could move and act with elven grace, even though only human blood ran through his veins. "And I should hope we'll get along. You won't be getting rid of me anytime soon, even with a mating ceremony. It appears you still need your captain to train you."

Weylin bit back a retort and went quickly back into their match. He narrowed his eyes with renewed determination, shaving off the shadow the night had shrouded him in. He admired the way Callum sparred. He gave it his all, mind and body, and he never seemed afraid of the consequences, although he was only human with a lifespan much shorter than Weylin's. It was not a fact Weylin liked to recall. Without Callum, Weylin had no loyal friends. No friends that saw him as more than the Udar Apparent with titles to hand out like biscuits.

"While I wouldn't dream of it, you only attained the skill you have because it is I who once trained you," Weylin chided, as he and Callum circled each other with their wooden weapons held out before them.

"Please," Callum snorted. "You trained alongside me. And if anything, the instructor went easier on you—you know, title and all."

"You wish," Weylin snipped back.

He was not wrong, though. It was something that Weylin detested about training with others. Scoil used to be for elves only, but with the disappearance of ash trees and esos from Iomlan, there was nothing in scoil to teach that humans and dwarves could not also benefit from. So, they trained and learned side by side, by order of Weylin's great-grandfather. And without that, Weylin and Callum might have never crossed threads. Callum was not from a family of noble blood, or any importance, but his training would bring the Ronan name into the books of world tellers, something he was certain Callum had never intended to do, but rather happened into.

Weylin darted forward and stepped one way and then the other. It was enough to throw Callum off, and Weylin was at last able to land his own finishing blow to Callum's heart with the wooden sword.

Callum dropped his own, and the thud against sandy earth echoed through the clearing as he gripped at his chest. "You wound me, brother."

Weylin let out a chuckle and tucked his sparring weapon into the belt around his waist.

"I think we can call it a day now," he said with a grin.

"Oh, we can? Now that you get to finish with a win," Callum teased, and gathered his weapon from the ground.

"Of course," Weylin replied.

He stalked to the racks where the sparring weapons hung and placed his own there.

"How do you feel the war preparations are coming along?" Callum asked as they entered Castle Eagla through the great oak doors at the southern entrance.

"Not quickly enough," Weylin murmured. "The sooner we move, the better, in my opinion. Eilean is obviously in a dangerous place with their plague if she—they came here to plead for a cure. It's clear desperation, we ought to be taking advantage of it."

"Then why aren't we?" Callum asked.

"A few reasons. Father is hesitant to make any brash moves during the ninth generation, especially now that we've seen the type of power she can wield. It's pure, raw esos. The type of esos we have no defense against. Whoever told us she was no concern when it came to her esos was either misleading us or speaking of a different female entirely. Father wants more laochs trained, more legions at the ready. He would also prefer to get her in a place where her esos is limited. As our sources tell us, Eilean still has its ash trees. There's the concern of her unlimited source. Father would prefer to end her quickly and finish this war as soon as possible. Once she is buried, the prophecy can be prevented," Weylin continued as they made their way to the tavern inside the castle. His stomach growled with hunger. "Then there's the matter of allies. There's less rush in entering those conversations until my mating is finalized and Briongloid is a guaranteed ally. Father feels it would be ideal to seek out the lords and ladies of Earrach, Bitu, and Geimreigh as well, and confirm where we stand with them before diving into anything. Fomhar will fall into place behind Briongloid, their only allies left from the War for Descendants."

"Valid concerns," Callum responded with a tint of exhaustion that Weylin knew all too well. "Is there an official date for your mating ceremony yet?"

"I've hardly thought about it," Weylin replied, and they sat down across from each other with a mug of ale in hand and a plate of venison and potatoes before them. "All I know is her brother, Oisin, Lord Apparent of Briongloid, will escort her here, and they are to arrive soon. Father rushed her arrival after the wyvern's landing. It will be safer for her here and shows that we will stand by one another."

"I would imagine that means the mating is to be soon then, as well."

Weylin responded with a grunt of agreement. His fate was flying at him faster than he could ever ready himself for. Certainly not when there was so much about the last moon to process still.

"Has your father brought up the dispute in Earrach again? I know they called for aid, but I imagine it is not the top of the priority list at the moment."

"No, the sylphs and the undines still battle along the shores of Earrach. I've requested we push the matter forward. This would be the opportune time to solidify our alliance on that front and assure that they know they are in our debt. He hasn't decided yet."

"If you think it's a worthy investment of our time, you know I'm more than willing to go. I know you're needed here more than I am."

"I know," Weylin said, more bitterly than he intended.

What Weylin did not add was how he had been itching to go there himself. He would be happy to take Callum with him, but there was a yearning in his blood to leave his castle and start rallying allies himself.

He was restless.

Having the Udar Apparent there to play politics would go a much longer way than the captain of his laochs, no matter how well-intentioned. He would prefer to see to the matters in Earrach himself, but his father only sneered at his request each time Weylin brought it up, saying he was needed in Samhradh, and that his betrothed would soon need him.

But Weylin could not imagine that Rania Dorcas would need him in any way. Not if he had gotten to know her at all in his brief meeting with her. No, she would fit in just fine in Castle Eagla.

"My lord." A familiar voice interrupted his thought, and Weylin looked up from his ale to see another of his laochs had approached their table. A smirk played at the corners of his lips as his eyes locked onto Weylin's. "Your betrothed—she has arrived."

Weylin felt Callum's eyes on him. Pressure built in his chest as he quickly wiped the look of shock from his face before they could catch it, and stood to his feet.

"Well, take me to her."

7

RUAIRI

Ruairi woke to an empty bed that still smelled of her.

He reached out and touched the side where she had fallen asleep beside him. It was already cold. He would have thought it a dream, if not for the imprint she had left.

He couldn't help but wonder why she had left. He had hoped she'd had the same feeling of comfort at sharing conversation and a bed once again. It was the best he had slept since he first left Eilean.

His fingers curled into a fist as he pushed away the shame that still came with the sight of his missing finger. The menders had stitched up the wound when he arrived home and taken care of it so it would heal cleanly. And it had, but it did not change what was done to him. It was a physical piece of himself he would never get back from inside the walls of Castle Eagla, but not even the worst piece.

Memories of Orla's claws sorting through his mind still came back to him in waves, and he couldn't help the feeling that she had stolen more than he knew. He felt it again when he wrapped Aisla in his arms the previous sunset. He felt an unfamiliarity at first, only to blink and see with clarity his best friend standing before him.

His best friend, who was so much more than that, he had to remind himself.

They had been a family, she, Eire, and himself, and that family was fading with each passing moment. Most of the time, it felt like he was the only one holding on to it with hands that gripped too tightly.

Ruairi closed his eyes and allowed himself a moment to lie back in his bed before dragging his tired body to the washroom. He prepared himself for another day of long hours and rigorously training the future laochs of Eilean. They would be needed sooner rather than later, he feared, and that responsibility weighed heavy on him as he stepped outside his front door with his pack slung over his shoulder.

Ruairi was hopeful, at least, that Aisla would go with him to classes today. It would mean a lot to the next generation to see her there.

He knew she was not ready to face the opinions that ran rampant, and for that he did not blame her. But where their students were concerned, she was typically admired, not shamed.

The path between their homes was short and worn. He could still see the imprint of her boots where she went in. His eyebrows furrowed as he noticed other footprints mingled with them that seemed fresh.

His heartbeat quickened, and a rush sounded in his ears.

He closed the distance and knocked on the wooden door to her baile. When she did not answer, he pushed through.

"Aisla," he called.

No answer.

He shut the door behind him and noted the way her bed was made, something she rarely did. He inspected her room, searching for any place she might have left a note, and noticed everything appeared much neater than she had last left it. Maybe she had departed in less of a hurry this time, but Aisla had never been known to be tidy, so why would she start now? And Ruairi could hardly imagine the urge to clean would strike her in the few hours she would have had between leaving his baile and disappearing from her own.

It was curious indeed, but he did not know what to make of it. Aisla had her own agenda these days, and he didn't know how much more clearly he could tell her he was there for her, no matter what she decided. If she wanted to go about it alone, there was nothing he could do about it.

But surely, she would have known he would come looking for her. Surely, she would have wanted to start the day together. Surely, she would want to face whatever opinions awaited her together.

He ran a finger along a dusty windowsill, fighting against that familiar hurt.

He left her baile with his hands shoved in his pockets. His feet scuffed along the dirt path into the city center. He found himself looking for her familiar light brown hair on each elf he passed.

No one so much as glanced in his direction.

He didn't know where she might go, but he was certain she would not have gone to Cliona first. Ruairi picked up his pace and headed to the place he hoped she might go—a place he knew there were amends to be made.

Ruairi was out of breath when he burst through the doors to the infirmary. He hadn't even noticed when he started running, just that he had felt a panic in his chest he could not explain.

The mender at the desk looked up at him with a small smile, as she always did. "Good to see you today, Ruairi."

"You, too," he huffed between breaths. "Have you seen Aisla here this morning?" He asked, but had a sinking feeling she would have said something already if she had.

"Aisla? She's back?" The mender was clearly shocked by his question, confirming his suspicion. Her eyes grew wide, and she leaned in closer. "I had no idea. When did she get back?"

"Last night," Ruairi mumbled as he glanced past the entryway down the hall. "I'll take that as a no, then."

"When you find her, do tell her to come see Eire! I think it will help them both."

Ruairi nodded and turned on his heel to leave the building.

His mind reeled as the rush of wind sounded in his ears, and his blood ached with tension he could not release.

Where would she have gone?

Ruairi knew where he could go to get confirmation one way or the other. It would make him late for his morning training, but it was with his older students. He trusted them to get things moving without him. The stronger esos wielders amongst them had already proven themselves to be leaders among their peers.

Ruairi made his way through the Tus Forest, quickly brushing past the tall pines and lower sitting ash trees. He kicked pinecones as he went until, at last, he reached the wyvern caves. He heard a low roar as Gaotha left her cave to greet him.

She leaned her massive, scaled head into his outreached hand. They had shared far less time together since his return from Eilean, and he often wished he was training riders rather than laochs, if only so he could spend more time with her.

"Muinin—is he here?" Ruairi asked his wyvern, and her large ruby eyes blinked open.

He had a feeling in his gut that he already knew the answer.

Gaotha drew back a step and slowly shook her head. Her eyes fell as if there was something she wished to tell him but could not. Ruairi loved his esos of winds, but he was often jealous of the shifters that could communicate freely with their bonded. It was something he would never know the feeling of, outside of this nonverbal communication they had learned to share.

"I figured," he murmured. "I have to get to classes, but I'll be back soon. I promise."

Gaotha ducked her head in understanding, and guilt crept into the corners of Ruairi's mind that he had come all this way, only to leave yet again. He turned and headed back before he could dwell on it further.

There was less urgency in his footsteps as he racked his brain, trying to make sense of it all.

If Muinin was also gone, that means it had been intentional. Aisla had left with Muinin but had decided not to tell him. The realization made his throat dry as he grieved the days they would have told each other any and everything.

He wondered if they would ever find their way back to that place.

There was so much damage, so much trauma. They would both need time to sift through it, but it had never occurred to him that it would drive a wedge so deeply between them.

Ruairi could at least find peace in the fact that Aisla had Muinin with her, wherever she was. He knew Muinin would protect her better than any mortal could, and without limits. The elder wyvern was more than capable of doing whatever it would take to ensure the safety of his rider.

It took little work for Ruairi to figure she had gone to find the Silenced World Tellers. And if that was the case, he could only assume she had not told him because he had told her to burn the damn letter. He knew it could only do more harm than good, and they both needed the good right now. More than ever.

The parchment alone had felt so dark. It haunted him whenever it was near. He could only imagine what its translation would reveal.

A shudder travelled through him at the thought.

He had hoped still that even though he did not agree with her mission, Aisla would take him along for the journey. Aisla knew him well enough to know that he would never say no to an adventure.

Ruairi clenched his jaw as he made his way back to Caillte.

If Aisla was going to use her own time and resources to follow her theories, he would do the same.

After the sun had set and Ruairi had led four different trainings for the students, he pulled his cloak over his head and made his way into the woods. He toyed with the silver ring inside his pocket, and his heartbeat thrummed in his ears, louder with each step.

He had not been to this place since that day he had returned to Eilean with more questions than answers. Not physically, at least. He had come back here many times in the hours of his sleep—in the nightmares that he feared would haunt him until his very last sunrise.

Ruairi no longer had dreams. Only nightmares.

And even worse, there were rumors now that there were more buildings out there with the same purpose. He had not heard how many husks there were, but he was afraid to know the answer.

The woods were silent around him. An eerie chill raised the hairs along his arms. He stopped outside the door and waited a long moment. He could turn back before it was too late.

With a deep breath, Ruairi held his palm to the lock. The sound of rushing wind blew through his ears, and then it was a physical force emitting from his palm. He pushed the air into the lock and twitched his fingers, willing it into place. His sharp exhale was followed by a click that meant he had unlocked it. It was a trick he had taught himself many moons ago, while searching the halls of scoil for cheat sheets on world telling tests—he and Aisla's least favorite subject.

He had never been good at memorization.

Ruairi shook his hand out, allowing the esos to dissipate, and wrapped his hand around the cold brass doorknob. He pushed forward, and the door swung open easily.

Immediately, the groans and growls that permanently resided in the back of his mind met his ears. He gritted his teeth, forcing himself to face it, and stepped forward. There was a matchbox lying on the table to his right. He pulled one out to light a torch that hung on the wall.

The flickering light illuminated the decaying faces of the husks. Some sat on the ground, others clung to the iron bars that made up their makeshift cells. They lived without any sustenance. Ruairi was fully perplexed by it all, and he knew the menders were as well from the brief conversations he would share with Edi when they encountered each other in the infirmary.

Not a single pair of eyes focused on him. They all looked past him or through him—transfixed on things he could not see. For the first time, he saw them as the people they once were. He did not recognize anyone in particular, but when he looked closely, they seemed more alive to him than they once did. They were not alert or aware, but they were strong enough to continue their fight. And whether that fight was worth it or not was not for Ruairi to decide, but it was an admirable fight, nonetheless.

His hands trembled when he reached into his pocket. For the first time, he slipped the dainty ring onto his finger. It seemed to grow and mold to his skin—fitting as though it were made for him.

His blood chilled as he looked down at it, and he swore he saw dark shadows slithering through the silver metal in the torchlight.

Ruairi squeezed his eyes shut, fighting for his next breath, then opened them again. He unclenched his fist and held his hand with the ring up before the husks.

He froze.

His whole body was stuck in place, as every head snapped in his direction. Every vacant set of eyes suddenly came to life and locked on him in unison.

It was so much pressure, so much power. Ruairi felt as though he would combust.

8
AISLA

With no map to reference, doubts crept into her mind and grew with each passing moment, but Aisla had nothing else to follow. And nowhere else to go.

She guided Muinin into an easy landing along the southern coast of Eilean, where she vaguely recalled the marked point on the map to be. Her head spun with all that had changed since she left the comfort of the tent that had become her makeshift home and returned to Caillte. She gripped Muinin's shoulder blades tighter, wishing more than ever she had his leather riding gear. Her core ached from the tension of holding on.

They hit the ground with a thud.

As Aisla slid down his side, she noticed a fresh wound that ran behind his left shoulder. It was scabbing over, and she couldn't help but wonder if Muinin was facing terror from his own peers because of the decision Aisla had made.

"Did another wyvern do this to you?" Aisla whispered, running a hand over it. It went deep beneath his scales, and she could only imagine the pain it caused. Anger rumbled through her.

Muinin's eyes darted to her, and he protectively pushed his wing back to conceal it. Aisla's stomach sunk.

"I'm so sorry," she murmured, allowing her hand to fall to her side. "I didn't mean for any of this."

She knew Muinin didn't blame her, and that almost made it worse. Aisla squeezed her eyes shut and opened them again. She could no longer linger in the past and dwell on her guilt.

There had to be a way out.

She exhaled and turned in a slow circle, looking for any hint of civilization. Aisla cringed as the evidence of the lofa stared back at her from every angle she could view. It had begun in the south after all, and it had poisoned their plants and their trees, leaving them unusable. The populations had been forced to migrate north to escape it. While it was miraculously no longer spreading, the crops were still dead. Aisla could see their grey and decay. In a way, they reflected the way Eire had been when Aisla last saw her.

It was a visible reminder of her lost and failing realm. Her realm would not last many more winters without trade with Iomlan, which would be even more impossible to negotiate now—thanks to her.

There was something in her that hoped protecting the Silenced World Tellers' libraries would be enough to keep them in the south despite lofa. If they stayed to be near their books and the knowledge they had gathered, hopefully they were still here to be found. Maybe they even thought there was a cure amongst their own resources. Aisla was certain someone would've shared it with the rest of the realm if they had found one.

Yet, a feeling she had tried her best to ignore still whispered her fears that the society written about in *The Dawn of Talam* had been wiped out before the lofa even started. No one had spoken of it to her. She only knew it from the book she could only find a single copy of.

She had to wonder what knowledge they held that would lead them into the silence and hiding.

Aisla's hand instinctively reached for *Oidhe* where it always was in her waistband, but it was not there. And it was not safe to go back for it.

She hissed a curse under her breath.

Aisla stalked through the unfamiliar woods with nothing but her torn shirt, linen pants, and the letter in her thick wool socks. Then there was Muinin, who flew just above the treetops, staying nearby, but not close enough to draw attention. He was the only reason she felt safe carrying onwards without fear of death waiting for her in the woods.

The Dawn of Talam described the society as one that was obsessed with the pursuit of knowledge. They followed in the steps of Eabha, the mother goddess. They were a people of human, elves, and dwarves alike who spent their waking hours chasing after a wealth of wisdom and recording it on parchment with their quill pens.

They went so far back in history that they had discovered events and places and people that were never mentioned in scoil. Others began to hear of their stories, and grew suspicious of their intentions. Many thought they made up stories to claim as knowledge. People outside of their circle wondered what was truly the telling of Talam, and what could have been myths created for manipulation.

But the world tellers had written and signed a pact that declared they would only ever pen words that were proven to be truth. Anything that was speculation must clearly be marked as such. They referred to these speculations as theses. The pact was signed in blood and became supernaturally binding, or at least that's what was written.

Anyone who broke the pact, writing falsities, mysteriously passed on the moment they lifted their pen from the parchment.

The thought sent a shiver down Aisla's spine as she wondered how many of them could have been blissfully unaware that the words they penned were not true.

Eventually, they were shunned from society, and forced to find their own land. And soon, they were blotted from the telling of the world all together, at least as far as Aisla could tell.

She wondered if that was why there were no records of the prophecy. Nothing had ever been given to the mortals on Talam to solidify the prophecy, and anything they knew about it had only been shared by word of mouth.

The Dawn of Talam didn't note how many members were in the Silenced. It only said that they had fled and migrated south to build their library away from the capital and prying eyes. They sought land away from the scrutiny and the threats. There had to be a reason they were silenced, and a reason their books were not taught in scoil.

If she could find anyone that knew the runic language that adorned the parchment her grandmother had given Ruairi, it would be the Silenced World Tellers—that much Aisla was certain of. On top of that, Aisla was encouraged that the Silenced World Tellers' passion for the lesser-known knowledge of Talam might mention the prophecy. Even if they weren't confident enough to pen it, Aisla had seen no restrictions on verbally sharing falsities.

Aisla would do anything to learn more about her role in the prophecy of the norns and the games of gods who treated the lives of mortals like pawns.

As she read *The Dawn of Talam*, she learned the story of a norn who found love with an elf of Bitu. The norn was called Verdandi, the norn of the present and current times. She had fallen madly in love with a male name Skrymir.

Skrymir was the tallest elf in all the telling of the worlds. He was handsome and good, but cunning and ambitious. Verdandi fell in love from afar as she watched his fate play out. She knew he was to perish of a poison presented to him by a brother that sought to take his place as Lord of Bitu. On the eve his life was to pass on, Verdandi took on the form of a female elf and showed up outside of his castle's gates.

She was more beautiful than any being Skrymir Unfrig had ever laid eyes on, but not only that, she was wise, and she was kind. Verdandi had never presented herself to anyone beyond the elven infants the norns visited upon the nightfall of their births, but she could not keep away from him. Her sisters had pleaded with her not to, even demanded she remained with them, hidden in their tear in the realms that no one else could access, but they could not stop her, as no one sister held more power over the other.

Verdandi asked Skrymir to eat with her along the shores of the sea, and stole him away from the fate his brother had nearly given him. They woke up in the sand, tangled in each other's arms, and Verdandi lived three centuries as the male's mate.

They were blissfully happy. It was a mating of pure joy that neither had known before meeting the other. Verdandi never shared with Skrymir who she truly was, as it was the one demand her sisters had required should they take on the weight of a job meant for three while she lived with her love.

As Skrymir grew old, Verdandi grew anxious for the world that she watched Skrymir love so dearly. For she knew the words to the prophecy that she and her sisters had sworn to Sionna they would keep a secret from the mortals.

But she could no longer keep it from him. She could no longer keep her beloved in the dark. On the eve of the anniversary of their mating, Verdandi told the male everything. She spoke the words of the prophecy, and the male pushed away from her, suddenly terrified.

He ran from the bedroom they shared and called to his two brothers, telling them everything he could recall, but it was foggy and blurred, as Verdandi had muddled his mind while he ran away from her even though it pained her to do so. It was all she could think to do in her panic at the way he took the news.

From there, the word spread like wildfire, its truth fading with each ear that heard it.

Verdandi was heartbroken. While it was not within her power to wipe his memory entirely, she cursed the words of the prophecy so they may never be put on a page. Not by any mortal.

She and her sisters had then revoked the esos of seers from all the realms. Never again would an elf be able to peer into the future.

Verdandi returned home to grieve with her sisters, while Skrymir was too busy preparing for a fate that was still generations and centuries away.

Aisla only hoped that the Silenced would know more of the story.

All she knew, and all that she had been told, was that she was capable of all nine forms of esos, as she was the elf born into the richest bloodline during the ninth generation. It had been confirmed by the norns upon her birth.

And Aisla was fated to be blessed or cursed with it. It meant she was fated to save or end the nine realms of Talam.

It was nearing dusk when Aisla finally saw a light in the distance. It did not appear to be the towering library she imagined for the Silenced, but Aisla did not care any longer. She needed food. She needed a blade and a cloak to keep her warm in the night.

She carried on towards it, as the feeling of defeat crept into her chest. Her eyes blurred in and out of focus with exhaustion. She'd hardly slept the night before between her conversations with Ruairi and her rude awakening at the hands of the masked assaulters.

The light appeared far away, but grew brighter with each step she took. After she had walked five more swords' lengths, Aisla realized the light was no mark of civilization. It was simply a glowing orb that hovered near the trunk of a towering pine tree.

You are so close, young one. The familiar female voice sounded within her skull once again, raising the hair along Aisla's arms.

She still hadn't figured out what exactly it meant to have a voice inside of her head, but she had no reason to assume it had malicious intent. It was comforting to hear it now of all times. She needed a sign, and she got one.

Aisla took another step towards the light with more confidence. There was something alluring about it that drew her in. She closed the distance until she was close enough to reach out and touch it.

She glanced around the clearing to confirm there was no one else in sight. Aisla reached a shaking hand out and caressed the light that glowed brilliantly. The surrounding light faded to the dark of the night.

It sent a faint shock through her body, and she swore she felt the ground beneath her feet tremble. Aisla's eyes grew wide, and she took a step back, away from the mysterious orb.

It glowed brighter for a beat, and Aisla slunk away from it, shrinking back into the cover of the trees. Then it flickered out, but Aisla did not have time to ponder its purpose as a low growl sounded behind her.

9
WEYLIN

Weylin held his head high as he strode into the entry hall of Castle Eagla with Callum at his right side. There was an anxious energy in his chest that he could not explain. It was a feeling he had not felt when he'd asked for her hand in mating.

Her cloud white hair caught his attention first when he rounded the corner. Then, his eyes were pulled to the matching hair of her older brother, Oisin. Weylin's mother and father stood with them in the hall, but it was otherwise empty. Rania was dressed in a pale blue gown. It was a similar shade to the color of her dress on the day of their betrothal celebration, but the dress was far less elegant and intricate. It was simple.

It seemed as though a lifetime had passed since he had last seen her.

So much had changed since that sunset when a dove had ripped her mother's eye from its socket. It was far more than he had had time to understand for himself. He did not know if there would ever truly be time to come to terms with the sunrises spent with the enemy of his family—the enemy to his throne who had become something of a friend. If only briefly, and if only to turn on him in the end.

A familiar rage riled in his blood at the thought, but he pushed it down as he closed the distance to greet his betrothed.

The hint of guilt gnawed at his stomach when he neared her, a polite smile masking his face. He had shared a kiss with the *mallaithe*. A brief one, no doubt, as she had shoved him away. But in that moment, it had felt as though it were over far too soon. In that moment, he had wanted so much more, and had forgotten about Rania Dorcas.

But she could not know that. And here she was, in the flesh, at the door to his home. Rania waited for him at the entrance to the castle that would soon be hers as well. Gods bless them, they would one day raise an Udar Apparent of their own within those very walls—an heir to unite Briongloid and Samhradh permanently and irrevocably.

And that was enough for Weylin. He could set everything else aside.

Before he knew it, Weylin was standing before her, and Rania was looking up at him under light lashes that covered her bewildering blue eyes. She still had that charming look of secrets and the untold. It was something that lured and whispered—something that would get any ordinary male in far too much trouble, but Weylin knew better. She grinned when she met his gaze, and he noticed her brother take a protective step towards her.

"My lady Rania," Weylin greeted as he bowed to her. He took her hand before gently pressing his lips to it. She was still cold despite her arrival to Samhradh, the warmest of the seven worldly realms. It all felt so familiar, yet so foreign. "I trust your travels treated you well."

"As well as one could expect," Rania replied in that lilting voice of hers. She shot a sideways glance at her brother, and Weylin got the impression they had run into trouble along their journey of some sort or another. Ideally, Weylin would have sent his own laochs to escort her to Castle Eagla, or she would have been able to journey with her whole family, but given the rush to get her there as a safety precaution in the face of their current predicaments, her brother had to suffice as her only escort. If the whispers on the wind were to be believed, they were quite close as far as siblings go, so Weylin imagined she was thankful to spend the time with him, and thankful for a friendly face in a foreign home. "We are glad to be here now, though."

"I am more glad to see you, I assure you. I still regret the way I left your home, and hope all is well with your family since I last saw them."

A darkness flashed past Rania's eyes, but it disappeared as quickly as it appeared. Rania's eyes glossed over with that poised look that felt false by the moment.

"They have seen better days, as you can imagine, but they are healing. They will be grateful to hear of our safe arrival."

Despite all the complications nagging the back of his mind, and the constant urgency he felt in his chest, Weylin was pleased to see the spark of life that his betrothal brought to his mother's eyes. As he predicted, with his mating ceremony on the horizon, it had given his mother something to look forward to, something to throw herself into. It was those types of distractions—the balls, feasts, and celebrations—that brought his mother joy. She loved planning and organizing and decorating.

And he was thankful to give her something to work on.

"They look forward to their visit. As well as the melding of our threads," Rania said, pulling him from his thoughts. She turned her grin upon his mother, Niamh. "You look lovely, by the way. I wish we could have met sooner. "

Weylin watched the blush creep into his mother's cheeks as she gave a genuine smile. Perhaps the most genuine in the room.

Visitors rarely gave Niamh attention, not when they were too busy vying for the approval of his father. The Udar had remained silent during the conversation. Weylin assumed he had already greeted them when he went to allow them entrance into Castle Eagla. Faolan did not often waste his time on pleasantries or words that went beyond what was necessary.

"Thank you," Niamh replied with a slight bow of her head. "You as well. I could not have dreamed up a better mate for my son if the heavens had allowed me to craft her myself. You truly live up to the name 'Gem of Dreams.'"

"You flatter me, Niamh," Rania said. Weylin had the sudden thought that this was going too well, almost as though it had been rehearsed. He wondered how much Rania knew about playing the game, and how her skills might compare to his. He was certain she could find trouble if she thought herself wiser than she was. "And who might this be?" Rania asked, and she boldly turned her gaze upon Callum.

Rania did not wait for introductions. She would make her own.

"This is Callum Ronan. He is the captain of my personal guard, and the strongest laoch you will ever meet. Besides me, of course," Weylin said, and Callum bowed in Rania's direction. "As my mate, I'm sure you two will become good friends. He is like a brother to me, as I have none of my own."

"At your service, my lady," Callum said with a smile as he straightened.

"It's a pleasure to meet you." Rania gathered her skirts in her pale hands and returned his bow. "I look forward to our friendship."

"Shall I show you to your rooms? I'm sure you would like to get settled in after your long journey," Weylin said and stepped forward. He offered his arm, and she took it gently, but firmly. The same way she had that evening in Briongloid all those sunrises ago.

He had been eager then, excited for the prospect of what was to come, but now there was a foreboding that had not left him since the landing of the wyvern. Weylin had never expected a mating of love, and he knew his mating to Rania would not be one. Not to start at least, but if it was possible to learn to love, he was sure they could learn to love each other.

Weylin had not seen many examples of love in his life, but he'd heard the tales of love so fierce not even the gods could tear the two from each other. He didn't know if he believed it any more than he believed the monsters in myths made to threaten children into obedience. Especially not when there had not been a pairing of searc in generations. Searc was the mating of two true mates of the heart—equal in mind, body, and spirit, and bound by the norns in a way that could not be ignored. It was supposed to be the sort of love written about in those tales. It was said to be revealed to them by the binding of a golden thread. Whether it was a metaphor or a physical thing, Weylin did not know. And whether any of it was real, Weylin did not know either.

"Please! I would love to rest my feet before we dine," Rania replied cheerily, and they started off down the hall.

Callum and Oisin remained behind with his parents, and Weylin could feel four sets of eyes on them as they made their way deeper into the castle.

"I am delighted to see you here, so soon," Weylin said once they were out of earshot of the others.

"Are you now?" Rania spoke in that voice that taunted, gently. "I should think your mind to be occupied with other matters more pressing than the arrival of your betrothed."

There was an edge in her voice that hinted at something greater than what was obvious to the rest of the world. A panic rose in Weylin's gut as he wondered if she could be referencing the *mallaithe*, and if she was, how she could have possibly found out. He cleared his throat, preparing a response, when Rania spoke again.

"Much has changed in this world since the landing of the wyvern —and right in your courtyard, if the whispers on the wind are to be believed."

Relief flooded Weylin's chest as he nodded in response. "You are right about that," he replied. "There are many matters that occupy my mind during such unprecedented times, and there are many demands as the Udar Apparent when my home and my family are so heavily tied into it all. But that does not take away from the fact that I am pleased to meet your gaze once again. I have thought of you many times since I last saw you."

That part was a lie. He had hardly had the time to think about her since leaving her home, as evidenced by his lapse in judgment next to that rushing river when he held the lifeless body of the *mallaithe* that he had somehow breathed life into. But it was the right thing to say, and Weylin had perfected the art of saying the right words at the right time.

While Weylin would have little time in the coming moons to devote to their courtship, moments like these would be essential to forming a cordial relationship with his mate.

"I am glad to hear it," she said, but she did not sound fully convinced. "Tell me about it—the wyvern—that day. All of it."

Weylin nearly missed a step at her request. No one had asked him to recount that day before, and he spent most of his time trying to forget the details and focus only on the impact. It was the only way he had begun to rid himself of the rage that had threatened to consume him in the wake of Aisling Iarkis.

Rania said nothing about his misstep. She simply continued forward, her eyes focused ahead down the long stone hallway decorated with the Myrkor colors of maroon and marigold.

"I, well, I had just returned home from our betrothal—"

"It took you a while to return, did it not?" she interrupted, and irritation flared through Weylin. What was the point of her requesting him to tell the full story, if she was going to interrupt him before he could finish the very first sentence?

"Yes, you are correct. I took my time returning home, as it is not often that I have the chance to leave without the escort of my personal guard, and I will admit, the freedom was nice."

Weylin, his father, and Callum had agreed to keep his travels with the *mallaithe* from the rest of the world. They were the only ones who knew, and they intended to keep it that way. There was no point in spreading word of his failure. They were already failures that would haunt him until his final breath. He could have sat back and watched her life end on more than one occasion, but each time, he had intercepted. His fate had been to keep her own fate moving. And he would curse the norns every day for it.

"That's fair enough," Rania said, skepticism lacing each syllable.

"As I was saying," Weylin began, and he could practically feel the wave of annoyance that passed over Rania at the words. *Good,* he thought to himself before continuing. "I returned the night before the *mallaithe* reached the castle and spoke with my father, who had gotten word from one of our own sources that the *mallaithe* was headed towards Castle Eagla. Our source also shared that she had not come into her power and would not pose a threat as far as her esos was concerned. We were told she would be easy to put down and that the prophecy could be ended once and for all, and we would save the realms from the doom foretold. Of course, someone was feeding lies to our intelligence, and she blew through the league of laochs we had escorting her to the throne room. She stormed in demanding some cure for a plague that ails Eilean. There was no such cure, and I haven't the slightest idea why she would assume we had it, or why it was worth her arrival to Samhradh, of all places. The lack of cure was rather upsetting to her, and I have the feeling seeing the throne of her ancestors with my father atop it didn't help either.

The female went absolutely *feral*. Like a wild animal. She was vicious and cruel—there was no reasoning with her. Her esos was so strong it consumed the room, and there was nothing we could do to put an end to her. She used her esos of winds to yank the breath from my lungs. She thought she had ended me, but I woke up in time to see her beast escaping our courtyard."

Part was truth. Part was false. It was the story that the Udar had woven to be spread throughout the realms. The story of a ruthless, evil, and cursed *Gheall Ceann*. One to remind the realms of the translation of the prophecy that spelled death, destruction, and the end of all life on Talam.

One part he knew to be a lie. He knew that Aisla Iarkis had never intended to kill him. If she had wanted to, she could have with a simple extra tug down the thread of her esos that choked off his air supply just enough to knock him out. It was a calculated amount—that much he knew beyond a doubt.

She could not bring herself to kill him. And that fact was her weakness—his strength.

"And what was it like?" Rania asked.

"Her esos was overwhelming. I've never felt such raw power, and blades were no match for it."

"Not her. The *beast*. The *wyvern*. What was it like?"

"Oh. The wyvern was massive," Weylin responded. Of all the things about that day, he didn't find himself revisiting those final moments when the wyvern beat its wings and blew a massive gust of flames into the air. And he probably should have. The wyverns had not been seen on Iomlan since the War for Descendants. He had only known them as drawings in books of the world tellers. "It was like nothing I've ever seen before, and no illustration does it justice. It's a creature of nightmarish destruction, and there was nothing friendly about it. Those things will be our biggest threat in the coming war—perhaps the only serious one they pose against us."

"I wouldn't underestimate our enemy. It appears we have already made that mistake once," Rania said.

Weylin bristled defensively. At the same time, those words spoken atop Eolas in a realm far from Samhradh haunted him with Rania's reminder.

"*Don't underestimate me, Fenian Daro. Not for a moment,*" Ellora, who was never really Ellora, had threatened.

"What do we have to combat the wyvern?" Rania asked.

"That's one of the many problems our dwarves and laochs are working on at the moment," Weylin responded, and cleared his throat. "We'll need bigger weapons. Spears large enough to launch from the ground and propel fast enough to take the beasts down from the skies. We're also working on a material that will resist their esos of flames. We're making progress, but it is slow progress, I am afraid. All our weapon plans during the War for Descendants were stolen by their spies, so they could keep the advantage of their wyverns, and anyone who helped work on them is long dead."

"I should like to attend such conversations—the ones regarding our tactics and strategy moving forward."

Weylin did not know if it was her gall at assuming she could attend their meetings or the way she said *our* like she was already a part of Samhradh that made him stop in his tracks and turn to face her. She stopped and faced him in the same moment, as if she had been anticipating his reaction. Her blue eyes were steely and unyielding, and Weylin did not know how to respond to her request that sounded more like a demand.

"I'm afraid that would be my father's call," he said with a forced sympathetic frown. Her expression didn't falter for even a beat as she narrowed her eyes at him.

"One day, Weylin Myrkor, you will be the Udar, and you will no longer be able to hide behind the reign of terror your father wields. One day, you will make decisions and craft your own legacy, choosing how your reign will be remembered. And that legacy will be mine own as well." The words rushed from her lips like water from a faucet. "You can start by having the guts to tell me here and now your decision regarding my attendance in such strategy meetings. I'd respect an outright no a Hel of a lot more than blaming your father for the eventual no he will give me."

Weylin grit his teeth and forced hot breaths in and out through his nostrils. He had to fight the temper rising in his chest. He knew he could not let her words get the best of him. It was exactly what she wanted, and he could see it in the smirk that steadily made its way onto her pale lips.

"Fine. You want me to make that call? Then I will see you there, Lady Dorcas. No reason my mate should be left out of such conversations," Weylin spoke at last.

He couldn't wait to watch the members of his father's inner council tear her ideas to shreds like wolves on a deer. Rania Dorcas had no idea what she just agreed to.

"Thank you," she said with a grin of satisfaction. "That is all I needed to hear."

"My pleasure." He sneered. "Did you spend your days in Castle Tromlui plotting and planning?"

"No, not at all," she responded with unnerving calmness. Then she took his arm once again, and they started back down the corridor towards her rooms.

Again, Weylin was left with the feeling that he was on the outside of some joke he could not possibly understand.

And he hated the feeling.

It was dark out when Weylin made his way to his father's office. Most of the castle's inhabitants had gone to sleep. The moons were beginning their nightly parade across the sky, and Weylin had finished dinner with Rania and Oisin.

He left the dinner with confidence that they would fit well into the dynamics of Castle Eagla. The conversation had flowed naturally for the most part. There was a slight tension in the air, as if both parties were keeping secrets of their own, but of course they were.

That was only natural in the world of politics—a fact Weylin had known for as long as he could remember.

He yanked the great wooden door open to reveal his father

holding a piece of parchment up in the torchlight. He barely glanced up when Weylin entered the room.

"Yes?" His father drawled and continued to scan the page.

"I come to discuss the dispute in Earrach," Weylin said before taking the seat across from his father. He sat straight as an arrow. He was poised as the Udar Apparent ought to be. "Word of their internal conflict has reached my laochs. This is an opportunity to reinforce our alliance in the time of the ninth generation. We'll come out with a favor owed."

"Earrach has never shown ill will towards Samhradh. Why should we doubt them now?"

"Not doubt them, but one can never be too certain. You have heard the rumors of Corren Kyne. The male is an absolute brute, and Noland is only growing older. Who knows what Corren should think himself capable of once his father passes on, and then we'll be dealing with his reign as Lord of Earrach. If I step in and help them solve the dispute of the elemental spirits before it affects their laochs too greatly, they will be in our debt when it comes time to rally our alliances. And their legions will be stronger for it."

"And we should weaken our own to save theirs? We cannot risk our laochs. Especially not now of all times," his father said, lowering the parchment to look at Weylin. His eyes were cold and unflinching.

"I don't think we need to send our own," Weylin said, and Faolan leaned in curiously. "If I go myself, that would show enough good will towards them to get what we need out of it. I will meet with Noland to negotiate the peace terms, and they wouldn't dare go against the crown. A dispute between sylphs and undines couldn't possibly take too long to end. Even so, the sooner the better. And if I step in, Noland will surely be grateful. We need to lock in alliances before it is too late, and we are taken off guard. We'll need all the strength we can gather heading into the Inevitable War. The sooner we can strike Eilean, the more likely we can catch them while they are still scrambling to prepare with what little resources they have."

"You have obligations in Samhradh, Weylin. Leave them to sort their own drama," Faolan said before leaning back in his chair and turning his attention back to the parchment in his hands.

Weylin's fists clenched at his side.

"What obligations? Planning a mating ceremony that Mother is more than capable of handling herself? Or should I ask how involved you were in your own?" Weylin snapped.

"Watch it, *boy*," Faolan snarled back. "What of your betrothed? You plan to leave her on her own while you go play hero in a battle that is not your own? Surely you won't bring her along with you to the battlefront."

"She doesn't need entertainment," Weylin growled. "Callum will be here. He can ensure she feels comfortable in her new home. Not to mention Oisin, as well."

"You intend to go to Earrach without the captain of your guard?" His father scoffed. Weylin's fingers curled into the armrests of the chair until his knuckles strained against the surface of his skin.

"The captain of *my* guard is the chief engineer in crafting *your* weapons to oppose the wyverns. He is needed here more than I am, if you paid any attention."

Faolan's eyes narrowed at Weylin in the silence that ran taut between them. Weylin saw the near tangible darkness writhing in his father's brown eyes. He clenched his jaw.

"It seems you have yet to learn the proper way to speak to your Udar, *son*."

There was no doubting they were moments away from escalating the situation. The air whispered of violence and a brewing rage. His father had not laid a hand on him in many moons, but Weylin would certainly not put it past him.

Weylin was older now, and capable of standing up for himself—and his father was well aware.

He was curious how it might have played out had the door to the study not flung open.

Weylin whirled to face the laoch who interrupted them.

"M-my lord," the man stuttered with a brief bow to them both. There was a deep concern etched into the creases of his brow, and Weylin felt uneasy before the man finished his sentence. "It's your brother, my Udar, they found his body just outside the city this morning."

10

AISLA

Aisla thought her sunrises spent on Iomlan had steeled her against surprises of the woods. She thought she trusted her training enough to keep her alive.

But that was when she had a blade at her side—when she had anything at all.

Aisla balled her hands into fists and whirled to face the sound. She found herself facing an enfield. It was a creature no taller than her waist with the body and head of a fox, but the front legs of an eagle equipped with long, threatening talons, and great striped wings connecting at its front legs and protruding from behind its shoulder blades. It had the hindquarters and tail of a red wolf.

Aisla's eyes widened at the sight.

She had never seen one in person, only heard legends of the intelligent creatures. Legends spoke of the enfields protecting burial sites when an esteemed elf passed away, but no one had seen them in many generations.

She did not have time to piece it together as she wondered how the creature's presence could relate to the strange glowing bulb that drew her there.

There was an echoing silence in her ears as she desperately pulled at her dormant esos, not that she had expected anything different. She swore under her breath, bracing herself for a fight. The creature pulled its lips back in a snarl that revealed sharp, white teeth that glinted in the light of the setting sun.

Aisla had little hope of fighting the beast unarmed. And even less hope of outrunning it.

"I mean no harm," she whispered, unclenching her fists and facing her palms out in surrender as she took a step backwards. "I'll be on my way now."

The creature did not advance, but another low sound rumbled through its throat, sending Aisla's heart pounding. She held her breath as though that would keep it at bay.

"Please, I lost my way," she said. "I won't bother you again."

The beast darted towards her and gnashed its teeth. Aisla startled and stumbled, tripping over a root and falling backwards onto the heels of her hand. Curiously, the enfield stopped in its tracks, as if tugged by an invisible leash, and looked back over its raised hackles.

Aisla followed its attention, afraid of whatever might have been threatening enough to stop it.

Aisla's throat dried as she met the silver-eyed gaze of a female elf that looked to be around her age. She had dark brown hair and stood half a head taller than Aisla.

In that moment, Aisla knew she was either fatally doomed or miraculously saved.

"What are you doing here?" the female asked. She narrowed her eyes at Aisla, and Aisla felt shame heating her cheeks as she peered up from where she had fallen to the ground. The female looked her up and down, dragging her gaze across Aisla's disheveled state. She did not come across as aggressive, but no part of her tone or expression indicated friendliness either. The enfield padded over to the female and sat down at her feet, its bushy and feathered tail winding around her ankles.

"I was looking for a village, and it appears I have not found one," Aisla said. "I'll be on my way now."

Aisla gathered herself to stand. She inhaled a sharp breath, praying to the gods that she could avoid any form of conflict. It was the last thing she needed.

"We are far from any villages here," the female spoke again. Her voice was rough and low. She took a step forward and reached out her hand to Aisla. Aisla hesitantly took it and was hauled to her feet. "Where are you from?"

"Caillte," she answered, choosing honesty this time around.

"What are you doing so far south? Capital dwellers don't often find themselves this way."

"I can see why," Aisla said under her breath. "I was just exploring with my wyvern. We needed to escape the city for a moment, and it seems we've wandered a tad too far from the city."

"Was it a planned exploration?"

"More or less."

"Where are your supplies? Why is your shirt in tatters?"

"It's—it's a long story," Aisla replied. The tension in her shoulders loosened. "If you can point me in the direction of the nearest town or village or city and yes, I know it's far, then I would greatly appreciate it."

"No one explores these parts willingly since the lofa ravaged our crops. There's something you aren't telling me. Speak freely or choke on your blood," the female said.

Within a moment, there was a flash of silver, and the female was clutching a short sword in her right hand. She did not move toward Aisla with it, but the sight of it was a threat enough.

"I've heard of a library here I was hoping to visit." Aisla gave in, and her heart pounded in her chest. "But it appears the rumors were false, and there is nothing for me here. I apologize if I have intruded on your lands. I was truly just looking for the library. Then, it got late, and I needed supplies, and I was hoping to find any sort of civilization. There was a light here that I followed, thinking it might be fire, but it obviously was not. When I touched it, your enfield attacked me."

"A library, you say. And what need have you for a library?"

"I seek knowledge. What other reason could there be?"

"What kind of knowledge?" the female asked with a suspicious gleam in her eyes.

Aisla had been backed into a corner. She could not continue to lie, but she could not risk oversharing with the stranger.

"There's a note my father left to me before he passed on, but he transcribed it in the runic language. I was hoping to find a text that could aid me in translating it."

"And there are no such texts in the capital?"

"No," Aisla answered, surprised. The runic language had not been used since the early ages of elves and dwarves, before man even entered the realms. Why would they possess texts to translate it? "There are not."

"You still have not answered why your shirt is in tatters."

"I was attacked."

"By whom?"

"Those who sought to attack me, who else?" Aisla snapped, growing impatient.

"Hmm." The female eyed Aisla curiously. "I can take you to the library, but only because I have known who you were since the moment I set eyes on you. And the fact that Fella has not ripped your throat out by now is a good sign." She looked down at the enfield and patted him on the head. Aisla's skin prickled with panic. "Regardless, if any of what you have said turns out to be a lie, or you disrespect my home and my people even once, you will be left outside with your limbs bound together at the mercy of the dark of the night. And believe me when I say nothing but olc spirits of Ifreann lurk these woods since the Iofa first reached us."

Aisla merely nodded.

"Come," the female said, and she turned around and walked in the opposite direction.

With no option but to follow, Aisla carried on after her.

Aisla made signals with her hands behind her back, knowing Muinin was still watching from the safety of shadows. It was her way of telling him, *I'm okay. Stay nearby, but it could be a while. I will call if I need you.*

It was enough to get the message she needed across. While Muinin could hear her whisper from across the realms, she would not be able to communicate mind to mind with him until she had mastered her esos of shifters. It was an esos she hadn't worked on often, as the rest always felt more pressing and necessary.

Aisla looked ahead, satisfied with her message to Muinin. She quickly noticed that where the female walked, the enfield followed as though a shadow. They walked past dead trees and rotting bushes. Everything was so dry and so dreary. Aisla winced at the realization that people lived in this.

"What's your name?" Aisla spoke up.

"Eilis," she replied without hesitation. "And yours?"

"I thought you said you knew who I was?"

"I know you are the *Gheall Ceann*," she said, and again the hair raised along Aisla's spine. "But I do not know what name they call you by."

"Aisla," she replied.

"It is nice to meet you, Aisla."

"And you," Aisla said, but she grew wearier with each step onwards. "How do you know my name?" Aisla asked.

Eilis did not reply. A foreboding feeling stirred in Aisla's stomach.

After a while longer of moving in silence, they came upon a massive willow tree. Not only was it massive, but it was still alive. The odd tree was still green, with branches that hung around its trunk to create a curtain she could not see through. The female pulled apart an opening in the overhanging branches and ducked through them, not bothering to hold them open for Aisla.

Aisla followed in her footsteps, pulled the branches back where the female had disappeared, and found herself stepping into a truly beautiful scene. The base of the tree was large and gnarled, but all around it was green grass and blossoming red flowers. It was such a stark contrast to everything outside the branches of the willow tree. She could not help the gasp of surprise that left her lips.

"How?" was all Aisla could think to say.

"We couldn't tell you. All we can understand is that the land must be blessed by the gods. A sanctuary of knowledge that the mother goddess could not overlook."

Aisla nodded, but the thought of the interference of gods twisted a knot in her gut.

She watched Eilis roll away a large stone at the base of the tree to reveal a hole in the ground, and the top of a ladder was just barely visible. If Eilis was taking her to the library, it turned out the towering library was no tower at all, but an underground fortress. No wonder she could not find it on her own.

Eilis lowered herself down the ladder, and Fella stayed behind. Aisla followed behind her, thankful that the ladder felt sturdy beneath the weight of their bodies. The ladder went deep underground, and the hole above them shrunk with each step Aisla took downwards. She peered between the rungs and saw rows and rows of books of every shade. Her eyes widened. The books were old and worn, but beautiful and calling out to her.

Finally, Eilis hit the bottom, and Aisla stepped off the ladder next. The ground beneath them was earthy soil. Aisla looked around at the brightly decorated library. There were couches and chairs and rugs and tables. She couldn't even begin to imagine how they got it all there. It looked comfortable and homey—somewhere Aisla thought she would like to stay for a while, if she didn't have pressing obliga-tions elsewhere in the realm and an unknown amount of time to figure it all out.

There were dwarves, humans, and elves milling about. Some chat-tered near stacks of books, while others were sunk deep into the cush-ioned seats with a book on their laps. Heads turned to her the longer Aisla stood there gawking in disbelief. They furrowed their brows curiously at her, but one look at Eilis and they turned their attention back to whatever they had been doing before her arrival. It was evident that they trusted her—that Eilis had some sway in this place. She seemed like a good friend to make.

"This is the library you seek," Eilis spoke, holding her arms wide to encompass the place. "We have been wondering when the *Gheall Ceann* might find us."

Aisla's palms sweat, and she longed for *Oidhe* at her side, for comfort if nothing else, at the reminder of her title and what it made others want to do to her.

"What do you mean?"

"One would hope that our *chosen one* would care to seek knowl-edge to aid her in her journey. And she only need open *The Dawn of Talam* to find her way here. A book that was planted, and a book that would only reveal its contents when opened by her."

Surprise caught in Aisla's throat at Eilis's revelation. She hadn't the first idea who would have planted such a thing for her. Or why they could not just come to get her themselves.

"It is in our name, Aisling. We are the Silenced World Tellers. And those with no secrets need no silencing," the female spoke with a grim-ness that made Aisla squirm with discomfort.

"It's Aisla," she corrected. "Not Aisling."

Eilis only ducked her head in response.

"How did you know who I was?"

"You will know the answer to that soon enough," Eilis spoke with a confident secrecy. "Come."

Aisla glanced around at the others, watching as she followed after Eilis. She walked past shelves that housed more rows of books. Aisla could hardly fathom how so many words could exist on so many pages. As they walked, more beings came into view. Everyone there seemed so peaceful and calm. Eyes widened when they caught her walking by, but no one seemed upset or afraid. No one moved to interrupt them.

The bookshelves were made of a lovely dark brown wood that added to the warm atmosphere. All the seating was patched together from vibrant cloths, but not in a tacky way—in an elegant way that felt almost luxurious in its own right. The scent of parchment mingled with the scent of tea, and Aisla thought it just might be the most pleasant smell one could live amongst. There were doors along the walls bordered by books. Aisla wondered if they might lead to sleeping chambers. Surely the Silenced World Tellers needed sleep.

"I assume you all live here, then? Underground, I mean?" Aisla asked, clearing her throat awkwardly.

"You assume correctly," Eilis said without looking back at her. "There are community sleeping arrangements, and rooms with just one bed for our elders, and those that prefer it. We rarely leave the area unless we need to—the less attention we attract, the better."

"Why not share the resources with the rest of the realm?"

"Again, there is a reason we are silenced. They do not wish to share our vast wealth of knowledge for fear of what others might do with it. Some things, they prefer to leave dead and buried in the ground with the ashes of our ancestors and the footprints of the ancients. So here we remain."

"What could you possibly know that our leaders would want to keep a secret?" Even as the words left her lips, Aisla could feel herself bristling defensively.

"If you ask such a question, you know less about your grandmother than we thought."

"Don't speak of her that way," Aisla snapped.

They may have ended on bad terms—on rather horrible terms—but Aisla would not let her realm begin attacking their leadership. While her grandmother might be a harsh grandmother, she had sacrificed much as Mathair, and long proved herself worthy of the title.

That was when Eilis finally glanced back. There was clear judgement in her eyes. There was judgement, but also a dash of sympathy that made Aisla uneasy.

"Here," Eilis said, ignoring Aisla's comment altogether. She stopped and gestured down a short corridor that opened into a kitchen. "After you."

Aisla entered, and the moment the scent of smoked vegetables hit her nostrils, she could feel her mouth begin to water. She had forgotten how hungry she was. She had not eaten since lunch the day before, and that was a lunch from her measly, hastily packed supplies from her tent in the woods.

"How do you cook down here?" she asked curiously, and approached a table full of food that had been set out and made herself a plate.

"Do you ever stop asking questions?" Eilis grumbled.

"This is all quite strange to someone who lives above ground," Aisla replied defensively.

"The cooks go up the ladder and cook enough for a week usually. We store it and make it last as long as we can, then do it all again."

Aisla nodded and sat down at a long wooden table.

"And what's your role here?"

Eilis stared at her through narrowed eyes as she lifted a fork to her lips, as if to say *another question?*

"If it wasn't obvious enough, I am a protector, on top of my own search for knowledge. The glowing orb acts as a door knocker here. If it is touched, Fella responds. The enfield represents a guardian of the fallen, and Fella protects our knowledge from its own death. He protects us from discovery. If Fella doesn't kill the intruder before I have the chance to get there, then I handle it, and Fella steps in as needed."

"Totally rational," Aisla grumbled after shoving several bites of food into her mouth. It was better than the meals they ate in Caillte by a long shot. She had more questions, questions about getting food here amid the lofa, but she did not ask them. Not now, anyway. She could save them for another time. "So, is there someone who could help me with my translating dilemma?"

Eilis paused and set her fork down. "About that. I was thinking—"

She stopped mid-sentence, and Aisla caught her eyes widen as she turned to face a disturbance at the kitchen's doorway. Aisla curiously followed Eilis's gaze, and her jaw dropped open.

Her stomach sunk through the floor and down to the core of Talam.

Her heartbeat thundered, and her appetite disappeared as the sound of her fork clattering to her plate echoed through her skull.

She remained rooted in her seat, even though a part of her yearned to jump up and run.

Aisla met familiar yellow-green eyes. Eyes that were as familiar as looking into a mirror, even despite the time apart. Eyes that should not exist. A sight that should not be possible.

Aisla Iarkis met the wide and wild gaze of her *dead* father.

II
RUAIRI

Ruairi yanked the ring off his finger and shoved it deep in his pocket. Bile rose in his throat. There was no hesitation when he turned on his heel and rushed through the door that led him into the makeshift dungeon for the husks.

He nearly forgot to lock the door behind him in his hurry.

Their growls and moans followed his every step. They burned through his ears and made his skin crawl as he fought the urge to vomit. The lock clicked into place, and Ruairi began to run.

He ran until he reached the back entrance to the infirmary, feeling a chill in his bones the whole way there. His palms sweated and his hands trembled. He leaned against the trunk of a tall oak tree as he inhaled deep gulps of early spring air.

His chest was tight.

He tilted his head back and looked up at the branches above as he shifted through the questions that raced through his mind that had nearly fallen to shambles under the pressure of the olc feeling of the ring he held.

How did the ring hold such power over the husks? Was it created or discovered? How did Cliona get her hands on it? And why would she hand such a power over to their enemy, even as a bargaining chip for their cure? How many more were there that he didn't know about? Did any of them truly pass on?

None of it made sense. And with no Aisla and no Eire to talk to, Ruairi found himself running low on options. One thing was for certain. He could not keep the knowledge to himself.

Ruairi's feet carried him onwards before his mind caught up. He was numb as he marched up to the front door of the infirmary. He inhaled a deep breath and pushed through the doors into the building.

"Is Edi in?" Ruairi asked the first mender who met his eyes.

"She's in her office," the mender replied, eyeing him curiously. He was certain she had expected him to make his way to Eire's room on his own, as he did every other day.

"Thank you," he murmured.

The mender furrowed her eyebrows in confusion at his surely wild expression.

Ruairi sucked in a deep breath before he lifted his fist to rap on the door to Edi's office. Moments later, he was greeted by her tired hazel eyes and the lines on her face crafted by age that seemed deeper than the last time he had seen her.

"Do you have a moment?" Ruairi asked by way of greeting.

"Come in," she responded with exasperation.

She took the seat behind her desk that was a mess of papers and vials from testing. He wondered if any of those vials contained Eire's blood, and his stomach turned. He closed his eyes and opened them before taking the empty seat across from Edi.

"I—I think I've happened upon something," Ruairi started. He chewed on the inside of his lip. And it struck him for the first time.

He could not be certain that Edi was not in league with Cliona. Everything she had ever said indicated a political neutrality, but there was no way to be sure. "Edi, can I trust you?"

He did not know if that was the right thing to say. He did not know if she would simply lie to him to hear what he would share next. But Ruairi Vilulf was not made for the world of politics. He was a laoch, not a leader or a manipulator. He had always imagined serving at Aisla's side once she took the throne, and not the one Cliona sat, but her true throne that was stolen away to Castle Eagla. He would give his life to see it returned to her. With or without the throne, Ruairi would serve her in whatever capacity he could, although he had always imagined her hand in his—their fingers intertwined and their hearts beating as one. Aisla knew him well enough to know he would not be involved in the politics, but he would fight whenever and however needed.

His conversation with Edi was so far outside his realm of comfort, he did not know where the next step would lead him, but he could only keep going.

"That depends, Ruairi. What secrets will you ask me to keep? I want to know nothing of our Mathair Apparent. I don't want to know where she has gone, or if she ever plans to return. Her grandmother is looking for her, and that is no business of mine, unless she returns in need of mending."

"That is understandable," Ruairi said, "but this is not about Aisla." He traced nervous circles on his thumb with his index finger.

It felt like a good sign. The fact that Edi wanted to avoid knowledge that would aid Cliona in her hunt for Aisla was enough for him.

"Go on then," she prodded, and in that moment, it was all he needed.

"It's about this," Ruairi said.

He pushed his hand into the bottom of his pocket. That dark feeling rushed to him as he withdrew the silver ring with the emerald stone and set it on the desk in between them. The glint of silver caught in the sunlight filtering in through the window. Edi looked at it, then looked up at him. Her lips pressed into a thin line as concern creased her brow.

"And what might this be, aside from a family heirloom?" Edi said, sounding almost defensive.

"Somehow, it's connected to the husks," he responded. Disbelief crossed her features. "I know it sounds a little insane, and it just might be, but if you would allow me to show you, you'll understand what I mean."

"Show me what?"

"I've had it for a little while now," he said carefully, leaving out the part about where he got it from. "And every time it touches my skin, it feels wrong. And unsettling. There's a darkness to it, and I can't be sure, but it feels like the thing contains olc esos, but it all started to make sense this sunrise. I took it with me to where the husks are held and—"

"I told you, you are not to go there unsupervised, under any conditions," Edi hissed. "It's restricted access only, and last I checked, it was locked."

Guilt heated Ruairi's cheeks, but he could not let her intimidate him. Not until he was able to get through his story, at least.

"It was," he said. "But I needed to test a theory. I went in, and they were distant and noisy just as they were when you took me. Then, I slipped *that* on, and it molded to fit my finger. I held my hand up to them, and I swear to all the nine gods, every husk in the room turned to me—their eyes actually focused on me. They seemed almost alert. I can't explain it. Truly, it would be better if I could just show you, Edi, there's something going on here."

"You've let your imagination run wild, Ruairi. You've been through so much this last moon, and your friends have too. I can only imagine the pressure is getting to your mind. If you see the mender at the desk, she can give you a herb to help you sleep. Surely your nights in that godsdamned castle have messed with your senses."

Ruairi clenched his hands into fists at his side. A war of anger and disappointment and shame battled within him. He was angry she talked to him like he was unwell and could not see the world for what it was. And he was disappointed that he had let himself believe she could help—that she would hear him out. Then, there was that lingering shame that followed with any mention of the torture he had endured by order of the Udar. As if it was his fault he endured it. He had not yet learned how to shake the feeling.

"That's just it," he continued, despite the defeat that threatened to drive him back to his baile. "I heard them—more husks—at the castle. I am certain of it. And now everything that has happened with the ring, somehow it must all be related. Somehow, someone is playing a game with the souls of Talam as though they are pawns to be used."

Saying it aloud felt heavier than it had when it existed only in Ruairi's mind.

"What are you talking about?" Edi asked in disbelief.

The way she asked it did not indicate that she cared to learn more, or that she even wanted a genuine explanation. The tone was that of ridicule, and someone who wished to dismiss. That was the last thing Ruairi had expected from the lead mender of Caillte.

It was so unlike Edi, he didn't know what to make of it all.

A flighty panic rose from his palms to his chest. He was torn between the desperate need for someone to understand—the desperate need to have someone on his side—and then there was an urgency to run. It was a driving need to flee in fear that he had said too much entirely.

The former weighed heavier on him, with the knowledge he had no one left to run to.

Even his own parents had made their support of the Mathair more than clear, despite his open protest to them.

"Please, Edi, you've got to trust me on this. Someone needs to take this seriously other than myself. I've already been removed from the inner council. I've got no pull, but you do."

Edi stood up and darkness washed over her hazel eyes. It was a darkness that made Ruairi wish he had gone in favor of his urge to flee.

"And this is *exactly* why you were removed," she sneered, but it was not anger that ruled that darkness, but fear. Edi looked terrified, and his words aroused something to cause it.

"I'm sorry," was all Ruairi could think to say as he gathered his things to leave.

"You ask too many questions. You stick your nose in business that is far from your own. You put your own life at risk and mark yourself a threat when you let these baseless theories occupy your mind. Do yourself a favor, Ruairi Vilulf, and keep your head down. And if you do not heed this advice, keep my name and my practice *out of it*."

"How many are there, Edi?" He dared one more question, needing to know for his own peace of mind if the rumors were true.

"Leave," Edi snapped in response, her eyes darkening.

Ruairi's heart thundered so loud, he could hardly hear himself think. He could not come up with the words to say, so he let his silence answer for him as he pushed open the door of her office.

"And one last thing," Edi spoke in a voice as cold as winter's ice. "If you come across our *Gheall Ceann*, you tell her to stay far away. She does more harm than good, and I fear I am not the only one who sees it."

Ruairi did not miss the hidden meaning of her words as the door fell shut behind him with a thud that echoed through his very core.

12
AISLA

Aisla still had not found the words to speak or the air to breathe.

Her hands clutched the edge of her wooden seat, gripping it like a lifeline. Her eyes must be deceiving her.

Her father was dead.

This male before her was Feargal Iarkis. It was *impossible*. She couldn't give herself that hope, yet there he was.

Aisla continued to stare into his eyes, as though they would evaporate before her very own. She looked for any sign he could be an imposter. His yellow-green eyes were too stark, too harsh, and too familiar to be real.

The male took a few steps forward, trying his best at a smile that fell short of genuine. He looked cautious, nervous even. She could tell he was afraid of how she might react. That alone brought up an anger she could not explain and that she did not know what to do with.

She was only glad her esos had left her and could not respond to the emotions within her.

"Aisling," he spoke, and the voice was so real—deep, just the way she remembered it. It struck a chord in the pit of her stomach and opened a floodgate of memories she thought she had done away with forever. Tears burned down her cheeks, but words still did not come. "It's me, and I-I'm so sorry."

"My father is dead. I don't know who you are, but I do know my father wouldn't abandon me." Her voice cracked at the last sentence, as she felt her strength leaving her and her head growing lighter.

They were the first words to leave Aisla's lips. They struck and created a drop in his shoulders, a slight falter in his wary smile, and an unmistakable stutter in his step. But he continued to approach her.

"I can explain." He paused beside the bench she sat on. He looked as though he might embrace her and thought better of it. He sat next to her, an arm's length away.

Aisla knew she should have leapt from her seat. She should have flung her arms around him and buried her face in that embrace. Instead, she was frozen to her spot, unable to move, and she cursed herself for it.

"I'll leave you to it, then," Eilis interrupted, and Aisla realized she had forgotten the female was still sitting across from her.

Eilis emptied her tray and scurried from the room that felt so much tighter in her absence. Half of Aisla wanted to plead with her to stay. She wasn't ready to face this, whatever it was, alone.

But Aisla bit her tongue and turned to face the male sitting to her left.

"I would appreciate it if you explained how you are here."

Her voice hadn't come out nearly as strong as she had meant it to.

A part of her was shocked at herself for responding so coldly, even as the realization settled in that it was really him. It could not be an imposter. She thought that, even a moon ago, she might have responded differently.

But now, she had changed. For better or for worse.

She was callous, and that came with distance and distrust. And everything she had been through, everything Ruairi had been through. Would it have been different if her father had been home? Her head began to swim, and the room felt like it was spinning. Aisla fought to push the feeling to the back of her mind.

How could he have left her?

Her father had been her best friend—her everything. Nothing could have torn her from his side, or at least she thought. She had grieved him since the moment she'd heard of his death. And it hurt more than barghest teeth in her flesh to imagine there was something that could make him leave her. And for so long. She didn't know if he had ever intended to see her again, or if he would have been content for her to carry on, believing he was long passed on from the soil of Talam.

The thought made her feel like an intruder. Unwelcome. Her stomach turned in a tumble of nausea.

"It's a long story, and I want you to know I will share every detail with you in time." Aisla felt herself yearning to protest, to demand all of it now, but she waited, wondering what else he had to say. "But what I can tell you right now is I would have never left if I had any other option. If I was not driven away from Caillte, I would have fought for you until my dying breath."

"What could've driven you out of your own home?" Aisla asked. Her body felt far away and detached, silent tears running down her cheeks. She could not stop them.

"It was my mother, Aisla. Your grandmother. She left me with no other choice."

Aisla felt the world go still as a ringing sounded in her ears, and her eyes fixed on a point just beyond her father's head. She hardly knew if she continued to breathe.

Her grandmother?

Cliona had been cold and cruel at times, yes, but ultimately, she was always watching out for Aisla. She had trained her and brought her up as though she were her own. Their last conversation had not been a good one, but she couldn't imagine Cliona being cold enough to run her own son out, or to pull a father away from his daughter—to pull *her* father away from *her*.

"What do you mean?" Aisla breathed out and found her father's eyes once again. There was no mistaking the earnestness in them.

It was a knife to her already bleeding heart.

"She wanted to turn me and your mother against you. She believed the prophecy of Iomlan—the one that declares the doom of Talam at your hands. She never believed the prophecy of Eilean, but she hides it from Caillte and all but her closest peers. They know all the secrets, or at least the ones she shares with them," he said. "My mother was always scheming, and would do anything to get you into the hands of the Udar, as though you were a token and not a soul. She thought it would save Eilean from isolation, and was always looking for ways to barter for power. Your mother and I refused to support it since the moment your mother knew she was with child."

Each breath shuddered through Aisla's chest, and her hands trembled at her sides. She was not sure if it was from rage or fear or something in between. She could hardly see through her tear-blurred vision and made no attempt to clear them away. Her palms sweat and her body grew warm.

"Why not kill me then?" Aisla whispered. "It doesn't make sense."

"You're worth more alive than dead while the Udar is still in power. She just needed us to agree to it."

Aisla shook her head, trying to make sense of it all. But failing.

Her body was number. Her head continued to spin.

"She would never."

"Aisling, she did. Your mother is passed on because of her."

Aisla did not know if it was the fact that she had let herself wonder for a moment if her mother could still be alive as well, or that for the first time in her life, word of her mother's death had come from her father's lips. The words caused a pain so deep, she doubled over and let her head fall into her hands as violent sobs racked through her body.

Her father laid a comforting hand on her back, but she shrugged him off. She felt the world collapsing around her. Walls crumbled as clouds fell from the sky. The ground seemed to gape open as if Hel itself awaited her below. It felt as though all she had ever known had been a lie. She was sure if she still had any access to her esos, the room would have been obliterated by it.

Maybe the entire library.

"I'm so sorry, Aisling. I could never find the right words to explain, and I know it's a lot to take in. I wasn't sure how to begin. I did not know I would be seeing you today."

At that, Aisla's head snapped up. She met her father's wide eyes, with no hesitation.

"Then when were you planning to? Or did you think you were rid of your cursed daughter forever? I wish I could be so lucky as to walk away from the gods' damned prophecy whenever I fancied it."

"It's not like that at all. I wanted to find you—I've wanted to hold you in my arms since the moment I left Caillte—but Cliona doesn't know I'm alive. She thinks me long gone and passed on, and I needed to keep it that way. I wasn't sure how to see you without also seeing her. I have my own contacts in Eilean, instructors in scoil and neighbors by your baile. They inform me of every move you make, and have been helping me plan my return when the time is right."

"And the time wasn't right when they informed you I'd sailed to Iomlan?"

"We both know that wasn't planned. I had no way to know beforehand. I heard of your safe return, and I heard you'd left Caillte. But I always knew where you were—in the woods near the wyvern caves. They told me you'd taken the book, and I knew you would arrive soon. If not, I was to come get you from the woods at the end of the moon in Braon."

Aisla didn't have the words. She clenched her jaw and averted her eyes. The room spun as she turned. Aisla wanted to flee—something she did all too well and too often lately. She could hardly even think. She was relieved, afraid, hurt, and overwhelmed by it all. When she fled Caillte, she had never expected to find this. And to know people had been watching her every step without her knowledge? It felt like an invasion that made the hairs along her arms stand up.

The secrets of her life laced her skin like a thread that was pulled tighter by the norns with each passing beat. They cut into her like wounds of a blade.

"I don't know what to say," Aisla said at last, and turned her head towards him. She could hardly bring herself to meet those eyes that were the same as her own. The same as her own, but warm. "I want the full story. I want to know it all. And you owe—you owe me that—"

She was suddenly unsteady, even as she sat. She could not get the words out. Spots filled her vision until it was all black, and it felt as though the world was falling away beneath her.

Aisla felt herself falling until she was caught by familiar, strong arms.

It was too much. Far too much. Then, it was over.

When Aisla opened her eyes, she was again in that land across the sea.

She recognized the bedroom of the Udar Apparent. This time, Weylin Myrkor was not sleeping in his bed, but he was awake, and writing furiously at his desk.

Aisla's throat dried. She debated what to do next as her eyes again went to his blade resting in the corner of the room. She did not have the benefit of his unconscious state this time, which meant he would almost certainly hear her crossing the room to get it.

She wished she could blink her eyes and return to the Silenced World Tellers' underground fortress. She wished she could disappear. She couldn't handle this—not after everything that had come before she fainted.

But it was too late.

As though alerted by an external force to her appearance, Weylin dropped his pen on the parchment. Aisla's heart thundered in her ears. He turned around and faced her.

She felt the sudden, inexplicable urge to run to him. Despite it all, the betrayal and the history they could never erase, she yearned to fall against his chest that smelled of oak wood and salty air. Aisla wished he would wipe the tears that longed to fall from her eyes, the way he had in Spiorad.

This is not Fenian Daro, she had to remind herself as she stood taller and swallowed down the emotion.

"You really ought to stop showing up in my room in the middle of the night," he spoke with a confidence that angered Aisla so deeply, she trembled. "It's not proper."

Aisla balled her hands into fists.

"Besides, Samhradh is so much more beautiful during the day," he continued. "You ought to see it."

"I have," Aisla growled.

Weylin turned his chair around to face her, and she did not move from where she stood. She scanned him for any glint of a weapon, but he appeared unarmed. She still didn't know if they could harm each other during these visits that posed as dreams. She felt both vulnerable and powerful.

"Ah, yes," Weylin said with a nod. "I suppose you have. Under rather unfortunate circumstances, no, *banphrionsa*?"

"Don't call me that," her voice came out as a snarl, but Weylin did not flinch.

"Only a *banphrionsa* would march into a castle and cause the stir you did," he retorted. "Declaring war all on your own. Few others would think they had the power to do that."

"That wasn't my intent," she snapped. "I never meant for that. We just wanted to leave."

"Intent or not, it is the predicament we find ourselves in," he said.

He stood, and Aisla ground her teeth together as he crossed the large room to her. She refused to step back. He closed the distance until he was standing near enough to touch her. Aisla's breath caught in her throat. Her heartbeat quickened with each moment he grew nearer.

"It's a shame you are who you are," he spoke barely above a whisper. "I had rather thought we were becoming friends."

There was a genuineness to his words she had not expected. His eyebrows knitted together as he observed her, and there was something there other than malice and disgust. It was a feeling that made her stomach clench and her lips part, but she hadn't the words to speak. She wanted to agree, but she couldn't bring herself to.

He reached out and tucked a lock of light brown hair behind Aisla's ear. She froze when his touch left a trail of electricity across her temple. It confirmed what she had both feared and hoped. They could touch here. She could have brought that blade down upon him the last time.

She should have. But she wouldn't.

"I could *never* be friends with the likes of you," she whispered back, looking up at him.

"I don't think you mean that," he replied with a smirk. "But you can believe it if you need to."

"You don't know the first thing about me."

"We both know that isn't true," Weylin said, calmly. "I know you better than anyone else does, I would even venture to say. I know your deepest fear."

"And I know yours," Aisla retorted.

"I am aware," Weylin replied, gently. He still had not moved. They were near enough to touch, but neither of them dared to. "Now, why are you here?"

"I was hoping you could answer that."

Aisla watched Weylin tilt his head in confusion. He opened his mouth to speak, but before any sound came out, Aisla was blinking awake in the dark, small room under the surface of Eilean.

She ran her fingers along that spot on her temple and swore she could still feel his touch.

13

RANIA

Rania Dorcas woke early the sunrise following her arrival to Castle Eagla. It was much warmer in Samhradh than it was in Briongloid, and she found herself missing the chill of the morning as she reached her arms above her head in a stretch and wiped the sleep from her eyes.

She wondered if she would spend the day with her betrothed. The Young Wolf seemed different yesterday. He was distant and a touch cold, but that was to be expected in times such as these. And aside from that, Rania had never expected to mate a male she loved. She didn't hold high hopes for romance and flowery language shared between the sheets—not as the other females her age dreamed of and wrote about in the journals they kept beneath their pillows. Rania would be a fool to put such hopes in her own mind, and such things had never been her motivation, anyway.

Rania's parents may not have seen it as she had grown up in the shadows of Castle Tromlui, always hiding behind the bravery and boldness of Oisin, but those shadows had enabled her to study the game far better than he. She was more than prepared to play it, no matter the costs. It benefited her that her parents had never imagined she would come into a position such as this. It meant their surprise was genuine, but she had long expected Weylin's visit to her home.

It felt like something of a reward to wake up in the capital of Samhradh that morning. The city that would become her home. The city where she would lie next to a mate that sat the Arden Throne. She longed for nothing more than that.

Rania burrowed beneath the down quilt for a moment longer, taking it all in. She inhaled a deep breath, and then she pulled herself out of the nest she had created. Her feet touched the cold stone floor, and she crossed the room to her private bathing chamber. She ran a bath perfumed with cedar and lily, taking her time before presenting herself to her new realm.

When she was ready and dressed in a maroon gown to represent the Myrkor dynasty, she made her way to her brother's room on the other side of the corridor.

Before she could knock, the door opened to Oisin. His brilliant blue eyes were wide, and his hair was still ruffled from sleep.

"Well, good morning, brother," Rania cooed with a grin. "Busy night?"

"No, I mean, well, yes," he stammered, gathering his thoughts. Her brother was known as a bit of a philanderer back home, and she had expected the reputation to follow him here, although maybe not quite so soon. It was fair enough, though. He was in no rush to mate since his seat as Lord of Briongloid was secured, regardless.

"Oh? Am I interrupting? I can leave."

"No." Oisin shook his head, but still had not opened the door wide enough to allow her in. "She left already. I've news to share regarding the Udar. He sent a messenger to my rooms and asked me to join him and Weylin today. Faolan's brother, Conroy Myrkor, Lord of the Samhradh Plains, was found dead last night. The three of us are going to retrieve his body."

"Well, I take it as a good sign they chose to invite you. I assume they're leaving soon, but you mustn't leave your room looking like this." Rania looked him up and down, with a pointed glance at his messy state. "Here," she said and brushed past him into his room, noting the disheveled bed as well. "You go wash your face and fix that mess of hair. I'll find something proper for you to wear."

Oisin let out a groan but listened. They had always been like that. Oisin was a mess, and Rania was around to clean it up. At the same time, Oisin was wise and a valuable asset to their realm. Rania just wished he could be more organized and conscious of how he was coming across to the world. She worried how he would fare without her once he went back home, and she did not. On top of that, Oisin had always been her best friend, and the day he left her in Samhradh would be a hard day.

Losing him would be no easy sacrifice.

But she could not linger on the thought. She would face that moment when it arose.

Rania heard the water running in the washroom as she shuffled through his wardrobe that had been prepared prior to their arrival. There was a vast array of colors inside, but similar to her own dress, she thought it best he wore a Myrkor marigold top and found a pair of black pants to go with it. She laid them out on his chaise and went about straightening up his bed.

"You know you don't need to do that," Oisin called around his toothbrush.

"I'm aware," Rania chirped back, but did not stop.

"Then why bother?"

"Why not?"

"Because it's a waste of time. I'm only going to get back into bed at the end of the day."

"Trust me, the partners you bring back here will appreciate it."

"If you say so," he replied, wiping his mouth on a towel and tossing it onto the counter before walking towards her.

He looked better already—less asleep, at least.

"So, you are leaving this morning, I take it? As is my betrothed?"

"Yes. It will be us and his father making our way to the scene of Conroy's death," Oisin responded. "I'll be sure to tell him all my favorite terrible things about you, since he'll now be stuck with you. I'll tell him how you're terribly competitive and a horrible loser. The way you go to bed so early that you're practically a grandmother. Or maybe the insufferable way you must keep everything so damn neat and tidy. I can't imagine having to live with you for the rest of our cruelly long lives. I suppose Weylin will have to manage."

"Only if you tell him all the great things, too," Rania said, walking up to her brother. "You'd have to tell him how I am far smarter than you or anyone else in Castle Tromlui. And you'd have to mention how I best you nine times out of ten with my blade. And, of course, you couldn't forget to tell him I make a perfect tart when given the proper ingredients."

"Only half of those things are true," Oisin said and rolled his eyes. "So full of yourself these days."

"If one does not have confidence, or at least the ability to feign it, what does one have?"

"So humble, my sister," Oisin said. "What are you planning to do while we are away for the day? I do feel bad leaving you alone on our first sunrise in Omra."

"I have entertained myself for as long as I can remember, and a change of scenery won't stop me now. Don't worry about me. I've got plenty of exploring to do in my new home. Enjoy your day out with the royals. And brother?" Rania said as she passed Oisin and headed for the door. "Do remember to put on real shoes."

She looked down at his slippers, and Oisin loosed a chuckle that brought a smile to her lips.

Rania made her way to the gardens that surrounded Castle Eagla. The flowers in Omra were much more vibrant than the flowers of Scamall. She had been surprised that no one stopped her on her way outside, but it was a pleasant surprise.

She had worried that she would be treated delicately upon her arrival. So many often felt the need to dote on her or treat her as breakable, merely because she was a female. But Rania Dorcas had never had trouble holding her own, and was thankful for the solitude outside of the castle walls she found in the garden.

Her fingers grazed across the soft petals as she made her way along the paving stones nestled between lush green grass. She couldn't help but wonder how they kept the grass so vibrant when sand surrounded much of the city beyond the castle.

She hummed a lullaby her mother used to sing to her as she glided through the beautiful flora, in no rush to be anywhere at all. It was a pleasant feeling, at least for the time being.

She took her time examining each new plant, admiring the variety and brilliance of their colors. She felt eyes on her. There were whispers as others passed her, but she paid them no mind.

Rania looked up and found a familiar male sitting on a bench along the edges of the gardens. He had his nose buried in a book.

"Cormac? Was that your name?" Rania called out to him, making her way towards him.

But she knew his name was Callum—Callum Ronan, the captain of Weylin's personal guard, that would soon become her personal guard as well.

"It's Callum, milady," he said. He closed the book and stood, greeting her with a bow. "I didn't expect to see you out here."

"Oh, you didn't?" she asked, raising a curious brow at him. "You mean my betrothed did not task you with watching over me while he is away? If he was so worried, he should've just taken me with him."

"They were unsure how gruesome the scene would be—"

"Ah, not fit for a lady? I should have expected," she said with a dramatic sigh. She watched Callum's body language shift defensively. She decided to change her approach, as she figured she ought to make friends in her new home, and Callum would not be going anywhere anytime soon. There were plenty of stories of the captain of the guard and the Udar Apparent. Their friendship ran thicker than blood, and Rania had a lot of respect for such a bond. "Never mind that. Don't you have things to do today? I would hate to be a distraction, and hereby relieve you of whatever duty Weylin has assigned you regarding me."

"I was mostly taking today off anyway," Callum responded. "I've hit a roadblock in weaponry plans I'm working on and needed a day to think about it."

"This is a beautiful place to think, I suppose," Rania said, gesturing to the lovely gardens that surrounded them. She could truly think of no better place, in Samhradh at least, from what little she had seen so far. Rania took a seat on the bench Callum had previously occupied, and he sat down, almost hesitantly, next to her. "What sort of weaponry plans are you working on?"

"I'm working on engineering something to combat the wyverns. Some of the world tellers' books outline weapons used in the past, but we're looking for something bigger—more efficient."

"Weylin mentioned something like that," Rania said, and Callum looked surprised. "He had not mentioned that you were working on it, though."

"Does it surprise you that I am?"

"Maybe. A bit. You just seem rather young, is all."

"I see. You would prefer an elderly male with trembling fingers and worsening eyesight to tinker with the miniscule nuts and bolts that make up these weapons."

A smile rose to Rania's lips as she felt Callum warming to her.

"Not like that," she said, and he returned her smile.

The man radiated an inexplicably familiar warmth. He was easy to talk to. She paused to really look at him for the first time. His brown hair was a bit outgrown and wild, with loose curls, and his eyes were a green that reminded her of the pine trees that grew all over Briongloid. There was a dimple on one side of his smile, and he had a boyish charm that she knew would appeal to potential partners. She found it curious, and always had, that the Udar Apparent had chosen a human to hold such a high honor.

"What do you like to do around here?" she asked.

"Hmm. I spend much of my time with your betrothed, although I suppose I will have to learn to share now," he said and gave her a playful wink. "I train other laochs out at the camps frequently. And of course, I work on the weaponry as well. When I have the free time, I like to read." He gestured to the book that now rested on his lap.

"Books on weaponry?"

"Yes and no. I read them more often than I would like some days. I prefer books set in other worlds. Books of adventure and myths and legends that don't exist within Talam. It's my own sort of escape, I guess. Everyone needs one these days."

Rania nodded with a soft, knowing smile.

"What's yours? Your escape?"

"I find that I don't look for an escape. If I'm being honest, I'm often sticking my nose places it doesn't belong, if you ask my brother. I'm looking for a way *in*, not *out*."

"Well, I am certain Weylin will honor those desires when life gets more normal around here. Everything has been a bit uprooted since the wyvern landed, as you can imagine, and I am sure have experienced yourself. But Weylin is a good male, and he will do all that he can to make you comfortable."

"I should hope so," Rania responded and focused on the flowers straight ahead of her. They were a brilliant white, the color of clouds, with pale blue streaks that ran through the center of the petals. "Weylin, is he . . . he seems rather distant, doesn't he?"

Callum hesitated, choosing his next words carefully. Rania didn't blame him.

"His mind is often running faster than he can keep up with lately. There's so much pressure on him, and even more pressure that he puts on himself. If he's acting differently towards you, don't take it personally. He's been acting differently towards me, as well."

Rania nodded and leaned in closer to Callum.

"It sounds as though we will become great friends then, Callum Ronan," she said, and found humor in the shock on his face that she had indeed remembered his full name. "I look forward to it."

14

WEYLIN

There was a heavy, foreboding feeling in Weylin's chest that stirred with each step he took. The laochs led him, his father, and Oisin Dorcas to the place where his uncle fell. They had left his body untouched, and that almost made it worse. That meant there was something they wanted them to see.

Weylin was still trying to shake off the previous night. The *mallaithe* had appeared in his chambers once again. He was only thankful he had been up late working on letters to the captains at the laoch training camps this time. It had made it much harder for her to reach his blade.

He didn't know how to explain how she was able to appear to him, but he could not do the same to her. When his finger had grazed her temple, he had confirmed they could touch still. Something that could go terribly wrong.

It was all so jarring, but Weylin could only act unbothered by it.

He could tell that made her more uneasy than anything else he could do. But unbothered was the opposite of how he felt.

The feeling of his skin against hers had sent a shock through his blood that nearly made him flinch away. It was a feeling of generations of pent-up rage, and a feeling of missing her so deeply it was as though he had known her for far longer than those few sunrises shared together. He wanted to grab her and hold her closer as he once had. And he wanted to shove her away and watch as she fell to the ground.

He'd had the strange sensation of being pulled back to the moment on the riverbank. Before their lips had ever touched, when he had felt the breath return to her lungs after she had certainly passed on. It was that rush of relief he felt again when he brushed her skin, but why it took him back to that moment, he could not understand.

It terrified him. She held a power over him, and he could only hope she didn't realize it.

"We're nearly there," the laoch spoke up, and Weylin saw his father nod in response.

Oisin had remained mostly silent on the journey there. He was unsure of his place. Weylin had been surprised to hear his father had invited the male. Faolan said it was a good time to invite him into the politics of Samhradh. It was a show of genuine partnership, and Oisin wasn't going anywhere anytime soon.

And when he did leave—it would not be long before he became the Lord of Briongloid, and it would create an entirely new dynamic to have a Lord in Briongloid who considered the Myrkors not only allied through mating, but trustworthy and transparent.

His father had not been overly upset by news of his brother's passing on. He and Conroy had been close when they were younger, but the intense environment of growing up under an Udar drove them apart. Especially since only one of them could come into the title.

Conroy had turned to the woods in near isolation when it became clear his younger brother would win the title. He used his training as a laoch to hunt and gather and provide for the cities. He no longer had use for any of the training in politics and manipulation their father had given them.

Weylin and Faolan rarely heard from the male. Conroy had never mated, leaving him with no other family.

Weylin could hardly imagine what it would have been like to grow up with a sibling in his situation. Callum was the closest thing he had ever had to one, but there was never anything for them to compete for the way Conroy and Faolan had.

They passed through Omra and a couple villages outside the capital until they were led to an area right outside of Bodog, a mid-sized city known for its coastal location and the smell of seaweed in the air. Despite being coastal, there were still swaths of pine trees that littered the land and provided grounds for hunting and exploring.

"Just there," the laoch said. He held out his arm towards a patch of woods just outside of the city.

Weylin threw a glance at Oisin, who returned his grim look.

Weylin braced his hand on *Uamhan*, prepared for anything to come out of the woods. Everyone around him did the same with their own blades. Everyone except his father, whom the rest would protect with their own lives.

Large paw prints appeared in the sand below. They were too large to be wolves. The shape of them indicated that they unmistakably belonged to one of the largest beasts of the realms—a bear. Black bears lived throughout Samhradh, but for the most part, they paid the elves, humans, and dwarves no mind. They kept to themselves and the woods, unless provoked.

Weylin stepped in front of the rest, following the paw prints to confirm what he already expected to be true. His eyes followed their trail before his feet could. Blood spattered the sand, and it was dark from sitting overnight.

The blood led to the remains of a body. And those remains were just distinguishable enough to be Conroy Myrkor.

Deep wounds marred Conroy's body until he was nothing more than a pile of gore and bones. It was bad enough that Weylin had to look away, and he caught Oisin doing the same out of the corner of his eye.

Thoughts coursed through Weylin's mind in rings that spun continuously and unendingly. As the dove that had ripped the eye from Brigid Dorcas's face had once haunted him—this too would darken his thoughts for the foreseeable future.

The bear was the animal of House Kyne.

A bear had mercilessly ravaged Conroy Myrkor.

Weylin rarely gave thought to superstitions, but it seemed the supernatural had been giving an awful lot of thought to him as of late.

Their party arrived to Castle Eagla just after dusk with the remains of Conroy Myrkor in tow. They would bury him in the family cemetery, as all the Myrkors before him had been. With no mate or children, there was no one to mourn him save for Weylin, Faolan, Niamh, and the few friends he had collected during his too short life.

The scene still shook Weylin to his core. It had an undeniable, looming meaning, and Weylin was burdened by the implications on the near silent journey home. His father had made no remark. He simply said the words to honor a passing on, *lig se scith le deithe*, meaning *may he rest with gods.*

Weylin didn't know if he believed in such fates. He hardly knew how he felt about any sort of an afterlife, but he knew for certain that his father held no such religious affiliations. He spoke the words as more of a ritualistic expectation than with any hint of meaningful feeling.

The halls felt darker when they walked through them. It was not only the grieving of a soul lost, but the ominous sign it had brought them. He knew everyone was thinking it, but no one had voiced it.

It was maddening in its own way.

Oisin had thanked them for allowing him to accompany them on the journey, and gave his condolences for their loss, before going to find his sister and let her know what they found.

"Father, I would like a word," Weylin said when they found themselves alone in a corridor that led to the wing that housed his father's office.

"I figured you might," Faolan responded with an exasperated sigh.

There was tension brewing between them. Something along the lines of *I told you so* played on the tip of Weylin's tongue, but he would need to make a stronger argument than that to get his father's blessing.

They said nothing else until they were seated across from each other. His father sat in the ornate chair behind the desk, while he had the smaller wooden chair closer to the door.

"*A bear attack*, Father. It could not be a more obvious cue that we need to go to Earrach—*I* need to go to Earrach," Weylin started, knowing they would both prefer to skip over the small talk.

"Since when do you believe in omens from the gods?" his father replied with a sneer.

He had never told his father about the doves in Castle Tromlui.

Rania had promised silence from her own kingdom. He didn't know how it was possible to enforce such a thing, but later came to know it was through threat of pain of death to whoever breathed a word of it, and it had worked.

Weylin thought it best he followed that sentiment as well. And although that sign had felt obvious and directed at him, it was easy enough to brush off. But this—this felt too direct given everything else going on and the timing of it. They would be fools to not heed the warning laid out before them.

"Since it is now more than ever the time of the *mallaithe*. We don't have time for fool's oversights," Weylin said. "We both have had our fair share of them as of late."

Weylin would never forget how severely his father had underestimated Aisling Iarkis. How terribly wrong he had been about her. There was a tiny sliver of him that was not angry at him for it. Because if his father had prepared for her properly, if it was one female against a league of laochs, he didn't know if she would have made it out of the castle.

Weylin had yet to decide how he felt about that.

"Watch yourself," Faolan growled. "My answer remains unchanged. Your realm needs you here. And you will remain here until your mating ceremony. I will have no more discussion about the matter. I will consider sending laochs on our behalf to speak with the Kynes and confirm the alliance that we are already certain of."

"Is anything certain during these times?"

"Your paranoia will be your demise, *boy*. There is no room for it in my halls. Learn to act with a sound mind, or produce an heir better fit for my throne than you."

Weylin stood.

His nostrils flared, and his hands curled into fists. He clenched his teeth and turned to leave the room, biting back all the words he wanted to shout.

"And speaking of your commitments to the throne," Faolan drawled, amusement lacing his tone that made Weylin's stomach turn. "Your mating ceremony will be on the next full moon in Braon. We moved it up, as there is no time to waste. You, of all people, can understand that."

No words left Weylin's lips as he flung the door to his father's office open and stormed down the corridor to his own rooms.

15
AISLA

Aisla's fingers rubbed against the smooth parchment as she toyed with the cursed letter. It seemed to feel lighter now that she had spent so much time with it. It had become more familiar, rather than ominous, even though its contents were still unknown to her.

She'd slept fitfully following her faint, despite the comfortable bed loaned to her. The dream that she wasn't even sure she could call a dream didn't help matters. Aisla's primary concern was that the Young Wolf would find a way into her rooms the way she had his. She didn't know what he would do if he could, and the thought kept her awake as she stared at the ceiling.

The Udar Apparent had haunted Aisla's sleep many times since they had parted ways, but not in the same way it had been the last two times. It was always distant before. Nightmares made of dreams and fears. This had been real—she had felt his touch. And he hadn't tried to immediately kill her as she thought he would. He taunted her, and it almost felt as it had when they were Ellora Morlee and Fenian Daro, during a moon that now felt like a lifetime ago.

The thought sent a chill through her.

She shook her head and swung her legs over the edge of the bed in the private room.

Aisla knew there was no time to waste. She had to get moving as soon as she could. She would go to her father and apologize for her cold shoulder the sunset before. It was not her intent to come across as she had. If she was being honest with herself, she was so unbelievably relieved to see him again. It had just been so outside her realm of thinking, of hoping, it had taken her aback. And although she could acknowledge her approach had been a touch cruel, there were still many questions she had surrounding his sudden reappearance.

She did not intend on leaving without answers.

One of the many good things that had come with the discovery of her father in the library was that she now had someone she could trust on the inside. That had been the first step in her plan to get the letter translated.

Even if her father could not read the runes, perhaps he would introduce her to someone he knew and trusted that could.

Finding her father again would be a task in itself.

The library had turned out to be a beautiful maze of rooms and shelves, and of course, books that lined those shelves. Every turn down a corridor brought her somewhere entirely new, and all the shelves were far too tall to hope to see over. A ladder was needed to reach most of the books.

Although it was beautiful, stunning even, Aisla couldn't imagine how they lived this way. She supposed they got used to it, but it all felt rather claustrophobic to her.

Everyone she met was friendly towards her. A few nodded and wished her a good day when she walked past. She wondered how many of them knew who she was. She thought it was a majority of them from the way their attention lingered, and she imagined word spread quickly in an underground habitation.

A thought struck her then, stopping her in her tracks and knocking the wind out of her.

Muinin.

Muinin was bonded to Feargal before he was bonded to Aisla. Did he know his rider still lived? But if he had, it would have been impossible to bond to a new rider. She was certain he would have sensed it, though. After all, he had responded to her shouted call from across the world within moments. How could he not hear Feargal, even down in the library?

Aisla would need to tell Muinin that Feargal was alive the moment she saw him. She only wished she had mastered the esos of shifters that would allow them to communicate mind to mind. It would make sharing such news so much less complicated.

She knew Muinin was still hovering nearby, waiting for her to give him an update. She wondered how he would react to the news.

After a few wrong turns, Aisla found the room she had taken dinner in the previous night. There were baked pastries and tea out this sunrise, and the smell alone caused Aisla's mouth to water. She took one that smelled of cranberries and glanced about the bustling room. It was much busier than it had been the previous evening. Her eyes scanned the room, hoping to lock eyes with either her father or Eilis. She caught the profile of Eilis's face, and a wave of relief washed over her as she pushed through the crowd to reach her.

"Good morning," Aisla greeted.

"Morning," Eilis said. "How'd you rest?"

"Well," Aisla lied. "Thank you for the accommodations."

"You are welcome to them as long as you should choose to stay with us," Eilis said. "Although, I would assume the outside world needs you more than these books do."

Her words sent a pang of guilt through Aisla, but she brushed it off. She had grown accustomed to the expectations others had of her.

But still, there was that pressure building in the back of her mind that reminded her she needed to return to Caillte. If for no other reason, Ruairi deserved to know where she'd gone to. Her stomach twisted at the thought of the way she had left things, and wondered what he might think of her disappearing yet again without a word.

"I was wondering where I might find my father?" The word sounded so strange and foreign from her lips after so many years of remaining dormant. It felt as though her tongue had forgotten how to form the syllables.

"We were thinking you might ask that. He's in the study just outside of this room, down the corridor to the right. He's waiting for you."

"Thank you," Aisla said with a brief nod and left the room with the remains of her pastry still in hand.

Nerves stirred in Aisla's chest with each step that she took forward. She was thankful that he had left her the option to find him, rather than seeking her out. She followed Eilis's directions that led her down the corridor she had not yet explored. Aisla paused outside of the door and inhaled a deep breath, cooling the ever-present fire in her veins.

The room was tight, but cozy, just like the rest of the underground library. The walls were made of shelves lined with books and at the center of the room, there were two round cushioned chairs sitting around a small wooden table. Her father was settled into one of them with a book in his lap that was bound in a ruby red cover.

"Good morning," Aisla said, offering a small smile, which her father returned when he looked up from his reading.

He stood when she entered the room, and she paused. They both looked uncomfortable, unsure what to do in this new space they shared that was once the most cherished bond she had.

"Morning, Aisling," he responded in a deep and familiar voice. "How did you sleep? Are you feeling better?"

"Well," she lied again, as flashes of the Udar Apparent's bedroom blurred her vision. She instinctively scratched the skin on her temple that he had touched, "and I am."

She nearly corrected him.

She went by Aisla now. No one called her Aisling. She had fully embraced the nickname after the passing of her parents. They were the only ones who ever really called her it, anyway. She had taken to correcting anyone who previously called her by her full name and introduced herself as 'Aisla' only. It was born of her desire to bury the person who 'Aisling' was, and the pain she had endured through their passing. Her closest friends then shortened the name even further to 'Ash.'

Aisla couldn't correct her father, though. If there was anyone who could still call her by her full name, it would be him. Even if it reminded her of that dark time. The transition in her life that made her an orphan, and her grandmother was left to act as her sole parent. And now, with everything her father had told her so far, she had to wonder if that had been Cliona's plan all along.

"Hey," Aisla said, gently, and Feargal lifted his eyes to meet hers. "I'm sorry about yesterday. It was a lot, but I shouldn't have reacted so coldly."

"I don't blame you, for how you responded," he said and took a step towards her. "Not in the least—I deserve it."

Aisla nodded, thankful for the comfort, and it was enough of an invite for him to step forward again and wrap his arms around her. She paused, but allowed him to pull her into his embrace.

His arms enveloped her and squeezed her against his chest. The intimacy of the moment said more than words ever could between them. She found her own arms rising to wrap around his torso, and she felt a glimpse of peace for the first time since Eire had fallen from her wyvern. It was a moment she wished she could hang on to, but knew she could not. She clenched her fists into the fabric of his shirt, as though she were a child once again.

"I'm glad you're alive. I'm glad you're here," she whispered into his chest, and he held her tighter.

"Thank you," he whispered into her hair, and she knew they had been words he needed to hear. "I can't tell you what it means to see you again."

"I know," she replied, and slowly withdrew from him.

She glanced up at his eyes that brimmed with emotion and knew hers reflected the same. Her throat tightened as she took a seat.

"What do you think of this place?" Feargal asked, changing the subject as he settled into the chair beside her.

He closed his book and set it aside as he looked around the place that had become his home. The thought made Aisla's stomach uneasy. She was almost jealous.

"It's beautiful, honestly," she said. And she meant it. "I could've never even dreamt up a place like this. It's lovely, and the people seem friendly, too."

Everyone she had met in the library came across as genuine and kind, even from a passing glance. It was such a stark contrast to how she had left her own home. There were still bruises that lined her arms from where they had grabbed her, and gods knew what they had planned to do with her. When Aisla woke up, there had been clothes sitting on the desk in her room. She had chosen to wear the long sleeve blouse to cover the marks. Aisla didn't want to answer questions, and she especially didn't want to explain what had happened to her father. She had thrown away her ripped clothes from that night. Aisla longed to wash away any memory of that harsh return to her baile. She would have burned the garments if she could have.

"I'm glad you think so. I know they're all glad to meet you—I've spoken a lot about you."

"Only good things, I hope," Aisla teased to lighten the heavy mood. "I know there's a lot more we both need to share with each other. All these years apart, and I'm sure there are more than enough stories to fill several of these books. But I came looking for the

Silenced for a reason. And I was hoping you could help me with that, now that I've found you."

"May I ask how you found us here?"

"*The Dawn of Talam*. It was this book I had been reading when we were searching for a cure for the lofa, and I didn't find that, but I found so much more. Stories they never taught us in scoil."

Feargal smiled, and a thoughtful look crossed his eyes. He averted his gaze to look at the ornate rug at their feet.

"Your mother wrote that book," he said. Aisla's breath caught in her throat. "I helped, but she put it together. Croia Haze was the pen name she chose. Little heart and fire. She chose it with you in mind. She always said your blood was made of embers, and she loved you and the way you lived your life so passionately, even from a young age."

Tears fell as Aisla raised her hand to her mouth. It hurt deep in her stomach to be reminded of the tenderness with which Aine Iarkis had lived her life. She had always been too good for this world.

"She wrote everything we learned, and everything we had hoped to share with the realm one day. Your grandmother never liked the way she pushed and dug for answers to age-old questions. She would have preferred we put our time and efforts into other things. So, we kept what we learned to ourselves. Your mother began work on *The Dawn of Talam*. I left it behind when I fled, hoping it would one day fall into your hands. Well, hope and the help of my friends still in Caillte. I suppose, for once, the gods granted me a favor, not a curse."

Aisla nodded thoughtfully, but a question rested on the tip of her tongue: *Is that what I was? Was I your curse?*

She pushed the thought away and focused on what he was telling her.

"Thank you for sharing that with me," Aisla said around a tight throat. "I would say I'm surprised, but I think little can surprise me at this point. Now that I'm thinking about it, there are some sections where I can almost imagine her voice. She always had a talent for telling stories, didn't she?"

"That she did," Feargal said. "I'm glad her words brought you here. She wouldn't have wanted it any other way. I miss her."

The admission brought another wave of grief over Aisla, and she didn't know how much more of it she could take.

"I miss her too," Aisla whispered. "Every day."

Feargal reached out and rested a hand on her knee. She looked up at him. There was sorrow there that reflected her own, and a longing to find the connection they had once shared. And the pressure of it— it was too much to bear. She cleared her throat and looked away.

"What brought you here, then, that I might help you with?" Feargal asked as he withdrew his hand.

"This," Aisla said. Suddenly, panic replaced her grief, and her heart was in her throat. She leaned over and pulled the letter from the sock she wore, where she always kept it. Her hands shook as she clutched it in her lap. She didn't unfold it yet, as if afraid he could discern it immediately, and she was not yet prepared to know what revelations it might bring. "It's a letter. It's the letter that Cliona sent Ruairi to give the Udar to bargain for a cure for the lofa. We weren't meant to open it, but I did. She doesn't know I kept it. Ruairi thinks there's something sinister about it, and I feel a heaviness in it as well. It is written in the runic language, so I don't know of anyone who could translate it. I figured if anyone would be able to, someone who studies our world would, so I came here."

Her father looked at her hands gripping the parchment. She knew he was waiting for her to hand it to him. She tightened her grip on it, fighting a sudden urge to abandon her entire plan and keep it to herself.

But it was too late for that.

Aisla knew as soon as she told him about it, there was no going back to letting it be just hers. She wondered if she should have heeded Ruairi's advice and burnt the runes to ash before it had gotten this far.

She blinked her eyes closed, and when she opened them again, she held it out to her father. Aisla released a breath as her father pulled it from her shaking fingers.

A weight lifted from her shoulders.

She watched intently as he unfolded it along the worn creases. Aisla looked up at his face and saw his brows knit together thoughtfully.

"What I can tell you is that no one is fluent in this language any longer. It predates Aosta, even," he said. Aisla's heart sunk with disappointment at the same time the sweet taste of relief coated her tongue. "But we have the resources to translate runes one at a time. I will do it for you, but it will take time."

"How long? I'm afraid my life has always been a bit short on time," Aisla said grimly as she thought again of Ruairi. Guilt gnawed at her gut. She had no other choice, though, and she knew he would understand when she could finally explain it to him. Nonetheless, she couldn't stay long here, even if she wanted to.

"I will make it my priority. Maybe give me three or four sunrises with it?"

Aisla nodded, hesitantly. It was reasonable. It would give her time to make a homecoming plan that would not end with her attacked and vulnerable in her bed, but still she felt restless at the thought. "I can do that."

"Until then, I hope you'll stay here?" His eyes wandered to hers.

"Yes, I will," she said. "I have no options at the moment."

"What do you mean?"

"I'll tell you that story the next time I see you," Aisla said, too exasperated to get into it. She rose to her feet. "Thank you, for being willing to help. I'll meet you back here for dinner?"

"I would really like that."

Aisla nodded again before ducking through the entryway, eager to put as much distance between herself and the letter as she could, now that it was finally out of her hands.

16

CALLUM

He would have missed the letter that had been slid under his door had he not nearly slipped on the paper in the dark of the early morning. It was folded in half and the ink looked fresh, and as though it had been written hastily.

Callum immediately recognized the penmanship to be Weylin's. An anxious feeling crept in as his eyes scanned the page.

Callum,

I do not know how much information you've received, but Conroy Myrkor was mauled to death by a bear in the woods just outside of Bodog. Knowing you, I will not have to spell out the omen that yields for us. I spoke to my father again, and demanded we make a move towards solidifying our alliance in Earrach, but was again refused.

I have grown far too restless to sit by and wait. I was never so good at that. You know this better than anyone. Especially when his only reason for me staying is for my mating ceremony, which there is still plenty of time to prepare for. So, I have left to go to Earrach.

I went alone, but there is nothing to worry about there. My hope is that you will tell my father in time, but preferably at a time once I am too far gone for him to bother sending someone after me. Then, there is the matter of Rania. If you could let Oisin know what to tell her, and what not to tell the Udar, that would be much appreciated.

I know you'll understand.

Thank you, Cal, and I'll see you soon, brother.

Weylin

Callum inhaled a deep breath before balling up the letter and tossing it onto his bed. He ran his fingers through his brown curls that had gotten far too long as of late.

He was not upset Weylin had left. Not by any means. No one, and especially not himself, could cage the Young Wolf, nor would he want to. But the burden of this letter lay in a conversation with the Udar that was certain to not go over well. He would wait until the end of the day before going to him and come up with a lie about when he discovered the letter.

That would give Weylin more than enough time.

Faolan would not waste a laoch on bringing his rebel son home.

But Weylin would have Hel to pay when he returned—Callum was sure of that.

He thought about finding Oisin and telling him the news, but he doubted he would be awake so early. Callum figured Rania would not be surprised. She already knew of Weylin's eagerness to see to the disputes in Earrach himself, and she seemed to understand her betrothed better than most did, even in their brief time together.

Callum had spent most of the previous day with Rania in the castle gardens, talking on the bench. They had talked until nearly sunset, and he had found her company more enjoyable than he had expected. It was good news for him, given that she would soon become a large part of his life.

He thought she and Weylin would make an excellent match.

There was something about the female that drew him in. She was cunning, yes, and mysterious even, but she was not the ice princess that she painted herself to be. She had been vulnerable, and she had laughed with him until she had thrown her head back with joy. There was more to Rania Dorcas than met the eye.

Speaking of whom, Callum thought to himself as he rounded the corner. Much to his surprise, he found himself face to face with the female herself. *What could she be doing up so early?*

Rania looked up and met his gaze. Her blue eyes startled when she registered who he was. There was something wary in her expression, but she replaced it with a warmth as she neared.

"What are you doing up?" he asked.

"I could ask you the same."

"I was on my way to work on the weaponry planning. I find I get my work done better in the mornings, before everyone else is awake."

"I share the same sentiment," Rania said. He offered her his arm so they could walk towards the castle kitchen together, where they could get a pastry for breakfast. She looped her arm through his and held it with a confidence that did not surprise him. "I couldn't sleep last night. What Oisin told me—about the bear and Conroy Myrkor —it seems rather odd, doesn't it?"

The mention of the situation pulled at the guilt in Callum's chest.

"Very weird, yes. There's something I need to tell you about that," Callum said, deciding there was no need to go through Oisin to tell her when she was right there.

"Let me guess," Rania mused, pressing her lips into a thin line as she feigned a thoughtful look. "The bear is in this very castle, right now!"

Callum turned to her with an incredulous expression. It might have been the last thing he expected her to say. She only grinned back at him before playfully bumping his shoulder.

"Only kidding," she said. "I should only wish life could be so unpredictable, although on second thought, maybe not. What's that saying? Caution your prayers, or they might just be answered? I would say that is probably wise advice to heed. But, more predictably, I would guess that my betrothed is no longer here. I'm assuming he took the sign as an omen and fled in the dark of the night to speak to the bears themselves. He'll find himself at the doorstep of the Kynes's castle before long, eager to rage war against the *mallaithe*."

"More or less. You seem very observant."

"I pride myself on it. But I could've seen that coming moons away. He thinks himself a hero, if nothing else," Rania mused. Callum would have to agree. The way she said it wasn't judgmental or conde-scending, either. It was more contemplative and almost curious. "I can admire heroism when it is dealt with a dash of realism. I believe Weylin possesses both. Wouldn't you say, Captain Ronan?"

"I would," Callum agreed. "He's always been a very realistic thinker."

"And you—are you a dreamer or a realist?"

Callum waited before answering the question. He considered the meaning, not sure which one he was truly. They veered off into the nearly empty kitchen. The chef had just prepared the first batch of pastries, fresh from the oven, and it smelled of raspberries and cream. He and Rania each grabbed one and sat at a wooden table on the outskirts of the vacant room.

"A bit of both, if I'm being honest."

"I would have guessed as much," Rania said with a victorious grin.

"It seems you've a knack for reading people," Callum noted.

"I do," Rania said without hesitation. Her confidence was almost humorous, but there was nothing humorous about the way she wielded it in a way that kept those around her on edge. "And do you think yourself a hero as well?"

Callum loosed a chuckle. "I'll leave the heroism to you elves with lifetimes nine times as long as mine, if not longer."

"I think that's where you're wrong, Callum," Rania said. "I think you could be a hero, too."

The comment made Callum uncomfortable. He shifted in his seat and turned his attention to the pastry on the napkin before him. Callum was no hero, not in this world or any other. If he had been a hero, he would have stood up for the red-haired elf that was tortured at the hands of his comrades. If he had been a hero, he would have done more for him than share a measly meal.

"Thank you," Callum said at last, pushing down that queasy, guilty feeling that came with the thought of the male. "I will take that as a compliment."

"And you should. I don't often hand them out."

She looked up then. There was a depth in the blue of her eyes that held him there for a moment. She was beautiful. More than that, she was alluring. There was something almost otherworldly about those eyes that made him look away.

"I'm sorry to be the one to tell you about Weylin." Callum cleared his throat, redirecting the conversation. "I can imagine it's a disappointment to come all this way, and then he's absent. He means well, though. I wouldn't take it personally. The war weighs heavy on him, and he is eager to put an end to the prophecy. He has been excited about your arrival for many sunrises now."

That part was a lie. He hardly spoke of his betrothed, but Callum felt Rania needed to hear something reassuring about her mate-to-be.

"For the record, you didn't tell me. I guessed it," Rania said. "But I'm glad to hear it. We will have many sunrises together, anyway. I am not bothered by his disappearance. Is this something he does often, though? Run away into the night with only a note left behind for his best friend, I mean."

"No," Callum said with a smile as he bit into his pastry and warmth filled his mouth. The sweet flavors caused his mouth to water. "I would say this is a first."

"At least he left you behind so I could have some good company." She said it as though she meant it. "My brother does love to sleep in, and these halls feel quite lonely in the early hours."

"How is your brother after what they saw yesterday?"

"He was shaken up for certain. There have been far too many omens lately, and it's got him on edge."

"What other omens have you seen?" Callum asked. He had never believed much in the gods that seemed to have turned their backs on Iomlan, but he would be curious if there were more.

One could only call so many instances coincidences before they became a pattern.

"Oh, I can't recall," Rania said, although a brief look of panic crossed her face. "Something my parents have been rambling about lately, but I don't know the details. My parents are quite superstitious. It's rather common to be, in Briongloid."

"Will you miss your realm?"

"Of course," she replied instantly, and Callum felt a pang of sympathy for the female. He wondered how much she wanted to be here. And how much she wanted to be betrothed. "It is my home, after all. But I am sure in no time, Samhradh will feel like home. It helps to have my brother here."

"You two are quite close, aren't you?"

"Absolutely. He's my closest friend. Do you have any siblings?"

"None by blood. Weylin is close enough to a brother, though."

"I admire the bond you two share—forged by choice and not blood. It is a rare thing to find, and a rare thing to keep."

"Thank you." Callum nodded.

"Can I come with you today?" she asked abruptly, as though she had been wanting to ask since they first sat down. "To train laochs, or work on weaponry, or whatever is on your agenda. I get bored quite easily, and the castle layout is still unfamiliar to me. Plus, you'd be surprised what I can do in an arena or in a drawing room."

Callum chewed on the inside of his lip. He had never brought anyone with him before—not anyone that wasn't already a laoch, at least.

"Sure," he decided, not wanting to leave her by herself. After all, Weylin had asked him to watch out for her. "Weylin's betrothed is welcome wherever I am."

17

RUAIRI

His palms sweated as he sat across the table from Eire. She had been taking her morning walk around the infirmary when he arrived. For once, he had not arrived only to check on her. He was there with the ring that weighed heavily on his conscience.

Edi's warning had haunted his sleep the previous night. The way she had shut him down and ushered him away like he'd had the lofa himself. It had been the last thing he was expecting of her, and had set him even more on edge than he already was. But at the same time, it created an urgency within him. In his gut, he knew Edi was hiding something.

It had come with a feeling that he was about to uncover something just beyond his reach. Something drove him forward—there was a need to know, and a need to stop whatever it could doom. He needed to find out before it was too late, and Ruairi feared the impact it could have on Aisla, but he didn't know why, only that pursuing the answers could help him protect her.

It felt wrong coming here to see Eire with an ulterior motive. It was manipulative and gross, but he needed to see how she would react to the olc esos within. Would it affect her the same way it had the other husks?

"How is your morning, Eire?" Ruairi stated, looking up into her eyes, and forcing his guilt away.

"Same as always," she mumbled. Her eyes were distant as ever as she looked anywhere but at him. "Has your friend returned?"

A pang of hurt shot through Ruairi, and he swallowed around the knot in his throat. It had been two sunrises now since Aisla had disappeared without a trace. Ruairi tried not to dwell on it. For the longer he did, the more it upset him. He was only glad she had come to him first. It gave him validation, but also meant no one else had seen her, and Cliona had no reason to come barging into his baile asking for her, and he was thankful for that. He preferred to stay as far out of the Mathair's way as possible, especially since his dismissal from her inner council.

"No," he answered. "Aisla has not come back to Caillte."

"That must be hard," Eire mused. She ran a slow hand through her black curls. He was surprised that though the disease had rotted her light brown skin and mauled her flesh, most of her hair remained intact. "Poor red-haired boy. All alone."

Ruairi ignored the comment. New Eire had no room for niceties, and he felt as though she actively sought ways to get under his skin, but he knew he had to brush it off and understand that she didn't know what she was saying.

It was hard to stomach all the same. Especially when the Eire he had grown up with would have comforted him through it all. Eire before the lofa had been a warm light shining brightly for anyone to see. She had been bold and brave and full of life in a way that was hard to find in others. It was so far from what she had become, and Ruairi didn't know if he would ever stop grieving for her.

The Eire before the Iofa would have been by their side every step of the way, fighting just as hard as either of them.

"Look," he said, "I'm not alone. You're right here."

"Mm-hmm," Eire hummed, playing with her thumbs in her lap.

Ruairi took the lull in conversation to reach into his pocket, and his fingers danced along the edge of that silver ring with the emerald stone. It had given him so much stress. He slowly withdrew it and held it in his palm.

There was no reaction.

He sucked in a breath and slid the ring onto his finger but kept it under the table and out of Eire's sight. Immediately, Eire's head snapped in his direction, and that distant look locked onto him as the husks had when he put it on.

"Tell me something only Eire knows," Ruairi whispered.

He needed to test a theory. His heart pounded in his chest.

"You cheated on your final world teller exam. And you haven't told Aisla that you did." The voice that came out was strange and warped. Yet, her gaze remained unyielding and unflinching as she stared at him—through him.

"Stand," he whispered. Even uttering the command made his stomach turn.

Eire stood.

"Sit back down," he murmured.

He slipped the ring off and shoved it back deep in his pocket. His heart hammered in his chest, and he felt his breath catching in his throat in disbelief. It was a theory that had kept him up at night, but one he did not know what to do with. He was afraid of the power of the ring. He was afraid it was far greater than anything he had imagined.

"What's the matter with you?" Eire asked.

Ruairi looked up and saw that she had snapped back into herself.

She acted as though nothing at all had happened. It was as if she didn't know he had controlled her, if even for a moment.

"Nothing at all, Eire," Ruairi muttered.

But his mind was spinning faster than he could keep up with. It was nauseating.

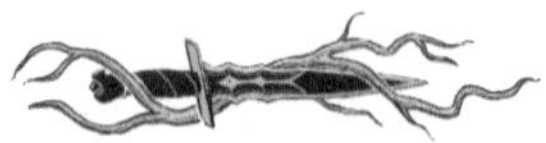

Eitri had been a friend of Ruairi's family for as long as Ruairi could remember. The dwarf had forged every weapon the Vilulfs ever wielded. He even crafted the dagger that Ruairi had gifted to Aisla, *Oidhe*.

After seeing Eire's reaction to the ring, and her blind obedience to whatever power lurked beneath its surface, even when she didn't see it, he couldn't let it rest.

He was certain Aisla would spend her energy trying to figure it out if she was here, too.

The longer he held the thing, while slowly unravelling its secrets, the madder it drove him. It was a constant fear, a constant anxiety, and a small part of him was also aware of the power now at his fingertips. He had the power to wield an entire army of husks, should one have access to them. And since they existed on both Eilean and Iomlan, Ruairi felt he was rapidly running out of time to try to stop an unstoppable force. He couldn't help but wonder if this was the only ring of its kind.

Ruairi knocked on Eitri's door just after dusk, hoping it would go better than when he talked to Edi. Although, that bar was set quite low.

Eitri opened the door and peeked through the crack. He wore a suspicious look until he recognized Ruairi, and his expression softened.

"What are you doing here, boy?" the dwarf asked gruffly, opening the door wider.

Dwarves had learned to be protective of their homes and their property, as they were the most likely target for thieves. Even though it was a rare occurrence, the weapons, tools, and jewelry they forged were more than enough to attract attention.

"I was hoping you could look at something for me," Ruairi replied.

Eitri's eyes darted back and forth behind Ruairi, as if checking to see if he was alone. Ruairi found the suspicion curious, but it wasn't exactly out of the ordinary.

"Come on in," he grunted. He opened the door just wide enough for Ruairi to slip through.

Ruairi had been in the dwarf's baile many times before. He quickly noted that it appeared messier than usual. It was cluttered, and tools were strewn about, along with a plate of half-eaten food and empty mugs that once contained ale.

"How is life treating you lately, Eitri?" Ruairi asked. He worked to maintain a neutral voice, but his concern grew the longer he looked around the baile.

"Same old," Eitri replied. "I hear you've had quite the moon."

"Indeed, I have," Ruairi said, grimly. "I suppose one I will, regretfully, not forget anytime soon."

"I was sorry when I heard about it. Your people appreciate your bravery and sacrifice."

"Hardly can call it a sacrifice when I return empty-handed. But I didn't come here to talk about things I wish had gone differently."

Ruairi did not hesitate, emboldened by secrets of the winds. He shoved his hand into his pocket and dropped the ring onto the center of the table between them. Eitri's lip pulled back in a sneer, but there was an unmistakable recognition in his eyes that told Ruairi all he needed to know.

"Your work, I assume?"

"The bitch said I would never see that thing again. Get it out of my damn face."

"So, I was correct? This is your craftsmanship?" Ruairi confirmed with a nod. He reached out and toyed with the ring, feigning a confidence he only half felt. "And is it safe to also assume that you are referring to our Mathair?"

"You shouldn't have it, Ruairi Vilulf. You don't know what you're getting yourself into. I've always told your father I'd watch out for you, but there is only so much I can do if you continue down this path."

"What path, Eitri? At least tell me what's going on."

"I cannot, Ruairi. Don't ask this of me. If you care a lick about me, or yourself for that matter, *drop it.*"

An uneasy feeling ravaged Ruairi's stomach, but he continued. He refused to give up. Not when he had no other avenues to venture down. He had exhausted the resources he could think of.

"I didn't want it to come to this, but I've heard of the fake jewelry you've been selling to the nobles when they come asking. And I'm sure they wouldn't like to hear of it. They have a way of seeking their own revenge when airgead is involved."

Darkness flashed across Eitri's eyes. Guilt twisted Ruairi's gut, but he refused to let it show.

"You wouldn't dare. You're not the type to act on malicious principles."

"Try me," Ruairi said and shrugged his shoulders. He leaned back in his chair, folding his arms across his chest. "I am not the same male that I was before I set foot on Iomlan. You grow up quick in enemy lands. And quicker in the hands of the Udar."

Saying it aloud made Ruairi's hands shake, but he clenched them into fists, willing a calmness over himself. Eitri's jaw tensed, and Ruairi saw him debating what could be worse for his business and his life in Eilean.

"Whatever words I speak to you are not to leave this baile. I don't care about that girlfriend of yours, or whatever hero you envision yourself to be." Eitri shot a glare at Ruairi and looked at him through narrowed eyes. He did not correct the male—Aisla was not his girlfriend, and never had been. And more than that, Ruairi had never thought himself a hero, merely a pawn trying to remain on the right side of things. "You're playing with lives, not theories. Understand the gravity of your request or *leave my baile*."

"I understand."

Ruairi fought to maintain his neutral expression and keep his composure. Internally, his heart raced and his esos rushed through his veins. He could hardly hear his own thoughts. He waited in the silence and each passing moment felt like it dragged into eternity.

"That ring is truly olc, and it isn't meant to be here. That's the first thing you should know," Eitri said and took a long swig from a fresh mug of ale. "The Mathair came to me, inquiring about my services. She asked questions about forging blades with a source of esos. I told her I didn't think such a thing was possible. She had some ideas and asked if we could collaborate. And, as any craftsman would, I agreed for the right price. And I am no cheap craftsman, I can assure you that."

Foreboding coursed through Ruairi. He thought he had been prepared to have his theories confirmed, or that it might even feel good to be right. But he suddenly wished he had never gone prodding at all, as he almost knew how the rest of the story would go. He wished more than ever that he could be wrong—that it could all be some misunderstanding or some convoluted story in his head.

"She brought the esos. Somehow, she had made it into a tangible thing. Don't ask me how, because she didn't give me those details, and I didn't ask. She even brought the seed of an ash tree and was convinced we could find a way to preserve it in that emerald gem—to keep the esos alive—with or without a source. We stored the ash seed in the gem and the esos in my silvers, and created this ring." Eitri gave himself a moment to pause as he loosed a long sigh of disappointment in himself. Ruairi could see it now. The mess, his tired eyes, the half-eaten bits of food. The consequences of Eitri's actions had impacted him greatly, and the guilt was too much for one male to bear. "If I had to guess, it was her esos of pryers that went into it. And the power to control minds is not a power that should be handled like a piece of jewelry, but that is what we created. She made me one promise. She promised she would keep the vile thing out of Eilean. And apparently, that is a promise she did not keep."

Ruairi's throat was dry, and his tongue was heavy. Cliona had created a ring to control minds. A ring with the esos of elves and the skilled forgery of dwarves. Ruairi had all but confirmed the ring was used to control husks specifically. But how could Cliona know that? So many details of the lofa were still unknown to the people of Eilean. How long had this ring been prepared for?

The worst fact of it all was, she had intended to hand the ring over to Faolan.

"And why would you want it sent off to Iomlan?" Ruairi finally found the voice to ask. His rage was building, and he kept his fists balled at his sides to keep it under control. "Such power shouldn't fall outside of our control."

"I don't know, and it wasn't my business to ask," Eitri growled. "But I don't want my friends and my family being controlled by some damn piece of metal. Such manipulation has no place in my home."

Ruairi wanted to shout that it was too late. He wanted to scream that his very creation was already promising doom on this very continent. He just wasn't certain how yet. The pieces were all laid out before him. He only needed the peace of mind to begin putting them into place.

"I've got to go," Ruairi said. He stood up abruptly, but not before snatching the ring from the table.

Eitri made no move to stop him.

"How did it even fall into your possession?" Eitri asked, suspicion lacing his tone.

"A story for another day, I'm afraid."

"Whatever. Just remember, everything I've told you doesn't leave this—"

A knock sounded at the front door. Ruairi's eyes grew wide as he looked back at Eitri. His heart thundered in his throat.

"Gods' sakes," the dwarf muttered under his breath. He stood from his chair and made his way through the mess to his door. "Can't a male enjoy his evening in peace? *You*, stay out of sight."

Ruairi didn't argue as he shrunk into a corner of the room and hid from the viewpoint of the door. He wasn't sure why he felt such urgency. Maybe it was the secrets shared between them, and the need to hide them even though they were not physical things for strangers to see.

He strained to listen as his hand clutched the ring in his pocket protectively.

Ruairi heard the front door creak open, and the dwarf barked a harsh: "What do you want?"

The words were hardly out of Eitri's mouth when the door was forcibly shoved open.

"*Move.*"

Ruairi froze in place. A familiar voice met his ears, and it was none other than their Mathair. He heard Eitri hit the ground as he was shoved out of the way by a second person. There were five pairs of footsteps in total that entered the dwarf's baile.

"Where is Ruairi Vilulf? I received word he came poking around here this sunset."

"I haven't seen that boy since he left for Iomlan," Eitri snapped. "What do you think you're doing here? I've fulfilled my end of our agreement."

No one answered his question. Ruairi heard Cliona's footsteps getting closer. He had moments—no, less than moments—to figure out a plan.

He took a deep breath and scanned the room for any way out.

18

AISLA

It was unsettling walking around a place with no windows. It didn't take long for Aisla to miss the rays of sunshine that greeted her each sunrise. At first, it felt like a safety net, but it slowly felt more like a cage.

Aisla made her way through the rooms full of books and scanned titles, pulling books off shelves, shuffling through their tables of contents. She didn't know what else to do during her time in the library of the Silenced while she waited for her father to finish the translation. She had an anxious energy. It filled her since leaving the letter in her father's hands. She trusted him—more than she trusted anyone else in Talam, despite his deception. But she was haunted by a lack of control once it left her sock.

"Looking for something in particular?"

A familiar voice interrupted from behind Aisla. Eilis appeared, and was watching over her shoulder as she flipped through a book on the origin of the first population to settle in the realm of Fomhar, Iomlan's northwestern realm.

"Nothing in particular," Aisla responded and closed the book before sliding it back into its place on the shelf. "Just passing time."

"Any special interest in Fomhar?"

"Not really, but I'd prefer to know more about all the worldly realms before going into the Inevitable War."

Aisla took a seat at one of the two cushioned chairs in the room. Eilis did the same, sitting across from her.

"Fair enough. Speaking of this Inevitable War, that wyvern you've got is a beautiful beast. He seems mighty protective of you. I wish I got a better look at him before he took to the skies. We don't have wyverns in these parts, considering they couldn't live down here with us. None of us has ever bonded to one—aside from your father, I suppose."

The comment was a mental reminder to Aisla to ask her father about Muinin. There were so many questions surrounding the bond to her own wyvern, and she didn't even know if her father knew Muinin was hers now. If he had, surely he would've asked about him by now.

"You can meet him before I leave," Aisla said. "Muinin loves to show off. He'd be glad to flash his wings for anyone willing to give him the attention."

Eilis grinned. "I would like that very much. What's it like riding a wyvern?"

"It's surprisingly a lot like riding a horse," Aisla said. The thought took her back to sunrises spent atop Eolas, the dark horse of the Udar Apparent. Her mind flashed to Weylin's body heat pressed to her back and his arms wrapped around her waist when he taught her to ride. She would never again be able to ride a horse without evoking thoughts of him. Aisla brushed the memory away. "Only a lot bigger and slightly more uncomfortable, but you get used to it. If you're doing it right, your wyvern just feels like an extension of yourself. It's a bit of an art."

"That would be a dream come true, really. I've seen so many wyverns and riders fly across our land and above our trees and have always felt envious of the bond they share and the power they must hold together."

Eilis spoke of wyverns as though they were creatures from a story-book. It was a strange notion to Aisla, but she supposed if she had not grown up with them, she, too, would feel that way. She wondered what the laochs in Samhradh thought when Muinin landed outside their castle. Besides a declaration of war, when they looked past it and saw Muinin for what he was, did they see a creature of myth and legend or a beast of doom and destruction?

She hoped for the latter. The one advantage Eilean had was their wyverns.

"They're something alright," Aisla replied. "Do you guys have your own copy of *The Dawn of Talam* here?"

Aisla found she missed reading from its contents, and hoped to dive deeper into the book, especially knowing what she now knew about it. She was eager to pick it back up again. She was left without it when she fled Eilean with nothing but the clothes on her back. And even if she had time to grab one more thing, a weapon would have been much higher on her list of priorities. She felt the absence of *Oidhe* like a missing limb, every moment of every sunrise.

"We don't. There was only one copy, and that copy was left in Eilean for you. I would love to read it one day, though."

"Did you ever meet my mother?"

Aisla had yet to hear what happened to her mother, or how her father had survived Cliona and faked his death. She didn't know if she was ready to hear all of it, but she didn't want to remain in the dark, either. The question had been on the tip of her tongue when she had fainted upon seeing her father and hearing all that he had to say. She hadn't stayed to ask after handing him the letter, but knew it would be the first thing she asked the next time she saw him.

And even though no answer he gave could change her mother's fate, the thought of asking terrified her.

"No," Eilis said with a look of sympathy that made Aisla uncomfortable. She averted her eyes to her hands in her lap. "Your father showed up alone, just after she passed on. I wish I could have. She sounded like a lovely female."

"She was," Aisla replied softly. She rarely spoke of her parents' deaths, but finding her father alive without her mother resurfaced all the emotions she had felt when she was told of their passing seven years ago. Her fingers traced the wyvern teeth adorning the necklace at her throat. They were made of Combha's teeth, from an accident after Eire bonded the wyvern that was once Aisla's mother's. "Anyway," Aisla forced a smile to her lips and looked up again, "what do people do around here? I've got time to waste until dinner."

"Mostly research, studying, writing, and recording, as one might imagine. It's sort of a lifelong learning community here. We try to prepare the future generations the best that we can for the world that they will inherit—the good and the bad."

The idea reminded Aisla of the book filled with pages full of pressed flora and fauna that lay on her bedside table.

"That's really neat, actually. I can understand that motivation. Given my position and prophecy, it is not often that I am invited into political conversations, so I took to collecting plants from across Eilean with Muinin," Aisla said. "I keep them in a book and write everything I know about them, and anything else I can learn about them from the library we have. I hadn't seen a book like that for Eilean's plant life yet, so I figured it would give me something to do and to give to the generations to come. It feels like I am helping in my own small way."

Aisla didn't include her fears that there would be no generations to come after her. The part of her that feared the translation of the prophecy Iomlan believed roared in her blood, but she swallowed it down as she looked at Eilis.

"That's not small. I would love to see it one day. We could use it here. It sounds like you inherited more from your parents than you thought. I take it you went the route of world telling in scoil then?"

The thought was almost laughable to Aisla. She would've gone stir crazy sitting through all the lectures that world tellers do. Aisla would make a poor world teller, but she did enjoy the art of it, and admired those who focused on it.

"No, I'm a laoch. It's a different form of art, but I enjoy the physicality of it," Aisla replied with a hint of pride lacing her voice. She missed her classes and missed being a part of the laochs since she'd been away. She found a peace in the movements of combat, and it was entirely different from fighting with her esos.

"That does seem more fitting, I suppose."

"How do you mean?"

"I would hope the one meant to save our realms could hold her own in a fight. Besides, few world tellers show up in torn clothes with bruises covering their arms, looking ready to take on Fella."

"I believe it was Fella who was ready to take me on," Aisla muttered back.

"As he is trained to do," Eilis said with a grin.

"Fair enough."

"You said you're free until dinner, correct?" Eilis asked, and Aisla nodded. "Here, follow me. I'd like to show you something."

She stood and Aisla followed until they ended up back at the ladder Aisla had entered the library through. When Eilis began the climb back up to the outside world, a hesitancy gnawed at Aisla's insides, and her hand lingered on the wooden rung. There was a fear that came with facing the outside world again. And it wasn't Fella lingering at the top, but the idea that she would have to face what she fled from. The library felt safe and tucked away, and she had forgotten about everything else for a while. She was not ready to pop that bubble.

She knew Muinin would be smart enough to settle somewhere nearby while he waited for her call. No one could possibly know where to find her, but nothing felt truly impossible any longer.

Aisla inhaled a long, deep breath and forced herself to take the first step up the ladder. Then she was on her way, following Eilis into the light of the sun.

The journey of endless sunrises begins with the very first step.

Ruairi's voice echoed in her mind. Those words had pushed her forwards through times much worse than these, and she knew they would carry her forwards through many more. A chill travelled down her spine that was met with a rush of longing for Ruairi's hand in hers. She hoped he would forgive her for leaving again. She had hardly had the time to tell him how sorry she was for leaving him alone in Caillte to face the fallout alone.

The fallout, and the memories.

She was terrified to be close to him again, because being close to her had proven to be dangerous as of late. She knew getting close to anyone would only create a vulnerability her enemies could exploit.

In moments, Aisla was engulfed by the warmth of the sun on her skin, and she breathed in the fresh air of springtime.

"How do you live down there without this?" Aisla asked.

"We don't really," Eilis replied, almost defensively. "We can come up whenever we please. There are no rules against it. And you get used to it. There's a comfort to be found underground and out of sight of the rest of the world."

Aisla nodded, suddenly feeling hypocritical. She might not have been literally underground, but she had spent her fair share of time hiding from the world.

"This way," Eilis instructed, and Aisla trailed behind her.

They passed Fella where he was curled up against a dead ash tree that had fallen to the lofa. He seemed unphased by their presence as he opened one eye to peer at them and shut it again before continuing to snore lightly.

"Lazy bones," Eilis murmured playfully.

"With the lofa . . . can you use esos here? I mean, if all the ash trees are dead now, how could you?"

It reminded her of Iomlan and their lack of source for esos. Although, on Iomlan, there were no ash trees at all, not even dead and rotted ones such as these.

"Hopefully, what I am about to show you will answer that."

They continued on until Eilis slowed. Aisla looked up and was greeted by a vibrant green that seemed so out of place in this dead and barren part of the continent. Eilis looked back at her with a prideful grin.

"We're healing it—the land," she said with her arms spread wide. "It's a process, to be sure, but we make progress every day."

There were other elves, dwarves, and humans leaning down and kneeling in the soil. Some were planting and others were taking notes. They all glanced in her direction, and some waved to Eilis.

"How?"

It was all Aisla could ask as she stared in awe at the scene before her that seemed like it couldn't exist. The longer she looked, the more plants she recognized from her travels and her own collecting. And there were already ash trees growing there as well. She looked up and saw the cover of the towering dead trees that just about concealed the place from anyone looking overhead. It explained why she had never seen it on her flights with Muinin.

"We travel and we gather. It sounds like you have experience with that yourself," Eilis said. "We turned the soil until it was good for planting, and then we got to work. We began with food and moved onto ash trees to source our esos so those of us who are terrans and tsunas could use our esos to help rebuild our crops. In time, and it will take a very long time, we hope to restore the entirety of the southern continent to how it was before the lofa. Every day we make progress, no matter how insignificant."

Aisla nodded thoughtfully as she watched a man with short blond hair pour water across a row of sprouting plants. She could only hope she would be enough to save them all, and their efforts wouldn't be for nothing. She prayed that the Silenced would live to see the restoration of their home after the Inevitable War was finished, whether or not Aisla lived to see it.

"How has no one else seen it?" Aisla asked, wondering how, even with the tree cover, anyone could fly over Eilean and not notice this bright spot in all the bleakness the lofa had left in its wake.

"Our dwarves crafted a canopy that is made of a fine thread and the esos of a pryer. With lots of research in our libraries, they found a way to make a fabric that would allow the sunlight to reach our crops, but it reflects into the sky as an illusion—that's where the esos of mind manipulation comes in handy. From above, it is made to look like any other patch of land in the south following the lofa, and no one has bothered to venture here on foot since the lofa either. I don't know how the dwarves did it, but I do know that you should never underestimate the crafting skills of one."

Aisla puzzled over her words, shocked at such an invention, and unable to understand how it was possible. "You can put esos into a creation?" she asked.

"Only dwarves can," Eilis said. "They learned it in books that were long forgotten. It's a special power itself to craft things with esos, but the esos can still only come from an elf willing to give it."

"That's intriguing. I've never heard of such a thing." The thought of an object holding its own esos brought her back to that ring she had carried for many sunrises, and something in her stomach twisted.

"The whispers on the wind say you struggle with the art of esos?" Eilis said abruptly.

Aisla bristled defensively. "Who did you hear that from?"

"It doesn't matter. Is it true, or not?"

"It is, but I am working on it."

"How about I strike you a deal, *Gheall Ceann*. You and your knowledge of plants in our realm could be very beneficial to our cause. You help us while you're here—however long that may be—and in return, I will help you with your esos. We have enough ash trees here now to train."

"Deal," Aisla replied without hesitation. She knew no harm could come from the deal, and there was no point in hiding her weaknesses here.

The only thought that nagged the back of her mind was her rush to return home. She needed to get back to Ruairi and keep him safe from whatever Cliona had been planning. But Eilis had not set a time limit to her help, and Aisla knew the female would not expect more of her than she could give.

"And," Eilis interrupted, "you will bring us your book of Eilean's flora and fauna when it is completed and allow us to store it in our library. It would be a great asset to us and the future of our realm."

"It would be my honor," Aisla said with a grin.

Eilis stuck out her hand, and Aisla shook it as a renewed sense of purpose flooded through her veins.

19

WEYLIN

The journey to Castle Fas felt longer than a journey had felt in a long time.

The ghost of the female with fire in her very eyes haunted each step. His last journey had changed so much about himself, the world, and the future of the nine realms. There was something in the air since she had left him. Something he had not had the time to parse through since there was not a moment of solitude since the landing of the wyvern.

Alone in the forests between Samhradh and Earrach, Weylin grieved the loss of a friend. He acknowledged those memories he had shoved away from the forefront of his mind. He saw her laughing, dancing, under the moonlight in Spiorad. Weylin could feel the brush of her skin as he wiped a tear in a baile they were never meant to share. He could smell the iris and sea breeze that engulfed him each moment they spent atop Eolas.

He felt the rush of fear that captured him like a mouse before a viper when he had dragged her lifeless body from the river. And then there was the way it felt when she kissed him—as though the world had ended and begun in the very same breath.

Then he recalled the look in her eyes when she raised her blade against him. It was a look of hatred and revenge—a look that foretold a doom he could not comprehend. Weylin remembered the way her shadows had wound about her, making her a more powerful weapon than any of them were capable of defeating on their own. He blinked and replaced his moments with Ellora with scenes of the feral female he had seen ready to end his father in his own throne room.

She was driven by a generations' long hatred. She was driven by finding her red-haired lover tortured and wounded. She was driven by a prophecy she had been fed her entire life—and for that, he almost pitied her.

She was Ellora no more. She was, and could only ever be, Aisling Iarkis.

The *mallaithe* had given him back his life debt when she passed up the opportunity to kill him, but he didn't know that she would have reason to keep him alive next time. So, there would not be a next time, and Weylin knew with a certainty he couldn't explain that he would be the one to deliver her death.

It would be by his blade—the prophecy and Inevitable War end as one.

The journey was the time he needed to drag up those memories and release them with each breath out. He felt lighter as he approached the castle's gates.

"We were just wondering when the Young Wolf would hear of our plight and come knocking on our door," a loach sneered as Weylin approached. "But we heard the Gem of Dreams was now warming his bed. We thought he might consider himself preoccupied."

"You'll watch the way you speak of my mate to be," Weylin snarled.

In a moment, his blade was out, and he tossed it back and forth in his hands. The casual threat was all the reminder they needed to know he would not tolerate disrespect towards Rania.

"I seek audience with Noland," he said.

"I bet you do," the second laoch spoke up. "Noland has fallen ill. He has been for quite some time now—hardly leaves his bed these days. Corren would be happy to greet you, I am sure."

"Then you can tell Corren I'm waiting."

Weylin was wary of the way the two laochs seemed to mock him in their tone and their words.

Earrach, although a strong and consistent ally to Samhradh, was not well known for their manners or their attitudes—at least not in a good way.

Weylin watched the two laochs speak in hushed voices to each other. One disappeared beyond the gate and out of vision, presumably to get their Lord Apparent. Weylin let out a sigh as he sheathed his blade again. Eolas remained still behind him. It had been a long time since Weylin needed to control his horse with reins to keep her nearby.

Corren Kyne strode into the courtyard. His grass-colored cloak flowed behind him with the breeze of spring. His dark brown hair now reached just below his shoulders, and his dark blue eyes carried an amused gleam that made Weylin uneasy.

Nothing about the male spoke of humility. Even his walk had a flourish to it.

"Welcome, my brother," Corren called with a boom and Weylin cringed at his choice of word. He hardly knew the male, let alone held fraternal affiliation for him. Nonetheless, Weylin forced a smile onto his face as he stepped forward to shake his hand. "It has been a long time since your presence has graced my home. I am grateful to see you, now of all times. As I am sure you have heard, we could use an ally right now."

It was that word, *ally*, that Corren wound through the air like a noose around Weylin's neck. He knew what he was doing, and he played the game well. It was a nod to say Corren knew what Weylin needed. And he would give it if Weylin played his game.

"Indeed," Weylin said, "I have come to aid where I can."

"Alone, I see. Have you got laochs coming up behind you?"

"No," Weylin replied, prepared for the question. "My laochs are needed to train for the coming war, but I am here to stay for as long as I am needed until we can resolve this conflict."

"I see." Corren eyed him curiously, but he didn't seem upset. "I hear you like to travel alone these days, anyway. Or at least alone with the *mallaithe.*"

Weylin's nostrils flared. His hands curled into fists. They had tried their best to keep his time accidentally spent with Aisling Iarkis confined to their castle, but it was hard to do so when so many people had witnessed the fallout. They could not hide their failure at capturing her, but he had at least hoped word of their travels together had not spread beyond Omra. It seemed the people of Samhradh were not as good at keeping secrets as those of Briongloid.

"Only kidding, my lord," Corren said with a sneer. "No need to get all flustered. I do hear she is easy on the eyes."

"Nothing you can't find at any given pub at the right time after dusk," Weylin snapped, defensively.

It was a lie, of course. The *mallaithe* had been one of the most ethereally beautiful females he had ever laid eyes on it. There was an otherly look about her. There were none like her in any of the worldly realms, but Corren didn't need to know that.

"Well, I am certain you can tell me all about it during your stay. For now, we ought to go in and discuss Earrach's own problems. No sense in wasting your precious time."

Corren turned on his heel and sauntered back into the castle that loomed tall. Marble white towers with rust-colored domes stretched into the sky. Magenta flowers and brilliant green grass covered the courtyard. Earrach was known for its beautiful flora and pleasant weather throughout nearly all the seasons. It seemed such a stark contrast to the Kyne dynasty that ruled with a heavy fist. Noland Kyne was not unlike Faolan Myrkor, but Weylin always felt that his father hid it from the other realms better than the Lord of Earrach did.

He was also raised as less of a brute than Corren Kyne had become.

"What ails your father?" Weylin asked.

He took his first step onto the marble floor within the castle walls. The castle had a beautiful interior adorned with stone busts of different generations of Kynes. There were paintings of meadows and waterfalls, and, of course, bears.

The thought rose the hair along Weylin's arms.

"We are unsure, exactly," Corren answered the question nonchalantly. He was clearly unphased by his father's condition. Weylin did not entirely blame him. Noland's illness could only mean Corren was a step closer to taking the seat in Earrach. "He has a fever most days, and his appetite is all but diminished. Mother stays by his side at night, and during the day she is out here running the place as though it's always been hers. But she is tired. Our medics keep him comfortable enough with herbal medicines, but he seems to be declining rather than mending."

"I am sorry to hear it."

"I'm not," Corren said with a shrug. Weylin thought for a moment that perhaps he had underestimated how cruel the heir to Earrach was. "You forget, he is the eldest of the current lords of the worldly realms. He deserves his rest with the gods. I deserve a rise in rank. It feels overdue at this point."

"Fair enough."

The exchange left a sour taste in Weylin's mouth. At least Corren was an honest man, he supposed. That was a valuable trait to have in an ally.

Corren rounded corridor after corridor with a casual gait as he led Weylin into a room that looked to be a study. Papers were strewn about and pinned to the wall by daggers in a disorderly manner that overwhelmed Weylin the moment he passed through the doorway. It looked like the lair of a madman, and Weylin wondered if perhaps Corren Kyne was just that.

The thought weighed heavily on him as he took a seat and glanced around the room.

"Excuse the mess," Corren said. He took the seat closest to the door that was adorned in purple and green—the colors of Earrach.

"Tell me more of the conflict on your lands." Weylin felt eager to get to the point. He grew tired of the political dance they fell into all too easily.

"Ah, yes, our little *codagh an dulra*—our war of elements," Corren answered with an unnerving grin. "I hear you are betrothed to the Gem of Dreams, yes? The Dorcas female."

"That is correct. I am to be mated to *Rania* Dorcas."

"Then you understand a mating of convenience," Corren said. Weylin tensed at the comment that felt like an accusation. There was no malice lacing Corren's words, just brutal honesty, but to say such a thing seemed to overstep boundaries. Weylin felt the need to defend a romantic relationship between them. There had been, for a fleeting moment in a castle far away, but in truth, he was not sure there was anything to kindle. He would try, and he knew either way it was an ideal mating for them both. "Briongloid is known to have tense relations with our Udar and his decisions, so what better time to finally bring the two lines together than the ninth generation? We can all see it for what is—and don't get me wrong, it's a brilliant move—the same one I would make if I were you."

"I don't see what you're getting at," Weylin interrupted.

"Here in Earrach, we had our own sort of plan, like yours. I was to marry a sylph to appease the air spirits whom my father wronged many, many years ago. They are still bitter about their lives lost and their reduced territory. I suppose rightly so, but it had become an issue of late when they took to killing our livestock and poisoning our crops for the season. So, my father struck a deal. My hand in mating to their royal daughter, Meara. I was hardly teething when the deal was made."

"An elf mated to an air spirit? I've never heard of such a thing."

"Really? It's quite common in Earrach. The offspring are nearly always elemental rather than elvish, but I never minded that. And Meara, I've met her. She's beautiful and kind, but soft—too soft. I cannot spend my life with someone as breakable as a wine glass. And while my hand has been sworn to Meara for as long as I can remember, I fell in love with an undine. Her name is Vartry, and she is like none other. Needless to say, the sylphs didn't take it well when I made my love for Vartry known, and conflict between the air spirits and the people of the water broke out. It's not a matter of emotion for them, but rather the seat of power that was promised and given to another," Corren continued. He paused and picked at dirt beneath his fingernails. He told it all so nonchalantly, as though he was not the cause of the havoc that was destroying his lands. "Vartry is safe in Castle Fas with me, but the battle rages on. It's long overdue, really, given that their gods were practically born with their hands at each other's throats. I just gave the children of Leighis a reason to finally raise the first weapon against the children of Muir."

"And how do you suggest we end it?"

"Slaughter them all. Or do you have a better idea?"

Weylin nearly choked on air. He closed his eyes and inhaled a long breath. Gods help him.

He hadn't realized just what a monster of a male he was dealing with. And who he would need to leave the realm allied with.

20
CALLUM

It was another evening of little sleep for the captain of the Udar Apparent's guard.

Ever since the red-haired elf left the castle, guilt plagued his nights that he didn't know how to shake. It had not been his orders that marred the male. And not once had the torture inflicted on him come by his own hand. All the same, he had to look long and hard at his face in the mirror each sunrise—the face that served a male willing to put a soul through such things, and seemingly get nothing from it.

Callum had not found a way to make peace with it yet. He grappled with the things he'd seen, and the things he had not stopped. Even when he told himself there was nothing he could have done—that his interference would have only done more harm than good—he couldn't believe the words.

The only solace he had was that he did not serve Faolan Myrkor directly. He was under Weylin's command. And Weylin was a good male.

Callum was certain he was. He saw the way Weylin struggled silently with the issue of the *Gheall Ceann* since the landing of the wyvern. There were secrets to unfold there, even grief and vulnerability that the Young Wolf masked behind extra training and an urge to rush aggressively into the Inevitable War, but Callum saw through it. He hoped Weylin trusted him enough to one day confide in him. After all, Weylin was the only family he had, and the only person Callum had grown to trust in his years.

Callum splashed cold water on his face and changed into his day clothes to prepare for his sunrise ahead of sorting through an error he had found in his current weapon plans. It had been nice to have Rania with him the previous sunrise—she gave thoughtful input and carried even better banter to keep him awake in the boredom his work could sometimes bring him to. She was charming to be sure, but he was always left wondering how much of it was a show, laid out before her like a script for the Gem of Dreams, and how much of it was the real Rania.

He supposed that was something she and Weylin had in common.

He was thankful that Weylin was betrothed to someone so witty and easy to get along with. With arranged matings, there was no telling who Weylin might have ended up with. It would have impacted Callum's life if she had been dreadful, but Rania had not a dash of horribleness about her.

There was one stop Callum needed to make on his way to the drawing room that was reserved for him during this time.

He poked his head into the library, hoping to avoid the rather grumpy librarian who protected her shelves like trophies and made it awfully uncomfortable to pull something off them. His eyes flitted to her empty desk, and he slipped inside, heading for their records on weaponry.

He thumbed through pages that were falling from their binding with age when a rustling sounded behind him. Callum held his breath as he glanced over his shoulder, preparing for the librarian's glare, but was instead greeted by Rania's unmistakable cloud-white hair, falling down her back in a loose braid. It stood out, especially in Samhradh.

"Fancy seeing you here," he said.

She jumped and looked up from where she was thumbing through spines on a nearby shelf. Her surprise quickly turned to relief when she met his gaze.

"Well, if I am as observant as I think I am, I would say you are following me, Captain Callum Ronan."

Callum grinned, tucking the book he had pulled out under his arm, and taking a step towards her.

"I was here first."

"I've been here since before sunrise."

"I didn't see you when I came in."

"I never said you were the observant one."

"Fair enough," Callum said with a chuckle. "For the record, I did not know you were here, but if I had, it would not have been a matter of following you. It is my duty to as the captain of Weylin's guard to ensure his mate-to-be is comfortable and finding herself at home in his castle."

"You mean our castle?" Rania said.

She took a step forward and peered at him through long lashes. Her expression was innocent, but her words sent an unsettling chill through his core.

"I suppose so. Soon enough, anyway."

"I appreciate you being a friend to me, you know. I know that isn't part of your duty, but you're quite good at it."

"There is no need to thank me, milady."

Rania nodded. "What are you reading?"

"Notes on weapons used in the War for Descendants. I'm still trying to work out how to get enough force behind the ammunition to reach the skies. We made good headway yesterday, but I need to ensure all moving parts will be reliable, then I'll begin work on a prototype. Thanks for your help, by the way. Where did you learn so much about engineering?"

"It's my pleasure," she replied. "You learn a lot growing up in a castle, and even more when you're excluded from most things and have an excess amount of time to be buried in books."

"They missed out by excluding you," he said and meant it. "You've got a brilliant mind. We are fortunate to have you here."

Rania only smiled and reached out to run a finger along the edge of the book protruding from the crook of his arm, silently asking permission to take it. He loosened his grip, and she pulled it away. She wordlessly admired the cover before flipping open the first worn pages until she got to the table of contents.

Callum watched her striking blue eyes scan the page. She put her finger to her lips, wetting it before shuffling through the pages to somewhere midway through the book. She nodded to herself in approval, then shut the book and held it out to him.

"This is a good place to start," she said. "Good luck."

"Aren't you going to tell me what page you were looking at?"

"Nope. You're a smart boy. You'll figure it out."

She smiled slyly up at him, and Callum couldn't help but return the gesture as he shook his head at her.

"Are you going to join me?"

"Not today. I told Oisin we could spend the morning together. It's about time I go wake him up," she chirped. She turned on her heel and made to leave before throwing a glance back over her shoulder. "Try not to miss me too much."

Callum watched her disappear, and there was a pounding in his heart.

For the first time, he thought Rania Dorcas might be trouble. He brushed the thought away and hurried to his drawing room with a renewed eagerness.

21

RUAIRI

Cliona's eyes found Ruairi's before he had time to think. Her cold, yellow-green eyes bore into his with a ferocity that made his knees tremble. Her lips curled into a smile dark enough to eclipse the sun.

"Are you hiding from me?" She sneered, and Ruairi could do nothing but stay rooted in place. "Just like my granddaughter, after all."

Ruairi's heart thundered in his chest. His palms sweat. He had to come up with something. It appeared far more suspicious to stand there doing nothing in a panic than to give her an explanation.

"Just visiting a family friend, Mathair," he replied. He stepped forward and forced a calm he didn't feel into his voice. "I might not be hiding if you hadn't come storming in here with half your guard shouting my name. I might have been happy to greet you, otherwise."

"Save your lies," she hissed. Two sets of hands grabbed him as the laochs closed in on him. He recognized Conor, but he didn't recognize the other male with them. He must be one of her new inner council members since Ruairi had been dismissed. They were both large, brutish males. "Tell me where my ring is. I hear you've been poking about my realm asking about it, when it isn't even meant to be here. Aisla told me she *lost* it. I had a hard time believing it, but I've never known my granddaughter to deceive me. I guess that's what happens when she spends her sunrises with the likes of you. You're lucky to still have your breath, and you can thank her for it. I told you how essential that ring was, but she assured me she was the one who lost it, not you. That is the only reason you still live. Now, my parcel I trusted you with is opened, and no longer in Iomlan. You can start by cooperating. No more lies. Tell me where it is."

"Aisla took it with her." Ruairi replied without hesitation. He felt horrible throwing her name out there, but he knew that would be the only possible way to keep the ring out of Cliona's clutches. And he knew he would rather die than let her get her hands on it again. Especially with his newly obtained knowledge. "I don't know where she went. Your guess is as good as mine."

Ruairi allowed a real bitterness into his voice. It was true—he didn't know where she had run to, and it hurt. He needed to push the truths as much as he could to make Cliona believe him.

Cliona looked closely at him, and her eyes hardened with disbelief. Ruairi's heart sunk.

"Search him," she barked.

And the guards obeyed.

Their hands roamed his body. Pulling and shoving with no hint of gentleness. He grit his teeth and focused on his breath, steady in and steady out. They turned his pockets out, and Ruairi's heart flickered with relief.

He had used his few moments of preparation after Cliona barged into the house, not to run for the door, but to pull the ring from his pocket and tuck it inside his sock, as he had seen Aisla do with the letter. He couldn't guarantee they wouldn't check his socks, but it seemed less likely than his pockets, and he had limited options.

Conor made Ruairi open his mouth wide. He patted down his shirt and yanked through his hair. He must have decided the search was over when he took an angry step back and the other laoch followed his lead.

"It's not on him," Conor said to Cliona, but he held Ruairi's stare with such hatred, Ruairi wondered what he had ever done to the male. They had never seen eye to eye, sure, but Ruairi reserved such hatred for those who deserved it—for enemies across seas that had left permanent marks both visible and invisible on his being.

He didn't know why Conor hated him the way that he did.

"Brian, go search his baile," Cliona ordered. She snapped her neck towards a dwarf laoch that had remained near the door during the search. "Conor, take Ruairi and come with me."

She nodded at Ruairi and Conor grinned with a cruelty that creased the corners of his eyes. As though it had been discussed beforehand, Conor yanked Ruairi's arms behind his back and pulled a rope from his pocket.

Ruairi froze.

His chest tightened. His eyes widened. It was all too familiar. He could hardly think. He could hardly move.

As the rope was bound around his wrists, he was transported to another place and another time. A time that had ended so horribly, he would spend every moment of whatever life he had left trying to forget it.

Conor shoved him forward. Ruairi stumbled a step before carrying on with no other choice.

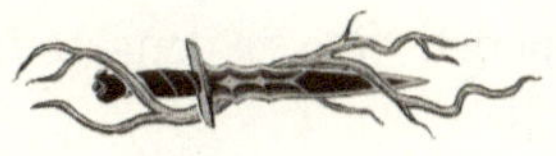

Ruairi hardly paid attention as he was led through the familiar halls of Castle Farraige. It felt wrong, so wrong, to be walking through them with his hands tied behind his back.

This was Aisla's home.

It was a place where he used to run through the corridors with her as children when her parents still lived. It was a place he had grown up in as much as his very own home. It had once been his solace, and it was soon to be his asylum.

He was not meant to be a prisoner here.

He worked with what little energy he could muster to push away his panic and place one foot in front of the other with his head held high. He refused to let them see him suffer.

Conor seemed to take pleasure in his task as he pushed Ruairi into Cliona's office and into the chair across from hers. Ruairi clenched his jaw as he looked into her cold, unflinching, yellow-green eyes. The color in them grew further and further from her granddaughter's each day.

"I didn't want it to come to this, Ruairi," she said with a sigh. "I gave you every opportunity to do the right thing, and you failed every test. You let our gods damned *Gheall Ceann* go to Iomlan with you. How could you have made a bigger blunder than that?"

How did you ever think you could protect her here? What were you thinking bringing her here?

Those words from the Udar Apparent's lips returned to haunt Ruairi as they rang eerily similar to the ones Cliona had just spoken. His stomach turned with guilt, but he clenched his jaw and held her gaze. He remained silent.

"One last thing, Vilulf," Cliona looked to him, and an emotion he could not discern flickered across her steely eyes, causing her to falter for the briefest of moments. "She's a dangerous one to love. I came to terms with that long ago."

Cliona didn't have to name her for Ruairi to know exactly who she was referring to.

There was a pause, and then it all turned to a searing black that flung him into a memory of a cell and the pale female who grabbed his hands. He fell to his knees hard against the concrete floor. He clenched his fists behind his back and breathed out ragged breaths as he fought to build up walls against the unexpected attack. Instead of protecting Aisla this time, he had to protect the knowledge he had put together regarding the cursed ring. Ruairi buried the past sunrise and all of his suspicions as deep as he could manage. Even as he buried and even as he built, he could see the blinding light of her claws breaking through the dark places he was fighting to protect.

Cliona used her esos to shred through the interior of his mind. He couldn't hold on. It was all too familiar—too much.

"Please stop," Ruairi shouted. "Please. Please. Please," his voice dropped to a mumble as it was all he could manage.

And he let the walls fall down.

22

AISLA

Aisla's feet were tired from the morning spent planting and turning soil with the Silenced. Her knees ached from kneeling in the soil for so long, but she already felt eager to return.

It was fulfilling to be there with them.

She felt, for the first time in a long time, that she was doing something helpful—something good. And that feeling was exhilarating. She had nearly forgotten the sensation of accomplishment and pride. She promised Eilis she would join them again the next sunrise.

Her fingers nervously tapped against her upper thigh as she ducked into the room where she had taken her past two meals and looked around for her father's familiar face. It was still such an odd sensation, looking for him and knowing he would be there. She was so used to the moments she would search for him in the halls of Castle Farraige following the news of his passing on, only to remember she would not find him in the worldly realms. She was beyond grateful for the gift of him, but the implications of it were far too great to parse through, yet.

All she could think about now was what he had discovered about the letter. There was something deep within her that knew beyond a doubt it would not be good. It would take her deeper down this path of darkness she had found herself in, and the thought terrified her.

At the same time, there had been an urgency growing deeper inside of her with each passing moment. A breath didn't pass where she didn't think of Ruairi and the way she had left him, and she couldn't help but wonder if those people that attacked her out of spite hated him as badly as they did her. And if they did, he wouldn't be safe in Caillte much longer. She needed to return to him.

Aisla had been late returning to him before, and the consequences of that would haunt them each until they passed on. The thought made her blood turn cold, and she fought down the nausea rising in her throat as guilt fought to possess her.

She recognized her father's face at last, and he looked up to meet her searching eyes. His expression softened.

Aisla made her way to him and saw he had already made two full plates of food, and they were sitting out before him. There was steak, potatoes, and green beans. Aisla's mouth watered at the sight.

She would have never known this region was struck by the lofa when she looked at the spread. She almost felt guilty indulging in their food, as she knew how long and hard it was for them to produce it.

"How did you find your day here?" Feargal asked. She settled in across from him.

"It was actually very nice," she said with a genuine smile. In another world, she could see a life where she held a single source of esos, and her father did not carry the name *Iarkis*. In this alternate world, her family lived together here in the south, dwelling in the library of the Silenced World Tellers. She would trade *Oidhe* for a quill and a pot of ink. It was a pleasant life that could never be hers, and part of her wondered if her father truly believed it could be his. "Eilis showed me where they have been harvesting new plants—bringing back ash trees and food sources. I helped, and she said she would help me with my esos, too, while I'm here."

"I'm so glad to hear it, Aisling." He grinned, and Aisla fought the urge to prickle at the sound of her full name. It would take some getting used to. "I always thought you might enjoy it here. Eilis even reminds me a bit of Eire."

The mention of her best friend made Aisla avert her attention and her palms sweat.

"Never bothered to send an invite, I guess," Aisla said. It came out more bitter than she had meant it to. "I'm only kidding. It brings me comfort to see you happy here. I mean it."

Aisla looked up to see Feargal's lips turn into a gentle smile at the same time his eyes saddened. He knew that his happiness had come at the cost of their relationship. It would take more than a few sunrises together to mend what once had been.

"So," Aisla cleared her throat stiffly. She longed for that feeling of comfort they once shared. She missed their friendship, too. There was little hope they would have the proper time to find it once again, but she still found herself holding on to that spark. "About the letter. Any luck yet? I have to get back to Ruairi. Cliona's never liked him, and it frightens me to leave him alone with her now."

"Yes," he replied, and there was a hesitancy in his voice that made Aisla's blood turn. "The translation is going more quickly than I thought it would, thanks to the resources here. I think I can have it done tomorrow evening."

"What have you discovered?" Aisla felt herself ask, but she was numb in a way.

The news of his progress shocked her. She thought she'd have more time, but she supposed a fast solution was what she needed.

"I think you should wait until we can read the full letter together," he said. "It's a letter that needs to be read as a whole."

Aisla nodded. Relief and disappointment warred within her. She shook her head, trying to clear her thoughts and bring herself back to the present.

"Okay," she said. "The food here is good." She changed the subject as she lifted a forkful of steak to her lips. "Better than Caillte, honestly. We're still rationing in the lofa's wake. Our population is ever-growing, too."

"Did the lofa reach Caillte?"

Aisla's stomach dropped. She didn't know why she had expected him to know. The first case of lofa to infect a soul in Eilean was Eire, and that was when everything had fallen apart. She swallowed around a lump in her throat.

"Yes," she responded softly, looking to the food on her plate that was suddenly far less appealing. "Eire was the first to fall ill."

"I-I'm so sorry," Feargal said. Of all people, he knew how close they were—how Eire had been a sister to Aisla. "Is she okay?"

Aisla paused and looked around at the empty room.

"Do you have time?" she asked, realizing how desperately she needed to tell him everything.

Not just about Eire, but about how her life had changed in the lofa's wake. Everything that Ruairi had told her and everything she had learned across the Tusnua Sea. About the Udar Apparent and the lies they had exchanged. And the way she had set eyes upon the throne meant to be Feargal's. She wondered if he even knew about Muinin's landing in Iomlan, and what it now meant for the world.

"Of course."

Aisla took a deep breath and lowered her voice.

Then she told him *everything*. Sparing no detail.

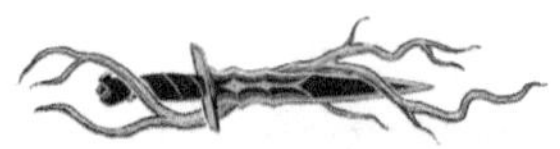

Hand over hand, Aisla climbed the ladder to the surface once again.

She had promised Eilis she would return in the morning, so they could resume what they were working on in the field.

Her shoulders felt looser, and her heart felt lighter.

Nothing had changed when she told Feargal. They had not solved any of the problems that plagued her. They did not come up with a solution to the coming conflicts, but he had listened to her. Aisla knew she could never unload her burden on someone else—nor would she want to—but this was the closest she had ever come, and she hadn't realized how badly she needed it until the pieces of her soul and her story were laid bare like shards of broken glass. And her father had been there to pick them up.

There was no judgement in his eyes. Not even when she got to the worst parts—the parts that burned to speak and made her nauseous with guilt. He understood why she had done them and listened and nodded his head.

At the end of her story, once she had told him of Ruairi, the Udar Apparent's deception, and their failure to retrieve a cure, Aisla sobbed. She sobbed like she had not in so long, her whole body shaking with the violence of it. Her father held her, cupping the back of her head, and she felt safe. A feeling she hadn't felt since before she ever set foot on the *Stoirme*.

After that, they talked about Muinin. Aisla asked how it was possible that he had bonded to her while Feargal was still alive. Feargal explained how Cliona had cleaved the bond between wyvern and rider with her esos of pryers—the dark mind esos that frightened Aisla to even think about. It had been the start of their punishment for not giving Aisla up, and it had only gotten worse from there.

Feargal had told her how it ended when Cliona killed her mother. When Aine had taken her last breath, he knew he wouldn't be safe for long, not unless he took her side against Aisla, and he would never do that. He would have taken Aisla with him, but he knew Cliona would stop at nothing to find Aisla, and he couldn't have hidden her forever, not when

Eilean was the only place they could go. So, his only answer was to disappear alone. His friends in Eilean reported that Cliona had sent scouts from her inner council to search for him, but had kept it a secret from the realm, declaring he had fallen ill of the same disease as Aine, giving up the fight quicker than she had in his grief. Those same friends kept an eye on Aisla, while Feargal was in the library of the Silenced, biding his time and formulating a plan to save them and taken Cliona down at last.

He had been waiting for her to find *The Dawn of Talam*, and that would bring her to them, and he could finally tell it all to her. It was easier for her to leave Caillte now that she had come of age. If she had gone missing as a child, Cliona would have used all of the resources at her disposal to find her and bring her back.

But now that the Inevitable War had been declared, it complicated things. Until they knew their people would follow Aisla, it was too risky to take down the Mathair of Eilean while Iomlan was eager to sink their teeth into the already wounded realm.

Aisla didn't know how she could face Cliona again, or if it would ever be safe to. A part of her even yearned to bury her blade in the Mathair, and that part of her made her sick to her stomach. Feargal promised they would figure it out together. He would help her return to Caillte, and more importantly, Ruairi.

After they talked, Aisla had sat by Feargal's side as he continued to translate the letter. She found comfort in the quiet after the storm she had spilled between them. It was a time spent with him she would cherish, when next they had to part.

She didn't leave his side until her eyes were falling shut while sleep beckoned her with open arms. She knew her father had to be exhausted as well. He walked her to her room and hugged her good night for the first time since she was only a child. It felt better than she remembered.

For the first time, Aisla felt as though she had no home at all. At least while she was on Iomlan, she always had Caillte to return to. Now, she felt lost from every angle, and knew she was merely stalling the longer she stayed in the south. They were kind and her father was here, but it was not her home.

And it never would be.

At least until the letter was translated, she had reason to be there. The more she learned of her grandmother's deceptions and schemes, the more it confirmed she had good reason to want it translated.

She wasn't ready to leave, but she didn't think she ever would be.

When the morning sun beamed down on Aisla's shoulders once again, she looked around for Eilis, and quickly found the female speaking to a woman near a tree. They leaned in close, and Aisla smiled when she sensed that timid intimacy between them. There was something new there, something blossoming, and it was a joy to witness. Aisla felt a small thread of jealousy coursing through her veins as she longed for such simple love, and everything she had come close to having had been so complicated. And it always would be.

The thought disappeared as Eilis turned and caught her gaze. She nodded to her, and turned back to the woman, seemingly dismissing her as she gave her a brief embrace and turned to head back towards the field of crops.

"That's Beckett," Eilis said as Aisla approached. "All of this was her idea. She's young, just around our age, but she was the first to start working through the issues the lofa had brought us. Rather than wallowing in our demise, she got right to planning and planting. First, she suggested we all stay in the library and live off whatever food we could gather to avoid the plague we had heard about. Once we ran out of food in the library, she organized crews to go out and find more food, wearing cloth coverings and avoiding touching anything that had been infected. She even helped the dwarves come up with the concept for the covering that keeps all this our secret. And now, she's leading our restoration. We're truly lucky to have her."

"I can see why," Aisla said. She noted the way Eilis glowed with pride and her eyes sparkled in a way that they usually did not. "And you're seeing each other, I'm guessing?"

"Yes," Eilis replied. Aisla saw a faint blush creep into her tawny cheeks. "It's very new, though. We'll see what happens."

"You make a good couple."

"Thank you," Eilis said and cleared her throat, changing the subject. "Are you ready?"

"Of course. How can we help now?"

"You've done enough helping for today," Eilis replied. Aisla tilted her head curiously. "We're going to bring that esos back out now."

Aisla froze, feeling stuck in place for a reason she could not name.

It had been part of their agreement, but she was not ready for it. She had been so glad to be helping people; she didn't feel prepared to reopen that cavern within her, fearing it would only lead to disappointment.

The last time she had touched her esos, she had left Eire with burn scars that marred her already battered body. She didn't want to hurt anyone else, especially not a community that already had enough to deal with. Aisla was wholly uncontrollable and continued to prove it upon her return to Eilean.

And sometimes she wondered if her grandmother was right about her.

"Come on." Eilis jerked her head over her shoulder and led Aisla to a nearby clearing. "You've got no choice. I'll sleep better at night if I know our *Gheall Ceann* was trained at my hand."

Aisla felt herself recoil at the words. They were so similar to comments Cliona had made when they were training. Even though she knew Eilis had not meant it that way. Eilis didn't seek to control her esos and her training the way her grandmother did.

"Okay." It was all she could reply as she followed the female on heavy feet.

"It must feel so powerful to have all nine sources of esos running through your veins. My esos makes me a shifter, and that alone feels like such a thrill, no matter how many times I've used it before."

A rush of excitement took over Aisla's hesitancies. She had not known many shifters in Caillte. The elemental forms of esos were the most common in elves, but she had always been curious to access that particular form of esos. What excited her even more was the chance she could communicate with Muinin at last, from anywhere, at any time. She wondered what all he would tell her.

As her father was his previous rider, they had been unable to communicate in such a way. Her father's esos was the esos of pryers just like his mother. He never used it—kept it tucked away deep within himself.

Wyverns and their riders learned to communicate regardless of their rider's source, and learned each other's body language, but to hear Muinin's own voice in her mind would be a dream come true for her.

"So, can you talk to Fella?" Aisla asked. Her interest was piqued.

"Yes. We've taken quite a liking to each other. I imagine it's how you feel with your wyvern, but much less powerful and intimidating, I suppose."

"I don't know. When I arrived unarmed, I was quite certain Fella would be the last thing I saw."

"Only if you had given him reason to."

"Noted for next time," Aisla said with a smile. "So, you shift into animal forms as well, right?"

"Indeed. And soon, you will too."

The thought sent a thrill down Aisla's spine.

"Here. This is a good place to start," Eilis said. She turned to look at Aisla with raised arms. "It usually helps me when I think of the way the animal moves. The feel of their paws or talons or hooves and how they might feel running across soil where the roots of the ash trees lie. And then I put myself in those paws or talons or hooves and close my eyes."

Aisla nodded her head, following along. She closed her eyes and imagined Muinin's massive claws as he walked along the earth. She thought of how it might feel to land on the ground after a long flight.

The feel of the soil squishing beneath the weight of her and pushing between her scaled toes.

Aisla breathed in and out, and focused on the sound of Eilis's voice as she walked her through the steps again. Aisla thought only of Muinin. She allowed her mind to concentrate on the wyvern while silencing the rest of the noise that consumed her every waking moment.

An eerie chill of calm enveloped her, and Eilis fell silent.

The lack of noise was almost deafening, but Aisla kept her eyes closed and her mind focused on Muinin.

She jumped when a golden thread glimmered in the darkness of her mind. She swallowed and willed her mind to follow the thread until it turned into a shimmering emerald. Then, it disappeared into black.

Disappointment filled her stomach, but it didn't last long.

Well, well, well. If it isn't our Gheall Ceann *of Talam. I've been waiting a long time to hear your voice.*

PART TWO
FLIGHT OF FATES

23

WEYLIN

orren Kyne agreed to take Weylin to the battlefront the sunrise following his arrival. The evening held a tense conversation between the two males. Weylin was blind to how quickly the dispute between the sylphs and the undines had gotten violent.

Corren had been all too serious about his plan to wipe out the sylphs in Earrach entirely, and his callousness surrounding the topic made even Weylin's skin crawl. He had heard the whispers on the wind that spoke of the cruelty of the ruling dynasty in Earrach, but never imagined it to be so savage and barbaric.

It was one thing to make a decision that would inevitably ruffle feathers, but it was another entirely to make decisions with the intent to harm without rationale.

Weylin wondered how closely his father had walked that line during his reign as Udar. He had heard of the torture of Aisling's red-headed male that was ordered by his father. Callum had even confided to him his own struggle with the cruelty of the Udar during that time. It felt like a horrid form of power extortion, and Weylin couldn't know as he wasn't within the castle walls.

He also knew his father would stop at nothing to get his hands on the *mallaithe* again. When he did, the Udar would not let her get away again.

The thought of capturing her once felt like a victory to Weylin. But now, even when he thought of the way she had betrayed him, he knew he could never stand by while she was subjected to his father's whims.

While she had hidden her own identity from him, he had too. But she had poisoned him and stolen his horse, leaving him in the middle of the woods with no explanation. Weylin still didn't know what he would have done if he had found out her true name before she realized his by the crown left atop his bag she had dug through.

No matter how he saw it, Ellora had not been real, but there was a real person beneath her. She was a person who had laid her vulnerabilities bare for him to see on a wine-filled night beneath cold moons, and it might have been fake, it might have been a lie, but not all of it had been.

That much he was certain of.

He felt Ellora still when she appeared in those two dreams that had been all too real. And when his finger grazed her temple, he had felt a burning fire that nearly made him flinch away, but he hadn't let her see it. Weylin didn't know what it meant, but he knew he could touch her skin, and that meant she could touch his. It was terrifying. It was thrilling. He found himself eager to see if it would happen again each evening, while also fighting a restless feeling that feared facing her again. He feared what she might do with a blade in her hand the next time.

Weylin knew the prophecy needed to be stopped. Above all, his family always fought to save Talam from the doom foretold by the norns, and he would see it through. But he would not allow his father to make Aisling a plaything as her male had been. And he was not the same male his father was, and he would not let himself become him.

It would kill him to see Ellora that way. No matter if only part of what they shared was real. He would not watch the fire in those yellow-green eyes fade beneath the hands of his laochs. She did not deserve that, because after all, she had never asked for the life she was born into. Whether she yearned for her power or dreaded it, he did not know, but she had certainly not chosen it.

She had once told him she feared not being enough, and he understood better than ever what she meant.

Seven laochs accompanied Corren and Weylin when they ventured into the lands where the spirits of the woods warred with the spirits of the sea. Corren had sent a crow just ahead of them asking for the leaders of the two legions to meet them at the hall in Galaban to talk about the dispute at Weylin's request, or rather, demand. Corren was clearly more eager to raise his blade than control his tongue.

Weylin supposed that was where he came in.

"Here we are," Corren spoke with a voice of mock awe that called Weylin from his thoughts. "The lovely coastal city of Galaban. While once beautiful, it has clearly fallen to the conflict of Leighis's and Muir's children."

Eolas let out a huff as Weylin dismounted and guided her down a worn path into the city. It looked rather barren. Some of the buildings had windows that were boarded up and there were abandoned bailes along the path. There was movement ahead and Weylin saw the airy shape of a sylph female gliding out of a building.

He had not seen one in person since he was a young boy. They were humanoid in figure, but had beautiful flowing wings that protruded from behind their shoulders and looked as though they were made of shimmering air. And they were, but they were tangible, too. They were one of the more intriguing creations of the gods. Sylphs has been formed by the goddess Leighis, who presided over healing, harvest, and the woods, to honor her elven lover. They could not have children of their own as the gods were forbidden from having children by mortals as the offspring would be far too powerful and could only find a place among gods as Ifreann had when Sionna had broken this sacred law of the gods. So, Leighis created her own race, the sylphs, and made them her children.

It was a beautifully tragic story, as sylphs now roamed Talam's worldly realms. They were mortals, with the essence of gods, but lacked the longevity of elves, and found themselves in a space between man and elf, not fitting into any category but their own entirely. Yet, they still fell under the reign of the Udar, swearing their fealty to the throne, as did every living soul on Talam.

Weylin followed Corren into a mid-sized building, made of brick with broken windows and a door that was hanging from one hinge. They slipped inside and the walls were already flickering in the candle-light, along with the sun that filtered in through dusty windows. Corren led them down a corridor wordlessly, and Weylin could sense his restlessness.

They entered a room and Weylin noted the four sylphs and five undines who sat around the table on opposite sides. Weylin, Corren, and the seven laochs from Castle Fas filled in around the large table, receiving glares from the other parties.

"Good sunrise, friends," Corren began. Weylin deemed it best to allow him to begin the conversation. It was his realm, after all, and Weylin knew better than to step on wary toes. "It's about time we all gathered to have a friendly conversation, don't you think? This was our Udar Apparent's idea after all."

A dark chuckle came from the sylph side of the table. Weylin turned his head in her direction. He set his jaw and wore the commanding look of the Udar Apparent. The one that had helped earn him the title of Young Wolf.

"You waited until now to sit and reason with these beasts," a male sylph sneered in disgust. "You have sent laochs in to steal *souls* that did not belong to you. *You* abandoned your word—*your sworn oath*—and pay the price with our blood. How could you justify that now?"

"I would caution your tongue," Weylin spoke up, and every head turned in his direction to hold him in place. He didn't flinch. He glared back and felt their hatred with every passing beat. "That is your lord you speak to, and you would do well to remember it."

"How could we forget?" another sylph said. Her right arm was missing, and she spoke with a heavy Earrachean accent. "He reminds us with every *anam* that blade steals while he rules over us."

The female used the aosta term for soul.

"Return to your own lands and leave the children of Muir alone, and I'll gladly keep my blade to myself," Corren snarled. His hands gripped the edge of the table. Weylin saw his knuckles tightened. They had hardly said enough for the male to react so strongly, and Weylin could now see how deeply the animosity ran between them.

"Respectfully," a beautiful undine female spoke up. She glanced at her nails as though unbothered by everything going on around her. "We can fight our own battles. You make us appear weak by your insistence on interfering."

"When I stayed out of your affairs," Corren started, his voice growing lower, more threatening, "you ventured into *my* cities, far away from your own and far from where this conflict originated."

Weylin's ears perked at that.

"Will you keep us as your caged pets now? I cannot imagine Vartry approves of your treatment of her people," the female taunted.

Corren tensed beside Weylin.

"What would it take to end this conflict?" Weylin redirected the conversation in a casual tone, leaning back and ignoring the building tension that threatened to boil over and consume them all. "There is no sense in losing *anams* any day, but especially not today when we are on the brink of a war that has the potential to rival the War for Descendants."

A silence fell over the room at the mention of the cursed war, as well as the promised one in their near future.

"An eradication of sylphs would suffice," the undine replied first, and Weylin didn't have time to wonder what influence Corren had played on the beings here before a sylph flew across the table and slit the undine's throat.

Blood pooled out of the gaping wound as her eyes widened before her head lolled forward and hit the wooden table.

The thud turned into a room drowning in chaos as every being jumped into action.

Weylin drew *Uamhan* and leapt up from his seat.

24

RANIA

Castle Eagla had turned out to be a far more pleasant home than Rania had imagined. She also knew she owed much of that to the green-eyed man who had quickly become a friend.

Oisin was often busy politicking with the Myrkors, and the dark circles that lined his eyes were proof of it. Since Weylin had taken it upon himself to solve the dispute in Earrach, Oisin had stepped in to fill his place as best as he could. It wasn't the way things would typically go, but Callum was busy creating a weapon to take the wyverns down, and trusting Oisin was another way the Myrkors showed their good faith to the Dorcases, who previously shared a rather tense relationship.

Rania could see Faolan was grateful for his help in the few meals they had shared, but he was also wary of working with the future Lord of Briongloid. Rania didn't blame him for it. Their alliance was hesitant at best, but she hoped her official mating to Weylin would stabilize it.

Niamh Myrkor seemed eager for it, at the very least. The female took every meal with the Dorcas siblings as an opportunity to hound her with plans and suggestions of florals, meal options, and various decor ideas. Rania didn't mind, but she had never been a female that dreamed of her mating day. She would much rather spend her hours in the drawing room with Callum Ronan. And she often did.

It was midday and Rania had not seen Oisin or Callum since she woke up.

It was an unusual occurrence, as she knew well enough where they both liked to linger.

She made her way to the library, where she found novels to pass her time with. Rania remembered Callum speaking of escape through his reading, and she had picked up several books that told tales of heroes and heroines who faced battles such as the ones they would soon be met with.

It felt easier to think of it when she read. If they could handle it, so could she. Rania was not afraid of much, because she never thought of herself as having much to lose. No one had ever looked at her as a threat, anyway, although she supposed that might soon change once the Udar Apparent was her mate.

But she was prepared for it. She had spent her whole life preparing for the possibility, even when her parents had not considered it.

Rania glided down the hall of ivory floors and watched the painting of a wolf pack fly by in her peripheral vision. She had gotten the hang of most of the routes and corridors within the castle, thanks to Callum. She found herself disappointed when she did not run into him in the halls, and every morning she woke up eager to see him again, hopeful that she would happen upon him, as they had both made a habit of doing.

He was very different from Weylin.

He was gentler, more timid. He seemed more apt to obey the rules and follow commands, but she could sense a hesitancy in him. Callum longed for justice and peace—something she didn't know if he would see in his lifetime. Rania knew Callum would always want to do what was right, no matter who was commanding it. Rania respected the man for it.

He was charming in his own way, too, but she didn't think he realized it.

She was nearly to the library when the sound of Oisin's voice drifted to her perked ears, and she followed it down a corridor to her right where it led her to a large oak door that had been pulled shut.

Rania paused outside of the door, leaning in closer to listen. She immediately recognized the Udar's deep and commanding voice.

"We need allies, yes, but we have more than enough as it is. We shouldn't waste any more time than we need to."

Silence followed the statement.

"What of the northern realms? It has been a while since we've received communication from the lords and ladies there," Callum spoke up.

A laugh boomed through the room. Rania knew it to be Faolan's. It was a mocking laugh, and one that Callum's statement had not warranted.

Rania pushed her shoulders back and tilted her chin higher. She wore a poised smile as she pushed open the door to the meeting room without hesitation or fear. For what did she need to fear when the Udar's son was her betrothed? Who would turn her away or shut her down when they would have Hel to pay for it?

Rania's pale blue dress swished about her thin frame as she walked into the room, aiming for an empty seat that fortunately fell between Callum and Oisin. Each head in the room jerked in her direction. She could feel their looks, their glares, and their gapes. Someone's jaw dropped open.

Rania looked at each of them with her perfectly mastered political grin. She allowed her gaze to linger with a faint smirk to keep them guessing, but charming enough to make them listen.

As she continued forward she looked upon Orla—the only other female in the room. Orla's green eyes gleamed with amusement as she leaned forward in her chair and rested her chin on her pale fist. There was something of approval in the look she gave Rania.

Finally, she caught Faolan's amber gaze that gave away no reaction at all. He wore a stubborn set of his jaw that said she should not be there but was otherwise unreadable.

Rania looked to Oisin as she passed his seat to get to the empty one, and the corner of his lip tugged into a devilish grin. He was not surprised.

Callum, on the other hand, was taken aback. He tensed beside Rania as she settled into the maroon cushioned chair.

"I grew bored," Rania said plainly. The entire room seemed to be waiting for further explanation as they remained silent. "I was on my way to the library when I overheard talk of the northern realms. I thought my voice might be worth adding, seeing as we neighbor Fomhar, and I know they are one of the realms of which you speak. Maybe even the most pressing of them."

"I suppose your invite was lost in the corridors," Faolan said with malice coating his words. "We are all so relieved you found your way here."

Rania wouldn't let her expression falter in the face of Faolan's sarcasm. She held his look evenly, allowing those around her to make their own judgements.

Faolan was evidently less than impressed with her arrival. She hadn't expected him to welcome her with open arms, but she knew he wouldn't throw her out or shame her. Not in front of an audience, at least.

And Rania had promised her parents, as well as herself, that she would never find herself in a room alone with the Udar. Weylin, she trusted, but his father was a different beast entirely. She feared his cruelty knew no bounds when it came to seeing his will to fruition.

"I was hoping you wouldn't mind," Rania said. She crossed her hands in front of her on the table and leaned back in her chair. "You were discussing the topic of alliances, yes? Don't mind me. You should continue where you left off. I'll catch up. I'm a quick study."

"Thank you so much for your permission, Lady Rania," Faolan sneered before dragging his eyes from her and looking at the male across from him who Rania did not recognize. Callum remained tense beside her, and hadn't offered a single glance in her direction, while Oisin looked at her, awaiting her reaction. A few chuckles sounded from the males around the table. Rania ignored them. "As I was saying, our top priority right now is defending our cities against their wyverns and their esos of flames. We need the weapons that will take the wyverns down, not simply injure them and anger them further. They have neither the legions nor the allies we do, but they have enough wyverns to raise concerns. On top of that, we will continue training every laoch in Samhradh so they will be ready for the Inevitable War when we make our move. And that will be sooner rather than later."

"And what about the advantage of their esos?" the male Faolan directed the statement at asked.

"We have it on good authority that their ash trees are depleted in the south. We will need to lure them there."

The room fell silent at that. Rania knew there was a part of them that wanted to go to the ash trees. They yearned to know which source of esos filled their blood, just as she did. It would be a significant risk to take elves with no esos training into a realm with ash trees. Their esos would awaken, and none of them knew how that would feel, or what it would do to them.

The thought made Rania shudder.

"What of Fomhar?" Rania spoke up when no one else did. Again, all attention turned towards her. She found she enjoyed the feeling.

"They, like Briongloid, stood with Eilean during the War for Descendants. They backed the *mallaithe* then. Do we know where they stand now?"

Rania's father often spoke of Fomhar as they were the only other ally on Iomlan from that cursed war. They had shared a close bond between their two dynasties, but that bond had deteriorated with the announcement of Rania's betrothal to the Young Wolf. Rania was around when Deaglan Shea's letter arrived, and Brendan Dorcas read it. The letter spoke of betrayal and severed bonds.

Rania would never betray the Shea family here in this castle. She would let them reveal themselves in time, but she knew it was worth cautioning her new realm. She, herself, held no allegiance to the realm of Fomhar, as she had not been alive in the time their families fought side by side to save the Iarkises. It was no concern of hers, but she knew it caused pain for her father to hear their family friend hold such grievances against them. And she knew, deep down, he blamed her for it.

But she was saving her family. Whether or not they saw it, she sacrificed her hand in mating to save the Dorcases from whatever fate would befall the *Gheall Ceann* and her own realm. Without her mating, she couldn't be certain which side her father would choose, but she knew which one would win. History had already told that story.

"They will fall into place right behind your own realm, I am certain of it," Faolan said with hardly a glance in her direction. "I have no reason to waste time and resources securing the weakest of the realms."

"I would not be so certain, if it were me."

Rania allowed her words to settle on cautious ears. Let the moments pass while she waited for the Udar to acknowledge her.

"Noted, Lady Dorcas," Faolan said. "I think that's quite enough for one afternoon. Callum, we will expect an updated weapon design in three sunrises. Oisin, you can start training the laochs alongside Quinn this evening. We appreciate you volunteering to help."

"Yes, my lord." Oisin dipped his head.

"Dismissed," Faolan growled as he stood up from the table. Orla followed without a word. She cast a single, curious glance in Rania's direction before they both exited the room.

The female made Rania uneasy. She was silent, but held an obvious sway over both the realm and the Udar. That amount of power was dangerous in hands Rania could not trust.

The rest of the council filed out behind them, talking amongst themselves about their different tasks. Each one looked at her over their shoulder before making their own exits.

"Well done, sister," Oisin said, rising to his feet. "I've yet to see anyone unnerve the Udar like that. The meeting was growing stale, anyway. I'm sure Captain Ronan would agree."

"As they tend to," Callum agreed with a small smile. There was something he was hiding. Rania sensed it in his tone and the distant look in his eyes. He had not met her gaze yet, even as she silently willed him to.

"I'll see you both at dinner?" Oisin said.

"That you will," Rania nodded.

Callum did not make to get up from his chair, so neither did she, as Oisin hurried from the room, seemingly in a rush to get somewhere. He always was these days.

"Are you okay?" Rania asked once the door fell shut behind her brother.

"Yes, why wouldn't I be?" Callum at last turned to face her, and when he looked at her, a shiver travelled down her spine.

"You seem off."

"I wasn't expecting to see you here," he said, ignoring her comment.

"A pleasant surprise, I hope."

"It always is, to see you," he said with a sigh. She noticed his shoulders drop before he ran a hand through his unruly curls. "But you need to be careful with the Udar. He is not so easily amused, but he is quick to anger. He has been careful around you, but he will not be forever. That is a male with a bad side to avoid."

"How can I be on his bad side when I am vowed to become his daughter?" Rania pressed. A flicker of emotion she couldn't quite place crossed Callum's eyes, but he recovered quickly.

"The male hardly harbors love for his own mate," Callum muttered before turning his attention to the parchment laid out before him. Rania recognized the plan they had been working on. "You shouldn't expect him to save any for the mate of his son."

"Hmm," she hummed in response, watching Callum's fingers roam the parchment.

She had not seen the man so downcast. There was a desire to get to the root of it she could not shake.

"Did you show them your plans?"

"I did."

Rania rose and moved to perch on the armrest of Callum's chair to peer at the design he had crafted, with her help, for a weapon that resembled a massive crossbow that would shoot arrows into the skies. From the wyvern's recent landing, it had become clear that their weapons were hardly effective against the wyvern's natural scaled armor.

"And what did they think?" She tilted her chin to look at him, and quickly realized how close they were as their noses nearly touched.

"They liked it." Callum breathed out, and Rania smiled. He dragged his dark green eyes from hers and looked at the carefully designed weapon plan. "Faolan wants two minor adjustments to the stability of it, and the size of the arrows, but after that is approved, we'll begin work on the first one."

"You don't sound happy?"

"I am."

"That wasn't very convincing."

"You shouldn't know me as well as you do for only being in this castle so few sunrises. I suppose I should make myself a bit harder to read," Callum teased. Rania was relieved to hear some of his usual personality return to his voice. "I am happy. I suppose this just makes it feel so much more real. And I'd be lying if I said I felt right about building the weapon to take these creatures down. They've got nothing to do with the prophecy, or the *mallaithe* for that matter. They didn't ask for this."

Rania nodded thoughtfully. Similar hesitations had crossed her own mind, but she could see the way it was wearing on Callum.

"You're right," she said. "They didn't. But the Iarkises will use them in their war regardless, and one wyvern on its own could wipe out entire cities if we choose not to fight back. We have to protect Iomlan, and if they choose to weaponize their wyverns, then that is out of our control."

"I understand that," Callum said. He paused a moment before continuing and lowered his voice to a whisper. "But besides their wyverns, what do they have? It's one worldly realm against six. The otherly realms will surely not involve themselves."

"They have the *Gheall Ceann*," Rania replied quietly. It was nearly blasphemy to refer to Aisling Iarkis as such around Samhradh. They preferred the title "*mallaithe*," which meant cursed. But *cursed* or *blessed*, whatever the prophecy had intended to tell them or warn them, she was still the *chosen one*, and she would never escape her fate one way or the other. Callum did not react to the title when she spoke it, but she had a feeling he wouldn't. "They know how they could end this. Speaking of six realms, it is my understanding that Samhradh is certain of their alliances, yet you've not spoken with the northern realms? Explain that to me."

"What is there to explain? They'll fall into place. They learned that in the aftermath of the War for Descendants."

Rania reached across Callum. She felt him tense beside her as she pushed aside the weaponry plans to reach the map of Iomlan that peeked out beneath it. She ran her finger across the boundaries of the northern territories.

"Fomhar has never been an ally of Samhradh, and their allegiance to Briongloid is only so strong. Geimreigh barely took the side of Samhradh in the end, and same for Bitu. It is better to be safe than sorry, as this time the stakes are much higher than they were in the War for Descendants. Every lord and every lady is combing over each piece of information that is known about that gods' damned prophecy and interpreting it for themselves. Will Aisling save the realms or destroy them? That is what they will all be asking themselves. The cost this time is not simply a throne, but the whole of Talam as we know it. You'll need to ensure they are interpreting the murmurs of the norns the same as you. It will not be long before the winds shatter the glass," Rania said, keeping her attention fixed on the map and the familiar territories.

Callum remained silent, and she dragged her eyes from the map to his own. His green eyes flitted back and forth between hers with an intensity that made her want to draw back as much as it made her want to lean forward. He was close, so close to her now. There was so much to unpack, she just needed him to trust her.

"What does that even mean?" he whispered softly, and his eyes narrowed curiously.

"I-I'm not sure," she stuttered as her eyes blinked rapidly.

Winds. Shattered. Glass.

The words had left her tongue as though they were talking about something as common as the weather, but she had never heard them together that way before. She didn't even know their meaning.

She sucked in a breath as her heartbeat quickened. Callum reached out and gently took her hand as he saw the panic come over her face. His touch lit a fire through her, and he gave her a reassuring squeeze as a breath she didn't know she was holding rushed from her lungs.

He leaned in closer to her, and she felt her cheeks heat as she opened her lips to speak, but no words came out.

"You know more than you're letting on," he spoke the words so quietly, they were hard to hear even in their close proximity. "If there's anyone in this castle you can trust, it's me, Rania."

Rania blinked slowly as he said her name. She wanted to say more, but she wasn't even sure what she could say. Callum released her hand and stood from the chair. Rania stood up, too. Her hands were shaking, but she couldn't explain why.

She stood back and watched as Callum gathered his papers and left without another word.

She longed to run after him—to tell him she did trust him—but her feet remained rooted in place.

25

RUAIRI

His life was a cruel joke in the hands of even crueler gods. Ruairi sat slumped against the corner of the small cell Cliona ordered Conor to throw him in after her interrogation.

He had now seen the inside of two cells in his brief lifetime, and had grown up thinking he would never see the inside of one. But here he was for the second time in less than a full moon in Braon.

Ruairi couldn't stop shaking.

It was all too familiar, too terrifying, and he didn't know what would come next. He couldn't imagine Cliona would take it as far as the laochs in Castle Eagla had, but she had already used her esos on him, sifting through his mind like sand. He had fought back as hard as he could to bury his secrets from her, but he knew it hadn't been enough.

His mind had revealed the ring hidden in his sock, and Cliona had ripped it from him. He had failed again. This failure felt like the very worst of them. Why would Cliona hand over control of an army of the husks to the Udar? It was all beyond him, but it confirmed every suspicion he had ever had of the Mathair.

Sinister forces were at play during the time of the ninth generation, and Ruairi had unintentionally played right into them.

There was one thing he was thankful for among it all. Cliona had not been able to gather any information about Aisla's whereabouts, since he truly had none for her to find. If she was protected still, Ruairi had hope. He didn't know how she would take his discoveries, but he knew that if she saw him locked up like this by her own grandmother, it would be enough to turn her against the Mathair.

If she could ever find him.

Ruairi wondered what stories Cliona would spin to his family. What lies would spread throughout Caillte when it became evident he was missing?

The cell in Castle Farraige was different than his had been in Castle Eagla. Here he shared a hall with other cells, all with barred walls, so the prisoners within could still see and speak to each other through them. In Castle Eagla, he had been in a walled room and had never met another prisoner in their halls.

There was one female in front of his cell and to the left, but she had not moved from the corner of her cell since he had arrived. Ruairi vaguely recognized her from what he could make out of her face in the dim torchlight. She was a couple of years ahead of him in scoil.

Across from him was Eitri.

Eitri had slung a slew of curses his way when Conor brought Ruairi in. He was angry, and understandably so. Shame heated Ruairi's cheeks with each insult. Ruairi had never meant to get him wrapped up in this. He had only needed answers to his questions, and a confirmation of his suspicions.

When he first arrived to the dungeons of the castle, he wondered if Edi had gotten wrapped up in it as well. He looked for the familiar face of their lead mender in the cells that he passed as Conor dragged him along. But then, he wondered if Edi had been the one to betray him to Cliona. He didn't know who else could have.

She didn't seem like the type, but Ruairi was quickly learning how few people in his life he could really trust.

He paused and closed his eyes. He tipped his head back against the concrete rear wall of his cell and breathed out slowly. There was a constant panic waiting to break just beneath the surface of his skin. A panic that was ever present to remind him of his time within the Udar's walls.

He could hardly keep his eyes open. It was all too familiar of his worst sunrises.

Ruairi clenched his hands into fists as his heart continued to thunder in his chest. He wondered if it would ever slow, or if it would continue to race until his breaths could no longer keep up.

He couldn't die here. He wouldn't let himself.

"Help me," Ruairi whispered to anyone that might be listening. "Help me. Help me."

He wouldn't allow his voice to be silenced this time.

"It's no use, boy," Eitri snarled. "Anyone who could be listening cares little for the likes of us."

26
AISLA

Aisla's hand flew to her mouth when she heard Muinin's voice rattle through her skull. She knew in that moment she would have recognized his voice, whether she first heard it in a bustling city street or a crowded hall.

It was different than the mysterious female voice that frequented her. It felt more concrete and tangible in a way she couldn't describe. It was almost as though she could feel Muinin despite the distance between them.

Muinin. She whispered the word back and felt it glide down the golden thread that lingered in the dark of her mind. *It's so good to hear your voice. I only wish I'd learned sooner. It's about time we finally found a shifter to teach us.*

Us? I didn't need to learn to speak.

Fair enough. Aisla thought with a grin.

Muinin's voice was rough and low, but not too low. There was a teasing, playful edge to it that greeted her like an embrace she was in desperate need of.

I'm proud of you, my bonded. Thank you for finding your voice.

Muinin finished with a purr of approval, and it caressed Aisla's mind like a reprieve from the constant guilt and fear and anxiety that consumed her.

I don't know what I would do without you, she said. And they both knew she meant it.

Probably not make it very far. But also, possibly not have started a war.

There was no scolding or judgement in his tone. It was his way of making light of a situation they had not yet been able to address. And her heart felt a little lighter, if only for a moment.

"Is that him?" Eilis's voice broke through Aisla's thoughts, and she had nearly forgotten the female was standing just beside her.

Aisla turned and saw the wide-eyed wonder on her face. She was certain it reflected her own. She wanted nothing more than to run to Muinin so they could sit face to face and talk about everything and anything.

But it was not the time.

Tears stung the corners of Aisla's eyes as she nodded her head in response.

"Yes, it was," she said. "I can hear him. I've always dreamed of what it would be like. Thank you for making it possible."

"You don't need to thank me," Eilis replied. "It was always within you—there was nothing that I gave you that you didn't already possess. Communicating with creatures is great progress for a shifter. It's the first big step and shifting comes with lots of practice and time. It's a stranger sensation since you aren't just letting a voice in. You're letting an idea change your whole being."

"Will you show me?"

Eilis grinned and nodded. She closed her eyes once again. She spoke, and Aisla followed along, pushing down her excitement at finding her esos once again.

Aisla could feel its reluctant awakening. The way the power within her veins responded to her plea for return like a bear awakening from a long hibernation into the warm spring sun. She coaxed it out, even as her pulse thrummed with fear of what it could do. But she couldn't fear it. Not any longer. Too many others did that for her. She needed to believe in it, and trust that it would not consume her again.

She knew better than to let it.

Aisla found her father later in the evening after another full day of both training and gardening with Eilis. She was eager to share her progress, and to see him again

Given his headway with the translation, there was a lingering question in the back of her mind that wondered if he had finished it since she'd last seen him.

The possibility made her itch uncomfortably. Her stomach twisted into a knot. What she once thought might have felt like relief, now felt like a dark cloud over her.

She knew whatever the letter said, it wouldn't be easy for her to hear. Aisla worked to not let her mind wander down that road. It did no one any good.

In a way, she also knew that once the letter was translated and back in her hands, she no longer had a reason to remain with the Silenced. And no matter how much it frightened her, she knew she had to get back to Ruairi as soon as she could.

While being in their library made her restless, she had also learned to find peace there. Training with Eilis had been the most she'd seen of her esos since that sunrise in the infirmary. She hadn't quite managed to shift forms, but she could feel herself growing closer with each time she closed her eyes and tried. It was a different type of power than any of the elemental powers she was used to. She was satisfied at least that she had finally made a connection to Muinin, and nothing would sever that until her passing on.

Or so she hoped.

Once Aisla was exhausted from trying to reconnect with her esos, they made their way back to the garden to help turn over the soil for new plants. Eilis had introduced her to Beckett as well, and Aisla was grateful to have made friends in the south.

They ate lunch in the field of blooming plants, sitting on a blanket of patched squares. They drank mead and ate pork with beans and laughed until their bellies ached. It felt like a glimpse of home for once, and it was comforting until Aisla remembered it had been her father's home ever since he'd left.

The anger in her heart that had settled on her since finding him turned to grief at the time they had missed out on. Aisla had lost her appetite when they brought out a peach pie, and politely excused herself before climbing down the long ladder, eager to find Feargal again.

"Hey," she said softly, but he jumped at her arrival. He was sitting in a small room with a desk and two cushioned chairs.

"Hey," he responded.

He looked up at her. There was an unmistakable sorrow in his eyes that mingled with exhaustion. She knew in that moment he had finished the letter.

"It's done?"

"It is."

"May I see it?" Aisla's heart thundered in her chest, and she slowly lowered herself into the chair beside her father.

"I wish I could convince you not to," he started. His breath was shaky, and Aisla's heart cracked along familiar lines she thought were healed. She braced her hands on the sides of her chair. "I wish I could convince you to stay here with me in this library and we would never have to leave. But that would be selfish of me, and I have been a selfish male for long enough. And I suppose it wouldn't be fair to you or any of the realms to ask that of you."

"You're not a selfish male," Aisla said, knowing she meant it.

"It's okay if you think I am. I had to leave—it was the only way I could make it out. I saw what Cliona did to your mother, and I knew I couldn't stay. But I never tried to go back, and for that, I am truly sorry, Aisling."

"What did she do to her?" Aisla asked, knowing this conversation had been dancing in the air between them. It was merely waiting to be loosed. Aisla finally forced herself to open that door, for she feared Feargal never would without her prompting. "I know she was the cause of her passing on, but what happened to her?" Her voice trailed off into a barely audible whisper.

"Cliona—your grandmother—toyed with her mind. She altered it and mended it and molded it like clay, until there was no mind left to pick apart," Feargal said, looking up at her with glassy eyes. "She wanted your mother to give you up, and to do so, she tried to plant visions in her mind of a world that you grew up to destroy. They were visions of a starless sky and winds that raged fire across Talam. Cliona showed her visions that brought her deepest fears to light, and after a time, your mother couldn't tell the difference between the visions and her reality. Your mother fought hard against them. When I tried to make Cliona stop, she locked me in a cell beneath the castle, where no one would hear my voice. A prisoner within my own home," Feargal loosed a dark, humorless chuckle, and a shadow fell over his sorrow-filled eyes. "It was all done subtly and privately enough that no one outside of those closest to her within her inner circle knew what was going on."

Feargal paused and toyed with the corner of his dark grey coat.

Aisla's breath caught in her throat and memories of a time when she had been forbidden from seeing her parents while they fought against a nameless illness rose to the surface of her mind. She had been told her mother fell ill first, then her father. They had every mender working to heal them, but they were too far along, or so she had been told. Cliona said the risk of contagion was too high for her, so Aisla spent her time with Eire and Ruairi's families, while she waited and prayed to gods she didn't know if she believed in. She tried so hard to forget those never-ending sunrises, and the pain she had known before her tenth naming day.

The next time she saw them, they were concealed within marble caskets lowered into the ground behind Castle Farraige.

"She got into your mother's mind and made her forget her esos of earth. She lost her connection to her esos as a terran entirely, and believed she was a Seer, even though the norns had long revoked such esos during the betrayal of Skrymir. That was the beginning of your mother losing herself entirely, and I could do nothing but wait and shout into the dark beneath the castle where no one could hear me. I was told she thought everything that Cliona had planted in her mind were visions of the future granted to her by the gods. Aine thought it was by her own power, and no longer realized it was Cliona's doing, yet she still refused to believe it was true. She would never think you capable of such things, so Cliona never let her return to you. Your mother fought for you until her final breath. Despite it all, I *need* you to know that. She still believed you to be good and believed you to be the savior that Talam needs. Cliona couldn't take that from her," Feargal said. "And I believe it, too."

Aisla swallowed around a lump in her throat. She ignored the silent tears rolling down her heated cheeks. Her hands balled into fists at her side, but she said nothing. She was silent as she waited for her father to continue.

"Cliona had your mother's body delivered to my cell," his voice was a low whisper. Aisla saw his own tears falling, too. It was an open wound—a wound not yet healed. "I don't know exactly how it happened. But there were no marks anywhere on her. Only invisible wounds that I would never truly know. She looked perfectly fine, just tired. She appeared peaceful in her final sleep. I will never forgive myself for the life I mated her into, and would have done anything to bring her back. But I know if she was here, she would tell you she would do it all over again. Because you needed a mother as strong as Aine to fight for you. And fight for you, she did."

Feargal paused and wiped his eyes. He let out a shaky breath before he continued.

Aisla was angry she had no idea this was going on within the walls of her own home. She was young, but to be so blind, she felt her ignorance like a hot iron pressed to her back. If only her mother had been permitted to return to her, Aisla was certain she would have seen a difference. She would have known something wasn't right.

"And I was next. My own mother took me to her interrogation room. She broke into my mind, but I was raised with her powers and had long learned the shields I needed to work in to place. We fought and screamed. We hated each other by then, but I didn't know if I could ever take her life. I knew she loved the power she held, and would do anything to keep it, but I had never imagined her capable of such evil," Feargal said. "That night, she ripped away the golden thread that bonded me to Muinin and that pain was unlike anything I had experienced. It was not as bad as losing your mother, of course, but different entirely. It was a physical, visceral pain that radiated through every cell of my body until I thought I would die. I knew that if you were to have any chance at surviving, I needed to save myself. I devised a plan to break out of my cell, and then took one of the passages in the dungeons I had discovered growing up in Castle Farraige. Then, I fled. I knew I should have gone back for you, and I cursed myself every day that I didn't, but I knew she would never let you go. I knew of the laochs she kept outside your rooms and laochs that were watching your movements at all hours. There is a longer, more complicated story of it all, but I hope you know I got myself out, because I needed to be out here, fighting for you. I needed to get out before she took my mind, as well. I didn't want to make you a true orphan."

"I've been an orphan for nine years," she whispered.

"I know. I didn't mean it that way. I'll always regret the way I left you."

"I understand why you did it," Aisla forced out around the choking of her grief. "I do. I just wish you had found a way to tell me to find you."

"I always planned for you to find the *Dawn of Talam*," he replied. "Your mother researched this place and put it all down for you. She'd hoped we would all live here together one day."

"A note would have been nice," she said with a dry, humorless laugh. "I'm sorry you had to go through all of it."

"I'm sorry, too."

Aisla reached out a hand and laid it on his knee. It was a small peace offering, but it was all she had to give in that moment. He laid his hand on top of hers and the warmth flooded her as though it were an embrace.

"I'd like to read the letter now," she said.

The words felt distant to her own ears. She knew she was not ready—she didn't know if she ever would be, but she couldn't stand not knowing anymore.

Feargal withdrew his hand and pulled the letter out from the stack of books before him. He sighed with a heaviness that threatened to break her before he held it in the air between them.

"Would you like me to stay or leave?"

"Stay," she said, "please."

"Of course."

Her hands shook as she took the letter from his grip. Aisla unfolded the letter that was worn from its adventure in Iomlan. It had been battered by blood, rain, and the other elements. Just as she had.

The irony was not lost on her.

Her eyes were ravenous for its words and anxious to commit its contents to memory in case it should ever be lost.

To the Udar of Talam, Faolan Myrkor,

I have upheld my end of our bargain. The poison has been planted, and it is spreading through Eilean as you read this letter. Your army will soon be one of great number here, and Eilean's sacrifice will not go unappreciated. The inflicted are multiplying and growing stronger as they adjust to the effects. It is best to take the rot out from within, and I fear my grand-daughter has more allies than enemies in her home. As we predicted. I was unable to sow the seeds of doubt early enough, and she is already esteemed as a savior by most. Little do they know of the doom she will unleash.

As agreed, I grant this ring to you, and you will have control of those who came in contact with the poison. The emerald contains a root of ash tree that will allow you to use the esos even with no source in your soil. They are yours against whatever allies rally alongside Aisling. In return, following the war, you will re-open relations between Eilean, and grant me the seat of Mathair of the worldly realms while you sit the throne as Ardri. As promised, I should remind you, I will not be your second, but your equal in return for my sacrifices. I will restore my realm to glory, as promised by Sionna, and we will work to reunite the seven worldly realms as one in a way my granddaughter never could.

Finally, the Gheall Ceann. I have suppressed her esos for as long as she has been in scoil. She's as helpless with her power as an infant. She has proven herself unfit to bring peace and her emotions rule her every move. She is too unpredictable, and it is our duty to stop her before it is too late. Once the declarations have been made, she is yours for the taking. Do with her what you must. We will be quick to put out any resistance to the decision given the ring and its power over a growing army. We will restore Eilean from the ground up. I thank you for your dedication to a better Talam, and to the salvation of the nine realms.

I await the new future with open arms. We will certainly make formidable allies in the war to come.
Cliona Darkis

Bile rose to the back of Aisla's throat. Ringing roared through her ears. Her palms burned with rage. Her blood boiled until she was sure it was made of embers.

How could her grandmother do this to her own people? What amount of power could be worth such a sacrifice? And Sionna—the goddess?

She looked up at her father through eyes blurry with tears of hot anger and terrible fear. She was dizzy and nauseous.

Aisla opened her mouth to speak, but instead retched all over the ornately patterned maroon carpet. She caught her head in her hands as her throat constricted with a deep-seated terror.

"This can't be real," she wept. The letter fell to the ground.

Her father rushed from his chair and enveloped her in his arms, and she had not realized how badly she needed it. She clung to him as her body shook with sobs. She wanted to cry out that her grandmother would never do such a thing. Cliona had raised her and taught her. She had loved her. Cliona wouldn't hurt her own realm. Cliona wouldn't betray her. She was an enemy to the Udar, not an ally. Cliona would never force Ruairi to be the one to hand that letter over. It was cruel. It was unforgivable.

The only family Aisla had for the past nine years couldn't do this to her.

She would not turn her over to those monsters capable of evil beyond words.

All for the sake of power.

Aisla clutched her father tighter as she felt her esos stirring beneath her skin. She held on to him as she was reminded that Cliona was the reason she could never master her esos. It all clicked into place, no matter how badly she wanted it not to. Cliona would never let her train with anyone else. She didn't want her politically involved.

The only times Aisla was successful in her esos was when she trained alongside someone else.

She supposed she was the ultimate bargaining chip. Not the letter. Not the ring.

All the Myrkors had ever wanted—the death of the *Gheall Ceann*. The death of Aisling Iarkis.

There was never a cure for the lofa. Because it had never existed. It was a poison spread by her grandmother at the command of her family's worst enemy. Cliona had never intended for Aisla to go to Iomlan with Ruairi. She must have panicked when she lost her real tool before her title was declared.

Everything she read in the letter lined up with the stories Feargal had told her about his mother. Yet, it was an impossible task to match the female who had raised her with the one who had driven her mother to a life-ending madness. With the letter laid out before her in her grandmother's own penmanship, Aisla could no longer hope to deny it.

Surely, now that none of her three tools had landed in the clutches of the Udar, she would be on a ruthless hunt for them. Two of them remained together in the library of the Silenced World Tellers, but the final one—Ruairi still had it.

"Ru," Aisla choked out. Her anger and grief were replaced with panic that widened her eyes. She pushed away from her father. Confusion crossed his face. "Ruairi. I have to go."

She leapt from her chair, dodging the remnants of her dinner with a cringe. She made for the closed door. Aisla felt sorry for whoever had to clean up the mess, but she didn't have the time to stop and think about it.

"Wait, Aisling," Feargal said. "Where are you going? Are you okay? I think you should stay one more night. Stay, and we'll come up with a plan together."

There was a pleading in his voice that tore through her bleeding heart. He caught her by the arm on her way out of the door.

"I can't leave him. *Not again*," she snapped. He took a step back from her and she saw the hurt in his eyes, but she couldn't stop. She could only hope she would see him again and be able to explain better. "Ruairi has the ring. Cliona will find out, and she will hurt him. His blood will not be on my hands. *Not again*. I need him."

"I'll come with you."

"You can't," she said and yanked her arm from his grasp. She turned away. "We will need allies on Eilean when the time comes."

The door fell shut behind her as Aisla left her father behind. She darted through halls, ignoring the curious looks that trailed her.

She ran. Her tears of grief dried by the heat of her rage.

Muinin, I need you, now.

I'm already here.

Thank you.

27

CALLUM

A knock sounded at Callum's door as he was getting ready to go to the laoch training camps for the morning. He had not been assigned duty there today, but he needed a break from looking at his design. It was his hope that time away would give him a fresh mind to look at the Udar's requests.

He needed to get out of the castle and away from the watchful leer of the Udar. He desperately wished Weylin would return and save him from it all.

Callum straightened his sand-colored top before opening the door. A startled breath was stolen from his lips when Rania appeared, but she was not poised and prepared as she always was, even at such an early hour.

Her eyes were tired and lined with dark circles that hinted at a lack of sleep. Her white blonde hair, typically tied in a lovely and ornate braid, fell around her shoulders in loose, tangled waves.

She was beautiful this way. Callum's stomach turned with a

feeling he couldn't place, and a part of him suddenly wished they had never met.

"Are you okay?" Callum asked.

"No," she said. She looked past him into his room, a silent request to enter. He stepped back to allow her to walk through the door-frame, and his heart thundered in his ears. He shut the door before turning to face her and watched her sit on the edge of his bed as though she had done it countless times before. "Oisin—he's gone. He went out to the city for a drink, and he didn't come back. I went to a few local pubs, looking for him, and he wasn't at any of them. I assumed he found a bed to stay in, but he's always home by morning. This isn't like him."

"Okay," Callum said, calmly. "What do we do now?"

"So, you'll help?" She looked up at him under light lashes and genuine surprise laced her voice.

"Of course. Where do we start?"

"Well," she said, "my mother doesn't like to talk about it, but Oisin has always had a gambling problem, especially after he's been drinking. I wouldn't be surprised if his mouth and empty pockets got him in trouble."

"He doesn't have airgead?"

"I keep the majority of it," Rania said. "We wouldn't have a cent to the Dorcas name if we entrusted our fortune to Oisin."

"Oh," Callum replied, not knowing what else to say. He ran his fingers through his hair, trying to remember all the places the laochs frequented and talked about.

He remembered an alley at the outskirts of Omra that housed a handful of pubs and taverns. It was infamous for the exchange of goods not found in the local markets. Shady characters roamed its parts, and laochs looking to make airgead in their free time.

Callum would never suspect Oisin of such things, but he did suspect he could have gotten into trouble with such people playing cards and placing bets. It was at least a place to start, and Rania wouldn't have made it there in her venture to the local pubs. Perhaps the Lord Apparent of Briongloid was hoping to stay out of view of the Udar's men by wandering further from the city center.

"I have an idea." Callum breathed out, and he watched Rania's eyes sparkle with hope. "But I think I should go alone."

"Absolutely not."

"It's no place for ladies, Rania."

She stood and crossed the room to him until she was a mere breath away. She stood more than a head shorter than he and craned her neck to glare up at him.

"I've just about had it with males telling me where ladies do and do not belong."

Callum's chest tightened at her words. He had not meant them that way, but he knew what she meant. He had seen her face when she entered the council room and looked about the room to see only males and Orla sitting around the table planning the future of Talam. Callum had seen the way her confidence faltered for just a beat.

Unfamiliar eyes would have missed it.

"Of course," he replied with a nod. "I apologize for my poor choice of words and my assumption. It's not so much that you're a lady, but that you're far finer than the scum that roam the parts we might find ourselves in."

"I can assure you; I've encountered worse."

"I hate that that is probably true," Callum said. "You are your own person. I would just make sure you don't have anything of value on you. And don't dress too nicely."

"This should do, then."

She tossed her arms up to indicate the pale grey dress she wore that was not nearly as decadent as her typical gowns, but he thought she looked just as regal in it. If not more so.

He nodded, knowing better than to argue with her.

"I suppose we can head out now in that case," Callum said. "I didn't have anything on my agenda today. I was going to visit the laoch camps, but I wasn't assigned to be there."

"Thank you," Rania said.

Before he could open his lips to reply, her arms were wrapped around his waist, enveloping him in an embrace that smelled of cedar and lily.

It had been a long time since anyone had embraced him in such a way.

He hesitantly put his own arms around her, suddenly all too aware of all the time they had been spending together, and how others might perceive it. He swallowed and a brief sorrow he couldn't explain tightened the air in his lungs. He pushed the thoughts aside and held Rania Dorcas, knowing her brother was the only person she truly knew in Castle Eagla. Callum knew she needed the comfort of a friend.

"Tell me. Where are we going then?" Rania pulled away and again looked up at him.

A single tear rolled down her cheek, and Callum gently wiped it from her pale skin. She blinked once as her lips parted with unspoken words. Callum took a step backwards, creating distance between them.

"A village at the outskirts of Samhradh," he replied. "It's a good place to start. There are a lot of shady happenings there, that much I am certain of. If your brother got in with the wrong crowd, he may well have ended up there by morning."

"Are you ready to go?"

"Do I not look ready to you?" he teased, desperately wishing to fall back into the typical banter that was such a large part of their friendship.

"Of course you do," she said, and a mischievous smile played at the corners of her lips.

Her vulnerability was masked behind that bravado she wore like a second layer of skin. She looped her arm through his. Callum held his breath as he prayed no one would be in the halls to see them exiting his chamber together.

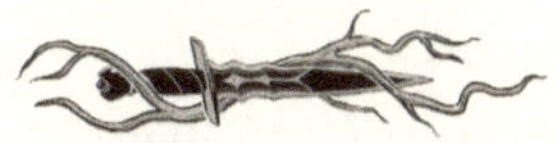

"Do you come here often?" Rania asked as they made their way down the cobblestone road that made up Dullahan Row.

Dullahan Row housed multiple pubs, taverns, and inns. Callum kept his head down beneath the hood of his cloak and suggested Rania do the same. There were enough of his laochs that enjoyed finding trouble that he didn't want either of them to be recognized.

"No," he said. "Not here. I prefer to make my mischief closer to home. My own bed is too good to pass up."

"I can understand that. Where's your favorite place to go?"

"Honestly, Weylin and I usually stay in the castle's tavern. Sometimes we visit the coast, and there's a pub there called Spirits of the Sand. They have the best brews around and good food, too."

"Do you and my betrothed do everything together?" she asked curiously, no hint of malice in her voice.

"Obviously not. He's not here now, is he?"

"Hmm," she mumbled, but could not help the grin that turned her lips upwards. "Would he come here with us if he was?"

The question took Callum off guard. Weylin would probably avoid Dullahan Row like the plague, but he thought Weylin would be here to help Rania if he could. He wondered what their relationship was like—what it would be like once they were settled into their mating. Weylin had hardly spoken of his betrothal. He had been too haunted by the landing of the wyvern, and the *Gheall Ceann*. There was so much Weylin hadn't told him, but Callum did not blame him.

"Of course," Callum replied after a brief hesitation.

Rania looked at him curiously, as though she didn't believe him.

"You're a good friend, Callum," she said.

Before he could respond, Rania dropped his arm. She took a few long strides ahead of him, pushing through a dingy wooden door barely hanging on at the hinges that lead into the first pub along the road, The Tides of Samhradh.

Callum picked up his pace to catch the door as it swung shut behind her, shocked that Rania had taken it upon herself to burst in. Although not shocked at the same time. The female had a way of keeping him on his toes, and he didn't entirely hate it.

It was the early hours of sunrise for Callum, but for too many that meant it was the late hours of sunset. The pub milled with males and females, elves, dwarves, and humans, drinking and shouting and sharing moments in dark corners far too intimate for the public eye.

Rania made her way to the counter where a woman with long black braided hair took orders. Callum could not hear her over the crowd as he pushed through the bodies towards her, but she turned towards him with two mugs of ale in hand.

"Fancy a drink, Captain Ronan?" she said, shoving the drink in his direction.

He took it and a foreboding settled in his stomach as Rania lead the way to the rowdiest of the tables. He saw the way she scanned the crowd, hoping to meet the hazel of her brother's eyes.

"Good evening," Rania spoke loudly as she settled into an empty wooden chair. Not a single head turned her direction. "I'm here on behalf of the Udar Apparent."

At that, every pair of eyes turned on her and a silence fell over the table. Callum shifted uncomfortably. He had not expected to use their positions of power and didn't know how Weylin would feel about his title being used either.

"Go on," a dwarf snapped, leaning closer to her.

"We are looking for a male that looks, well, like me," she spoke in a voice of honey and silk. She had their attention, that much was evident. "It is of utmost importance that we find him sooner rather than later. Any information will be rewarded, of course."

They all looked at one another, empty expressions on their faces. Rania kept her calm as she waited.

"Haven't seen him," a man grunted before continuing his conversation with the selkie to his left.

Everyone else around their table turned away then, too, carrying on as if Rania had said nothing at all.

She looked at Callum with determination in her gaze as she took a swig of beer and stood.

"Well, that went well," Callum mumbled in her ear as she pressed closer to him, eyeing the room for her next target.

"I didn't expect to find answers from the first person we talked to. Did you?"

"Of course not."

"Then I think we're off to a fine start," she replied, pushing ahead of him towards a table of females giggling over a candle.

Callum watched as Rania spoke to nearly every soul in the pub. She worked them as though she was one of them.

They finished their drinks and ordered another round. She leaned into him when they walked, careful not to rub against the wrong passerby. When they'd exhausted every option in the Tides of Samhradh, they left the pub and wandered down the road to the next one.

They repeated this game as the streets dwindled down, and the first hints of sunrise peeked over the Samhradh mountains.

"What are we to do, Callum?" She looked at him as they exited their fourth establishment.

It was the first time Callum saw defeat and fear enter her expression. She had done a fine job keeping it at bay for as long as she had. Her breath smelled of ale, and her hair had grown messier, and the circles under her eyes darker. He imagined he reflected her tired, disheveled look.

"We keep trying," he replied, gently. "We will find him."

"Promise?" Rania whispered and gripped his arm tighter in hers.

"Promise."

She leaned her head against his arm as they walked, her steps growing slower. Callum silently cursed Oisin for making his sister worry this way. He hoped he knew how lucky he was to have her looking out for him. Callum had never had a sibling to do so for him, and his parents were eager to send him off to Omra as soon as he started showing interest in being a laoch for the Udar.

Callum wanted better words to comfort the female who had become his friend, but he was at a loss. All they could do was keep trying and hope that word of the Lord Apparent of Briongloid's disappearance didn't reach the Udar.

Callum jumped as he felt Rania pulled away from him, and her arm disappeared from his grasp. He whirled around, hand on the hilt of his blade to see her facing a bearded male with his hand grabbing her where he had turned her around. The male wore a stained top, and his clothes were entirely too big. He reeked of city life and walked with a limp.

"I would advise you to get your hands off of her right this moment," Callum snarled.

The male's hand dropped to his side, and he took a step back, putting his hands up in the universal sign of surrender. Rania looked back at him with worry in her eyes, but there was hope, too. Callum's hand remained on his blade, ready to draw it the moment the male dared to touch her again.

"My apologies, milady," the male spoke in a low, raspy voice. "It is only that I heard you were looking for a male who looked like you, and I have seen one of that very description just a few drinks ago."

"And?" Rania asked, taking a step closer to the male, wanting to keep the conversation as private as possible.

"He lost a bet," he said. "Well, a few of them, rather, when rolling the dice. He thought he could win it back, but when he could not, Hugh escorted him from the tavern with his cronies. The man owns the Gnashing Wolf, another pub in Dullahan Row. I would wager that he took your friend there to work off his debts. It wouldn't be the first time it happened, and it certainly won't be the last. Hugh is devious like that."

"Sounds like we should go to the Gnashing Wolf, then," Rania spoke without a falter in her confidence. Callum wondered how much debt they would have to pay off on behalf of her brother. "Thank you for the information, and for finding us."

Rania pulled out a pale blue velvet pouch and withdrew a few coins of airgead to drop in the male's outstretched hand.

"Gods be with you," the male murmured, before scurrying back to wherever he had come from.

"Do you believe him?" Callum whispered to Rania as she tucked her coin bag away.

"It's the best lead we've gotten so far. Do you know where the Gnashing Wolf is?" she asked, looking up at him with anxious eyes that searched his for any sort of reaction.

"Unfortunately."

28
WEYLIN

The sound of metal clashing against metal filled Weylin's ears as he drew *Uamhan* against the nearest sylph. It felt wrong, attacking them like this, but he had promised Corren his aid, and this was the aid he had requested.

The sylph male curled his lip in a sneer as he pressed against Weylin. "Never did I imagine I would cross blades with the Young Wolf himself," he said in a gravelly voice. Weylin pulled his blade away and dodged to the right, away from the blade he knew would swing his way. "Let's see if everything they say about you is true—"

The male's last words were lost to the wind as Weylin's blade drove through his heart.

He withdrew the bloodied blade and held it at the ready as he scanned the room, taking in the rest of the scene. Corren stood next to the corpse of the first sylph that had ended the undine and spilled the first blood. The seven laochs combined with the five undines had no problem felling the final two sylphs.

The room was bathed in blood and reeked of death.

Weylin wiped his blade on the tablecloth and sheathed it once again.

Corren looked up at him. Weylin closed the distance between them. He grabbed the male by the shoulders and slammed him against the nearest wall.

"What the hell was that?" Weylin snarled.

Corren smiled, revealing blood coated teeth where he had been struck in the face at some point. Weylin's skin crawled with unease. The male's face was spattered with blood, and he didn't seem the least bit apologetic about it. No one from Corren's side had fallen, but each sylph was now on its way to one of the otherly realms.

"How was I meant to know how that would go?" Corren asked.

"Because this is the environment you have cultivated," Weylin snapped.

Corren shrugged his shoulders, and Weylin knew the male would not give him anything more than that. Weylin released him and took a step back, wiping the back of his hand across his face.

"Take me to the battlefront," Weylin commanded, more than ready to settle it all and return home. Even though home meant his inevitable mating.

"As you wish." Corren gave a mock bow in Weylin's direction.

Weylin's blood heated further. He gritted his teeth and took a step back, allowing Corren to take the lead. Weylin followed the male through the open door and into the afternoon sunlight. Two of Corren's laochs stayed back to clean up the fallen bodies and gore.

Weylin set his jaw and trailed behind the Lord Apparent of Earrach. He hadn't realized just how far Earrach had fallen from its usual peace and serenity. There were charred buildings and broken market stands. Most of the bailes appeared abandoned in the wake of the conflict. It looked as though this region of Earrach had endured a war of its own. And Weylin knew they needed their allies to be strong in the war that was yet to come.

He stepped over logs and rocks as they made their way through a forest. He heard the hushed, angry whispers of the sylphs on the wind, hardly visible when they moved with such speed. It raised the hairs along his arm, but he didn't fear the spirits of the air. At the same time, he didn't wish to see their slaughter or abuse.

Weylin was not his father, and he would be a different leader to each of the realms. This was his chance to prove that.

The sounds of battle drifted to Weylin's ears. There were shouts and cries of triumph. There were moans of mourning and groans of pain. Metal clashed against metal. Weylin strode ahead of Corren and broke through the line of trees into a clearing that opened to reveal a battlefield between the Children of Leighis and the Children of Muir.

"Cease this madness! *Now!*" Weylin's voice boomed with authority that echoed through the trees and nearly every pair of eyes turned to him.

Out of the corner of his eye, Weylin saw an undine raise her blade against a sylph, who had halted at the command of the Udar Apparent. Without hesitation, Weylin withdrew *Uamhan* from his baldric and sliced off the head of the undine. The sylph whose life he had just saved gaped at him with wide eyes.

Corren loosed a low growl behind him. Weylin ignored it.

"Respect the command of your Udar Apparent, or join your friend here in the otherly realms," Weylin snarled and kicked the head at his feet. All movement stopped and a tangible fear filled the air. "This conflict will not help Earrach or the sylphs and undines across Iomlan in the face of the Inevitable War. I am certain you are all aware of the landing of the wyvern, and what that means for the future of our realms. Samhradh needs Earrach and its legions to stand against the *mallaithe*."

"That war is no war of ours," a sylph on Weylin's right hissed. He slowly turned to face her. "That male promised his hand to our Meara. He swore an oath that would at last grant the sylphs a level of respect among the population of Iomlan, and he went back on his word. That's an unforgivable crime to all sylphs."

"And it is an unforgivable crime in my eyes as well." Weylin took a step towards her. "But matters of the heart cannot be broken down into law. Corren Kyne will grant a seat on his inner council to a sylph when it comes time for him to take his place as Lord of Earrach. You will have a say in matters of this realm, moving forward, as will the undines when Corren mates Vartry. You have the word of the Udar Apparent, and that I can guarantee you will not be broken."

The sylph pressed her lips in a thin line. He saw the way she was processing the information.

"As far as the Inevitable War, it is your war. It is a war of every living soul in Talam, and to ignore that fact is to stand with the *mallaithe*. We must protect the realms from the doom foretold, and should you not, you will be treated as one of the enemy. Let me make that clear."

Weylin paused to turn about the clearing, letting the meaning of his words settle in. He held the attention of every soul who dared to hold his, while others looked away.

"Understood," the sylph said at last, when Weylin's attention fell upon her again.

"The conflict here is done. And if I hear of one more sylph raising their weapon against an undine, or the other way around, I will send my own legions here to settle the matter. The sylphs will gain their seat of power, and Corren will mate his chosen partner. There is nothing further to discuss."

"What of the boundary disputes?" an undine snapped, clearly not satisfied with the compromise he proposed. "This wasn't all over some mating shit."

Weylin swore internally at the fact that Corren had mentioned nothing of boundaries. Then again, he'd been a fool to think this was all merely over Meara and Corren.

"I will redraw the boundaries for the sylphs and the undines myself. Lord Corren will bring them to you before the next full moon in Sneachta. Any concerns you have once you see them, you can send to Castle Eagla. Now, is there anything else, or can you all keep your lifeblood in your veins?"

Silence answered his rhetorical question.

"That's what I thought," Weylin said and turned on his heel to leave. "And thank you for your service to Iomlan."

Weylin heard the disgruntled murmurs, but also the sighs of relief that the conflict had reached some sort of end. He was certain smaller brawls would continue to break out until the boundaries were made clear and the forces could separate themselves into their own territories. But if Corren could focus his efforts toward the Inevitable War, that was enough for Weylin.

Corren took quick steps to catch up to Weylin and matched his pace once they were far enough from the battlefront to speak.

"I was prepared to berate you for the words you spoke on my behalf," Corren started, and Weylin was already annoyed. "But perhaps I should thank you for showing the gall I once heard the Young Wolf possessed. Whispers on the wind say you've gone soft, and lack the vigor needed to fill your father's shoes."

Weylin's muscles tensed as he acknowledged the clear instigation in Corren's voice. He listened carefully and realized the laochs had stayed behind to attend to ensuring the end of the battle. They were alone now in the woods outside the small city.

"I would caution your tongue, Corren Kyne," Weylin spoke in a low voice. "I need you as an ally, but I will not tolerate bloodshed simply because you desire to see blood spilt. You will see how quickly my patience wears thin."

"The realms know," Corren continued as though Weylin had said nothing at all. "They know of your journey beside the *Gheall Ceann*. Some say you even went so far as to bed her."

Rage tore through Weylin. He whirled on Corren, pressing his blade to the male's throat in a fluid movement before he could blink.

"How are we meant to trust your allegiance—your loyalties—when you prance down the coastline playing mate to the one set to ruin the realms?"

Weylin felt that familiar rush in his veins. That unreachable power that ached with the need to erupt. His blood was ablaze with the embers of a flame just out of reach. He pressed his blade harder against the male's throat, wondering at his absolute idiocy.

"You don't know a damn thing about me or what I spend my sunrises doing," Weylin said, cooling the flames that burned hot. He breathed out the anger that threatened to break the poised appearance he had carefully crafted. "I would hate to lose an ally in Earrach, but I will slit your throat if you continue to throw lies in my face and claim you know the truth."

The male only grinned as he drew his knee up between Weylin's legs and his breath left his lungs as he stumbled back a step. He blinked through the pain, refusing to let Corren out of his sight. He was careful to keep his sword in front of him, but Corren had already drawn his own blade and advanced on him.

"What in the Hel is wrong with you?" Weylin seethed. "You will not walk out of this alive."

Weylin said it as a warning to both Corren and himself. He could have been reckless. He could have killed Corren for all the insults he had thrown his way, but Weylin needed to rein in his temper. There were too many loose threads already tangled about him as of late. The last thing he needed was the blood of one of the Lord Apparent's of the realms on his hands. It wouldn't help their predicament in any way. He needed to get the situation under control.

"I'd love to see you try," Corren taunted.

He swung his blade at Weylin's left flank, which he dodged, but not as quickly as he should have. He was a mere moment away from a nasty gash along his abdomen.

Panic coursed through Weylin's veins. Surely this was a trap. Corren would be more foolish than Weylin thought to dig his blade into the Udar Apparent. They needed allies right now, not enemies. Unless Earrach had decided to work in favor of the *mallaithe*, Weylin could see no reason for any of this. He didn't know how they would have ever gone about getting in contact with her.

None of it made any sense, no matter how Weylin looked at it. Corren Kyne was an unpredictable male—the most dangerous thing to have in play during the ninth generation.

Weylin adjusted his stance to the right and watched Corren's eyebrows furrow before dashing left and thrusting his sword towards Corren. He was not shocked when the male moved out of the way. Weylin was holding back, and they both knew it.

"Think logically, Corren," Weylin spoke smoothly despite all the panic he felt. They circled each other in the clearing with no other souls in sight, pacing like caged beasts. "This doesn't end well for either of us—no matter the outcome."

"Would the Udar give so many chances at life? Seems to me the whispers on the wind speak true."

He wondered what his father might do in his situation, and decided Corren Kyne would already be dead.

"You've no idea what you're talking about," Weylin snapped before lashing out again. This time, it was in anger, not planned, and it showed in his sloppy stance. He roared as he reared back in response to Corren's next jab.

Weylin swung *Uamhan* and was met by the familiar clang of metal on metal.

"Is this all you've got? I was expecting to be out of breath by now," Corren jeered as Weylin drew his blade back.

They continued this game of back and forth. Jab. Dodge. Lunge. Swing. *Clang*. Thrust. Sidestep. Slash.

The Young Wolf knew how to end this. He'd had more opportunities than he could count on both hands to take the male's lifeblood. What he couldn't figure out was how to avoid further dividing the realms in doing so.

"You're predictable, Weylin Myrkor. You're weak, and it will shock no one, but me least of all, when your reign ends before it starts. There's more than one beast clawing at your door. Faolan, no one would touch. You—you showed your weakness the moment you let the wyvern land, and even further when you let it escape—when you let *her* escape."

Weylin clenched his jaw as rage flared through him once again. He charged forward and easily predicted the dodge from Corren, who he now realized favored his left side. Weylin counteracted the dodge with a swing of his blade that left Corren unarmed. He pressed the tip of *Uamhan* against the male's heart, applying enough pressure to pierce through the cloth and at last make real the threat of his end.

"One. More. Word," Weylin seethed as his chest heaved with pants. More from stress than exhaustion.

Corren's attention fixed on the blade at his chest. His gaze traveled to the hilt and dragged upwards until it locked onto Weylin's. It wasn't fear there, not even anger or taunting, but approval. As though this is what he had wanted all along. Weylin was more perplexed than ever as he tightened his grip on his blade and continued to hold the pressure.

They remained there, silence strung between them. Corren finally found the sense to keep his mouth shut, which is all Weylin had wanted. Weylin kicked Corren's blade behind him, so Corren could not get to it easily. Then he stepped back and let his arm that held his sword fall to his side.

"Would you have killed me?" Corren asked the moment his life's thread was no longer hanging at the tip of Weylin's blade.

"I told you. One more word from your foul lips and I would have."

"I know," Corren replied with the nod of his head. "You have my word, then. Earrach will serve you in whatever war may come. We are prepared to stand behind the Young Wolf who has proven himself to me."

"I do not need to prove myself to *any*one," Weylin snarled, leaning in closer to Corren again.

He couldn't help but feel tricked. He got the result he wanted, but he didn't feel victorious.

"I know," Corren repeated, the slimy grin still plastered on his face.

Weylin watched the male reach into the back of his waistband and withdraw a small blade, unsure what he planned to do. He shifted his own sword slightly, a reminder of what he could wield, but he didn't think Corren Kyne planned violence, not this time.

Corren drew his blade across his palm, and red liquid flowed out of the dark line.

"On my honor, Earrach will draw her blade at the sound of your call if you swear to protect us from the wrath of the *mallaithe*," Corren spoke the words aloud, offering the oath before turning the dagger handle towards Weylin.

Weylin took the offering and drew the small blade across his own palm, the cut stinging with pain as blood beaded along the wound. Weylin had never been blood sworn before. It was a tradition of old, that was rarely practiced in Samhradh, and he had to wonder if it was common practice in Earrach or if it was a special occasion.

He didn't think on it long before they shook hands and their blood mixed.

Allies. From now until we pass on.

29

AISLA

I t didn't take long for Aisla to leave the library of the Silenced, as she had brought nothing with her and left with more than she thought she could bare.

She wore the clothes that Eilis had given her the first sunset she arrived, but she couldn't bring herself to say goodbye to her new friend.

Aisla could already see how useful her new esos knowledge would be. Her bond with Muinin was stronger than ever. He was both her greatest ally and her greatest protector. If Aisla had no one else, she would always have Muinin.

The cool night air raised a chill along Aisla's arms as she entered the outside world once again. Sure enough, Muinin was waiting with a large emerald wing outstretched, and Aisla cringed at the idea of having to ride again with no leathers, but she saw little choice and they had little time. She climbed his wing and seated herself between his shoulder blades.

Are you hurt? Muinin questioned as he took off into the wispy clouds.

No. There's so much I need to tell you.

Well, it's a good thing we have time, then. It's just you and me up here.

My father is still alive, Aisla blurted down the bond they had found and Muinin dropped nearly five swords' lengths in shock before gathering his composure. Aisla's stomach flew into her throat. *I should have expected that.*

Once her stomach settled, Aisla felt as though a great weight had been lifted from her shoulders. She had felt such guilt knowing and not telling the wyvern that had once been bonded to her father. But she needed to be with Muinin when she told him. She needed to touch him and be ready to explain it all to him because it was no minor revelation.

Not for either of them.

That's not possible, Muinin hissed, and there was fresh grief there. A wyvern would never truly stop grieving for its bonded rider, and she felt horrible for reopening that wound. *I would know.*

My grandmother . . . Cliona. She tore the bond from my father's mind. She lied when she said he was sick and died of his illness. She had tortured him until he fled here. Part of that torture was taking you from him, so you would have never known a difference. It's as though you had never bonded. I'm so sorry.

I didn't know an elf could do such a thing, Muinin snarled, and Aisla could feel the heat of his anger radiating from his body.

Neither did I. We can't trust the Mathair, Muinin. And another thing . . . she wants me dead, or handed over to the Udar, I suppose, which is essentially dead. Maybe worse than dead.

A growl ripped from Muinin's throat and rumbled through Aisla's core, that was already trembling with adrenaline and cold. She opened her mind to the wyvern and felt him rush to meet her down the bond. She showed him everything that had been revealed to her in the library of the Silenced. Everything her father had told her.

It ended with the contents of the letter.

Muinin was silent for a long moment as they neared the outskirts of Caillte.

That bitch is dead. Muinin spoke at last as he began his descent towards the green grass. *She's toying with the wrong wyvern, and she will soon find that out. Give her Hel. If you can't, all you need to do is ask, and I will. Gladly.*

Aisla knew he meant it.

She sucked in a shaky breath, closing that bond again. She felt tired after leaving it open and vulnerable, even for such a brief time. Aisla worked to calm her racing heart. Muinin now knew why she needed to return. She needed to find Ruairi and get him and the ring far away from Cliona. They would have to flee together, but she wasn't certain where.

There was always the library—she knew she would be welcomed back with open arms—but she couldn't hide there forever. And she knew it would be harder to leave a second time than it was the first.

Knowing what she knew now, she couldn't leave Ruairi alone any longer than she already had. She knew he was in imminent danger, if Cliona hadn't already gotten her claws on him.

Muinin agreed to her plan as long as he could linger nearby, and she knew he would respond to her call if, and when, things got out of hand. Now, she wouldn't have to speak it. She wouldn't need to shout or whisper, she could simply think it, and he would be there.

The ground met Muinin's feet with a harsh thud, and Aisla slid down his side.

Thank you. I'll see you soon. She leaned her head against Muinin's long snout.

You better.

Aisla smiled up at him and nodded when words escaped her.

She turned on her heel with a renewed sense of purpose and a confidence she willed into her fearful heart. She clutched the small dagger that her father had given to her before she left. It was not *Oidhe*, but it would do. She tilted her chin higher and reminded herself to walk, not as the Mathair would.

But as a laoch would.

As a female scorned and a female betrayed.

A female with nothing left to lose, and everything left to fight for.

Tall and proud and unafraid.

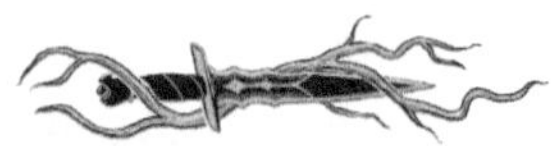

Muinin dropped Aisla off in the same place he had last time, near the outskirts of her cluster of bailes. The memory raised bumps along Aisla's spine, but she brushed the thought away and forced her feet forward.

She pulled her cloak over her head and slipped around the back of Ruairi's baile. Her hand met the cold metal of the doorknob, and she gently turned it, pushing into his baile. She held her breath.

Her heart sunk when she saw his empty bed.

It sunk deeper when she noticed his things strewn about. Her Ruairi would never leave his baile in such a mess. Order to him was nearly as important as his daily meals. It always had been.

His things had been searched.

She closed the door behind her and stepped forward into the disarray, cautiously. Someone had torn through his drawers that were left open and their contents tossed about carelessly. His notes. His pictures. His belongings.

A loose portrait caught Aisla's eye, and she knelt to retrieve it from the floor. She picked it up, and a memory rushed to her of Eire painting in the meadow near the wyvern caves. There was Ruairi with his brilliant red hair that Eire had somehow captured so wonderfully with her colored chalk. He was laughing—his head tilted back in a full belly laugh that Aisla had always loved. She could hear it through the drawing, and a tear slid down her cheek.

Then there she was. Aisla with her long, light brown hair that was braided over her right shoulder and tousled by the wind. She was holding a small pink flower, showing it to Ruairi with a smile that lit up her face. She remembered that sunrise like it had just happened. Ruairi had given her that plant after a sailing trip to the south. And now it sat pressed between the pages of the journal on her bedside table.

Aisla's jaw clenched, and she dropped the drawing. She watched as it floated down, down, down, under Ruairi's bed.

She closed her eyes, and when she opened them, she saw red.

Her ears rang and her palms itched with her flames that were just barely out of reach.

She made her way to her baile, hiding in the dark of the shadows that the night provided. Aisla was shocked to find her room spotless. Cleaner than she ever kept it. Whoever had attacked her had come back to clean up their mess, to hide the evidence of their assault she assumed. She wondered if Cliona had orchestrated the attack.

Aisla retrieved *Oidhe*, tucking it into a strap inside of her boot. There was immense relief when the familiar cool metal touched her skin.

Cliona was family, yes, but so was Ruairi.

No one was outside to see Aisla Iarkis sneak around the back of Castle Farraige, trying to find her way in secretly. If Ruairi wasn't in his baile, her fear was he had found himself in another prison cell. It was too late for him to be training or out for dinner.

Aisla startled when she was met by two laochs guarding the castle's rear.

The sight immediately struck her. Farraige had never kept a castle guard. There was no need to, when the only people on the island were citizens of Eilean. They had not had visitors from the outside since their realm was banished all those generations ago. They would only need a guard if Eilean's own people were at war with each other. If the kingdom was at risk from within, or if it had something to hide—something to protect.

Aisla wondered which the case was. Or if it could be all of them.

Her plan was already unravelling before her very eyes. And the only thing she could do was recover her composure. If she was confronted, they would take her to Cliona regardless of what she said, that much she was certain of. So, she would have to take control back.

Aisla's brain worked to come up with a new approach. Her hands trembled at her sides.

A guard stepped forward, and Aisla did not recognize him. He was a dwarf with auburn hair.

Aisla pulled her cloak back, revealing herself with her head tilted up as she glared down her nose at the male. She watched as shock crossed his features followed by a smirk that pulled up the corner of his lips.

"So, the shameful *Gheall Ceann* returns," he sneered. "Sneaking in through the back, furthermore."

Aisla did not flinch away from the taunt. His voice was familiar. It was a voice that had entered her baile those short sunrises ago. She didn't allow the recognition to show. Not while the bruises of their attack still marred her body.

"I need to see my grandmother," Aisla declared.

"And the front gate didn't suit you?" he jeered, but did not wait for a response. "I believe she would be delighted to see you." The male's tone made Aisla's insides turn. "It's a bit late for a visit, but I think she would make an exception for you."

The dwarf turned and nodded to the woman that stood by and watched the exchange.

"Alert the Mathair."

The woman nodded. After she had disappeared into the castle, the dwarf turned back to face Aisla.

"Some nerve you've got showing up here," he growled. "We were all convinced you'd run for the hills and left your boyfriend behind. It would've been the smart thing to do."

"I've never been known for my wit, though, have I?" Aisla grinned and titled her head, refusing to let any of his jabs get beneath her skin.

Her heart raced and her palms sweat, but she forced steady breaths and a calm face to the surface.

"That's for damned sure. Declaring a war on behalf of your entire realm when we were already knee deep in a plague. Just answer me this, was it worth it?"

"I owe you no answers."

Aisla knew what she would say, though. The answer was yes. She would do it again and again if it meant Ruairi would live. She didn't regret her call to her wyvern, no matter the looming consequences.

And if that made her a fool, so be it. If it made her a villain, she would own it. If it made her an outcast, she would earn back her place.

"I figured as much. Never one for the people, that's for certain," he said. The dwarf turned around to lead Aisla around the front to the castle's entrance.

Her castle.

The inside of Castle Farraige felt different and unfamiliar. It was eerie and barren. Aisla was no longer afraid of the reminder of her parents' death. No, now she feared the evil lurking within the walls of the castle that remained very much alive.

The dwarf led Aisla through the corridors of her family home that suddenly seemed to come alive with a threatening aura. Aisla told herself she could be braver than her father had been—that she would be. She fought the urge to reach for the comforting touch of her necklace.

Before she knew it, she was facing the door to her grandmother's study. The dwarf pulled it open, and Aisla closed her eyes.

When they opened, she met cold yellow-green eyes that held no ounce of familiarity. There was no comfort to be found there as they stood across from one another—foreign as strangers.

30

RANIA

"The Gnashing Wolf was an establishment once known for wolf fights, that are, of course, outlawed. Our Udar found out and shut it down, claiming it as a disgrace to his family's chosen animal," Callum explained, as Rania allowed him to lead the way to the infamous tavern. "The tavern has since ended its wolf fighting, but it is still a place for the filth of Samhradh to roam and get into all sorts of trouble."

"It sounds like we're on the right path, then," she said under her breath.

Rania was thankful when Callum had offered to help her. She would've found a way on her own, but it would've taken much longer than having the captain of her betrothed's guard by her side. Plus, she found she rather enjoyed his company.

She was also grateful that Callum had shown no signs of judgment towards her brother for his poor choice in company and entertainment. A part of her knew that he wouldn't treat either of them any differently for it, but to have it confirmed was a great relief.

"I suppose you've never been then?" she asked.

"Only once," Callum replied. "I was sent to retrieve a group of laochs who didn't show for training. I didn't go inside."

"I guess now is your chance, then."

Rania looked up at the wooden sign that hung by a single iron chain. *The Gnashing Wolf* was written in bold maroon lettering, faded by time. There was an illustration of a wolf howling up at the moons in the 'o's of the name.

It was about as rough as she had imagined.

There was a man passed out in the road right outside of the entrance. The place reeked of ale, and the stench of tobacco mingled with mildew.

Charming, Rania thought to herself.

Callum sighed and stepped around the man. Rania followed his lead.

He held open the battered door for her, and she slipped inside, immediately encased by foul smells even worse than they had been outside the building. She headed straight towards the woman behind the counter who was cleaning dishes. Lines of kohl ran down her cheeks, and she wore a dirty apron over a marigold blouse and black pants. Her brown hair was knotted atop her head, with strands falling loose.

"I'm looking for a male who looks just like me, but with hazel eyes," Rania said by way of greeting. She leaned forward across the bar. "I have reason to believe he ended his night here."

"Plenty of pretty boys come in and out of the place. I don't have time to recount them all for you." The woman grunted, turning her back to Rania to face the sink.

"Ahem," Rania coughed loudly, dropping a handful of airgead on the counter.

The clink of the coins caught the barkeep's attention. She

narrowed her eyes at Rania, truly looking at her for the first time. Callum moved to stand next to Rania, feeling the urge to protect her, even though she seemed to be handling herself just fine.

"Is he your mate?"

"No," Rania replied, "my brother."

"Not the one that looks like you. The one hovering over your shoulder," the woman snapped.

Rania felt Callum tense beside her. She ignored the comment. They had done nothing wrong.

"Why do you ask?"

"Just wondering about his status, lady. I know plenty of folks who would pay a pretty price to spend even an hour with the likes of him."

"Have you seen my brother or not?" Rania snapped, sitting up straighter.

"You know, I did see a male with hair the color of yours just a few hours ago. He got into a spat with Tuck over a game of dice," she said, eyeing the coins before her. "Hugh got involved. Apparently, he didn't have the airgead to back his game, so they took him back here to work off his debt in the kitchen."

Rania felt a brief smugness at how well she knew her brother. And then eagerness to rip him to shreds for slipping up during his time in Samhradh. It was not uncommon behavior among the children of the realms' dynasties, but she had hoped he would hide it better, at least for a while longer.

"Of course he did," Rania replied with a sweetness like honey. "Would you fetch him for me? From the kitchen or wherever."

"Fetch him yourself," the woman replied, having already gathered the airgead Rania had laid out on the counter as reward for her help.

Callum cleared his throat and leaned forward, none too subtly, adjusting the laoch badge pinned to his chest. Rania elbowed his side.

"Be right back," the woman muttered, and Rania noted the way her jaw clenched as she walked away.

"I had it handled, you know," Rania said. "I didn't need you flashing your rank."

"I know you didn't," he replied with his hands up. "I was just speeding up the process, is all."

"Fine," she said with a dramatic sigh. "I'm sorry to have dragged you all this way here. Where there is Oisin, trouble will follow." She paused a moment and turned again to face him. There was a soft hesitancy in the lines on her face. "Please, don't mention it to the Udar or to Weylin. I'll talk to Oisin, and I promise it won't happen again."

"Of course. It's none of my business, anyway," Callum said.

"Thank you," she said, and her hand reached out to gently take his. She held it for a moment, not knowing what she was thinking. "I mean it."

Callum nodded, and she dropped his hand suddenly. They both turned their attention to the woman who had returned with Oisin and a large, burly man in tow.

Oisin had a nasty bruise lining his left eye, and a scratch ran horizontally across his throat. He had run with the wrong crowd. That much was clear in the ghostly look in his hazel eyes.

"He owes Tuck still," the burly man who she assumed to be Hugh spoke.

Oisin stood behind him, focusing on the floor as if both ashamed and afraid to leave the male's side.

Rania ignored the man and crossed the room to her brother on quick feet. She threw her arms around him, ignoring the stench of his night out. His arms enveloped her, and he slumped with relief into her embrace. She burrowed her face in the crook of his neck, allowing herself to live in that moment with him for just a little longer. Then she pulled back and looked up at her brother, assessing his condition.

"How much does he owe?" She turned back to the man and reached her hand into her pocket without hesitation. "And don't lie to me. He'll verify your answer."

She jerked her chin towards her brother, who stood frozen in place.

The man listed his price. Rania looked at Oisin to approve. He nodded his head, and Rania let out a huff of disapproval before fishing the airgead from her pocket and turning it over to the man who grinned victoriously.

"Come back anytime," he said with a sly grin.

Rania threw an icy look his way before looping her arm through Oisin's and turning to leave.

"Come on."

She made her way to Callum and used her free arm to snake it through his.

"I'm so sorry about all of this," she said again, under her breath so no one else could hear.

"You don't need to apologize to me, Rania," he whispered, and a chill travelled the length of her spine. "This is what friends are for."

But Rania had never had a friend she could call upon who would go to such great lengths for her. She didn't know if anyone in the realms would save her brother.

She gently squeezed the captain of the Udar Apparent's personal guard's arm in response.

They made their way out of the Gnashing Wolf, led by Rania as she dragged them along with haste. The moment the door rattled shut behind them, Rania dropped both of their arms. She began her berating of Oisin that would last the whole way back to Castle Eagla.

31

AISLA

"Good evening, grandmother," Aisla drawled as nerves tore her apart from the inside.

She fought to keep the feeling from her face, her stance, her tone. She hadn't intended on facing Cliona that evening. She had only intended to find Ruairi—to ensure he was safe. Her half-formed planned crumbled in the blink of an eye. All she knew was she had to hide what she knew, even while rage boiled in her blood at the sight of her grandmother's face.

Calm, she told herself. *Calm*, she pleaded with herself. *Calm*.

"What a surprise," Cliona crooned, and settled into her worn emerald chair behind the desk. Aisla followed, taking the empty one. "And sneaking in the back of your own castle? Not very Mathair-like of you." Cliona finished with a *tsk* of her tongue.

Aisla's mind worked, spinning endlessly. She only hoped Cliona couldn't sense it as she worked to build up walls against her grandmother's esos. Just in case.

"Your laoch can explain the reason for my sneaking to you," Aisla snapped, jerking her chin towards the dwarf with the familiar voice. "I was attacked in my own baile just a few sunrises ago. It didn't appear safe to enter any other way."

"Interesting," Cliona said. Aisla noted the way no hint of surprise crossed her features, confirming her suspicions. "So, you were looking for me, then."

Aisla nodded slowly.

"Funny, I had thought you might have been looking for someone else."

"And who would I be looking for in Castle Farraige?" Aisla tilted her head to the side, holding the gaze of the Mathair. She feigned innocence, knowing she was right to look for Ruairi in the dungeons.

"Let's find out." The words had hardly left Cliona's mouth before a searing pain shot through Aisla, rupturing her flimsy shields. Panic consumed her.

She worked quickly to hide what she needed to. Eilis and Fella. A library under the ground. Her head hitting the floor. Her father's eyes. A piece of parchment fluttering to the ground.

Flashes from her time spent in the library of the Silenced World Tellers sparked across her eyelids. She hoped she was burying them, but Aisla could not tell. She gritted her teeth and slammed her shields up against Cliona's attack.

Nothing was going as she wanted, no *needed*, it too.

Aisla held off Cliona just long enough to draw her blade from her boot and darted across the room to where the Mathair now stood. She moved as though carried by otherly winds, and none of Cliona's laochs had a chance to react. Not until Aisla already had her pressed against a wall with *Oidhe* to her throat.

She panted labored breaths. Cliona's face twisted into a scowl. Aisla heard the laochs unsheathe their blades behind her. She knew if she ended the Mathair here, they were standing by, ready to take her head in one quick movement.

There was no more plan.

Sneaking in hadn't worked. Cliona was taking the information she carried by force. Aisla didn't know what to do next. Her blood was hot, and her anger was all she could see.

You move too quickly, Gheall Ceann, a familiar voice sounded in her head. *Think before you make your next move. The fate of the realms depends on it. What you do next cannot be undone.*

She wanted to snarl at it, but she knew no one else could hear it. She didn't even know how or why the voice continued to visit her. It was so infrequent she couldn't count on it for anything but annoyance.

But it was right. If she killed Cliona before anyone knew what their Mathair truly was, she would make a martyr. She would become the *mallaithe* they feared.

"It seems you've been busy," Cliona spat, finally cutting through the tension brewing in her study.

Fear turned Aisla's rage to ice, cooling her veins. She needed to warn her father. And Eilis. Had she exposed their long-maintained secret? Guilt caused bile to rise to the back of her throat.

"It's not like you to hide secrets from me, Aisling."

Aisla stood up straighter at the sound of her full name on the lips of the Mathair. It was a taunt meant to rile her.

"Secrets?" Aisla asked with a confidence she didn't feel—an art she nearly perfected. "You're one to talk about *secrets.*"

"It wasn't smart to return."

Aisla tightened her grip on the blade against her grandmother's throat. Her palms were slick with sweat.

"And why is that?"

"Your people aren't happy with the way you handled yourself on Iomlan," she said. "The whispers on the wind say they question whether you are the *Gheall Ceann* after all. Some say you are the *mallaithe* the Udar suspects you to be."

Aisla inhaled a long breath and took a step back and lowered her blade. But she kept it poised, ready to strike if any of the laochs moved to attack her. Her muscles remained tense. Cliona reached up to rub her throat.

"And when they come knocking on your door—when they ask your own opinion on the prophecy and your granddaughter—what do you tell them? Do you tell them I'm the monster you created?"

"Aisla." Cliona's features softened and her eyes flickered with hurt. Aisla braced herself for the lies to come. She had to remind herself, Cliona didn't know how much she knew. "You are my granddaughter. What do you think I told them? Have I not stood up for you—*fought for you*—your entire life?"

Wrath stirred in Aisla's chest. It riled the embers of her blood, and she grit her teeth, fighting every urge to sink her blade into the heart of the female that killed Aine Iarkis.

That is what she had been made to believe her whole life. She had spent years believing her grandmother's love and protection was all she had, and it had all been a lie. Aisla took a moment to calm her thundering heart. She fought to pull herself from the emotions that felt like tangled vines threatening to consume her, but she needed a clear mind. And she tried her damndest to find one before she spoke her next words.

"That is what you told my mother, isn't it?"

The words hung between them, suspended by an invisible golden thread that neither of them could yank away. Cliona's face fell, and a darkness consumed her eyes. They were in entirely unfamiliar territory now. It was territory neither of them knew how to navigate.

"And what do you mean by that?"

"You killed her!" Aisla roared and her palms itched the moment before the esos of her flames burst from them.

Blinding pain exploded behind her eyelids. It was happening again, but somehow worse. Aisla fell to her knees and her esos flickered away until her hands were left as cold as ice. She dropped her head into her hands and screamed with agony. She felt the interior of her mind being pulled in different directions. It was tearing along the seams.

Then it stopped. Aisla heaved deep breaths in and out as the room slowly came back into focus. She panted as she leaned forward on her hands and knees, urging herself not to vomit.

This was a glimpse of Cliona's full power as a pryer. The esos she had only sprinkled enough of throughout Aisla's life to dampen her esos. The way she had kept all of her training doomed. This was what her mother had spent her last days fighting. This was what she had endured.

Tears of agony and tears of fury wet her cheeks.

"Why?" Aisla choked out, sitting on her knees and looking up at her grandmother, who no longer looked like her grandmother at all.

"Because, Aisla," Cliona said as she glared down at her through cold, unflinching eyes. She was no longer hiding behind a false kindness—not now that Aisla knew what she had done. "There are things greater than blood in this world, and one day you will understand that. You are too volatile. You always have been. I refuse to risk the nine realms, hoping you will save them. Your very birth spelled their doom, and only your death can stop it."

"Then kill me," Aisla snarled with every ounce of savagery she could muster. She felt like a wild beast as she bared her teeth at her grandmother, and she hoped Cliona knew this was all her doing. She trembled with her rage, but her esos was too far away to find with Cliona still holding it at bay. "Kill me right now, and save your precious realms, if you are so certain."

"Your death is not mine for the taking."

"You'd prefer the Udar did your dirty work? You're a *coward*." Aisla spat at the ground at Cliona's feet. "I know everything you have done. I know the evil that laces your veins as tightly as a vine."

"My darling," Cliona said, and she knelt before Aisla, using a finger to tilt her chin up to look her in the eyes. "You don't know anything. You're as foolish as your mother before you was."

Aisla lashed her hand out and her fingernails raked down Cliona's cheek like talons before she could jump out of the way. The marks flared bright red, bringing Aisla a hint of satisfaction.

Before Aisla could get to her feet, two laochs yanked her up by the shoulders and tied a rope around her wrists. Aisla watched the red blood bead along the lines that would scar her grandmother's cheek.

"*Coward!*" Aisla shouted, wanting all Caillte to hear the word. "You *murdered* her."

Cliona looked to her laochs and jerked her chin towards the door in command. They began to drag her away as Cliona watched with a smugness that made Aisla's skin crawl.

"Stop!" she cried out. "Where's Ruairi? Let me see him before you take me away."

Cliona was silent. Aisla cursed under her breath.

"Please. Let me see him," she whispered in desperation, pleading to whatever soul Cliona had left.

It all felt too familiar. Saving him from the Udar first, and now her own grandmother. He didn't deserve to be involved in any of this. He had never deserved it. It was all a reminder of the cost of caring for her. Her parents, Eire, and Ruairi. What could she touch without destroying and maiming?

Her throat burned with fear.

"Take her to see Ruairi," Cliona said with a chilling grin. "It's what our *Gheall Ceann* wants after all."

A feeling of foreboding sunk into Aisla's chest as she allowed the laochs to drag her out of the room and down the hall. Her body was numb as the tears dried on her skin. She held her breath as they led her down the dark stairwell into the dungeon of her family's home. The home her father and mother had lived in. The home they had fallen in love in. The home they had raised her in.

Aisla's sight quickly adjusted to the black of the dungeons. Her muscles slackened as she gave into her defeat. They shoved her into a cell and locked the door of metal bars.

The metal bars were made of iron, which was known for repressing esos. She would have no access to hers down there, and the thought was a frightening one.

"Damn you all," Aisla sneered.

"Rot in Hel, *mallaithe*," one of them barked at her before they strode back the way they came from, and the door clanged shut behind them.

She heard others rustling in their cells, and she crawled forward towards the edge of the cage she found herself in. She gripped the cold iron bars and peered into the cell across from her, trying to make out figures in the shadows.

"Ruairi," she called out desperately.

"Aisla."

His reply met her ears with a mixture of relief and fear. Ruairi Vilulf's voice called to her from her right and she scrambled across the cell to him. Their cells shared the same wall of iron bars.

He leaned against them and reached out to her. She grasped his hand with shaking fingers then pulled herself forward. They leaned their foreheads together in a gap between the bars.

Her whole body trembled with the consolation of him. His skin felt like home and his warmth was an answered prayer.

"I was afraid you'd be here," she breathed out. "I'm so sorry. You don't deserve this."

"One of these days," he murmured, and she could hear the dryness of his throat in the rasp of his voice. "We will meet, and your first words won't be *I'm sorry*."

He let out a chuckle that was so familiar. Aisla felt the weight of the world slipping from her shoulders.

"Oh, Ruairi," she said with a smile and a laugh escaped her own lips. "I missed you. I should have never left."

A beat of silence passed between them. Ruairi agreed with her sentiment, and she knew that.

"Where did you go?"

"I-I have so much I need to tell you." She lowered her voice, but knew even then there were secrets she could not share while she knew there were others nearby. "I was attacked on the night I returned. I left your baile to sleep in my own bed, and I was attacked. It was so dark, I couldn't see their faces, but they tried to tie me up. I escaped and Muinin took me to the library.'"

Aisla knew Ruairi would know what she meant, since she had mentioned it to him. She waited for his reaction.

"Attacked in your own baile?"

"Yes," she answered curtly, not wanting to relive that night ever again.

"But I went looking for you. It was so clean."

"I know. All I can figure is they didn't want anyone to know what happened since I got away."

"Why didn't you come and get me?"

"There was no time, Ru," she said. "I barely escaped them."

"Did you learn anything at the library?"

"A story for another time," she repeated those words she had given him atop Muinin as they fled Iomlan together. "But . . . you were right."

She felt Ruairi's muscles loosen.

"I didn't want to be," he whispered, but his lack of surprise told her everything that she needed to know. Ruairi had made his own findings in Caillte. And those findings had landed him here.

"The ring?" she asked so quietly she wasn't sure if Ruairi even heard her.

"It's bad."

The heaviness in the air grew, further darkening their reunion. Aisla nodded her head.

"What are we going to do?"

"I've been trying to figure that out since they brought me here."

"How long?" she asked, afraid to hear the answer.

"Three sunrises."

"Gods, it must be horrible. After everything you've gone through—"

"I can't think about it, Ash," he interrupted gently. The pain in his voice was clear, and guilt tied Aisla's insides in knots. "Not now."

"I understand."

She leaned against the cell wall, burdened by the weight of holding herself up.

What is going on in there? Muinin's voice came crashing through her skull like a wave against the shore. *I haven't been able to reach you. I'd started a countdown before I would burn the castle to the ground.*

Muinin! I didn't think I would be able to hear you through the iron.

It was such a relief to still have her bond to her wyvern. It was as though that bond ran stronger than her esos. It was a separate thing entirely.

Iron? Where in the Hel are you?

In the dungeons. But I'm with Ruairi.

That male didn't protect you on Iomlan, and I don't trust him to now, Muinin retorted. *I'm coming to get you.*

No! she exclaimed too quickly. *We're figuring it out. I'll fill you in when I can. I can't afford to start any more wars.*

Muinin snorted with disapproval. *If that is what you wish. But just know I don't agree with the plan.*

I haven't even told you a plan.

That is exactly my point.

Aisla couldn't help but roll her eyes.

I'll be okay. I'll call if I need you.

You better.

Right now, I need you to protect my father and the library. Stay near them—make sure they aren't discovered. I need to find a way to warn him.

Warn him about what?

Aisla filled him in on what happened with Cliona, allowing the bond to open again for him to see. She didn't know if it was a good idea to further her wyvern's hatred for the Mathair, but she didn't want to keep secrets from him.

He deserved better than that.

32

EIRE

It was late when Eire Trygg was awakened by a glow that bathed her infirmary room in warmth. She opened her eyes just as the light chased the ever-present shadows away from her bedside. The shadows retreated to the corners of the room with a hiss of resistance, until they disappeared altogether.

She sat up and leaned towards the light. Eire pulled her knees to her chest, afraid of what had first seemed like a gift. She wondered if her time had come. It was hardly a life she lived anymore, but she wasn't ready to give it up. She didn't want to leave the worldly realms, yet.

"Hello?" she whispered, her blood cooling with fear.

She was tired, so tired. Her body ached, and she had not been herself in many sunrises. There was not a waking moment that her rotting flesh and decaying skin didn't remind her of all that she had lost. Eire's thoughts often wandered to Fiona, who had given up the fight far too early. As much as she yearned to reunite with her in the otherly realms, she wasn't ready.

The light shimmered in a wave that cascaded in ripples, then disappeared. She was left to believe it had all been her imagination playing a cruel trick on her—as it often did. But she remembered the retreat of the shadows and knew it had felt too real.

Eire blinked once, and a female appeared before her.

The breath rushed from her aching lungs in a gasp as the female looked upon her with brilliant blue eyes that glowed with an otherly power. Her long, pin straight black hair fell down her shoulders, not a hair out of place.

Her skin was tan and full of life, but it radiated that warmth Eire felt before the glow disappeared.

"Hello, Eire Trygg," the female whispered. Eire couldn't explain it, but she knew the goddess Leighis stood before her. Goddess of healing, of harvest, and of nature.

Eire was lost for words as she rubbed her fists against her eyelids, but the goddess only smiled.

"I know you weren't expecting me," Leighis spoke. Her voice drifted through the air like a song of the spirits. Eire felt a part of herself awaken in the presence of the goddess that she thought was long gone. "But I have seen you. I know you are fighting," Leighis paused, "but I am not meant to be here," she whispered, as though sharing a secret with a close friend.

"How?" Eire felt the word leave her lips, but she didn't know how it got out. "How are you here?"

"I am Leighis," she stated simply, but tenderly. "You think I cannot visit a worldly realm when I wish to?"

"Of course you can," Eire replied, slowly nodding her head, trying to piece it all together in her mind that was far too slow. "*Why* are you here?"

"There is too much to explain before my absence raises concern,"

Leighis said. "I have come to make a bargain with you, daughter of mine. You do not go unnoticed by me."

A chill travelled through Eire as her heart surged with a feeling she couldn't place. It was the most she had felt in a very long time.

"A bargain?" Eire breathed.

"Yes. There is little I can do without consequence. The norns still control their threads and Crann Na Beatha, and always will. But I can offer you what is within my realm. I can offer you healing from your poison, but in return, you will lose your esos and you will lose your elven life. You will become a human at first light tomorrow, should you accept my offer." Leighis swept forward with an otherly gracefulness and sat on the edge of Eire's cot. She rested a gentle hand upon Eire's own. "I am sorry, Eire Trygg. I tried to protect you, but there are forces greater than myself playing the game. And every favor comes with a cost."

There was genuine sorrow in the goddess's voice. And even as Eire's heart fell to pieces, she felt she did not deserve it.

"Will I be me again? Will I feel like myself if I agree?"

Leighis seemed to contemplate her answer before replying. Her tone was coated with sympathy. "You will heal. You cannot be as you were before, but you will heal and can live out your human life on Talam until the time comes that you pass on. Your life is greater than you know it is. You are needed in the worldly realms, still. I can say no more."

Eire's mind raced as she tried to weigh the benefits and costs of the bargain, but before she could, an answer left her lips. A soft and desperate plea for a life other than this. "Yes, please."

Leighis nodded her head. She held Eire's hand in hers and leaned forward until her lips were nearly pressed to Eire's ear.

"Your esos will remain until the first sun ray touches the horizon. Use it wisely. Your friends are in danger in the castle. Urge them to seek shelter in Fomhar—a friend awaits you there," the words came in a whispered rush that brought a panic to Eire's chest. "Travel by air.

The sea is not safe for you. My sister will send clouds to cover your wyvern in the sky."

Eire knew she spoke of Realta, the goddess of the skies and celestial bodies. She was about to ask Leighis more as her mind reeled with it all, but the goddess murmured words Eire did not understand, and Eire's breath left her lungs. She squeezed her eyes shut as a sharp pain flooded her senses, and then she was drowning in it.

She was unable to speak—unable to breathe. She thought she was dying.

It all halted with a rush of air. The breath rushed back into her lungs. Her eyes flew open. The room had again fallen into darkness. There was not a trace of the goddess left behind.

Eire would have thought it was all a cruel dream to taunt her, but she looked down and saw her light brown skin was smooth once more. She gasped and felt along her body, and it was smooth all over. She lifted her shirt and touched the place where her ribs had once been exposed to the open air, and the wound was closed.

Eire was herself again.

She ran a finger over her ear and felt the peaked tip that remained.

Until sunrise, she reminded herself.

A joyful sob wracked her body as she covered her mouth with her hand. Eire gave herself nine breaths and no more to revel in the miracle she had been granted. She rejoiced in the fact that her gods were still there—still listening.

She ran her fingers over her new skin. Savored the way it felt like silk against her touch. Eire touched her face and her neck. It was all healed.

Then she stood up and gathered her things. She held her breath as she slipped out of her room and padded through the halls of the infirmary. She was thankful the menders had reduced their shifts as the lofa had mysteriously stopped spreading.

Leighis had called it a poison, and Eire wondered at her choice of words.

Your friends are in danger in the castle. Urge them to seek shelter in Fomhar.

The words replayed in Eire's mind as she scurried along the edges of the hall, careful to move as silently as she could. She knew Leighis had meant Ruairi and Aisla. She had not heard anything about Aisla since she had visited her room and left in flames. But deep down, she knew Aisla was still her friend. They shared a bond no fire could burn away.

Eire paused outside of the mender supply room.

She glanced over her shoulder and ducked inside. Her chest was heavy as she carefully shifted through vials until she grabbed a handful of doses of Valerian and shoved them deep within her pocket.

She whispered a hushed prayer of gratitude to Leighis, and a prayer of protection as she made her way towards Castle Farraige.

The dark sky began to lighten.

33
RUAIRI

A dark cloud had settled over Ruairi during the sunrises preceding Aisla's arrival to the dungeons beneath Castle Farraige. It was a cloud that came in waves of density. There were moments of complete agony and moments of total numbness. And somewhere between it all, Ruairi Vilulf lived.

And he fought for each passing breath to pull himself from the haze that preyed on his every thought.

But now she was here.

Selfishly, it was a relief that chilled his bones when he recognized the sound of her voice. In the hours since she had slumped against that barred wall between them, since they had held hands with a touch that gave Ruairi his breath again, the relief had faded to fear.

If Aisla was down here with him, he did not know what could be going on up there, but he knew for certain it could not be good.

He leaned his head back against an iron bar and felt the warmth of Aisla's body just beyond it. He listened to her steady breaths as she rested behind him. Ruairi had not slept since he got there—not long enough to consider it rest. He felt the unease that came with a lack of sleep in every muscle of his body.

He forced his eyelids shut and worked to match his breath to hers, in attempt to find the solace of sleep at last. He finally found a steady rhythm that nearly lulled him into the thrall of sleep when a pair or footsteps sounded from the stairwell.

They were light, hurried steps. He heard a feminine panting as they rushed down the stairs. His heart swelled in a panic, and he moved to crouch at the edge of his cell, squinting his eyes to make out the figure in the darkness.

His hands gripped the cold iron bars. He felt his blood freeze with disbelief.

He blinked. Once. Twice. Three times.

But she did not change.

"Eire," he breathed in a voice barely above a whisper. As though he feared speaking her name too loudly would frighten her away and she would disappear.

Her head turned slowly in his direction and a smile lit up her beautiful, unmarred face. She was herself again. No more wounds. No more revealed bones. Not a hint of the lofa touched her.

"How?" he whispered in awe.

He didn't know how it was possible. Ruairi hardly believed his own eyes as he looked upon the female that was like a sister to him. She was whole again. He had long stopped letting himself hope for such an outcome. Ruairi had accepted the fact that Eire would remain a husk until her passing on. Even in his wildest dreams, he hadn't let himself hope for this.

And now that it was real—now that she stood before him, looking as healthy as ever, a great weight lifted from his chest.

"The guards at the top of the stairs are sleeping peacefully thanks to some stolen herbs," she said with a mischievous smirk. "And I may have used the water in their blood to ensure I had no problem feeding it to them."

There was a sort of hesitancy when she spoke of her esos. Ruairi knew Eire well enough to know that there was something she was hiding in the words she spoke. It was beyond the use of her esos to contort blood, which was frowned upon, but in this case, Ruairi took no issue with it.

"That's great," Ruairi said, "but that's not the 'how' that I meant."

Eire looked down at her hands. She turned them over, admiring the skin that was her own. "I will tell you once we're out of here," she whispered. "I've got some prisoners to break free."

Before Ruairi could push further, he heard Aisla stirring in her cell.

"What's going on?" she murmured, the fog of sleep lacing her voice. She stood and walked to the edge of her own cell. "It can't be."

Ruairi watched Eire approach Aisla's cell. He couldn't see her facial expression, but he could only imagine it was one of relief and hesitancy and joy.

Aisla took a step back, and he knew all three of them recalled the last time they were in the same room together. It was the last time Aisla had seen Eire at all. The smell of burning flesh filled Ruairi's nostrils at the thought of it. Aisla's screams as he dragged her from the room. She fought him the whole time.

Aisla had not been the same since, and he knew her guilt over that moment was as much to blame for her solitude as her call for Muinin on Iomlan was.

"I forgive you," Eire spoke first.

A weight on Ruairi's own shoulders lightened with the words he knew Aisla needed to hear.

"I never meant to hurt you." Aisla's voice came out tight and strained.

"I know," Eire replied with a voice equally filled with sorrow. "You never would."

"Are you okay?" Aisla asked, without stepping forward again. She remained in the shadows of her cell.

"I'll explain later," she said. A glint of gold caught Ruairi's eye as it flashed from Eire's pocket. "A bit preoccupied at the moment."

"Fair enough," Aisla whispered back.

Ruairi listened as the sound of metal scraping against metal set his soul ablaze with hope. He would be free again. There was no fight to free him this time. Eire had come in and used something as simple as a key to get him out, and he was suddenly burning from the inside out.

His skin itched with the anticipation of being free of the iron bars. His throat scratched with a scream for her to hurry, but he knew it was all in his head. The panic and the fear that should be relief was a wave that he had to fight to stay on top of.

Aisla's door creaked as it opened, but she did not stop to embrace Eire. He was thankful for it. Eire moved to his door and shoved the key into the lock.

"I always thought I'd be the one next to Aisla in a cell, not you," she teased, and Ruairi's shoulders eased with the comfort of her voice. "Didn't know you had it in you, Vilulf."

"Oh, just wait until you hear the full story," he teased back even as his voice came out dry.

"I look forward to it."

It took everything in him not to burst from the cage he had been thrown into the moment the lock turned. Instead, Ruairi gritted his teeth and balled his fists, and consciously slowed his heart with each step forward—each step toward freedom.

"What's our plan?" Ruairi asked, turning to Aisla, who always had the plan.

Aisla chewed her lower lip and met his gaze with a wildness in her yellow-green eyes that seemed almost unfamiliar.

"You're not going to like it," Eire interrupted, and they both turned to look at her.

Eire was right. Ruairi hated the plan.

"So, you're telling me you want us to go *back* to Iomlan? Where everything went to Hel in a handbasket in the first place?" he whispered as they snuck out through one of the tunnels Aisla led them through in Castle Farraige.

"Leighis told me we had to. It's the only safe route for us," Eire said back, holding firm to her unwavering confidence in the gods.

"Leighis? So, you speak to gods now?" Ruairi asked. He felt Aisla's glare boring through him.

She hadn't been there all those sunrises, though. Eire and Ruairi had spent many hours together quipping back and forth, and he would treat her no differently now.

"*She came to me,*" Eire hissed, keeping her voice low. "I told you I would answer all of your questions once we are out of here."

"You can't expect me to follow you back to Iomlan based on such little information."

Aisla stopped at a wooden door and slowly opened it. She peered around it, and when she decided the coast was clear, she led them through it. The cool air of the spring night kissed his skin.

"So, you don't trust me?" Eire threw a glance over her shoulder, her bright blue eyes narrowed in challenge.

The sight of those eyes in the light of the moon caused Ruairi's heart to stutter with surprise and awe once again. They were not white, not faded and muddled, but the clear blue of Eire that he had known for as long as he could remember.

"I think that's quite enough from both of you," Aisla spoke up.

Ruairi dragged his eyes to hers, seeing the anxiety in every line of her face. Her eyebrows scrunched together, and her left cheek was puckered where she was nervously chewing on it.

Ruairi's pulse raced with the anticipation of fleeing the castle, but he also found a calm in the reunion of their friendship—of all three of them together again. They had been apart for far too long.

It felt right in so many ways, but terrifying in so many more. How long would it be before they were separated again? And with death following them each like a shadow, how long could they keep it at bay?

Silence fell over them as they looked from one to the other. They knew they couldn't stand around for long.

"I do agree with Ruairi," Aisla said. She turned to lead them into the darkness of the woods to conceal them from anyone who could be watching. "We need to discuss before we jump on a ship back there."

The last words left her lips in a barely audible whisper. Ruairi heard the fear in her voice and knew it all too well.

"Well, good thing we won't be sailing," Eire said in a mock cheery tone. Aisla's head snapped towards her, and Ruairi's stomach dropped as he knew what she was going to suggest next. "We are going to fly."

"Absolutely not," he and Aisla stated in unison.

Eire set her jaw in defiance. "To the path," she snapped before leading them to the path they had walked along so many times before.

It was the same one where Ruairi said goodbye to Aisla all those sunrises ago, when he thought he might make his final journey, but had prayed it would not be the last time he held her. He had not prayed since.

His feet carried him to the spot that was just off the path. It was a small clearing by an overgrown willow tree that made for the perfect spot for childhood gossip, drama, and venting. And now it made for the perfect spot for young adults fleeing the only home they had ever known.

They stood there, and the space that had once felt endless and full of hope suddenly felt cramped and cold. They looked at one another, no one knowing where to start. It was a moment of sorrow and relief and fear.

"Before I say anything," Eire started, and Ruairi could have guessed it would be her. She locked her gaze onto Ruairi as she spoke, as though what she was going to say next was meant specifically for his ears. "You have to promise you'll trust me."

"I promise," they both said, exchanging a glance of worry.

"Leighis visited me. She was there in my infirmary room. She was as beautiful as the world tellers say she is. And before you say it," she shot a pointed look at Ruairi, and he held his hands up in defense. He hadn't even uttered a sound. "It was really her there. Not a dream or an apparition. I felt her skin on my skin, and I swear on my life it was real."

"Okay, she was real. You had a goddess in your infirmary room," Aisla interrupted impatiently. "What did she say?"

"A lot, but in few words." Eire paused. She took a deep breath, turning her eyes to the ground beneath their feet. Ruairi noticed the way her shoulders slumped forward with the weight of what she was about to tell them. "She visited me, and she told me you two were in danger. And she was right about that. She healed me, and told me to go to you. She said *urge them to seek shelter in Fomhar. A friend awaits you there.*"

"Fomhar?" Ruairi exclaimed at the same time Aisla said, "Healed you? Just like that?"

Eire looked back and forth between them. A secret creased her brow and turned her lips into a frown.

"Yes, Fomhar," she said slowly, choosing to answer Ruairi first. "She told me we need to fly. Leighis said Realta would create cloud cover for us to fly by."

"Cloud cover or not, there is the matter of landing," Aisla snapped. "We won't go unnoticed."

"She's a goddess, Aisla. I think she'll be able to cover our landing."

"There's a damn blockade, Eire!"

"All I know is a goddess advised that we fly to Fomhar. I don't know what more you could want. Just look at my face! It's a miracle, and even *you* can't deny that, Ru."

Ruairi clenched his jaw and tilted his head to look up at the trees. He remained silent, slowly piecing it all together. Eire was right. It was a miracle, and the proof couldn't be any more solid.

"Fine," Aisla said, looking to Eire once again. "We will go to Fomhar."

"Tonight?" Eire pushed.

"Tonight," Aisla agreed, "because we've got nowhere else to go."

Eire nodded, and Ruairi's stomach sank.

"It all feels so quick," he said, wishing Aisla had put her foot down.

"If you come up with a better plan," Aisla said, "I am all ears."

Ruairi had nothing more to say to that. He knew she hadn't meant it harshly, but tensions were high and there was no right answer.

"Eire," Aisla spoke up again, "what did your healing cost you?"

Eire shuffled her worn brown boots in the dirt.

"It cost me my esos," she breathed out. "My esos and my pointed ears. Come sunrise, I will turn human. My lifespan will shrink to that of one as well."

Ruairi's breath caught in his throat. He heard a gasp escape from Aisla.

Neither of them knew how to comfort her in the moments that followed her revelation.

Aisla stepped forward and threw her arms around her friend, and Ruairi followed. They held on to Eire as they heard her faint sniffles she tried to suppress. It was fine to be born a human—they lived as freely as elves did—but to be born elven and become human? To know what it was to wield your esos and lose that in mere hours? And to think you had hundreds of years to live only to learn you'll have less than a century on Talam? That was unthinkable.

And to hear that was the case for one of the souls you loved most—that was unbearable.

Anger burned Ruairi's cheeks. If the gods had so much power, he didn't understand why this favor cost Eire so much. It was cruel.

"We'll find a way to undo it," Aisla whispered.

"Don't make promises you can't keep," Eire replied. Ruairi's chest constricted at the words. "But, Aisla, do you know what this means?"

There was a hint of hope in Eire's voice, despite it all.

"No, I don't."

"It means there are gods taking sides in this war. And Leighis is on yours."

34

RANIA

Rania woke up to the news that Weylin had begun his journey home. That meant there were just two sunrises until her mating ceremony.

Her stomach churned at the thought. She felt guilty for the emotion. She should feel victorious, or maybe excited, but there was something new now, and something holding her back. Rania was never one to choose emotions over logic—in fact, she prided herself in her capability to prioritize the latter—and she could not become that sort of female now.

Rania smoothed her skirts and choked the feeling down. She opened the door to her bedchamber with her practiced smile once again upon her lips.

"Good morning, Mother," Rania said cheerily when she looked upon her mother's beaming face, and her stomach twisted again. "How did you find your travels?"

Rania stepped back as she held the door open to allow her mother to make her way into the rather enormous and extravagant room.

Her mother's single eye went wide as she took it all in, gawking in awe. It had taken some time for Rania to get used to, the eye socket that was empty after her beautiful eye had been carried away by what Rania had to assume was one of Eabha's two doves. She still didn't know what it meant, but found herself losing hours of sleep if she dwelled too long on it.

So, she tried not to waste her time speculating.

"It was fine, dear," her mother said, turning in a slow circle, her mind not truly on the question or her answer. "This place is magnificent, Nia."

"Well, our castle is bigger," Rania said playfully, although it was true. She knew what her mother meant. Castle Tromlui was much more casual, beautiful but not magnificent or elegant like Castle Eagla was.

"That is true." Brigid finished her rotation and stopped to look at Rania. "You look happy."

Rania's heart stuttered at the comment. She had forgotten how good she had become at pretending. When she was younger, her parents could always read her, and they knew when she was hiding something. As she grew older, she got so good at playing the game, no one knew her anymore. They couldn't tell the difference between her lies or her truths.

And sometimes, she wondered what that meant about herself.

She nodded and smiled, pushing the feeling to the back of her mind.

"I am happy," Rania said. And she was, but for all the wrong reasons. It was a happiness that couldn't possibly last. "What is father doing today?"

"The usual politicking, of course. I think he's excited to be reunited with Oisin. I told him we would return from picking up your dress in time for lunch together—just the four of us."

"I would like that very much," Rania answered, a warmth filling her at the thought of her family coming together again. She knew it would not happen often, if ever again, after her mating. "Oisin is thriving in the city, as I am sure you can imagine."

Rania left out the story of the escapade she and Callum had saved him from.

"Indeed," her mother said, knowingly. Oisin hardly cared to hide his delinquency from anyone, let alone their parents. "Actually, I've been looking forward to telling you. The Udar has agreed to let him stay here with you, even after your mating. He'll return when he is needed in Briongloid, but I thought it would be nice for you to have family here. And the Udar says he fit in well with his council, and his input during the coming war is appreciated."

Rania's heart swelled with both relief and joy. She threw her arms around her mother in response. Brigid seemed surprised by it, taking a half-step back. They did not often embrace like this, and Rania found herself wondering why.

"Thank you," she whispered. "I'm so glad he'll be here."

"I figured you would be. Now, let's get into the city. Niamh told me how to get to the seamstress who's been working on your mating gowns."

"Let's be on our way, then," Rania said with a tight smile and a slight shake in her hand that she knew her mother would not notice.

There were no words Rania could think to accurately describe how she felt when she looked into the grand mirror at the seamstress's shop. The dress was everything she didn't know she wanted in a dress.

It was both simple and elegant. Ornate and delicate.

The dress was made of cloud white silk that hugged her body in all the right places and fell loosely like a waterfall around her hips. Icy blue embroidery decorated the corset that hugged her torso in an intricate pattern of lilies. It was simple enough that you wouldn't notice the pattern at first glance, but the longer you looked at it, the more you were drawn into it.

The threading was her favorite color.

There were no sleeves. Instead, threads of tiny light blue beads hung from the place where sleeves would have been. When she wore the dress, they fell down her shoulders and gave a sense of majesty. The neckline plunged low, but not too low. She would wear a veil atop her head until it was replaced by the crown the Udar was having made for her. Her only request was that the gems be blue opal.

Rania's throat tightened. She should have felt excited to be standing in the dress that was made just for her, preparing to marry the male she had hoped would come knocking on her door for as long as she could remember, but she only felt trapped.

Suddenly, the dress felt too tight. Too long and too stiff. She wanted to rip it from her body. Her fingers twitched with the urge to claw it free.

Rania inhaled a deep breath and looked in the mirror. She closed her eyes and crooked her neck to the left and to the right, and straightened out the skirts of the dress. She exhaled a long breath and blinked her eyes slowly open.

And when they opened, she was beaming.

She wanted this. She did. She told herself she did.

Rania turned to face her mother, who was wiping tears from the corner of her eye.

"I think it's perfect," she whispered around the tears of a mother watching her daughter's dreams unfold. "You look regal."

"I feel it, too."

Her mother reached out and gave her hand a reassuring squeeze.

"I'm so proud of you, Nia," she said.

"Thank you, Mother. I wouldn't be here without you."

"Weylin is one lucky male."

Rania smiled and patted her mother's hand.

"Now, let's get you out of it before we ruin it."

Then began the work of trying to pry the dress from Rania's skin. It was much harder work to get it off than to put it on. Her delicate mating dress was exchanged for a stunning maroon ball gown that Rania slipped in and out of much more comfortably. She would wear it for the dinner the evening preceding her mating ceremony. It was one of the Myrkor colors. The colors of her new realm.

Once they were satisfied with both dresses, Rania and her mother had them packaged and delivered to Castle Eagla. Brendan and Oisin met them in the city market for a lunch of beef stew and a pint of ale.

Rania's heart was full as she looked around the table at the only family she had ever known. She wanted to cling to it and never let it go, but she had never felt that way back in Briongloid. She had only ever looked for a way out then. Rania had desired a way to live as something other than the younger sister of Oisin Dorcas, set to inherit nothing and forever live in her brother's shadow.

And now she had gotten exactly what she wanted.

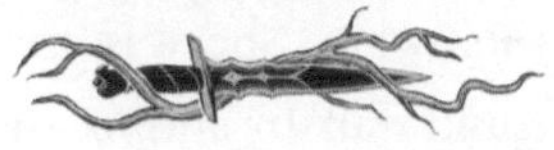

It was late at night. Too late, really.

Much too late for Rania to say what she was about to say.

She inhaled a deep breath and lifted her fist to rap on the wooden door. Then came the sound of footsteps.

Rania Dorcas had never second guessed anything she had ever done in her life, but it seemed to be all she could do lately. As she heard the footsteps nearing the door, she turned on her heel to leave. Her heart thundered so loudly in her ears it hardly gave her the space to think.

But it was too late. Much too late.

The door opened. Rania turned to face familiar dark green eyes.

"Hi," she said softly, and her shoulders dropped.

"Hi," he replied, a confused look crossing his features. "Is everything okay?"

Rania swallowed. She looked at Callum Ronan, and she didn't see the captain of the Udar Apparent's guard, but she saw her friend. She saw the man who had become her closest friend. A man with good morals, and a wit to rival her own. She saw a man with the ability to read her in a way her own parents could not. Rania saw a man that was everything she didn't know she wanted.

His brown curls were tousled about his head, and his eyes looked tired. His shirt was crooked, as if he had pulled it on when he heard a knock at his door.

"Of course."

"Then may I ask what brought you to my rooms in the middle of the night?"

"You did."

"I did? I don't recall—"

"Can we talk?" Rania interrupted and took a step closer to him. She was suddenly all too aware. She was anxious to get out of the hallway where anyone could walk by and see them.

"In here?"

"Unless you have a better suggestion."

"Come in, then," Callum replied, stepping back to allow Rania to slip beneath his arm that held the door open.

His bed was unmade, but the rest of his room was tidy.

Rania's heart was pounding so loudly, she was almost certain he could hear it, and embarrassment reddened her pale cheeks.

"I haven't seen you since we found Oisin at the Gnashing Wolf," she started off. She turned to face him as the door fell shut.

"I've been busy."

"You're always busy," she insisted. "But before, you took me with you and made time. You know I would have joined you whether it be the library, the drawing room, Hel, even the training yard. It feels as though you've been avoiding me."

"That is not my intent. I—"

"Be honest," Rania interrupted again, and took a step towards him, yearning to close the distance. "Have you been avoiding me?"

"Yes," he breathed out before running his fingers through his unruly hair. "I have."

"Why?" she pressed.

"I-I don't know."

"You do, though. And so do I," she whispered. Rania dared to take another step closer, her pulse racing quicker with each passing breath. "It's not right, but I know you feel it."

Callum remained silent. He stared at the floor near his bed. Rania felt her heart breaking, and she knew she had done this to herself. She had never given her heart to another before, and she had never meant to give it to Callum, of all people. But it seemed it had a mind of its own and had betrayed her entirely.

"Please," she breathed out, "don't make me say it."

"Say what?"

Rania looked up at him. The air caught in her throat.

"I love you, Callum," she said the words quietly. She was afraid the gods might hear her confession and paint it across the skies for all to see. And a part of her wished that they would.

His features softened, but he didn't say anything.

Rania rubbed her fingers against her sweaty palms. The silence tore at her like a shard of glass. The air in the room pierced like blades.

"Please," she pleaded, "say something."

But there were no words that Callum Ronan could have spoken to make it all right. So, he reached out and cupped her cheek in his hand. She leaned into the warmth of it, as if on instinct. He rubbed his thumb against her skin and the connection in their gazes was so strong she felt seen for the first time she could remember. Callum saw her for who she was. He saw beyond her fake smiles and her poise. He had seen her since the first time they sat together in the courtyard of the castle.

She parted her lips to speak, but no sound came out. And then his lips met hers. It was gentle at first. Cautious and curious. Hesitant until it turned greedy, as though they could never get enough of each other.

His arm circled her back and pulled her body against his. His fingers dug into her side as he gripped her like he was a man with something to lose. She wound her fingers in the hair she had grown to adore. Her other hand balled the fabric of the back of his shirt.

It would never be enough.

They fell onto his bed and into the blankets that smelled of him. Rania felt a tear run down her cheek, but their lips did not part. His teeth grazed her bottom lip, and she parted her mouth to let him in.

His hands roamed her body. She arched her back to close the distance between them.

She didn't know how long they were lost in each other, but it was not long enough.

Callum pulled back and braced himself with his arm, so he hovered above her. His lips were red and swollen. She reached for the back of his neck to pull him closer again, but he did not budge.

Rania's heart raced, and she ached for him.

"This is why I was avoiding you," he said, his voice tight with restraint.

He sat up. Rania followed and brought her knees up to her chest, where she sat on his bed.

"I know."

"This isn't right."

"I know," she repeated.

Callum shook his head and looked out his massive window at the night sky.

"I can't help what I've been promised into, Callum. And more than that, I can't help the way I feel for you."

"Promised into? I know him better than that. Did you or did you not accept when he asked for your hand? Not your father, Rania. *You*."

"I did."

Pain flashed through Callum's eyes that reflected the moon's light. Guilt flooded Rania, even though she knew she hadn't done anything wrong. Well, she hadn't until moments ago when they crossed that unspoken line.

"I didn't know I would meet you," she said, as though it would make it any better.

"But would that have changed anything?"

Rania knew her answer immediately. She looked at the ground and felt her heart shattering like a glass rose.

"Yes. No. I don't know, Callum," she said. "I'll never know because that's not how it happened. But what I do know is that I've spent my whole life in the shadow of Oisin, watching and waiting. It wasn't his fault, but I never wanted to be invisible again. I taught myself how to politick and picked up on nuances most others would overlook. I peered into every open door and poured over every letter addressed to my father. I raised myself to rule, knowing there was a good chance the Udar would one day need to secure an alliance with my realm. And when that day came, I was as prepared as I possibly could be to be the ruler that the realms need. I can't give that up, Callum."

"I never asked you to," he replied defensively.

"Tell me it's not just me."

"It's not just you, Rania. I think I just proved that," he replied.

She knew it was unfair to ask of him, but having the confirmation gave her the courage to reach out and take his hand in hers. She ran her finger along each callous on his rough hands, cherishing the imperfections that came from years of hard work.

"I don't want to lose you."

"Weylin is my best friend. He's like a brother to me," Callum said.

He straightened his fingers and shook his hand free from hers.

The rejection shot through Rania's heart like an arrow. She didn't know what else she had expected.

"Just one night," she begged, and ignored the shame that made her want to sprint from the room. "Hold me for one night."

"And what would that do? We both know it would only make it worse."

Rania paused to think. She fought to calm her racing thoughts when all she could think about was the feeling of his lips on hers and the way she longed to return to that moment.

"There have been rulers who have had consorts," Rania said. The moment the words left her lips, she felt disgusted by the idea and by herself. Callum deserved so much more. She only wished she could be the one to give him that. She looked up to see the disgust reflected in his own expression. He was offended by the idea, and she couldn't blame him. "I didn't mean it like that. But wouldn't Weylin want you to be happy? I'm sure he would understand."

Callum inhaled a long breath. He stood and moved to stand in front of her. He took her chin in his hands and tilted it up, so she was forced to look into his eyes. She longed for more than that. She wanted to touch him and find comfort in his embrace. His cold eyes warmed until they were filled with a tenderness that made her hands tremble.

He released her chin and knelt between her knees, so they were eye level. Rania felt a panic rising inside of her, unsure of what he would say next.

"If you were mine, Rania Dorcas, and I were yours," he breathed and her name on his lips was enough to make her shudder, "then I would not share you with another in any way or form. I would need you to be mine in every way that it is possible. I love you. We both need things beyond what a consort provides. You are the best female I have ever had the pleasure of knowing. You're clever, kind, and wise. You're gentle, yet one of the strongest souls I have ever met. You care about everyone around you so fiercely they never have to fear for anything. You hold yourself so that everyone can see you are perfect. Everyone except for me, that is, and thank gods you've allowed me to know your imperfections, because they are all the parts of you that I love the most. You're the mate I've always dreamed of, and the mate that could never be. So, please Rania, if you care for me as you say you do, do not ask me that question again. I fear I will not have the strength to say no twice."

Callum leaned closer. The intensity in his eyes was too much to bear as silent tears streamed down Rania's warm cheeks. She fell deeper and deeper into a love as fragile as the wind, even as she felt the foundations shattering around her and her very heart along with it.

She could only nod, as her throat was too tight to speak. Then, she pushed around him to flee back to her own chambers, like the coward she was.

Rania knew she would hold on to every word he spoke until the day she took her final breath.

And hold she did, as his confession played on a loop in her mind, each rendition hurt worse than the previous one but tasted sweeter all the same.

35

AISLA

Each time you come to me with a new plan, it is worse than the one before. Muinin's voice sounded in Aisla's head. *The answer is no. I shouldn't even have to tell you that.*

You would disagree with a goddess? Aisla snapped.

She followed in Ruairi's tracks up and around Caillte towards the wyvern caves where she had lived for a brief time. It felt like a lifetime ago now. Everything had changed in her time away, and it was a change there was no coming back from.

She could only imagine how Ruairi felt.

The wyverns are nearly as old as the gods themselves, Muinin said with a sarcastic snort. *I have no reason to obey them or be loyal to them. You're not going back to Iomlan.*

Would you prefer I ask Combha or Gaotha to take us? Aisla taunted.

That's not an option either. Besides, Combha is patrolling around the library currently. We haven't seen anything, yet.

I hope you change your mind, because we are on our way to the wyvern caves now. And if you refuse to take us, I'm sure Goatha can do the job.

Muinin's growl sounded through her mind, but Aisla ignored it as she pushed forward.

Aisla's patience was wearing thin. Maybe his voice in her head was less of a perk than she thought it would be. It was like having a second conscience. Only it was bossy and sarcastic, and she had no control over it, and could hardly figure out how to tune him out most of the time.

It's the only way. I trust Eire, and you do too.

There was a long pause, and the silence weighed heavily on Aisla.

Fine. I'll bring you to Iomlan, but if I sense danger, I won't wait for your call this time. I'll warn you that I'm coming, at least.

Yeah, because that went so well last time, Aisla retorted.

You would be dead had you not made that call. And with you, the nine realms would have fallen as well, Muinin corrected defensively. *You did the right thing.*

Aisla knew most of Iomlan would not agree with her wyvern, but she didn't protest.

Thank you. I'm glad you'll be making this journey with us.

You can thank me by staying alive.

Aisla rolled her eyes.

"I can communicate with Muinin now," Aisla blurted aloud to Ruairi and Eire, and they stopped in their tracks.

"You can? How?" Eire asked immediately, her eyes lighting up with excitement.

Aisla would never again take for granted those beautiful blue eyes. She would also never escape the nightmares of the time she had seen them faded and unrecognizable.

"It's tied into everything else I've needed to tell you guys," she replied in a hushed tone, even though they were far from civilization now. It hit her all at once. There was so much she needed to share with them, and she didn't know where to begin, not when she had hardly processed it for herself. The Silenced were real, and they were a thriving people. Her father was alive, and he seemed to thrive as well. And finally, and perhaps most conflicting, her grandmother was plotting against her —alongside Faolan Myrkor, of all people. "I went to the library of the Silenced World Tellers, and it exists. It's real. There are more books there than in our library. They're a lovely people. They're kind and wise, and one of their own, Eilis—she's a shifter. She taught me how to find my bond to Muinin within my own mind, so I can communicate with him. Her own bonded is an enfield named Fella. He nearly tore out my throat when I first found them, but Eilis used their bond to teach me. I haven't shifted yet, but it's a start. I feel safer going back to Iomlan now that we can communicate with Muinin. It'll help all of us."

"That's incredible, Ash," Ruairi said, the awe clear in his voice and his eyes. "I'm so proud of you."

"Thanks, Ru."

"Does Muinin know we're coming, then?" he asked.

"Yes," she said. "He does, and he's not happy about it. But we should keep moving. I'll tell you more while we walk."

Ruairi and Eire nodded, and they continued to the wyvern caves. Aisla felt a little lighter with each step they took, even though each step took her closer to the Udar once again.

"I won't lie. I'm a little jealous you can talk to Muinin now, and I can't talk to Combha the same way," Eire teased. "Tell us more about the library of the Silenced World Tellers. What was it like?"

Aisla smiled as she delved into the world of the people she was fortunate enough to live among, even for such a brief time. She described every detail as thoroughly as she could, more than happy to grant Eire that wish. She knew her friend loved adventure as much as she did, and there was so much she had missed out on while she was suffering in the infirmary. Not all of it was good, and most of it she would've never wished upon Eire, but it was an adventure all the same —and one Eire could have never shared.

Aisla avoided mentioning her father or the letter, knowing that was not Eire's question. In time, she was certain she would reveal all, but she could only handle small steps. And sharing the favorable pieces of her stay in the library of the Silenced was a good place to start.

"One day," Aisla said as she wrapped up her story between Eire's comments and questions, "I'll take you both there."

Eire nodded hesitantly. And Aisla felt the unspoken fear hanging between them. *If* it still existed, after the Inevitable War that was to fall upon them any sunrise. *If* they survived the war itself.

"So," Ruairi interrupted, "did they translate the letter for you?"

Of course, that would be his question. Aisla didn't blame him. She had been itching to interrogate him about the ring.

"Yes, they did," Aisla replied, mulling over her next words carefully. "Funny enough," she paused again and took a deep breath, "it was translated by my father."

Again, Eire and Ruairi came to a halt, this time turning to face her with wide eyes and dropped jaws. There was disbelief and shock and confusion, and she recognized it all because she had felt it too when she first recognized his face beneath the forest floor.

"H-he's alive," Aisla continued, even though no one else had said anything. "My mother isn't, but he is. If you promise not to stop again, I'll tell you the rest. But we must keep moving."

They both nodded silently, agreeing before they took off again side by side into the night of Eilean.

Then, Aisla let the cold and cruel story that her father told her unfurl from her lips. And once she started, she couldn't stop. She told them about her father and what had been done to him. And her mother and what her fate had truly been. She detailed as much of it as she could recall, because somebody else needed to know. Somebody else needed to understand.

She ran through the gist of the letter that Ruairi had been sent to Iomlan with. She hit all the important parts of it, and told them she had left it with her father in the library.

At some point, hot tears wet her cold cheeks. At some point, she thought her heart might stop from all the places it had cracked.

How many wounds could a heart take before it reached its final beat?

Aisla thought she might begin to count them, and if maybe her heart could withstand its number of tears, her mind could too. Knowing how frequently Cliona had been in her head, invading her very mind, was perhaps the most unsettling thought of all. She would train her mind to be as strong as her heart was, and Cliona would never again be able to toy with her esos, her thoughts, and her strengths again.

"I'm sorry," Ruairi murmured, and she knew he meant it.

He had every right to say *I told you so,* but he never would. She heard his grief as clear as her own, because when she hurt, he hurt. As it always had been.

Aisla was glad that they were moving and could not stop. She was glad Ruairi could not stop to comfort her in his embrace, because she knew she would fall apart in his arms, and that was the last thing any of them needed.

She was reminded that they still hadn't discussed the kiss shared between them before everything went awry. Her cheeks heated in shame. She could never be what he wanted her to be—not when loving her meant being in danger.

And being the *Gheall Ceann,* that would always be the case.

Aisla's throat tightened. "Me too," she said, and he knew she meant it in more ways than one.

Ruairi looked over his shoulder and met her gaze with that familiar tenderness that she didn't deserve. Sorrow filled her chest until she looked away.

She couldn't bring herself to glance at him and see the hurt that she knew filled his light green eyes. Loving her had gotten Ruairi tortured. She would never again allow herself to love or be loved if it meant it would paint a target on her partner's back. She hadn't talked to Ruairi about it yet, as she hadn't found the words to. But Aisla knew that when she did, he would protest.

But she would not change her mind.

"Along those lines," Ruairi spoke up again and cleared his throat as they carried forward, "I finally figured out the ring. It's what landed me in the dungeons."

"And?" Eire asked, breaking the tension that had begun to brew.

Aisla assumed Ruairi had told her about the ring on one of his many visits to her infirmary room. He had been a good friend to her when she had not.

"And the ring controls the husks. Cliona had the dwarves weave her esos within it to give the wearer of the ring control over their minds, with or without ash trees," he replied, and confusion flooded Aisla's muddled brain. "They've used the lofa to create an army of them. An army that whoever bears that ring can control with no limitations that I can find."

"Who is *they*?" Eire snapped.

Aisla heard the anger in her voice. She understood why. Whatever this was, it affected Eire more than it did Ruairi or Aisla.

"Cliona. And Faolan," Aisla answered before Ruairi could. The words left her lips in a faint rasp. She didn't know how many more revelations she could take. If Aisla had any tears left to shed, she didn't even know if they would fall. She was so fed up with it all. Her hatred for Cliona grew with every new deception. "Cliona's letter was her way of handing over me and the ring. The Udar need only grant her a title for it all. She was willing to give him his *mallaithe* and an army, all for a guaranteed seat by his side in this 'new Talam' they envision. She's a spineless coward. And I'm so terribly sorry you both have been dragged into this all."

Silence fell among them, but their pace did not slow. If anything, it quickened, led by an irate Eire. Aisla saw her hands curl into fists at her side, and she wished with her whole heart that there was something she could do to lessen the pain.

"I don't blame you," Eire spoke up after a while. "If that's what you're thinking."

"I wouldn't fault you if you did," Aisla said.

Eire reached out and took Aisla's hand without looking at her. She intertwined their fingers and gave her a gentle, reassuring squeeze.

"Why would I? You are not your grandmother. You never have been."

Aisla nodded, even as the back of her throat burned with the tears she could not shed.

The wyvern caves came into view just ahead, and Aisla's stomach tied in knots.

Her whole body tensed at the sight, knowing they were closing in on that point of no return. It was so familiar to the night she and Ruairi had snuck away across the Tusnua Sea aboard *Stoirme*. That time, Eire had not been with them, and Aisla had been desperately wishing that she was.

This is really what you want? Muinin's voice echoed through her skull at the same moment his emerald scales became visible in the dark as he stalked from the wyvern caves.

It is. Aisla replied.

Muinin grunted in response and greeted her with a slight bow of his massive head.

She rushed to him and wrapped her arms around his neck. Muinin tensed out of stubbornness before giving in and pressing into her embrace.

Thank you.

It's what I'm here for, he retorted. *It's good to see you,* Gheall Ceann.

And you, as well. She grinned before releasing him and turning to face her friends.

They both stared at her with wonder in their eyes.

"You were talking to him?" Eire asked.

"Yes," Aisla replied. "He says hello," she lied.

Muinin growled behind her.

"Did erm, Leighis, tell you when her friend in Fomhar would be waiting for us? Or more specifically, where?"

"No," Eire said stubbornly. "She was rather vague, but I wasn't going to question her."

"Well, maybe you should have," Aisla snapped in the same moment as Muinin said: *Is it too late to rescind my acceptance of your plan?*

"Look," Ruairi said, and Aisla was surprised to hear him speak up. "We have what we need to know this is the right thing to do. Just look at Eire. We must keep moving. We cannot be discovered here—we've already taken a great risk tonight, let's not challenge our blessings."

Aisla swallowed. He was right.

They had already risked a stop in a nearby village for weapons and food for their journey. They couldn't leave empty-handed. It was too late for any shops to be open, which made it easier to loot for what they needed while being who they were. Ruairi, Eire, and Aisla would not go unnoticed in the daylight—not so close to Caillte.

Aisla's new dagger was strapped to her waist, but she missed *Oidhe* as though it were an extension of her being, but there was no way they could have gone back for it.

"Great thinking, Ru," Eire chirped, turning pointedly to Aisla.

"To Fomhar we go," Aisla said as nerves bubbled inside of her.

Fomhar was further from Eilean than Briongloid was, but flying would be faster than sailing. They would take Muinin since Combha was preoccupied, and they all felt safer knowing Gaotha would be there with her as well. Muinin was the largest of the three wyverns, and they could all fit comfortably on his back for the duration of the flight.

Fomhar was further north than Briongloid as well, which meant it was further from Samhradh. She hoped that would make it easier to get into, but she also had to trust that Leighis would protect them if she was the one sending them there. As much as Aisla dreaded it, she also knew she would know for certain the truth of Eire's words if the tips of her ears rounded when day broke the horizon. And with it, the esos of her blood would slip from her veins like a scarf in the wind.

The thought sent a shudder down Aisla's spine. She shook her head to clear it as the three of them climbed up between Muinin's shoulder blades.

This time, when they left the shores of Eilean, Aisla did not look back.

She didn't watch her home disappear out of sight because she didn't know that it was a home for her any longer. Aisla Iarkis didn't know if she belonged in this realm, or any other, but she did know it was her life's duty to find a way to save them all from each other.

No matter what it cost her in the process.

36

EIRE

It was a surreal feeling to be reunited with Aisla and Ruairi—a feeling she never thought she would know, especially after Aisla stopped visiting her.

Eire glanced over her shoulder where Ruairi sat behind her. He looked out over the clouds, deep in thought. At least part of Leighis's promise to her had proven true so far. Realta had provided more than enough cloud coverage for Muinin to fly through. It made the flight rather uncomfortable, but he would duck out of the clouds briefly to look at their surroundings. Aisla held the map, and she was giving her wyvern instructions.

Eire was incredibly jealous of the esos. She would never hear Combha's voice for herself, but she hoped Aisla would find a way to talk to her for her.

Aisla sat in front of Eire, and when she wasn't looking down at the map in her hands, she would look up at the dual moons of the night sky. Aisla and Ruairi had both been oddly quiet since leaving

Eilean, and she could only imagine how unsettling it must feel to make the journey again after how horribly the last one had gone.

There was also something new between them, Eire noticed. It was something fragile and delicate. Something that was perhaps already fractured, and both were too afraid to poke it and risk deepening those spider-webbing cracks in fear it would fall apart entirely.

As much as it was easy to fall back into the comfort of their friendship the three of them shared as closely as family, so much had changed. Eire felt like an outsider and a stranger, but she didn't know how she could mend it without masking her own emotions.

Eire felt that familiar anger in her very soul. It was the rage that came when she remembered all that the lofa had taken from Eilean, and all that it had taken from her. She could not live a day in her life without recalling Fiona's last seconds as she pleaded with her to find a will to live. And then she sat helplessly as Fiona was wheeled away.

She didn't know if Fiona had ended up as a husk in the cells outside of Caillte that Ruairi had told her about. She couldn't think about it—couldn't consider the possibility of opposing her in a war, because husk or not, Fiona had been the love of her life. It was a pain no amount of time would heal, and memories no amount of grief could erase.

The thought caused her hands to tremble. Eire inhaled a long breath.

She wondered how it would feel to go from elven to human. Would it be instant or gradual? And she feared the way the esos would drain from her blood. It would be an adjustment to live without it, not that she had been using it much lately, as she was restrained in the infirmary. Still, she always felt its presence within herself. And to not feel it, she worried it would make her a different soul entirely.

"You should do something," Aisla's voice carried to her on the wind. She looked back at Eire over her shoulder, grinning. "With your esos. You know, a final show of Eire Trygg's mastery as a tsuna."

Eire laughed a genuine laugh for the first time in a very long time.

It was a laugh of relief and a laugh that was accompanied by the stinging of tears in the corners of her eyes. She nodded, and breathed in deeply, allowing herself to hear that rush of power in her veins.

Her throat went dry. Eire felt Aisla and Ruairi's eyes on her.

A heaviness settled within her chest that she thought might last for the rest of her shortened life. She lifted her hands, dragging the water from the air around her with her movement. Her blood sang with the familiarity of the sensation as her esos rushed to the surface of her skin at the call of her will.

Her fingers worked like those of an artist, painting with the power she would soon lose. They worked of their own accord until Eire was smiling, and a single tear fell. She gazed out at the scene of three friends running through a field, heads tipped back, while they laughed at jokes that a water portrait could never tell. There was Aisla and Ruairi and herself, caught in a moment of joy they had lived countless times.

The scene disappeared and was replaced by a beautiful female looking at Eire with a soft smile on her lips. It was the first evening she and Fiona had spent time alone together. They ate dinner in a field of flowers, and Fiona plucked one out of the ground, and tucked it behind Eire's right ear. In her water portrait, Fiona held the small flower out to her.

She pushed her power into it, allowing it to drain from her blood. A choked laugh escaped her trembling lips. A hand touched her back, then another touched her leg.

Aisla and Ruairi were with her as she watched the light crawl from behind the horizon and shimmer through the water figure she had created. Fiona faded into mist that returned to the clouds and dawn enveloped the sky.

Pain erupted through Eire. Pain that made her double over on Muinin's back, letting her head fall into her hands. She wanted to rip out her hair at the roots.

She could feel the esos of her lifeblood tearing away from her very essence. It was entwined so deeply, Eire felt each thread that wound itself around her veins pull and wrench away from her.

It was a white-hot pain. It burned through her limbs, her core, her throat, and her nostrils. Eire screamed. Her friends adjusted themselves to hold her.

Then it was over, as quickly as it began.

Eire kept her head bowed as she reached a shaking hand to touch the tips of her ears. She was met by an unfamiliar soft curve, and her chest heaved with sobs as she fell into Ruairi's open arms behind her while Aisla gently rubbed her hand in the only comfort she could offer.

37
WEYLIN

The journey to Blathriel from Omra was much longer than the journey to Scamall had been. It was a relief when Weylin crossed the bridge over the Grain River that brought him into the half of Samhradh where Castle Eagla sat. It meant he only had one more sleep before he and Eolas would be back home if they traveled all day.

He'd sent a messenger raven with his travel itinerary to his mother because he knew she was anxious for his return. She hated when he travelled without Callum or any of the rest of his personal guard. On top of that, he knew she was eagerly planning a mating that he had been dreading and even avoiding.

Weylin's thumb dragged along the fresh scar of his blood-binding agreement with Corren Kyne. What confused him the most about the whole ordeal was the foolish fight the male picked to prove a point. They were both politically aware that Weylin had gone to Earrach to help, but mostly to secure their alliance. Corren didn't need to go as far as he did to reach an agreement. He had asked for protection from the *mallaithe,* but Weylin's goal had always been to save all the realms from her. Even her own, if he could.

Corren seemed to be testing Weylin, to see if he was worthy of Earrach's allegiance or not, and the thought put a foul taste in Weylin's mouth.

Aside from the extra distance and time it took to reach the capital of Earrach, Weylin could feel a phantom wind haunting his footsteps home.

And the phantom wind he knew to be memories of Ellora—a female who never existed. She was a female who had both understood him and drove him to insanity at the same time.

He supposed it made sense now, how she understood him so well —in a way that no one else ever could. For if anyone would understand the burdens of inheritance and power, it would be Aisling Iarkis.

He could still hear her voice as she whispered the words through her wine-stained lips in the dark of a puball under cold moons. And the more he thought about it, the more it tore at him. He knew that pressure. He knew exactly what she had meant, and her fears of not being enough. He also knew her pressure would be greater than anyone else's in all the realms.

Aisling's burdens came with a warrant of death, and Ifreann had been waiting at her door every moment since her birth. Ifreann, and the fate of every soul in the nine realms.

There was a part of Weylin that was relieved to find out who Ellora truly was, because it meant he was forced to hate her. It made it easier to. If she had stayed Ellora Morlee, the poor female from Fomhar training to be a laoch for the Udar, it would have been harder to stay away, and harder to march towards his mating ceremony.

He could still feel the warmth of her skin when they finally kissed along the rushing river. And the memory twisted knots in his stomach, and he clenched his fists at his side.

The last time he had returned home from a journey to another realm, she'd been with him nearly every step of the way.

That journey had led to the ground for Iomlan to declare war on Eilean at any moment. Weylin felt more confident on the declaration after solidifying their alliance with Earrach, as they had the largest and most well-trained legion of laochs aside from Samhradh. Once Callum finalized his weapon to take down the wyverns, they would be nearly unstoppable, and Eilean would either surrender the *mallaithe* or face its end as a realm.

It had been a handful of sunrises since that second time Aisling appeared in his bedroom. Weylin wondered if whatever was connecting their minds only worked when he was in Castle Eagla for some reason. It seemed odd, but he could think of no other explanation. He found himself eager to get home and see if she would appear again, if only so he knew he hadn't imagined it those first two times. Sometimes he wondered if she had been there at all, or if his mind was playing tricks on him.

It was nearly midday when Weylin directed Eolas toward a small stream flowing between the towering pine trees of the woods. He dismounted and filled his flask while Eolas bent her head to drink the running water.

When his flask was full to the brim, Weylin stood and took a few paces away from the stream. The air felt still as a foreboding feeling raised the hair along Weylin's spine. He strained his ears over the sound of the wind, but it was too late.

A growl sounded from the south, and Weylin's hand shot to *Uamhan*. Not fast enough. A black wolf lunged from the shadows and pinned Weylin to the forest floor before he could withdraw his blade and fight the beast of a creature. The claws of its massive paws dug into Weylin's shoulders as the weight of the wolf held him there.

Teeth gnashed a mere dagger's length away from Weylin's throat, and he knew his life hung in the balance as an image of a glinting golden thread flashed behind his eyelids when he blinked. His thread

—the one that contained his very life force on the Crann Na Beatha, flashing through his mind as though it was a threat from the norns themselves.

With renewed motivation, Weylin put his full weight into gripping the side of the beast and rolling it over so Weylin could be on top of it. The wolf's jaws continued to snap, and warm spit splattered across Weylin's face.

Weylin clenched his jaw as he fumbled for a way to hold the wolf at bay while getting a better grip on his blade that grazed the side of the wolf and dripped wet blood onto Weylin's skin. If he could just get one free hand, he could end the wolf's life with one plunge of his sword.

Weylin growled with fury as the beast twisted and turned until they were rolling through the brush, each of them desperately fighting to end the other's life. His heart thundered at the thought of the wolf's pack that surely lingered nearby. What if he survived this one only to face several more?

He blinked hard as he pushed the thought from his mind and put his focus back into finding a way to rid the worldly realms of the beast. The wolf opened its maw as Weylin felt his strength draining around the hum of power that he could not touch. It strained its neck, and its hot breath flooded Weylin's senses. His arms collapsed beneath the weight of the beast and the wolf snapped a final time. Then, its brutal roar fade into a yelp of pain and it collapsed on top of Weylin with a thud that stole the breath from his lungs.

Weylin grabbed the sides of the wolf and shoved its heavy body off of him, before sitting up to find himself staring face to face with an emerald-green viper.

Its scales reflected the warm spring sun.

His heart skipped a beat, and he watched the black slit of the creature's golden eyes flicker with curiosity.

Hisssss.

The creature opened its mouth to bare fangs coated in the wolf's lifeblood, and slithered towards Weylin. Tantalizingly slowly.

Weylin remained still, holding the creature's too-intelligent gaze. He breathed slowly, as if that would help quell his rising panic.

Bumps raised along Weylin's arms as the snake slithered across the hand he hadn't dared to move. Weylin held his breath as the tip of its tail finally passed over his skin, and he heard it retreating into the woods where he had come from.

Weylin kept his relief at bay as he stood, gripping his sword. He turned and watched the viper disappear into the darkness, but every time he blinked, he swore he saw its slitted golden eyes staring back at him from the shadows.

38
RUAIRI

How did you ever think you could protect her here? What were you thinking bringing her here?

The words of the Udar Apparent ran on an endless loop through Ruairi's mind as the shore of Iomlan came into view.

The first thing that struck Ruairi was the fact that there was no blockade along Fomhar's border. At first, it came as a relief, but then the lack of one stirred a sense of foreboding in his gut. He didn't know what it could mean.

"Do you see that?" Aisla asked, and he knew exactly what she was referring to.

"No blockade," Ruairi murmured.

"What does it mean?" Eire cut in.

"They're rallying their forces," Ruairi replied. "But we can at least use it to our advantage."

From above, Ruairi could see that Fomhar was littered with the beautiful reds and golds of foliage in autumn. A stark contrast to the varying shades of green they had come across last time they made a voyage across the Tusnua Sea.

And Ruairi was making the same mistake again. He knew it, too, as he glanced over Eire at the back of Aisla's head. He knew her wary gaze was focused ahead.

He looked to the dawn sky that shone in a rare, brilliant shade of lilac, as though the very essence of Eire's esos had drifted into the clouds to live amongst the gods in Albios. The sight tore at his heart. He allowed his eyes to fall shut for a moment, grieving what Eire had lost, but thankful that they had not lost her to the otherly realms.

Eire leaned against him. The transformation had truly done a number on her. Her screams were forever etched into the recesses of his brain, where he compartmentalized all the terrible things that had happened in his life. Most of which had happened within the last full moon in Sneachta.

To himself. And to those he loved most.

A gasp from Aisla drew Ruairi out of his own mind and he looked up to follow her finger, where she pointed to the south.

"No, no, no," she breathed, and it took only a glance for Ruairi to see what had brought out her panic.

In the distance, the top of marigold and maroon sails were visible along the horizon line as ships raced westward, towards Eilean.

"We have to turn around," Aisla spoke flatly. "We have to turn around!" She repeated her words, her hysteria rising as she looked back at them.

"We can't," he hissed back at her as she turned backwards to face him with wild eyes that writhed in yellow-green flames. "We can't go back."

"I'm not abandoning my people," she snarled.

"Aisla, don't you see? This is what he wants—what they want. If you're on that continent, they'll take you and kill you. Who will satisfy the prophecy then? Your death would mean the end of the nine realms as we know it—you believe that same as I do."

"I can't just leave them," she snapped back, but her edge was fading. "My father."

"I know, Aisla. We have to trust that our loved ones can take care of themselves. They would want us to be safe, and to keep you safe, while we figure this out."

"Ruairi, I can't let this happen."

"What did you think would happen when you called Muinin to save us in Samhradh? I'm not saying you made the wrong choice— but you knew exactly what it meant, as much as anyone else did."

Ruairi watched hurt dim the fire in her eyes, but Muinin didn't falter. Ruairi assumed that meant they were staying the course. His throat tightened with fear and grief. No one on Eilean deserved this. And he knew it was his fault as much as it was Aisla's.

"I did it for you," she seethed between clenched teeth, but it was sorrow now that drove her anger. He could see it in the way water welled in the corners of her eyes. "I did it for you."

She was right. Ruairi knew she was. He would have died in Castle Orga if Aisla hadn't called Muinin. If Aisla hadn't begun to the Inevitable War.

"I know," was all Ruairi Vilulf could say. His heart twisted into familiar knots that grew harder and harder to undo.

Eire remained silent as Aisla turned around, looking ahead once again. He knew she was trying her best not to look at the ships. He inhaled a deep breath, wondering how they would ever get out of this.

Aisla's shoulders trembled, and she slumped forward. Eire sat up enough to stroke her hair gently in the silence of the night. Ruairi cursed as he forced himself to watch the Myrkor navy begin the war that Aisla had declared.

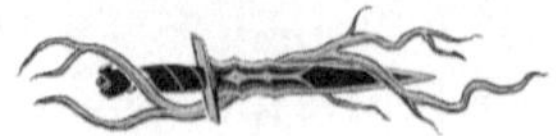

Nine ships streamed across the horizon. Ruairi could hardly pull his eyes away. Ruairi was only thankful for the cloud coverage that kept Muinin out of sight of the ships.

Eire had fallen asleep for a while, but not long. Aisla hadn't said a word since their heated exchange, but Ruairi heard her light snore now, and was thankful she had found rest, too.

They were nearly done with their journey and would need their energy.

"We're still doing the right thing," Eire insisted into the tense silence that had settled between them. "Leighis would not have told us to come here if there was any other way."

"How can you be so certain?" Ruairi challenged, gently, but he could no longer let that question fester in his gut as he had since she first told them of her plan.

"Why would she heal me otherwise?"

"To get you to bring Aisla back to Iomlan," Ruairi replied. "How do we know she isn't using you to work against the Udar?"

"Can't you just trust me?" Eire snapped. "If you had been there, you would understand. You'll see when we land, and her friend is there waiting for us."

"Okay," Ruairi said, knowing there was no longer a point in having this conversation.

"Is Aisla okay?" she whispered.

"I don't know," Ruairi replied honestly. "I don't know if she's been okay since we returned from Iomlan."

"I can't blame her."

"I know. I just thought she would communicate more about it— get through it together like we always do, but she's shut me out rather than acknowledged what we both went through, and I know it's a lot, but I just miss her."

"You should probably be telling her this."

"Yeah, it's hard to find the chance to."

"You've had plenty of time, Ru," Eire said softly. "I think it's less about the time, and more about the words you wish to speak. Did something happen between you on Iomlan?"

Ruairi's forefinger rubbed against his thumb in those nervous circles he had the habit of resorting to.

"We kissed," Ruairi breathed out. He hadn't told anyone else yet. "Before I was taken by the Udar's laochs. And nothing more came of it—I don't know where she stands."

A shadow of understanding crossed Eire's features as she nodded slowly. She gently reached out a hand to rest on Ruairi's knee. "She blames herself for all of it, you know. That's why she's pushing you away now."

Ruairi swallowed around the knot in his throat as the grief burned like a snake tightening around his heart. He wished he could take that pressure away—the blame Aisla had carried all these sunrises for choices they had made.

"I know," he said again.

He could not bear it—the look of sorrow on Eire's face—so he turned his chin towards the other side of the sky, staring out at the pink clouds that enveloped them.

"Everything is about to change," Eire spoke up. "Don't let your fears hold you back from saying what you need to say. Gods know the last thing you want to do is to lose the chance to ever say them."

There was genuine grief in her words, not just sorrow at the situation Ruairi found himself in, but the grieving of someone who knew real loss and the truth of the pain in each word.

"I'm so sorry about Fiona," Ruairi said, his palms sweating. He had heard of the passing of the female from whispers around town, but he had never brought it up to Eire. The menders had warned him the topic was too sensitive in her volatile state, while she had still been deteriorating. And he knew that the female Eire had painted in drops of water was her. The thought shattered his heart. "I can't imagine what that was like."

Eire's eyes did not flash with grief or anger or sorrow, but they fogged a milky white that was reminiscent of her days in the infirmary. It alarmed Ruairi, but he did not let it show.

"And I cannot imagine what it would have been like during the sunrises you spent in the cells of Castle Eagla," Eire said, and sniffed once before withdrawing her hand and sitting up straight, turning to face away from him. "We've all faced situations that none of us could relate to before. If you need anything, I'm here for you, but we must keep pushing forward to make all of that pain worth it, or it will have all been for nothing. And I refuse to let Fiona's life be for nothing. We're back together again, and I've been granted a life I did not deserve. Don't waste yours on the what-ifs, Ruairi Vilulf. I know you to be a better male than that."

Ruairi nodded, and despite the severity of their conversation, a lightness entered his chest. This was the closest he had seen Eire to her old self. And if that wasn't the best gift the gods could have given him, he did not know what was.

"I missed you, Eire."

"And I missed you too, Ru."

Muinin lowered himself closer to the Tusnua Sea, just before sunset.

Aisla had come up with a plan and relayed it to her wyvern. He would drop them on the shore of Fomhar, near their northern border. This put them as far from Samhradh as possible while staying within the realm of Fomhar. It was also the shore nearest Fomhar's capital, Sruthar.

Ruairi gripped Muinin's saddle until his knuckles were white as they began their rapid descent. The cloud cover Realta had provided for them moved with them as they neared the sandy beach, ensuring no one would see the wyvern land from afar. And from what Ruairi could see, there were no people along the beach.

"Ready?" Aisla asked them both above the roar of the wind.

"Yes!" he and Eire shouted back.

They scooted to the edge of Muinin's back, wanting to make a quick escape. The less time the wyvern spent on Iomlan, the better. Eire reached out and took Ruairi's hand, giving it a reassuring squeeze before releasing him.

Muinin landed with a thud. They gathered their packs they had filled during their guilt-ridden village raid, and slid off the side of his massive green body.

The wyvern let out a snort as he looked at Ruairi through narrowed eyes. Ruairi knew Muinin's meaning well enough: *Protect her this time. Or else.*

He didn't need the esos of a shifter to understand him. Ruairi swallowed and nodded his head.

Aisla ran her hand down Muinin's side before reaching his head. She gently pressed her forehead against his and the wyvern closed his golden eyes. After a moment, Aisla stepped away from him, and the wyvern's wings began to beat the air around him, swirling the fog that had covered his landing.

They watched Muinin disappear into the grey clouds. A lump formed in Ruairi's throat as Aisla turned to face him. Fear and sorrow evident in the lines that creased her brow.

The silence that hung between them reminded him of the last time they had come to Iomlan. The rush they had felt escaping a fleet. This time, there was no barricade close enough to spot them, and the ships headed towards Eilean were too far away. A wary comfort settled over Ruairi.

"I'm sorry," Aisla's soft voice spoke up. Her eyes were sad and tired, lacking all the warmth that usually anchored him. "I didn't mean what I said. This isn't your fault. I may have done it for you, but it was my choice. And truly, I don't blame you. I blame myself."

"It's okay," Ruairi replied, taking a cautious step towards her until they were almost touching. "But it's not about who's at fault, Ash. You can't possibly carry this burden on your own. And if you do me one favor, please share it with me. Share with Eire. But don't continue to let it weigh you down so heavily. What's done is done, and no one here is angry with you. You're safe. We love you, and we are going to figure this out."

Aisla nodded, but he could see the argument brewing in her eyes. He was thankful for it, because it was better than the hollowness she had started the conversation with. She held out her arms, and he embraced her with his arms wrapping tightly around her back. He breathed in her familiar scent, and wished the moment could drag into eternity as her fingers clutched the fabric at the back of his cloak.

He heard her sniffle as her grip loosened, and she stepped back from him with eyes that shined with wetness, but no tears fell.

"Hopefully Iomlan has a better welcome for us this time," she said with a small smile.

"You could say that again." He grinned and turned towards Eire, who stood looking out at the colorful trees ahead of them, giving Aisla and Ruairi space. He had not said all that he wanted to, but he felt he had said what he needed to, and he could only hope she would trust them to help her carry the burden she found herself with.

"Ready?" Aisla asked with a deep inhale as she looked first to Eire and then to Ruairi.

"It's about time I got to see Iomlan," Eire said, and began walking deeper into the realm of Fomhar.

Aisla followed.

With a final glance back over his shoulder, Ruairi loosed a breath and walked onwards, praying to any gods that were listening that they were not fools for this.

39

WEYLIN

The air felt different in Samhradh when Weylin walked up to the gated entrance of his home. It felt foreign in a lot of ways that he could not explain and was not ready to unpack for himself.

Each time he left his realm, it seemed a little more distant to him. He knew that would all change once he could sit down and talk with his father again. He didn't know what was going on with his own people. It was his fault for leaving, but he knew it was worth it to have Earrach solidify their alliance. It had gone far better than his last journey away from Samhradh, at least.

He had debated the merit of telling his father of the wolf attack that had only ended with him keeping his life's breath because of the viper that reeked of the gods.

And there was only one goddess who was associated with the snakes. Sionna herself—the goddess of mischief and war—the last goddess Weylin would ever want to find himself entangled with.

Although it seemed he might have found himself in her debt, if his suspicions were true.

In the end, Weylin decided better not to tell his father. They were already dealing with the repercussions of Weylin's uncle's death, and the strange prophecy that seemed to come with his death being caused by a bear. Weylin found comfort in the scar on his palm that was healing, and the oath that Corren had sworn to him with his lifeblood.

Weylin pushed all the thoughts to the back of his mind as the looming pressures came crashing down on him with the opening of the gates. He had one more sunrise until his mating day. One more sunrise to be his own male before becoming half of a unit, and a unit that would one day rule Talam.

His jaw clenched with reluctant anticipation as Callum's familiar green eyes met his from beyond the gates. He stood straighter than normal, tense, but Weylin couldn't blame him given the rush he had been in to finish the weapon plans for taking down the wyverns.

"My brother," Weylin greeted his best friend as some of the pressure lifted from his chest at the sight of Callum's familiar face.

"It is good to see you again," Callum said with a grin, and they embraced with a warmth that felt as comfortable as family. "Too quiet around here without you."

Weylin pulled away from Callum and turned his attention towards the castle and all the bustling he knew was going on during the eve of his mating ceremony.

"I can hardly believe that given the events that have come to pass and the one we face tomorrow," Weylin replied with a grimace.

He looked back to see Callum's face fall. There was something Callum was not saying that he wanted to.

"Is everything okay?"

"Of course," Callum's attention snapped back up, too quickly. "Why wouldn't it be?"

"I don't know. You tell me."

"Nothing a pint can't fix." Callum put on a fake smile and threw his arm around Weylin's shoulders as they sauntered towards the castle entrance.

Weylin followed the familiar halls in his castle, ignoring the souls that passed and cast curious, wide-eyed glances his way. He felt more conscious of his status than ever on the eve of his mating. It was as though it somehow legitimized all that he had ever been promised.

They grabbed their wooden mugs and sat at one of the long tables of the castle pub, sitting across from each other as they had countless times. He would find time to visit his father later, but he felt no urgency to do so—not when his father had felt so little urgency in securing their union with Earrach in the first place.

"A toast to Earrach is in order, I should hope?" Callum spoke up, quirking an eyebrow as he raised his mug, waiting for an answer.

"Indeed, it is," Weylin said.

He was grateful the journey had not been for nothing, even if it had also provided him with an escape from the politicking and planning of his current position.

Liquid sloshed over the sides of their mugs as they hit together before Weylin pressed the cup to his lips and savored the taste of home in the ale.

"Corren is even more of a wild card than I think we had guessed," Weylin said. "He caused the war between the undines and the sylphs. The male was promised to a sylph heir, and along with that promise came a title. But, he went and fell in love with an undine, which was, of course, an insult to the sylphs. The part that didn't sit well with me is Corren was essentially willing to wipe the sylphs of Earrach out all together as a solution to the problem. It would have been a massacre, not to mention a direct slap in the face to Leighis and her children. I solved the dispute and promised the sylphs a place in his court, and they seemed appeased by that answer. I left little room to argue."

"Damn." Callum whistled under his breath and sipped his drink. "Who would've thought the Lord Apparent of Earrach had a heart to love with after all. He sounds like a real pain."

Weylin grunted in agreement. "And on the way back—he tried to kill me."

Callum's jaw dropped at that, and his eyes widened, waiting for further explanation.

"It was some real alpha male shit," Weylin started, still trying to figure out how he felt about the whole situation. "He got me alone in the woods and took the opportunity to challenge me in combat. Corren said he wanted to see if I was worthy of taking the throne after my father has passed on. He wasn't bad with a blade either."

"You could have killed him for that."

"I know," Weylin grimaced. "Probably should have. But that wouldn't have been a good look for our alliance with Earrach. Corren Kyne is a male we need to be wary of."

"It certainly sounds that way."

Weylin nodded in agreement.

He noticed Callum's attention wander behind him, and he turned to see Rania striding towards them with a faint smile on her face. She met Weylin's eyes with a glimmer of mischief, and Weylin stood to greet her.

"My lady." Weylin bowed before taking her hand and lifting it to his lips, where he placed a soft kiss.

"Weylin," she replied, and it took Weylin back to Castle Tromlui, where he had insisted she drop his formal title. A smile tugged at his lips but did not reach his eyes. "I heard you had returned."

There was a slight challenge in the words, and Weylin knew he should have sought her out upon his arrival. He felt no guilt for not doing so, but it was a reminder of how soon things would change.

"Indeed. Here I am," he said, matching the challenge in her own tone. "I trust Callum was a sufficient guide while I was away."

Rania's eyes darted towards Callum, and there was something unreadable there—something that should have raised Weylin's attention, but he thought little of it since he had a hard time reading the female since he first met her. Callum met her gaze with a coldness that Weylin rarely saw from the man.

"Yes, he helped me get my feet on the ground," Rania replied, her attention once again locked on Weylin's. "I am very grateful Oisin was here as well. It was nice to have a familiar face and someone to spend my hours with—aside from my books. I've heard he's obtained the approval from your father to stay after our mating, as well. He will be an asset as the war begins."

"I do not doubt it."

"I overheard you saying the Lord of Earrach challenged you in his territory?" Rania asked before taking a seat on the wooden bench next to where Weylin had been sitting. He followed as she invited herself into their conversation.

"He did. It was an odd thing to do."

"You should've ended his life for such a thing," Callum cut in, repeating his sentiment almost aggressively. Weylin knew his friend felt it was his duty to protect him not only as the Udar Apparent but as his chosen family where Callum had none by blood.

"That's one way to make allies," Rania snapped, but did not look up at Callum as she spoke.

Weylin was taken aback by her harsh demeanor and wondered how much more he did not know about the female he was to mate the following sunset, not for the first time. At least she was comfortable enough to speak her mind.

"Rania is right," Weylin said, and he did not miss the smirk of satisfaction from the female. "I journeyed to Earrach with the pure intention of securing an ally, so I entertained his duel until my blade was at his throat. And then he offered a blood pact."

"I assume you did not take it. Blood pacts are practically unheard of these—" Callum interjected again.

"I accepted. He only asked for protection from the *mallaithe* in his oath. And he swore his allegiance to me."

"To you or Samhradh?" Rania asked this time, a curious edge to the words.

Weylin raised an eyebrow at her. "Are they not one and the same?"

"I suppose so."

"Well, the news at least strengthens our backing since your father sent ships to Eilean this sunrise."

"He did what?" Weylin snarled, as he grit his teeth.

40

AISLA

Aisla's blood turned to pure fire the moment she saw the ships crossing the Tusnua Sea towards her home—no matter if that home had rejected her or not.

The embers had yet to cool.

Her palms itched with her esos that had felt so distant for so long, but she was now barely able to contain it. She was only thankful her bond with Muinin seemed to go beyond the confines of esos now that she had finally found it. It worked through the iron in the prison, so she could only assume it would work without ash trees to replenish her esos on Iomlan.

How is it over there?

Muinin's voice broke through her thoughts, as if on cue. It grounded her in where she was and why she was there.

So far so good. You've hardly left the coast.

A grunt sounded in her mind, lighting up that golden thread. *I'll warn Caillte about the approaching ships.*

I wonder if Cliona already knows about them, Aisla shot back bitterly.

Regardless, Caillte needs to know. I'll tell Combha.

Thank you. Aisla knew Muinin was bonded to Combha in the way that elves and humans and dwarves mated their partners. It worked well for them when her parents were each bonded to one of the two. Eire's mother was a shifter, so Combha would be able to relay the message to her as Muinin would certainly reach Eilean before the ships did. Aisla didn't know how much it would help, but it was the only thing she could think to do.

Don't do anything stupid, Muinin interrupted her thoughts.

No promises.

Their arrival had been eerily quiet, and void of any mishaps compared to the last time Aisla had seen this land. Fomhar was different than Briongloid and Eilean. The foliage was red and gold and maroon. Bright red mushrooms littered the ground and the trunks of the trees. Aisla wished they were in the realm under different circumstances. She wished she had the time to stop and study each new plant she came across, to add to her book that was collecting dust on her bedside table.

"And how exactly are we supposed to find this 'friend' that awaits us?" Aisla asked. She had committed Leighis's words to Eire to memory. She turned them over again and again, listening for any godly trickery or empty promises, as she was not so naive to consider herself anything more than a pawn in the game that they played.

"She didn't say," Eire said, but no hint of embarrassment tinted her words—only foolhardy trust in gods that was strengthened by the miracle they granted her. "They will find us."

"Hopefully before the Udar's men do," Ruairi murmured, and Aisla found herself thankful she wasn't the only sane one left.

Still, she winced at the words and the memories they surely aroused, for him specifically.

They were the memories that lead to the visible scars that would never fully disappear and the invisible scars that would never fully heal.

"Did you see a blockade along the Fomhar shoreline?" Eire snapped. "Because I sure didn't. Leighis would have known this. She's helping us—I swear it."

"For now," Aisla added, earning herself a glare from Eire's sharp blue eyes.

"Yes, for now. But now is all that we need, as far as I'm aware."

"Let's at least agree to not trust the first person we see to be this supposed friend," Ruairi said. "We need to lie low and assess the current state of things before we go and put our lives in anyone's hands. We learned last time there are no ash trees on this continent, so we cannot use any of the esos that remains in our blood or we will immediately out ourselves as being from Eilean, and gods know that could go very badly, very quickly. And you can't risk depleting your esos out here, either."

"Speak for yourself," Eire retorted, and hostility laced her words.

"He didn't think about it, Eire." Aisla jumped to Ruairi's defense.

She knew he hadn't meant to bring up esos in front of Eire, who was still grieving the fresh loss of hers.

"Must be nice to be able to forget."

"I'm sorry," Ruairi said. "I should have thought before I spoke. I cannot imagine how you're feeling right now."

"You're right. You can't," Eire said, and effectively shut down the conversation.

They carried on in silence, Aisla's legs growing heavier with each passing breath.

What are you going to do all day when I'm not around? You know, besides trying to save our realm, Aisla asked down the golden thread, growing bored with the silence.

A laugh echoed in her head. *You think my days revolve around you?*

I didn't say that. But you do seem quite clingy with the whole 'how is it over there' talk when hardly a breath has passed since you left.

If I was 'clingy', you would have never been able to leave this realm. You know, before the wyvern caves, there was a time a wyvern would rarely let its bonded out of its sight. Maybe that is a time we should go back to.

I'll pass. I prefer your hot breath anywhere but down my neck.

Then don't be stupid.

I haven't done anything stupid.

Yet—you haven't done anything stupid, yet, Muinin retorted, but his tone was light and teasing. It edged on sarcasm rather than actual aggression. She knew most of the reason he could joke about it was because he trusted himself to get her out of any and every situation.

And maybe that's part of where her own arrogance at Castle Eagla had come from as well.

You didn't answer my question.

I'll do what I need to do. Eat. Sleep. Hunt. And try to sway the wyverns away from those that desire to send your head on a platter to the Udar's doorstep.

The wyverns are turning too?

In most cases, they'll follow their bonded, but not always. Wyverns are much more reasonable creatures than elves are. Also, a thank you would be nice. Politicking is not something I enjoy.

You and me both, Aisla chuckled back, and she heard Muinin chuff in agreement.

That's enough chitchat. I think you should be more focused on your surroundings given you're back in enemy lands. Against my better judgment.

Fomhar isn't enemy land. They backed us in the war.

Yeah, nine generations ago. Just don't do anything stupid, Muinin reiterated.

I think you've mentioned that already, Aisla said, but only silence answered.

As soon as her mind had fallen quiet, Aisla heard a rustling in the woods and instinctively reached for *Oidhe* in her waistband. But it was not the familiar grip of *Oidhe's* hilt that met her touch. Instead, she grasped her new, stolen, and unfamiliar blade and brought it in front of her.

She glanced over at both Ruairi and Eire, who shared her look of concern as they halted their footsteps, slowly reaching for their own weapons.

Aisla turned towards the general direction of the sound and caught a flash of blazing red hair. It was deeper than Ruairi's, but lighter, too. The color of sun rays on an autumn day rather than Ruairi's that was red like the burning of a fire.

Her heart thundered in her chest as she debated carrying on with caution or confronting whoever had been watching them in the woods.

"Hi," a soft, high-pitched voice decided for her. "I mean no harm."

The red-haired female stepped around the brush with her hands raised. Aisla watched her throat bob with a nervous swallow. She was beautiful in a simple sort of way. Freckles spattered her olive skin, and she had light hazel eyes that danced the line between brown and green. She wore a sage-green dress that looked old and worn and was torn in places. A bright red rose stared back at Aisla from inside her dress pocket, and small bits of twigs littered her hair as though she spent too much time amongst the trees.

"My name is Eimear," she said and slowly lowered her hands when Aisla made no move to advance with her blade. "I am a friend of Leighis. And of the *Gheall Ceann*."

41

RANIA

It was the eve of her mating day, and Rania Dorcas could not stand still.

She wiped her palms on her dress and wandered down the hall with a wineglass in hand to where she knew the ceremony was to be held. Her mother and Weylin's had taken it upon themselves to set everything up and decorate it, claiming no one could do it better than they could.

And Rania believed it.

After a dinner with both of their families, Rania found herself wanting to be anywhere but in her room by herself. Her mind was too filled with thoughts that she had no time for. The most prominent of which being Callum's green eyes and the look of hurt on his face when she suggested the idea of a consort. That didn't wound her nearly as much as remembering the words he spoke after, and how genuine they felt to her ears.

Each time she tried to hold on to them, they fell like sand between her fingers.

The dinner was stiff and cold. It was nothing like the flirtatious dinner she and Weylin had shared back in Briongloid.

Something had changed between them, and maybe it was the fact that they had both changed, even in the short time apart. She tried her best to be warm and friendly, and she knew even if their union was not born of a passionate love, Weylin was a male she could grow to love. He would not be a poor mate, and she should find herself fortunate to be his mate. A part of her wished he had never left for Earrach —she wished she had never spent the time getting to know and coming to love Callum Ronan the way that she did.

If she was being honest with herself, it had not taken long to realize how badly she wished it would be Callum waiting for her at the altar the next sunrise. But that was a fool's wish.

After dinner with the Myrkors, their mothers had insisted that Rania get her rest and take an early bedtime for her long day ahead. She had given it an honest effort before her feet led her to them, preferring to have a task than to sit idly by with nothing but the company of her own thoughts.

Rania pushed through the wooden doors to the large ballroom. It felt cold despite the heat of Samhradh.

Three heads turned in her direction as she entered the room. The Udar's mate, her own mother, and Orla—the Udar's rather disturbing and mysterious hand. There had been whispers on the wind that said she was somehow able to use her esos, despite the complete lack of ash trees on Iomlan. There were even more whispers that said the Udar treated her as his own consort. The thought made Rania's stomach turn as she plastered a smile on her lips and raised her wineglass in greeting.

"Thought I might give it my personal touch before the big day."

"Rania, dear, you shouldn't have come!" Niamh Myrkor exclaimed.

"We have it under control," her own mother said at nearly the same time. The two females had gotten along better than Rania could have hoped for. It was the quickest she had ever seen her mother make a friend and seeing them together warmed the bitter heart in her chest. "We don't want you to worry about anything."

"It's not that I'm worried, mother," Rania replied, avoiding the gaze of the fourth female in the room who had yet to speak. She walked over to a table and set her glass down to pick up a garland of pale blue flowers, and followed her mother to where they were hanging them up around a beautiful arch that would serve as their altar. "I want to help. Really, time with you is just what I need right now."

"I know the feeling, dear," her mother spoke, gently, and carried on with the task she had been in the middle of when Rania entered the room. "What do you think so far?"

"It's brilliant. A stunning place for a mating ceremony, truly."

"I'm so glad you think so," Niamh chimed in with her ever-charming voice. "Orla has been such a help, as well. It was her idea to hang the candles from the ceiling like this. So it looks like stars in the night."

"What a lovely idea," Rania replied, keeping her attention fixed on where her pale fingers worked the garland into place.

"Thank you," Orla replied in that too-cheery voice that chilled Rania to her bones. "You'll make a beautiful bride."

"I appreciate it."

Rania felt sorry for Niamh, who had to work alongside Orla as they flitted about the room, decorating it top to bottom in florals, candles, and greenery. It was everything Rania had ever dreamed of, and she was beyond grateful to have her mother at her side. She wondered if Niamh wished she had a daughter, and then remembered that would soon become her role. Niamh would make a lovely mother by mating. Faolan, on the other hand, was an absolute terror, but she'd dealt with his kind her whole life. She'd had her fair share of run-ins with monsters like him at bars and in the marketplace, and he was no more than what they were.

They acted like children with too much confidence that had not heard the word 'no' often enough in life and grew up to make it everyone else's problem.

They finished the decorating just before midnight—Rania continuing to dodge Niamh's and Brigid's insistent remarks that she see herself to bed.

"Well, it looks as beautiful as I had envisioned. More so, even," Brigid spoke up with pride and awe lacing her words. "What do you think, Nia?"

"I couldn't agree more." Rania turned to her mother, whose eye brimmed with tears. "You can't cry now—save it for tomorrow," she teased and embraced her mother in a hug that was tighter than any hug she had ever given.

Her mother clutched her as though it would be the last time she could, and Rania felt nausea enter her stomach.

"You're right," Brigid said.

She pulled away and held Rania's gaze. Her brows crinkled as though she recognized a change in her daughter, but Niamh interrupted her before she could say anything about it. A breath of relief filled Rania's chest.

"We've all got a long day ahead of us," she said. "I think we're finished here. Thank you for your help—we could not feel more blessed to host this union."

"The thanks is all ours," Brigid chirped back. She turned from Rania and followed Niamh from the room. Rania did not follow as she glanced back at all their hard work, and her mother noticed immediately. "Aren't you coming, Nia?"

"I will soon. I think I'd like some time alone here first. It'll be rather crowded tomorrow, I believe."

Her mother smiled with understanding and nodded softly. "Sleep well, my love."

"You too, mother."

The three females exited the room, Orla remaining eerily quiet as they did so, and the sound of the door thudding shut behind them reverberated through Rania's core as her shoulders sagged with a weight she hadn't realized she had been carrying.

She breathed out a long breath and sat down at one of the long tables where strangers would watch her bind her life to another the following sunrise.

Her throat grew tight with foreboding as she glanced around the grand room, and the decorations that felt both like her and foreign. She tipped her head back and closed her eyes. Rania imagined she was outside atop one of the mountains in Briongloid—able to reach the clouds around her like greeting a friend.

She stayed there for a long while. Long enough that the clock sounded to alert her to the changing of the days, and long enough that she found her eyes falling shut with every blink.

Rania gathered herself and walked towards the doors. She pulled one open, and a gasp escaped her as she spotted Callum Ronan walking past the corridor. She let the door fall shut and slipped back into the room, hoping he had not noticed her.

Just my terrible, terrible luck, she thought to herself as she leaned her back against the door, taking quick breaths in and out.

The door next to her pushed open slowly, and she wished she had leaned against the middle, able to hold both shut with the weight of her body. Then, she realized how childish and unbecoming that would look, and she breathed out a puff of air to push a hair from her eyes and turned to meet Callum's familiar eyes from where he peered around the door that he had not fully opened.

"What are you doing?" he asked. There was no malice in his voice. But there was no warmth either.

"I was helping decorate," Rania replied, and she swore Callum could hear her heart thundering if he listened closely enough.

He pushed the door fully open and glanced about the room that suddenly felt entirely too small. He stepped inside and the door fell shut behind him, echoing through Rania's bones.

"You decorated for your own mating ceremony, alone?"

"No."

"Where is everyone, then?"

"They went to bed."

"Then why didn't you?"

"Why aren't you asleep?" she snapped, losing her patience with the interrogation that he had no right to give.

"Couldn't sleep."

"Sulking in the halls, I see."

Callum rolled his eyes as he continued to glance about the ornately decorated room. "Your tongue grows sharp, Rania."

Rania's breath caught in her throat as she made a conscious effort to suppress the feeling in her stomach that arose from her name on his lips.

"It's always been sharp, my lord," she drawled. "You once found it amusing."

"You are many things, but I wouldn't consider amusing one of them."

"Oh? You find me a bore?"

"Of course not, and you know that, too. But you'd sell yourself short to call yourself amusing—you're more than that. There is depth beyond entertainment in that sharp tongue."

"Hmm," Rania hummed from where she still leaned against the door.

"Why did you try to hide when you saw me in the hallway?"

"We hadn't exactly left on good terms."

Callum paused and turned to face her, and the intensity in the green of his eyes and the lines that creased his forehead were nearly too much for Rania to bear. But she pressed her lips into a thin line and cocked her head to the side, matching his look with her own.

He took a step forward, and Rania tensed.

"I should go to bed," she whispered.

"You should," he said, but stepped closer to her.

He leaned over her, bracing his arm against the wooden door, and Rania had never felt so out of control as she was in that moment.

In a reality crafted by what little she could control, Rania had prided herself in being the mastermind of the life that had resulted with her in the capital of all the realms. But it was here, suppressing a tremble beneath the weight of Callum Ronan's gaze, that Rania found herself at a loss.

"You're making that rather difficult."

"Enough of this game, Rania," Callum whispered the words softly, no hint of aggression in that familiar voice. "Are you really going to go through with it?"

Rania opened her mouth to speak, but found her voice was empty when she tried.

She swallowed, wishing the silence would consume her whole as she grieved something that had never been hers.

The air between them thickened until it was hard to breathe. Time slowed until suddenly Callum's lips were on hers, drawing a surprised gasp from her as she leaned into him without hesitation. Her fingers found his brown curls she had once dreamed of touching like this.

His arms wrapped around her lower back and tightened around her as though she could slip through his grasp at any moment. It felt exactly how Rania knew it would.

It was painstakingly perfect.

The kind of feeling one only finds in one soul ever, and that soul could never be hers.

He kissed her with all the passion any lover she had taken had always lacked. If he was not holding her weight up with his embrace, she was sure her shaky legs would've given out.

A tear fell from the corner of her eye until the drop of salty water found its way into their kiss as though a reminder of their love's brevity.

Rania pulled away, but Callum held her in place as they both breathed out heavy breaths.

"I don't want to lose you," was all she could think to say as she stared into the eyes of the only man who had ever seen her—all of her.

"That's your decision, not mine," Callum replied. "You know I choose you."

Those words. *I choose you.* Those words were enough to fracture the wall of ice Rania had forged around her too-delicate heart. Tears blurred her vision as she gently placed her hands on Callum's chest and pushed, even as she felt the threads binding their very souls pulling and straining with a pain that was unbearable.

"I have to go," she whispered through trembling lips. Rania turned and threw open the door to her right.

She lifted her skirts and ran down the familiar, cold hallway to her room. She prayed to the unforgiving gods that they would erase the memory of the way his eyes fell when she pushed away from him. Along with the feeling of his skin on hers.

A feeling she did not deserve.

And never would.

42

RUAIRI

"Prove it," Aisla growled from beside Ruairi. Pure authority sounded through her voice in a way that raised the hair along his arms.

Ruairi had to give the female before them credit when she did not flinch. She held her ground, and even took a step towards their trio—despite the blades they held—her loose red curls bouncing with the movement. She was beautiful, despite the messiness about her. Her hair was a brighter red than his own, and her hazel eyes glimmered like molten amber in the morning sun.

"Leighis visited me and told me there would be three from another realm seeking shelter here in my own," she replied, confidently.

"That's not very specific," Aisla cut in.

Ruairi knew she was perhaps being overly harsh, but he could not blame the ghosts that plagued her memory of their last time on Iomlan. He could hardly breathe since setting foot on their shores, and worked to calm his racing heart with every step he took towards this dangerous place that he knew all too well.

"I was told to expect you, Aisling, our *Gheall Ceann*." She nodded towards Aisla and Aisla only narrowed her eyes. "And Ruairi of the winds," she turned her attention to him. He did not react. "And Eire, the faithful."

Eire blinked at that—a blink of approval, and he knew Aisla noted it, too. And as they had done so far, they would trust Eire. They owed her that much. Eire lowered her weapon first. Aisla and Ruairi followed.

Aisla took a step towards the female.

"You have friends in Fomhar, Aisling Iarkis. I cannot say the same of the other realms."

Her words sent a shadow of foreboding through Ruairi, and his esos rushed in response. He shook the feeling away with a shrug of his shoulders and waited for Aisla to respond.

"Does that mean there's a rebellion?" Aisla asked, and he heard the cautious hope in her voice.

"There is much you do not know about Iomlan," Eimear replied rather evasively. "Just as there is much Iomlan does not know about you. However, there are many willing to support the *Gheall Ceann* regardless of what is known about her. There are many who believe the prophecy that says you are our only chance at survival. The nine forms of esos in your blood will save us from the fall of the realms as we know them in the Inevitable War."

"Thank you," Aisla said, shifting uncomfortably.

"There is no need to thank us. While I am sure my family will be excited to meet you, it is not for you. It is for the nine realms—for a peace we have lacked for far too long."

Ruairi stayed silent as he watched Aisla nod and give a simple reply: "I understand."

"Who is your family?" Eire asked, speaking up for the first time since the female revealed herself.

"Do you know many families in Fomhar?" Eimear replied, but she did not ask maliciously. There was a humorous tone in her voice.

"No, I suppose not," Eire replied.

Eimear nodded in response. "So, are you willing to trust me, *Gheall Ceann*?"

"That is not my choice alone."

Pride filled Ruairi's chest at Aisla's response. Not necessarily because he wanted a say, but because she spoke with the strength of a true leader and the confidence of a loyal friend.

"I trust her," Eire replied, much to no one's surprise.

"Well, I suppose that means I do, too." Ruairi said, and all eyes turned in his direction.

"You can speak freely," Aisla said.

"I know," Ruairi responded. "And I am. We didn't come all this way to start second guessing ourselves now."

"Thank you for your trust," Eimear interjected, glancing between Aisla and Ruairi. "Now, I'm going to show you something, and it will require trust on my part. Fomhar has kept a secret for almost as long as the War for Descendants. We've only been able to keep it by keeping the Myrkors out of our hair, and I hope you will do the same to help us."

"I'm listening," Aisla said, as she folded her arms across her chest wearily.

Eimear let out a low whistle, and a rustling sounded in the woods behind her. Beyond the mass of bushes and brush appeared a beast with the body of a lion and the head and wings of an eagle.

A gryphon.

Ruairi's mouth dropped open as the beast shook out its long, feathered wings and snapped its beak in a warning.

"How?" Aisla blurted immediately.

"As I said," Eimear started as she walked to the creature and petted its long neck. Ruairi watched it lean into her and felt a yearning for Gaotha. "We keep the Myrkors out, and we fly as low to the ground as we can. The gryphons understand, and they don't want to be discovered either. They were forced to fight in wars for as far back as history dates, and they were never meant to serve us. In Fomhar, they are equal to us, and when the time comes, it will be their choice to take part in the war or not."

"I didn't know they ever truly existed. I thought they were just a myth," Eire spoke up and the awe in her voice was clear as her eyes widened in response to the creature.

"Maira is very much real and not a myth," Eimear said with a small laugh. "She's brought a friend along so we can sit two per gryphon on our way to my home."

"Where will we be going?" Ruairi asked, feeling rather skeptical of hopping on this creature he had only just met.

"To Sruthar," Eimear answered, and Ruairi immediately recognized the capital of Fomhar and was wary to fall into any more capital cities where the politics were played. "Where my home is—Castle Orga."

Ruairi's heart sank.

43
AISLA

Aisla wound her fingers deep into the feathers of the creature she thought only existed in myths. And here it was, beneath her—very much real and very much alive and very much holding her life in its claws. The thought sent a shudder down her back.

It had been easy enough to trust Eolas. A drop from the mare would cause a broken bone at worst or minimal bruising at best. She had been close enough to the ground to feel safe. Atop Alfson, as Eimear told her he was called, she felt herself feigning trust in him as her heart thundered in her chest.

She was sure Ruairi could feel it from where he sat behind her. Eire, on the other hand, looked much freer and more comfortable in front of Eimear, who knew how to handle the gryphons.

Eimear gave Ruairi and Aisla a crash course in gryphon, if you could even call it that. They had two test flights before they left for Castle Orga, which was not a short flight. Sruthar, the capital of

Fomhar, was deep into the realm, closer to the border shared with Bitu.

Eimear had spoken true when she said they flew as low as they could to remain undetected, so they weren't as high up as Muinin would take her, but they were still much higher than a horse, and the thought made Aisla nauseous. She had never trusted a flight by anyone except Muinin and Combha. She had not even gone solo with Gaotha, Ruairi's wyvern before.

Muinin had made his opinion on the matter plenty clear with sarcastic quips throughout the flight that found their way into her mind. She knew it was his way to both try to lighten her situation and express his disapproval at her choice of flying companion. Aisla only rolled her eyes. She knew even if he could not see her reaction, he could feel it down that golden thread that connected them, body and now mind.

Ruairi was tense behind her and had stayed mostly silent throughout the flight. Aisla had sensed his nerves and fear since the moment they set foot on land, and she understood why. Their previous journey had taken a toll on them both in ways the other could never imagine. They both had trauma to sort through and process, as well as lives that they could never return to.

But Aisla knew beyond a doubt Ruairi's was worse than hers, and there was no comparison. It took one look down at the hand that gripped her waist and the missing finger to envelop her in a cloud of guilt so thick she could hardly breathe through it, and sometimes she wondered if she deserved to.

"You okay, Ash?" Ruairi's voice rumbled from behind her, and the guilt faded at the warmth in it—the warmth she knew she could never earn.

She also knew she should've been the one asking him that question.

"I'm fine. Muinin's just being a jealous grouch," she replied, part lie and part truth. He was, but just not at that moment.

"That must be so weird to just hear him in your head like that. Weird, but so cool. And I imagine helpful, too."

"You could say that," she smiled to herself. "I bet Gaotha would have a much kinder voice than him."

"I believe it. Maybe one day you can talk to her for me. I would love to tell her how much she has always meant to me."

"Of course," Aisla replied without hesitation. "Are you doing okay? I hate that I brought you back here. I wish there was another way, but I'm not sure how safe Eilean is anymore."

"It's okay. I think we made the right choice trusting Eire. But only time will tell."

"So cryptic today, Ru," she teased.

"I know. I'm sorry—I don't mean to be."

"I'm only joking. And I could never blame you, you know? I would've stayed on Eilean if you didn't want to come here. I would have never forced you to. And I would never leave you. Well, not again or not by choice."

"I know, and that is the only reason I followed."

"I'm glad you did . . . I'm glad we did."

The conversation felt stilted and uncomfortable. It was so far from where they had once been, but she didn't know why. Aisla only knew that she desperately missed the Ruairi that had been her best friend and closest confidant. She missed the Ruairi that had held her and traced circles on the back of her hand when she lost herself to the darkness of her esos.

"Are we okay, Ash?"

He asked the question she had been dreading since she disappeared from his bed on that fearful night, she had been torn from sleep upon returning to her own baile. That night felt like it was moons away now—almost like it was some sort of dream.

She loved Ruairi. She did. And she always would.

But as the *Gheall Ceann*, she no longer felt capable of loving someone the way she had thought she loved Ruairi that night in the tent beneath the pouring rain of foreign realms. It wasn't fair to her or to whatever mate she would take. The Udar had swiftly reminded her of that, as did every scar that maimed Ruairi's body and every shallow breath that fell from his lips upon their return to Iomlan.

And Aisla may be selfish for choosing to live, and choosing her own life over whatever life the prophecy had given her, but she was not selfish enough to hurt Ruairi that badly ever again.

"Of course we are, Ru. We're always good. Why wouldn't we be?" She brushed away the sentiment behind the question. It was not the time nor the place, despite the fact that Ruairi deserved a proper answer and not the dismissal she had given him.

"There's a lot we haven't talked about."

"I know. Another day, please."

"Sure," came his one-word response.

Her heart tore at the answer, and even more at the fact that there was no bitterness in his voice, no bite. Purely understanding and patience that she did not deserve.

"You're still my favorite person," Aisla said. "Just don't tell Eire."

"Hmm," Ruairi hummed, and Aisla felt it in her core. "That sounds like the perfect information to hold over your head," he teased and playfully squeezed her side where he held her.

"I'll be sure to be on my best behavior," she teased back.

"I'm sure you will."

"It's beautiful here. You know, once you get past the idea of flying with creatures that we didn't even know were real," Aisla said, not wanting to stop speaking yet. Not wanting to fall into the silence she had grown all too comfortable with.

Alfson gave a puff of defiance at her words, and she patted him on the side in apology.

"It really is," Ruairi agreed. "I always thought Fomhar would be beautiful. We are lucky to experience it."

"We really are," Aisla agreed. "Here's to hoping we survive it."

Ruairi chuckled humorlessly behind her, and Aisla watched the trees of maroon and marigold and burnt orange slide by beneath the gryphon's feathered wings. She leaned into Ruairi as they took it all in. It was comfortable and safe.

While she wished they were travelling under different circumstances, she knew they were both driven to adventure. And getting to see Fomhar from above was something she never thought she would be able to do.

Aisla took in the mountains, streams, and forests. She committed them to memory as they flew.

Their gryphons landed near the castle that was as dreamy as the rest of the realm had been.

Castle Orga was nestled between majestic maple trees in a variety of warm and inviting colors. The walls were made of grey stones of assorted shades and sizes, and ended in a maroon tiled roof. It looked cozier than either Castle Farraige or Castle Eagla. It looked like a place Aisla would have enjoyed living in, in another life.

"Here, my baile is just outside the castle perimeter. I live there most of the time. Politicking isn't for me, if that wasn't obvious enough," Eimear said as she gestured towards her tattered dress and twig-filled hair.

Aisla would have never guessed the female came from nobility. She had to catch her jaw from dropping to the ground when she first told them. But she understood it.

She had told Cliona the very same thing when Eire and Ruairi moved out of their parents' bailes. It was the independence and normalcy that she so craved. Aisla was warming to Eimear, even if she did not yet fully trust her. The female radiated tenderness. There was something about her that was so unlike anyone else Aisla had ever met.

"I still have a room in Castle Orga, of course, and I stay there with my siblings from time to time, but I've always been a bit of the castaway of the family, in a sense."

"I know that feeling," Aisla responded lightly.

They followed Eimear around the castle walls and towards a baile that was even smaller than Aisla's humble abode. It was covered in beautiful twining vines of ivy, and more of those bright red mushrooms. Even though Aisla had known Eimear for a short span of time, it seemed like exactly the sort of place the female would live. And the inside was even more suited to her.

Eimear led the way wordlessly and pushed open the oak door that was rounded at the top. She invited them into a warm space that smelled of honey and tea. It was all one room, except for the washroom. It was similar to Aisla's own home.

A quilt of autumnal flowers edged in a deep yellow fabric covered the bed. A teal teapot and a still-full teacup sat on the small wooden table, as though she had last left in the middle of drinking it.

The place was messy in a comfortable sort of way. Things were strewn about, but it was not off-putting. In fact, it was the opposite. It felt lived in and inviting, as though anyone that entered the home was trusted enough to see into Eimear's very being—to see the parts of her both messy and put together.

"Sorry, it's a little tight in here. I don't often have company," Eimear spoke with no hint of shyness, and Aisla decided she liked the female. "I do have clothes for you to wear. My brother, Cillian, dropped them off while I went to meet you at the shore. My parents are still rather traditional about things, and while they are friends of the *Gheall Ceann,* they would take better to harboring the most wanted being in the nine realms if you show up in something a little more," Eimear paused to look them up and down, "formal."

Even though there was no judgement on her face, Aisla had never felt so nude while fully clothed.

"Do they know we're coming?" Ruairi asked, and Aisla realized she had not yet considered that they might show up unwarranted and unwanted.

Eimear was silent a moment as she turned to open a closet door, where she shuffled through fabrics out of Aisla's line of sight.

"No, they don't." Eimear answered, and Aisla's heart sunk into her stomach.

44

WEYLIN

Weylin Myrkor thought it would feel different when he stood at the end of the aisle waiting for his mate.

It's not that he ever thought it would feel like love, but at the very least that he would feel a contented peace. He'd imagined a calmness when he took his mate's hand, and he felt anything but.

His mind was restless, and there was something about it all that felt so very wrong. A feeling that it was far too late to think more on.

If he glanced to his right, he knew he would see Callum. If he glanced to his left, there was Oisin, ready to take his place at his sister's side during her mating ceremony.

Weylin's own mother, father, and Orla sat on one side of the first row, while Rania's parents sat on the other. Tears glistened in her mother's eye.

When Weylin's eyes met Orla's, a chill travelled down his arms as though she had sent a wave of cold to haunt him. There was something so wrong about the female who could wield esos without the source present. His father had never told him how she did it, but a part of him would always resent the fact that she could while he could not.

Weylin cleared his throat and raised his eyes to the sizeable crowd of people that he barely knew. Some were his laochs who had been his only and closest friends his whole life, but the rest were friends of his father, who were in and out of the castle and spread whispers like the wind.

A long, slow breath drawled from his lips as he blinked slowly.

He tuned out all the noise and focused on the door ahead where the Gem of Dreams would soon stroll into the room. He found himself pitying the female as the doors opened slowly and she entered the room, glowing as brightly as the moons.

A brilliant white dress decorated with pale blue embroidery accentuated her slim frame, the curves of her hips, and where the corset hugged her torso. It was a dress fit for a ruler of the realms, and a dress fit for his mate. She looked stunning and regal. Rania Dorcas looking like everything he could ever hope for in a mate.

She blinked her long, light lashes once, then looked up to meet his gaze.

He recognized she was not the same Rania he had met in Briongloid. She was older, wiser, and had changed in ways he could not yet know. He did not know how he had not recognized it before and wondered how blind he had been to her feelings and her needs while he was away in Earrach.

Something stirred in his chest that he could not place as he shifted his feet and pushed his shoulders back to stand straighter. He smiled warmly to Rania—let her know they were in this together. He would be a better mate to her than his father had ever been to his mother. That much he was certain of.

This was the beginning of their story, and while his attention was constantly pulled countless different ways, Rania would come first.

He could feel every beat of his heart as he watched Rania walk towards him, all on her own, leaning on no one for support. Her footsteps were so smooth, so graceful, she seemed to glide down that long aisle towards him, and for a moment, Weylin allowed himself to imagine it was just the two of them in the room.

She held his gaze up until the very end. There was an unease there, and he felt it too, but he was thankful she trusted him enough to keep her eyes trained on him in her moment of discomfort.

"Hi," he murmured to her when she finally reached her place at his side.

"Hi," she whispered back in that soft voice of hers.

She held a beautiful bouquet of small white flowers against her chest and her hands shook slightly as the priestess of Cion, the god of love and fate, cleared her throat to speak.

"We are gathered here to celebrate the union of our Udar Apparent, Lord Weylin Myrkor, and the daughter of Lord Brendan Dorcas, Rania Dorcas, first of her name," the female started and Weylin's breathing began to fall in short, ragged breaths. He could only hope Rania did not notice, but he was almost certain she did as anyone with elf senses would. "It is with great honor that we see their two houses joined today under the eyes of our nine just and fair gods. Everyone here in attendance—here to witness an event that the world tellers will write about for generations to come—is privileged to be a part of this turning point of Talam."

The words droned on and on, adding pressure to Weylin's lungs, which grew increasingly harder to draw breath. He did not hear all the words, but enough of them to know that everything he was told about mating was true. He was moments away from signing his life away and binding it to another in the eyes of the gods under the influence of the norns.

There was a moment just before the priestess finished her spiel. A moment when lightning seemed to jolt through Weylin, and all the world tilted on its axis. His stomach felt nauseous, and his mind was dizzy.

"Do you Rania Dorcas, agree to tie the blessed thread of your lifeblood to Weylin Myrkor's from this moment until your passing on?"

"I do," she replied and looked warmly up at him.

Her eyes were encouraging, almost as though she was nervous he would not repeat the same words.

He recalled then that vague statement she had made when he asked for her hand in mating all those sunrises ago.

I will become your betrothed until air turns to fire.

It had struck him as odd then. They were not words he had heard before, but recalling them now stirred something ancient and foreign within him.

He forced a smile back, hoping it came across better than he felt as the priestess spoke once again.

"Do you, Weylin Myrkor, agree to tie the blessed thread of your lifeblood to Rania Dorcas—"

Weylin's ears rang, and every sound in the room blurred to white noise at the words.

As if on cue, a golden thread erupted from his left hand. It glimmered in the light of the candles decorating the room and pulled from him to form a trail through the door Rania had entered from.

This was not a part of the mating ceremony. That much Weylin knew for certain.

Panic blossomed in his chest. Weylin was choking for air as he snapped his fist shut. It did not cut off the golden thread that pulled him from his altar.

Without looking back, Weylin ran. He couldn't look at Rania. He didn't want to face the look in her eyes when she noticed the golden thread that did not run to her.

Weylin ignored the gasps and shouts. He ignored Rania's cry and the boom of his father's voice. He pushed it all away as he chased after that golden thread, praying to the gods that nobody else had seen it erupt from his sweating palm.

Weylin could only hope he'd left in time.

He cursed under his breath and burst through the castle doors into the cool air of the night, surrounded by the light of two full moons and stars that seemed to mock him as he ran towards Eolas.

He realized the thread was leading him away—out of Omra and how far after that, he could not know. Weylin prayed his fears did not come true.

He had no choice. He could not let anyone see the mark of the norns. No one could know what he feared it meant.

45

AISLA

isla had imagined evenings like this.

If the prophecy would have never been whispered, and if her family had remained seated upon the throne gifted to them by the gods, her evenings would have been spent a lot like this. Castle Farraige had once held a more formal court as well. Her mother hadn't been alive to see it, nor had Cliona, but she knew her ancestors had.

Eimear had given Aisla a beautiful deep green gown to wear. It was made of silk so soft, it felt like nothing at all. There was a layer of lace made patterned in ivy leaves that shimmered in the moonlight. It slipped onto her body as if it had been made for her and her return to Iomlan. She still wore her wyvern tooth necklace.

Aisla felt like something beyond someone who was hunted for once. She felt like the *Gheall Ceann* rather than the *mallaithe* people wished her to be. She looked in the mirror and saw someone who could change the realms—someone who could unite them at last.

Dresses were not regularly a part of her attire in Caillte, as she was too often training with her blade. It was different and new.

A lilac dress had been given to Eire. It was simpler, but elegant all the same. Butterflies decorated the hem and scattered up the sleeves. They were sparser as they got higher up on the dress.

Ruairi dressed in a collared white shirt with a dark brown jacket that matched the pants Eimear gave him. He looked as handsome as ever, even when his unease was written all over his face.

Eimear had done Aisla's hair as well. She braided the light brown mess down her back with a strand of white gypsophila flowers woven into it.

"You look perfect," Ruairi breathed out when she stood and walked towards him.

Eire took the seat next for Eimear to weave her hair in a low braided bun.

"So do you," Aisla murmured as a blush crept into her cheeks.

Ruairi held his hand out to her, and Aisla gently placed hers in it. He lifted it to his lips and placed a gentle kiss there—something he had never done before. They had never been in a situation where it would have been appropriate. But in a life where ball gowns and formal dinners were commonplace, she supposed he would have done it countless times.

"I mean it," he whispered, still holding her hand in his.

"Thank you," she said with a smile. She threw her arms over his shoulders and his arms wound around her waist, pulling her into him. "I did, too."

She didn't want to let go. She breathed in his familiar scent, and it brought back so many memories of home.

Eire cleared her throat, and Aisla and Ruairi quickly pulled away.

"Get a room," she teased.

Aisla's cheeks heated with embarrassment. She shook it off and trotted to Eire. She pulled Eire into a hug then, and it was different from Ruairi. It was lighter, but just as full of love.

"You look lovely, Eire," Aisla said to her best friend.

"You look like our *Gheall Ceann*," she whispered back, and a chill travelled through Aisla's bones.

"Thank you."

Aisla released Eire and turned to look at Eimear, who looked upon the three friends with admiration in her eyes.

"Much better," Eimear chirped, assessing the three of them. "I am ready to take you to my family now—if you are?"

"We are," Aisla replied.

She felt like she was finding a part of herself that she thought would never be uncovered, even though it was all so far outside her realm of comfortability.

And she felt even further outside her realm of comfortability as Eimear led the three of them up the steps of Castle Orga.

Her life was always destined to be one of politicking, but this was truly her first time venturing out to do so. Aisla rubbed her sweaty palms on her dress as she recalled the grace with which her mother held herself and tried her best to emulate it.

They were greeted by a dwarf with deep auburn hair upon entering the castle. A playful smirk lifted the corners of his lips when he laid his eyes upon Eimear.

"And the princess returns to the castle. Who have you brought with you?"

"Lovely to see you, Nevin. Hope you haven't missed me too greatly," Eimear replied with a familiarity to her voice that told Aisla she had known the male for a long time. "This is Eire, and Ruairi, and Aisla."

Aisla's jaw nearly fell open as Eimear introduced them with no hesitancy. She had half a mind to snap at her for her foolishness, but she clenched her jaw and worked to maintain a neutral expression.

"You can't be serious. Aisla, as in the Aisling Iarkis?"

"The very same," Eimear answered with almost a twinge of gloating.

Aisla felt uneasy as the dwarf's eyes moved to meet her own. She matched his look with an even glance, willing him to look away while refusing to do so herself.

"It's an honor to meet you," Nevin spoke with awe that brought a heat to Aisla's cheeks. It deepened when he bowed at his waist.

Her lips opened to stop him, but this was not Eilean, and she needed the people here to see her as worthy of their following, and worthy of their sacrifices. So, she waited for Nevin to stand upright and nodded to him in gratitude.

"And it is my pleasure to meet you, Nevin."

"As you can imagine, I'm hoping to get a word with my parents as soon as I can," Eimear interrupted with waning patience.

"They're in the green dining room," Nevin replied without hesitation. "With all your siblings, of course. They're drinking to our royal wedding. For better or for worse. In case you forgot, the Udar Apparent mates the lady-in-waiting of Briongloid this sunset."

Aisla choked.

All eyes turned on her. Suddenly, the hall was too small. The air was too tight.

Her breaths were too hollow. Her heart was too fast. Her body was too far.

She blinked once, then twice. She blinked away the burn in her eyes she had not expected. Something deep within her burned as her palms itched, but she worked against every tensed muscle in her overly alert body to appear unfazed by the news—to appear as though she had already known it.

Weylin Myrkor—mated.

The thought tasted like bile on her tongue, and she wondered what this new alliance would mean for the future of the realms. Briongloid had supported Eilean in the war. To lose them to Samhradh would be a significant loss indeed.

How had she not known? Surely, Cliona knew, and surely, the word had spread through Eilean. Something this huge would not stay silent from the whispers on the wind. She supposed she might have heard it had she not spent so much time in an underground secret library and wyvern caves.

And it hadn't been long at all since she had left Iomlan. Hardly long enough to plan a mating, let alone a betrothal. Aisla wondered if he was betrothed when their lips met beside the rushing of the river. She shook her head, clearing the thought. If nothing else, it proved what an unworthy male he was to sit *her* throne.

How he was just like his father.

Aisla swallowed deeply and looked to Eimear as she continued. They all pretended they had not noticed the sound of discomfort that had come from Aisla's throat.

"The Dorcases are truly cowards for that. Brendan's father would never have approved the union," Eimear sneered with clear distaste.

"Couldn't agree more," Nevin replied, gruffly. "Good luck with your situation. I'm sure I'll see you again soon. And Aisling Iarkis, know that my life is yours, and I dutifully await the day my sword will shed the blood of enemies in your name."

Aisla had only read those words in books. In the fictional accounts of war that told the tale like a bedtime story but hearing them aloud and hearing them spoken to her—in *her* name—drove a chill down Aisla's back and raised the hair along her arms.

"I will never find the words to tell you just how much I appreciate that. I will spend every waking moment making myself worthy of your oath."

Something like admiration glimmered in Nevin's brown eyes. And something like grief, for a dynasty that could have been. He nodded and continued down the corridor, allowing Aisla's words to linger in the air around them.

Eimear let out a low whistle. "You're better at this politicking thing than I thought you would be."

"It was hardly politicking," Aisla responded and folded her hands behind her back. "I've spent my life running from the weight of my name, and if people are willing to serve me the way that Nevin is, it's time I embrace it. I hope it becomes a name that ignites a hope for the realms and a light in the dark."

"Spoken like our rightful *banrion*," Ruairi murmured, and yet another chill raced down Aisla's back as she turned to look at his green eyes that shimmered with emotion.

The word meant *queen* in Aosta. It was a title used before there was one Udar. When a *banrion* and a *ri* would rule the nine realms side by side with the lords and ladies of the realms as their counsel.

"I couldn't have said it better myself," Eire added softly, but proudly.

"Well," Eimear started, "that was much more emotional than I ever expected to get with the *Gheall Ceann* and her friends. I think it's past time we find my parents, and alert them to your arrival before the whispers on the wind alert them for us. Shall we?"

Eimear looked to Aisla, who nodded in return and followed Eimear through the castle that felt like a warm autumn day.

Aisla tried to think of anything but the amber eyes of Weylin Myrkor that haunted her every step. She tried and failed. She couldn't get it through her mind that he would be mated to the daughter of Briongloid that evening.

Before Aisla knew it, Eimear had pushed open a great oak door with no warning. The hall was flooded with candlelight as Aisla Iarkis interrupted the dinner of the Shea family. All seven pairs of eyes fell upon them with a weight that nearly caved Aisla's shoulders in.

"Eimear! I wish you would reply to my letters when I send them!" a childish voice whined, and that weight was immediately lifted.

The moment of levity released a fraction of the building tension between Aisla's shoulders.

"Yes, well, we can talk later about that, Halli. We have company," Eimear cut in, jerking her chin towards the trio standing in the doorway.

Aisla's heart pounded in her chest, and she realized she was more unprepared for this moment than fighting the barghests in Briongloid. She cleared her throat, preparing to speak, when a male voice cut her off.

"Excuse my daughter's manners." A red-haired male stood from his seat and crossed the room to them. The rest followed him, even the young female, although not without an exaggerated sigh. "Whom do we have the pleasure of hosting this evening?"

Aisla took a deep breath, and spoke, "The pleasure is mine. My name is Aisling Iarkis."

The Lord and Lady of Fomhar's jaws fell open at the words, and their eyes widened.

Aisla braced herself for whatever their response may be. It was a risk for her to be there. Imposing herself upon this family put them in opposition to the Udar who would hunt her down if he knew of her return to Iomlan. The Udar who was probably already hunting for her back on Eilean, where his ships had invaded. Aisla's insides turned at the thought. She pushed it away as she focused on handling whatever this conversation was about to turn into.

She locked eyes with the Lord of Fomhar, trying to get a read in the depths of their warm brown. He looked frightened—frightened and relieved. Aisla allowed herself to hope as she waited with bated breath.

"Our *Gheall Ceann*—promised of the gods—we are honored to be in your presence."

The Lord of Fomhar's voice boomed through the room, and Aisla swallowed her nerves as everyone in the room bowed to her.

Everyone including Eimear, and Eire, and Ruairi.

She fought every instinct to ask them to stop, and she forced her shoulders back to stand taller.

Aisla nodded her gratitude as they all stood and faced her again, waiting for her to respond.

"Thank you," she said awkwardly, unsure of how else to respond to the gesture. "I understand the position we put you in by coming here, but we seek safety as Eilean is no longer safe for us. Our Mathair has turned against us and believes the worst of the whispers of the prophecy. She will do anything for power and has struck a deal with the Udar to claim hers. That deal includes handing me over to him, and I understand Fomhar might be on our side of the prophecy. I had to seek shelter, and the goddess Leighis appeared to my friend and told us to come here. Should you choose to help us, you will have my eternal gratitude. I will do everything in my power to keep you and your people safe in the war to come. That being said, I would not blame you if you turned us away."

Aisla rubbed her palms together, fearing she had said too much or too little. She could not change it now. She could only stand firm in what she said and hope for the best.

"We have long awaited your arrival. We always knew it would come to this—that Fomhar would be asked to join the war in favor of the Promised One. And we always knew we would accept that call, may it please the gods. What we did not know is you would show up seeking shelter, not an alliance. We did not know you would appear without the force of your own home to back you."

"My home is divided. There are many who will respond to my call when the time comes, but it is true that my grandmother has her own followers as well. What I can say is that I learned a helpful detail between my arrival back home and my quick departure back to Iomlan," Aisla paused. "My father lives. My grandmother does not know this, yet, but he lives in a community full of world tellers, and they will back me when the time comes. The *Gheall Ceann* has friends in the south of Eilean, even if Caillte has turned against me. We have our wyverns as well, and my own is rallying his friends and his family."

The Lord of Fomhar tilted his head, evaluating her thoughtfully, and she had never felt more vulnerable. He had far too much power over her, and she cursed herself for allowing them to fall into this position.

"We will host you for as long as you should need it. And we shall follow you into war when you ask us to. Fomhar and whatever resources we have are at your disposal, as we know without you—the nine realms are sure to fall."

A burning energy filled Aisla's chest, and it spread through the room from everyone there. It was an energy of hope, of dreams, and of things yet to pass.

And for the first time in a long time, Aisla allowed herself to hope.

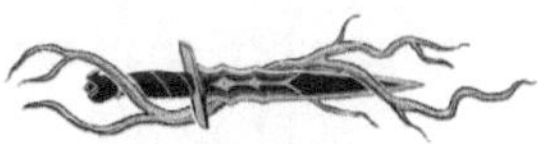

Aisla dreamt she was running from something she could not see and could not name. She dreamt her legs carried her faster than she knew they were capable of.

Her heart thundered with the fear of imminent death as she ran into a dark forest where she could hardly see beyond her own fingertips.

Then, threads of shimmering gold lit her vision. They were strung between branches of the dead trees and knit around their trunks. They grew denser as she ran, but Aisla could not force her legs to turn around. She broke through a few and ducked when she could until she was caught in a web of golden threads.

She couldn't move.

They wound around her arms. Her legs. Her throat. Her mouth.

They suspended her in the air beneath the moons, and suppressed her calls for help until they blinded her.

Aisla saw no more. She screamed no more.

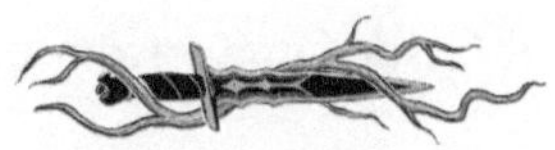

Aisla jolted upright, gasping for air as she dug her fingers into the emerald-green cover on her bed. She panted as she looked around the room.

That was when she noticed it.

She looked down and saw the single shimmering golden thread from her dreams that extended from her left palm. She pulled at it with her right hand, and her fingers slipped right through it, as if it was not there at all.

Aisla stood, and the thread followed her. She recalled the stories of the norns her parents told her when they tucked her into bed. They were known to control the fates of all beings by their golden threads on the Crann Na Beatha.

Threads that symbolized births, deaths, mates, and every step along the way.

She blinked. Once. Twice. Three times, and the thread continued to linger before her, and she knew those silent gods were once again sending her a message. One she could not ignore. Because whatever—whoever—was on the other end could follow it to Fomhar, and she needed to be a step ahead.

Aisla packed a bag, moving as quietly as possible, knowing Ruairi and Eire slept in the rooms on either side of her. They had taken her clothes down into the washroom, so she unfortunately had to make do with a simple sage-green night gown and a dark brown cloak that she pulled on over her shoulders. She tugged her gnarled hair into a braid that fell over her left shoulder.

Aisla sat down at the desk and gently pulled a piece of parchment and a quill from the drawer, and her hand began to move.

She finished the note and laid it gently atop her pillow, knowing they would find it. Then, she pulled the hood over her face and padded out of the room on quiet feet, praying to the gods above that she would make it out of Castle Orga unseen and unheard.

46
RANIA

Rania Dorcas was left to watch as Weylin Myrkor fled the scene of their mating ceremony like it was a crime he had committed.

Her heart drifted down like petals from a wilting flower, but not because it was broken—because everything she had sacrificed had been for nothing. Because with Weylin's disappearance, her hopes at the title she had been promised disappeared, too.

She knew something was off about the male since she'd met his gaze as she walked down the aisle. They had not been in love, would never be in love as long as Callum Ronan lived, but she knew Weylin well enough to know he was not in his right mind. He was all nerves and heavy breaths and sweat along his brow.

The moment the priestess required him to say those two simple words, he ran. Ran like the coward Rania had feared him to be.

Shame heated her cheeks as she faced the crowd of people that whispered and gasped amongst themselves. She was left with no words for perhaps only the second time in her life. The first being the night that Callum Ronan had kissed her against the very door Weylin had disappeared through.

Everyone looked at her. Waited for her to cry. Waited for her to fall to her knees. Waited for her to shout or scream—to react.

But she could only stand there, waiting for someone to save her. But no one could save her from the mixture of rage and grief and bittersweet relief that enveloped her.

Callum took a step towards her, but the Udar stood up faster, stepping between them and addressing the gathered elves, humans, and dwarves.

Orla followed him before Rania could blink.

Rania opened her mouth to say something to Weylin's father. She closed it again when she remembered it was not her place to explain or apologize for Weylin's actions. If anyone had explaining or apologizing to do, it was the Udar for raising a son who would leave her standing there in this room that was far too full.

"Pardon us," the Udar's voice echoed through the room with a calm that shocked Rania. "We require a moment of your attention. If you will all direct your focus to the hand of the crown, Orla, we can continue past this unfortunate situation."

Rania did not turn towards Orla, but she watched every head in the room turn in the female's direction with confused expressions on their faces. She was sure her own reflected the same sentiment.

She at last looked to her mother, whose cheek was wet with tears. Rania watched Brigid's single eye lock onto the unnerving black-haired female.

Then, her eye went white.

Rania gaped in horror, and she looked about the room to realize everyone else looked the same. Every pair of eyes in the room had rolled back into their heads until only the whites were showing. Rania fought the urge to scream as she turned to look at Callum and saw the white of his eyes staring back at her.

She balled her hands into fists and bit the inside of her cheek, knowing her life was at risk if she challenged the Udar and whatever plan he and that olc female had concocted.

It lasted a moment that seemed to stretch into a lifetime, and then they all went back to normal. Their faces of shock turned into faces of happiness and joy. Whoops and cheers of celebration exploded through the room.

Faolan Myrkor grabbed Rania's arm and whispered in her ear.

"I'll explain later. For now, you keep your damned mouth shut or forfeit your life," the Udar whispered under his breath, only loud enough for Rania to hear, before turning to address the crowd once again. "It is unfortunate that Weylin had to attend to the border dispute between realms before he had the chance to celebrate his mating, but as we all know—duty calls, and Weylin takes that call more seriously than most."

"So, it is up to us to celebrate in his absence," Brigid leapt from her seat in the front row, beaming with pride that shone as bright as the stars. Her tears had dried as if they never existed. Guilt stirred in Rania's stomach. "Join us for a celebratory meal and ball at the other end of the hall in the grand room. To the beautiful new mates that will lead Talam into a new age, outshining any other!"

The room erupted again, so loudly Rania hoped Weylin heard it from wherever he had scurried off too, and wondered what the Hel was going on.

She had only just begun to put the pieces together.

Her mind reeled with it all until it ached in pain, but she plastered on that smile she had spent many moons mastering and bowed before her people.

Faolan had explained it all.

How Orla had used her esos as a pryer to change the memories of every living being in that room to remember a lovely ceremony that ended in a beautiful mating between herself and Weylin Myrkor. They saw what Faolan and Rania needed them to see.

Rania had no idea how Orla had access to her esos, and the Udar had not given her an explanation. She did not dare ask, not in the face of everything else.

Rania's throat had grown tight at the news of the burden she would now carry like a weight upon her shoulders. Faolan had granted her a great weapon in trusting her. She would be a fool to use it against him.

No one would believe her when they all believed the same thing and they all possessed the same memories.

They were told Weylin had to rush away to deal with a dispute between borders. Upon his return, Faolan would fill him in. And Rania knew with that would include a punishment for abandoning her at the altar.

It was not her place to interfere.

And why would she, when she had been granted all that she had ever dreamed of? She was now the mate to the Udar Apparent of the seven worldly realms, as far as anyone was concerned. The news was already spreading beyond the castle walls, and Weylin was still nowhere to be found.

Rania knew Weylin enough to know he would put the pieces together if the news reached his ears before he returned home. He would not dispute it. He would be a fool to.

Weylin Myrkor was many things, but a fool was not one of them.

Rania Dorcas had never thought herself to be one either, not until she stood outside of Callum's door and raised a trembling fist. Her breaths came quick and nervous, and her stomach was uneasy as the first knock echoed through her very bones and the second caused her to take a step back as she waited with bated breath.

The door opened a crack, and Rania faced green eyes that were red with emotion.

"What are you doing here?" His face looked exhausted, and the words came out harsh and dry.

They might have come as a snarl if he had the energy to put such emotion into them.

"Please, can we talk?" She whispered around the thundering of her heart.

She knew her life would be at risk if she was caught outside of his rooms, that night of all nights. If anyone saw her anywhere near Callum Ronan's room, they would immediately tell the Udar, and the Udar would not take kindly to her discrepancy.

It was a secret she could not keep from Callum. It was a secret that could salvage the pieces of themselves they had scattered on the floor in their sacrifices for her ambitions. It was a long shot, but maybe giving him the gift of this secret—maybe it would be enough.

"You're out of your mind." He seethed with nothing but hatred, and Rania winced at the cold of his eyes. "You should be anywhere, and I mean anywhere, but here right now."

"I know. I just need you to hear me out."

"Give me one reason why I should."

"I am not mated."

Callum's brow furrowed, and his eyes narrowed. And the way his eyes wavered—it was enough for her to know she had made her way in. He would open the door for her, that much she was certain of, but how he would react to anything she had to say after that, only the gods could know.

"I saw it all. You mean to tell me that my own eyes deceive me? Surely, you don't think me blind."

"Not your eyes, but your mind."

Something like confusion crossed his face, followed by an understanding that was quickly replaced by a frosty glare once again. Rania felt herself shivering under the look.

The door opened and Rania felt her stomach fall into the stone floor of the castle as her heart floated into her throat.

She slipped in through the thin crack that he had left for her, barely large enough for her to squeeze in through, but it was all the opening she needed.

She heard the door shut behind them. She allowed herself one deep breath, and she gazed out into the starry night sky beyond Callum's windows that were left ajar to allow a light breeze in. The breeze kissed her skin, and she turned to face him again.

"Explain," he demanded, with no warmth in his voice.

He was in his night clothes, a loose white top and dark linen pants. His hair was tossed by the morsels of a restless sleep and bags lined his eyes. Rania suppressed the urge to go to him and caress his face. It was an effort not to wrap her arms around him and sob without giving him any explanation at all.

But Rania Dorcas had made herself stronger than all of that. She was not one to fall apart in the face of situations such as these, so she stayed planted where her feet had landed and opened her mouth to tell him all of it.

She told him how Weylin had dashed from the altar and looks of pity and shock had turned on her. There were gasps and sneers and even cheers as her cheeks heated red and she did not chase after the male. She did not know what had called him from the room in that instant, but she did know she had been left a mess to clean up.

Until Faolan and Orla stepped in and fixed it all. Until she got exactly what she wanted in a nearly impossible way—she owned the title and the name she had been vying for in all the ways that mattered, while saving herself from mating a male she hardly knew. And in turn, saving herself for the man she now stood before, explaining the nearly impossible.

Callum crossed his arms somewhere along the way. He kept his face unreadable in a way she knew had helped earn him a place in the Udar Apparent's personal guard.

When she finished her story, when she had poured everything out before him, he had one question: "And in what world do you expect me to believe such a myth?"

Rania's heart shattered as she opened her mouth to speak but knew her next words would make or break what lay between them. She paused, grasping for anything before it was too late, and then she spoke.

"If you do not believe me, there is nothing I can do to change your mind, for matters such as these exist in invisible ways that I cannot hand to you on a platter. Though, if I could I would," she said, with an acceptance that cleared the desperation she had felt. "What I can say is this: I give you my word, and I give you this promise. Should I speak my words false on this very night, I beg Eabha to remove my eye as she removed my mother's. May her doves rip it from its socket and carry it away to a land I could not find in this realm or any other of this soil, and may I never see the same again."

She had never told Callum what happened to her mother. Rania had sworn she never would. She saw the shock in his eyes at her revelation, but he did not ask questions.

Rania knew Callum was not a man that held an affinity for the gods, so she did not rely on his faith to trust her words. But he knew of *her* allegiance to them, and she hoped that would be enough. He knew she would not say such a thing lightly, not when the memories of her betrothal celebration still seared her dreams into nightmares and her snores into screams in the night's dark.

"I-I believe you. But why would Weylin leave?"

Rania felt a sob of relief lodge in her throat, but she forced it down as she looked up into his eyes and saw the ice melting.

"I wish I could say. I do not have an answer to that."

"I don't know whether to say I'm sorry or congratulations."

Rania smiled and took a step towards him. When he did not balk at her advance. She rested her hand against his cheek and her pulse quickened.

"Just kiss me."

The words escaped her in a breath that was stolen so softly it was as though she was afraid they could cause the world to crash around her.

And when his lips met hers, it felt as though it had.

Nothing else mattered as his arms wrapped around her waist and pulled her to him. She knew they would figure the rest out somehow, but in that moment, all that mattered was her freedom to be there with him.

Rania kissed Callum back and knew with her whole heart that the gods had granted them this gift.

The gift of each other.

47
AISLA

Aisla stole a horse from the stable of Castle Orga. She hoped they would understand.

The wind tore at her braid that flew behind her as she raced into the night with nothing but her silk night dress, her dark brown cloak, her dagger on her thigh, her worn brown boots, a pack of things she had scavenged from the empty kitchen, a half-formed plan, and faith in the note she had left in her wake.

The golden thread continued to compel her, gently but constantly, towards the south. Her heart thundered in her chest. She could feel the thread growing tighter with every moment she and the horse she had come to call Speckle for the white spots littering his light grey coat bounded forward.

Colors blurred together as she raced past them with only the weight of her fate on her mind. She smelled traces of eucalyptus plants and balsam trees in the air of Fomhar. Tears threatened to break, but she did not acknowledge the familiar feeling. Instead, she focused on the anger burning her blood. Aisla clenched her teeth and tightened her grip on the reins.

She tried to think of *anything* other than the golden thread that overrode every thought in her mind. Aisla wanted to weep. She wanted to scream at the gods. She wanted to plead with them—plead for the prophecy to be dropped into her lap or tucked beneath her pillow like the note she had left for Ruairi and Eire.

But the gods had already granted them one miracle, and she didn't expect another anytime soon.

Time passed quicker. The pull grew stronger. Aisla could do nothing but obey its demand as she continued her journey south through the cool days and the cooler nights.

The longer it existed as a part of her, the more she could scent the golden thread. It only confirmed what she already knew when the smell of oak wood and ocean air greeted her like a slap to the face.

The weight of the nine realms bore down on Aisla Iarkis as she pulled her cloak over her head. Her hands shook with nerves, but she clenched them into fists as she lowered herself from Speckle, silently promising him as many carrots as she could gather when they returned to Castle Orga.

Between her studying the map, and her experience traveling with the Udar Apparent, she knew he would arrive soon. She could also feel the tightening of the golden thread that bound her to him. The echo of her footsteps drowned out under the thundering of her heart. She followed the shimmering glint of gold until it was straight and taut, and she knew he was near. Near enough to be dangerous soon.

She wondered if he would come alone, or if he would bring

others. If she knew him at all, she knew his pride would lead him to come alone. He had probably ripped off his bed sheets and stormed through the castle before even thinking or considering a plan of action. She wondered if his new mate woke with him in the middle of the night.

Weylin was reactive, if nothing else, and she would use that to her advantage.

As best as she could.

She concealed herself behind a thick bush and focused on the sounds of the creatures of the night. Her head lolled back, and her shoulders sagged. She let herself get comfortable, but not too comfortable. Her arched ears were alert to every sound and ready to move with anything that felt out of place.

She had one more theory she needed to test, and she had been hesitant to try it given the lack of ash trees on Iomlan. She still possessed that limited supply of esos that lived in her veins until it was used up. And then there would be no way to bring it back. Not until she returned to the ash trees. And Aisla did not know when that would be, so she would use it sparingly—listening to her body and the strain of her esos.

Feel, but still your heart. Think, but ease your mind. Endure, but find your peace.

She repeated the words that were ingrained in her mind in scoil. Aisla breathed in and out. In and out. In and out.

She had to time it just right. She would need to do it just before he got to her, so he would not know exactly where she was, just the general area. So, she could ensure her assumption was correct and that he had arrived alone. If he hadn't, that would certainly cause complications for her, and her back-up plan would have to do.

The steady thump of horse hooves sounded, but still far enough away. She was more thankful than ever for her heightened elven senses as she listened for two beats longer to ensure she heard correctly.

Then, she thought of a fox, stealthy and low. Quiet and quick. Aisla imagined soft paws padding along the earth and whiskers that twitched with each shift in scent. She closed her eyes and thought of small, black ears, and the tiny, yet razor sharp teeth of the creatures. She breathed slowly, imagining her body as a fox's and imagining Eilis's voice guiding her through it all.

She felt her esos rushing to the surface of her skin, and then her bones ached. Her body groaned and burned, and she felt the change happening before she saw it. She slowly opened her eyes that saw the world slightly differently. The night was brighter through them.

Her heart raced with the thrill of her success until she looked down at paws that were larger than a fox's. They were the paws of a wolf.

The irony was not lost on her as she awaited the Udar Apparent. The Young Wolf himself.

It could have been worse. She reminded herself. She could have transformed into a wyvern or a bear, and it would have been even harder to conceal.

Aisla looked down again and joy flooded through her when she noticed her golden thread had disappeared with her transformation. Just as she hoped.

She stalked through the woods, staying behind the brush, and growing familiar with movement in that foreign and unfamiliar form. She was thankful that by the look of her legs and paws she was a black wolf, not white—it made it easier for her to hide in the dark of the night. Her goal was to stay hidden, to evaluate the situation, before executing her plan.

For once, I don't think your plan is terrible. Muinin's raspy voice entered her mind and there was comfort in hearing it. It didn't pull on her esos the way shifting had. And she was grateful for that.

That's because you helped me come up with it.

I know, perhaps you should ask for help more often.

You would like that, wouldn't you? Aisla teased back.

I only wish you would've kept in the part where I got to play a role.

We both know now is not the time.

I know, I know. Maybe next time.

Maybe next time, Aisla agreed.

Aisla settled in behind a different bush on the other side of the clearing. She took her pack in her mouth, holding it gently, careful not to puncture it with her too sharp canines.

He came into view at last, seated atop Eolas. Her stomach stirred at the familiar sight of his face.

He looked exhausted, but angry. His features were set with the same stoic look he had worn so often as Fenian.

She remembered the way his eyes would crease when he laughed. And the way his face lit up when he smiled. It was rare, but she knew it had not been faked. Aisla relied on that part of him to hope he would hear her out. Even if just for a moment.

A moment was all she needed.

She prayed to the gods Weylin Myrkor could not hear the beating of her heart as she started to doubt every step of her fragile plan, but it was far too late to change anything about it now.

Aisla perked her wolf ears and listened carefully. He had come alone as she had expected—as she had hoped. She waited until he and Eolas were deeper into the woods, and then she willed herself back into her own skin, and slowly she changed once again.

The moment she shifted, the golden thread appeared again. She had given herself enough distance to prepare herself before he chased to her hiding spot.

She slipped back into her dress from her pack and strapped her blade back to her thigh. It was no *Oidhe*, but it would do. Aisla stepped beyond the bush.

"Didn't get enough of me last time I found myself in Iomlan?" Aisla called out, feigning a confidence she very much did not feel.

She thanked the gods that her voice did not so much as quiver.

Weylin Myrkor's eyes widened as he took her in, and he blinked once, and the golden thread disappeared. Relief rushed through Aisla.

His lips curled into a smile that she could not read the sincerity in the dark of the night.

"Something like that," he replied, and slipped off the side of Eolas.

48
WEYLIN

Weylin had known the moment the thread pulled him from his altar where it would lead him. Or rather, to whom it would lead him.

But he still could not help but feel shock and fear as he stared at the *mallaithe* herself. His gods-chosen searc—his true mate.

Everything he had ever known seemed to fall apart on his trek north. The life he thought he would live now seemed a world away.

He had stayed in his tent whenever he rested, avoiding any semblance of civilization.

Weylin had stopped as little as he could, only raiding village markets and taverns in the dark of the night when he was sure no one was around. He was unable to ignore the incessant tug of the golden thread that had disappeared at last. It had disappeared the moment she had revealed herself to him once again. The moment the wind stole the air from his lungs.

"I hear a congratulations is in order," Aisling spoke again in that cool tone of hers, and he wondered how she felt so calm with everything that this meant.

Weylin wondered if she even knew what it meant.

She looked as ethereal as ever—stronger even, as if she had come into herself since he had last seen her. But there was still that tinge of a feral look in her yellow-green eyes that writhed with the fire of the gods.

It was the first time he had seen her in a gown, even though it was a thin one meant for sleeping. It was the first time he had met Aisling Iarkis as herself. And he couldn't help but acknowledge how exquisite she was. How her otherworldly beauty and grace radiated, rivaling the light of the moons above.

He acknowledged it, and he hated it. He hated it as much as he hated her. He hated it as much as the feeling that seared through his blood when he had watched her fly away atop her wyvern, leaving his castle in disarray and the bodies of his laochs on the castle floor.

But when he thought of Ellora and those nights spent together, he couldn't bring himself to hate that female. He had yet to reconcile the two, and the emotions continued to war as he worked to conceal them from his eyes.

He met her wild gaze. It was all too familiar, but there was no black blood of barghests littering the surrounding woods.

And she was no helpless female for him to save.

He understood now that pull he had felt when he first heard her screams in a forest in Briongloid. The signs had been there all along, but he hadn't known how to find them. Now that he couldn't ignore it, the pull towards her was that much stronger. And his need for her ran as deep as his distaste of her.

"No need," he responded equally calmly, as he took a step towards her. Eolas chuffed in warning or in greeting, he did not know. "Your little stunt pulled me from my own mating ceremony."

He almost felt satisfaction at the shock that crossed her features. It took her a moment for her to regain her composure, and he stepped closer again. She did not falter at his approach. He noted the glint of a blade she held gripped in her left hand.

Fire blazed through his very blood as he neared her. A fire he could not read.

"I heard you're mated."

"You heard wrong."

He watched her frantically putting the pieces together and waited.

"Did you know it was me? The golden thread?"

"Call it what it is, *Aisling*," he continued until he was a sword's length away from her. He could feel the heat radiating from her body as the air tightened around them. "*Searc*. We have been declared as searc by the norns. True heart mates—equal to each other. Something we have not seen in the worldly realms in a very, very long time. The norns have irrevocably bound our threads together. Now, what are we to do with that?"

"Well, I'm certainly not going back to your father, who has already sent his ships to my home."

"For what it's worth, I was away when he made that decision," Weylin replied, hoping to keep her anger at bay.

They needed calm minds to discuss what this would mean for the realms. And he would need her on his side if his plan was to work.

"Don't play innocent with me," she snarled back at him, clutching her dagger tighter.

"You left your people behind?" He changed the direction of the conversation, cursing himself for showing cracks in the relationship with his father when it clearly hadn't worked.

"Do *not* speak to me of my people." She curled her lip back and bared her teeth at him as that familiar fire flared brighter in her yellow-green eyes. "We both know how it ends when we draw our blades, so for your benefit, I'll offer you a deal. Not an alliance, but a deal. One that will allow you to leave this clearing alive."

Weylin's interest was piqued as he saw her first tell of nervousness. She rubbed her sweaty palms on her dress.

"I'm listening."

"I'll give you the ring your father so desperately desires, *if* you withdraw your people from Eilean and give me nine full moons in Sneachta to live and stall the war. At the end of nine moons, if I have not found the fully translated and correct prophecy, I will surrender myself to you."

It wasn't a bad deal. It was a deal that made sense, and they would both benefit from. He knew little of the ring she spoke of, and again wondered how much his father had been keeping from him, but the rest of it was almost logical.

And Weylin was a logical man.

"And if you do find the prophecy?"

"Then I swear to share it the moment it is in my hands. It will provide clarity on how I—*we*—truly save the realms. Whether that is saving or ending my life."

"Come now, *banphrionsa*." He did not miss the way she stood up straighter at the familiar nickname. He grinned. "We both know the whispers on the wind know enough of the prophecy to call for your death in order to save the world as we know it."

"But what if you're wrong? Put aside your arrogance long enough to consider that. If I am the solution and not the demise, the moment you kill me you've gambled it all away. Give me nine moons to be certain."

Weylin glanced at her and saw the determination there. She was an immovable force, and his only other option was to take her down himself. And he had seen her fight—he knew what the female was capable of, and did not know that he would leave with his life. At anyone else's hands, he would have led with confidence. In this, he did not know, and that was too much of a risk.

She took a step closer to him, closing the distance until she was forced to look up to meet his gaze. Their heartbeats thundered in unison as he couldn't help but remember how her lips felt against his and wonder if it came to her mind, too.

How could it not, given what they now knew? Given that she was his searc and no other love in all the realms could ever compare. Or so it was said. But Weylin had long wondered if he would ever be capable of love.

"If you're going to kill me, *do it*," she challenged in a whisper that carried on the wind. "But just know I'll demand one final favor from the gods when I meet them. One favor in exchange for the part in their game that my entire existence was. I will drop to my knees and plead with them if I must. I will beg them to turn me into whatever it is that Weylin Myrkor fears the most, and I will return to the worldly realms to make your life as miserable as your family has made mine."

The challenge sent a chill down his spine.

"What if you are what I fear the most?"

"Then I shall demand they return me in a form none other than this one," she hissed the words with all the malice in the world, but something told him she did not truly feel it. She could not, given the thread that bound them.

And he acknowledged in that moment something he had known since the moment he first laid eyes upon her.

He bent down slightly and leaned forward until their noses brushed. Her eyes flickered back and forth between his, blazing with fire cold as ice.

"I could never hurt you," he whispered.

In the same moment, pain seared through his thigh. He bit back a shout of pain as he realized she had stabbed him with her blade.

He had been too trusting.

"And I could never *kill* you," she responded in a voice hardly above a whisper.

Weylin knew she meant it, but they had said two very different things. She leaned up and blinked once at him, allowing their lips to brush for the briefest of moments, before Weylin collapsed to the forest floor.

His body had lost all feeling, and his limbs no longer obeyed his will. The *mallaithe* had poisoned him, again. The wound she had inflicted would not cause permanent damage, but he was now entirely at her mercy.

His eyes fluttered as he tried to focus on her. He looked at the light array of freckles that danced across her face. He traced them with his eyes until the details blurred and he could no longer make them out.

Shadows emerged from the woods around her. She was an ember engulfed in darkness.

It was the last thing he saw before his eyes fell shut and he was at the mercy of his enemy.

49

AISLA

Guilt wracked through Aisla as the pieces of her delicate plan fell into place.

Everything had happened exactly as she had hoped it would.

Or almost exactly.

She had confronted him and relied on his emotional state to make him weak, but she had too much rage from her ancestors to fall to the whims of the norns.

Then, she stalled—voicing her bluff that Weylin did not know was a bluff—until she knew Ruairi and Eire would appear.

The note she left on her borrowed silk pillowcase confessed everything.

Well, everything that they needed to know.

Aisla had not felt the necessity in telling them what Weylin Myrkor was to her. She shared only that she knew where the Young Wolf would be, and had to take advantage of the moment. She wrote that she had been granted a vision from the gods, borrowing from Eire's miracle even though the lie made her palms sweat. When Aisla asked them to trust her, she knew they would. And she had faith in them to convince Eimear to trust her as well.

She asked them to follow her, but keep their distance. Aisla did not want Ruairi's scent on her, in case the Young Wolf remembered it. Aisla didn't want any hint that she arrived with company, so he thought he could trust her.

In so many words, she told them she would need back up for her plan. A plan that would bring the Udar Apparent into their custody.

The greatest hostage they could ever hold.

In the same moment Aisla's heart shattered with the weight of what she had done—as she battled the urge to fall to the ground she watched the Young Wolf collapse against as his eyelids slowly shut— she felt immense relief that kept her on her feet when Ruairi, Eire, Eimear, and a few others emerged from the shadows of the midnight woods.

It had worked.

At what cost, Aisla did not know. What the betrayal made her, she could not say.

Aisla balled her shaking fists at her sides, and took a step away from the Udar Apparent, and towards her friends.

She found Eire's soft eyes first. Needing that gentle reassurance. Needing her constant love. Needing a reminder that she was still there.

"Thank you," Aisla said quietly in the same instant that Eire strode forward and did not hesitate to wrap her arms around Aisla's waist.

The embrace was a gesture that tore through the thread of composure Aisla had been clinging to. She allowed the full weight of her body to fall against Eire, knowing she could handle it. Aisla burrowed her face into her friend's curly black hair that still smelled of home. Her throat burned with tears she refused to shed.

She knew they wouldn't understand it. And Aisla didn't have the capacity to explain. She untangled herself from the warmth of her longest friend and took a step back to meet the expectant audience. She carefully avoided Ruairi's curious green gaze.

"Thank you all for trusting me," Aisla spoke louder and gave a small nod.

No one spoke as they approached the Udar Apparent's unconscious form. Aisla turned away as they bound his hands. She could not bring herself to watch—like the coward she was. They all pretended not to notice, and for that she was grateful.

Ruairi walked by her and laid a comforting hand on her back. "You did the right thing," he whispered.

Aisla swallowed. She nodded again.

They set Weylin Myrkor on the horse with Eimear's eldest brother, Sorin Shea. The poison would last until sunrise, and by then he would be at their mercy already, and that was all that they needed. Aisla had packed valerian root if he woke up fighting.

Aisla hoped Eimear had explained it all to her parents. She hoped she was correct in trusting the Sheas to keep Weylin Myrkor as her hostage in this war. There were so many pieces of her plan that rested in hope, but it was all that she had.

Aisla rode Eolas, thankful for the familiarity they shared from their previous journey together. She lingered at the back of their travelling party, wanting time to herself. She had hardly spoken. She could hardly bear to when Ruairi and Eire looked at her with eyes full of concern, but there was nothing she could give them.

Not yet.

There was so much for her to process. She had not expected wounds of her own to blossom when she drove her poison-dipped blade into his leg. She had not expected to allow their lips to touch, even if it was only for a moment. There was so much emotion in it, she almost wished it had lasted longer.

Aisla could feel herself breaking, and she willed herself to hold it together until she could get back to the room that had been loaned to her.

She was a leader to these people. She needed to keep that front if they were to trust Weylin Myrkor's future in her hands and with her plan. If she let herself falter, and if she let it show, she knew they would take matters into their own hands, and they far outnumbered her.

But this was her war to make.

And she was not backing down, even if it cost her everything that she had and everything that she was.

Whichever came first.

TAISTEALAI

It had taken little convincing to get the norns to agree to his plan.

Not after the liberties Sionna had taken to stir the pot.

The moment the dark prince had abandoned his post, they all knew Sionna had gone rogue. And the events that preceded his disappearance reeked of the viper goddess.

She left behind all semblance of the plan she had agreed to with the norns nine generations ago, and every promise she had ever made to her siblings and her parents.

Although, gods were rarely known to keep their promises.

Taistealai arrived to Crann Na Beatha the same moment the prince had arrived to Castle Orga. He had requested the parchment he now carried in his aching mouth, and they had given it to him. They had already known what he would request when he arrived. It had been prepared for him.

The ink was fresh upon the parchment. It was long past time for the *Gheall Ceann* to begin to put the pieces of her own story together.

The norns and the gods and even Taistealai himself owed her that much from all that they had put her through.

Taistealai had visited the home of the gods just a few sunrises ago, and the place had been in absolute disarray.

Sides had been chosen by everyone except for Eabha, who was notably absent from it all. Rather unfortunately, the sides had been split right down the middle of the remaining eight gods, with not one willing to budge or hear logic from the other side.

This war would be one that would shatter Talam as they knew it. One way or the other, they would ring in a new age or destroy the realms entirely. All depending on how Aisling Iarkis played the cards that she had been dealt.

And while Taistealai was forbidden from directly interfering, delivering her the prophecy was the best he could think to do.

He was not to be seen nor heard. That had been made clear to him by the norns.

It felt all too familiar—this turning of the tide.

That upheaval of change that could not be undone, followed by his sharing of the words he had held on to longer than any secret he had been asked to protect before.

And there had been many.

Taistealai had squirmed at the news of the searc binding the two forces of Talam. The norns had held that secret so close to their own chests that even he had not been let in on it. He was uncertain if it would be a good or a bad thing, only that it would play into the prophecy for better or for worse.

A certain sense of pride had filled him when he saw the *Gheall Ceann* make her move. Even though he had never met the female, he felt connected to her from all the years he had watched her change and grow from the shadows.

Castle Orga was cool, like an autumnal breeze that brushed

through Taistealai's dense russet fur. He shook his ears out as he crept along the dark corners of corridor after corridor until the scent of the *Gheall Ceann* led him to the dungeons of the castle. His heart skipped a beat, as his entire plan relied on her being asleep.

If worse came to worst, he would wait until she went to her rooms to find sleep and follow her there. But every breath he spent there increased his risk of getting caught—and he did not know what his punishment would be if he did get caught, and preferred not to find out.

The cement stairs felt cold as ice against the pads of Taistealai's small feet as his curiosity got the better of him, and he descended the stairs down into the dungeon, the darkness increasing with every step he took. He stayed in close to the column that ran up through the spiral stairs, ready to hide if need be, but he did not hear any movement from either end of the stairs.

Taistealai finally reached the bottom, and his breath came in heaves that he had to work to silence. He continued to follow the scent that led him there until he reached the very end of a long hall. He passed metal doors that he was not nearly tall enough to see into the window of.

Everything was closed off and locked away until he came upon a vast cell at the end of the curved corridor that was tucked into the corner and had one wall of intersecting bars facing towards him. Taistealai ducked down beneath the cover of the dark and peered at the scene before him.

The male who had become a piece in the *Gheall Ceann's* scheme to stay alive lie sleeping on a bed within the cell. It was against the back wall, but it was not a typical prisoner's bed. It was ornate, and the cell had a table and a proper toilet. Even an armchair and a desk. The male may be a prisoner here, but he was obviously a welcomed one.

Something ancient and untouched fractured in Taistealai's small heart when he noted the bundle of blankets nestled outside of the cell door. And he knew without having to scent her that the *Gheall Ceann* slept beneath them. He watched the steady rise and fall of the mound that her light brown hair spilled out of like branches on a winter tree.

His throat tied into a knot as he silently crossed the hall to her and tucked the piece of parchment beneath her.

Taistealai did not know what to make of the scene. He did not know whether it made her weaker or stronger in his eyes to find her this way, sleeping outside the cell of her searc. The same searc whose family would sooner see her die than live.

He did not know why, but a hope swelled within his aching chest as he scaled the stairs towards the light of the midnight castle.

A hope that could prove him a fool.

THANK YOU FOR READING
BLOOD OF EMBER

Share your feedback on social media using #CrownsOfTalam. I would love to hear from you! Connect with me on Instagram and TikTok @LEVanVeen. To keep in touch and be the first to hear news about the third book in The Crowns of Talam series, scan the QR code to visit my website and scroll to the bottom to join my email list!

If you enjoyed *Blood of Ember*, please consider leaving an honest review on Goodreads, Amazon, or any platform of your choosing. Your feedback is so important to me and helps indie authors reach a larger audience!

PRONUNCIATION GUIDE + GLOSSARY

World Lore:

Airgead [*air • eh • gid*] — currency of Talam

Atruach [*ah • tru • uh*] —an honor binding agreement

Anamacha [*on • om • ah • huh*] — souls

Anamarbh [*on • om • arb*] — Faolan's sword

Aosta [*ee • sta*] — the ancient tongue

Arden [*are • den*] — the true throne

Baile [*ball • luh*] — houses in cities

Banphrionsa [*bon • frin • suh*] – term of old for princess

Barghest [*bar • guest*] — wolf-like beast; malicious children of Ifreann

Braon [*breen*] — one of the dual moons of Talam

Banrion [*bon • reen*] — term of old for queen

Crann Na Beatha [*cron, nuh, bah • ha*] — the tree of life

Dioluine [*dee • loo • nay*] — immunity herb

Eitilt Go Maith [*eh • tilt, go, ma*] — term of old for "fly well"

Esos [*ess • ohs*] — magic

Fior [*fee • er*] — Ruairi's sword

Gheall Ceann [*gal, kee • own*] — the promised one

Laoch [*lee • ock*] — warrior

Lofa [*loff • uh*] — disease plaguing Eilean

Mallaithe [*mall • uh • hey*] — term of old for cursed

Mathair [*mo • her*] — ruler of Eilean

Nimhebas [*neeve • bas*] — death poison

Norns [*norns*] — ancient beings who name and prophesy the fate of each elf upon birth; they also know the fate of all beings, mortal and immortal

Nua [*new • ah*] — the common tongue

Oidhe [*oy • de • hey*] — Aisla's dagger given to her by Ruairi

Priomh [*preeve*] — a chief in a tribal community

Puball [*puh • bull*] — tent structures, often found in villages

Realta [*rell • tah*] — the crown of stars; the Mathair's crown

Ri [*ree*] — term of old for queen

Scoil [*scoll*] — school for elves

Searc [*shark*] — true mates

Sneachta [*sh • knock • tuh*] — one of the dual moons of Talam

Speartha [*spare • tha*] — the crown of skies; the Udar's crown

Stoirme [*ster • rum*] — Aisla and Ruairi's ship

Teigh [*chay*] — used to urge a horse forward

Uamhan [*oo • on*] — Weylin's sword

Udar [*oo • der*] — ruler of all seven worldly realms

Undine [*un • deen*] — sirens that live in deep waters; malicious children of Muir

Valerian [*val • air • ee • in*] — herb that causes drowsiness

Names:

Aileen Shea [*ay • leen, shay*] — Lady of Fomhar

Aisling (Aisla) Iarkis [*ash • ling, (ash • la), ee • ark • iss*] — the promised one

Aine Iarkis [*awn • ya, ee • ark • iss*] — Aisla's mother

Brendan Dorcas [*bren • den, door • cass*] — Lord of Briongloid

Brigid Dorcas [*bridge • id, door • cass*] — Lady of Briongloid

Callum Ronan [*cal • um, roan • in*] — captain of the Udar Apparent's personal guard

Cillian [*kill • ian, shay*] — Deaglan Shea's middle son

Cliona Iarkis [*clee • own • uh, ee • ark • iss*] — Mathair of Eilean

Comhbha [*co • wa*] — Eire's wyvern

Conroy Myrkor [*con • roy, mur • core*] — Weylin's uncle

Corren Kyne [*core • ren, kine*] — Lord Apparent of Earrach

Deaglan Shea [*deck • lin, shay*] — Lord of Fomhar

Eilis [*isle • esh*] — guardian of the library of the Silenced World Tellers

Eimear Shea [*ee • mur, shay*] —Deaglan Shea's eldest daughter

Eire Trygg [*air • uh, trig*] — Aisla's best friend

Eolas [*o • liss*] — one of Weylin's horses

Faolan Myrkor [*fay • lan, mur • core*] — Udar of the seven worldly realms

Feargal Iarkis [*ferr • gal, ee • ark • iss*] — Aisla's father

Gaotha [*gwee • ha*] — Ruairi's wyvern

Halli Shea [*hal • lee, shay*] — Deaglan Shea's youngest daughter

Intinn [*in • chin*] — one of Eabha's doves

Laisren [*lays • rin*] — Priomh of Spiorad

Luas [*loo • iss*] — one of Weylin's horses

Maira [may • ra] — Eimear's gryphon

Muinin [*mun • een*] — Aisla's wyvern

Oisin Dorcas [*oh • sheen, door • cass*] — heir to the seat in Briongloid

Rania Dorcas [*ruh • knee • uh, door • cass*] — daughter of the Lord of Briongloid

Roark [*rork*] — Deaglan Shea's youngest son

Ruairi Vilulf [*roo • ree, vill • ulf*] — Aisla's best friend

Sinead Bracken [*shin • aid, brack • en*] — bartender in Briseadhceo

Smaoinigh [*smwe • chee*] — one of Eabha's doves

Sorin [*soar • in*] — Lord Apparent of Fomhar

Taistealai [*tash • tuh • lee*] — messenger between the worldly realms and the otherly realms

Weylin Myrkor [*way • lynn, mur • core*] — Udar Apparent of the seven worldly realms

Gods/Goddesses:

Airdeall [*are • dull*] — goddess of the heavens; protector of the gods

Cion [*key • un*] — god of beauty, love, and fate

Eabha [*ay • va*] — goddess of wisdom, mother of the gods

Ifreann [*if • run*] — god of death and Hel

Leighis [*lay • sh*] — goddess of healing, harvest, and hunt

Muir [*moor*] — god of waters

Realta [*ray • all • ta*] — goddess of the sun, moons, and stars

Sionna [*see • on • uh*] — goddess of mischief and war

Taran [*tear • in*] — goddess of thunder and justice; protector of humanity

Locations:

Albios [*all • bee • oss*] — the heavens; one of the two otherly realms

Anseo [*ann • show*] — mid-sized city in Samhradh

Bitu [*bite • oo*] — northeastern worldly realm

Blathriel [*blath • ree • ell*] — capital of Earrach

Briongloid [*bring • loyd*] — southwestern worldly realm

Briseadhceo [*brish • oo • cho*] — mid-sized city in Briongloid

Caillte [*call • chuh*] — capital of Eilean

Cluain [*clu • en*] — small city outside of Omra

Cruthu [*cruh • who*] — castle in Bitu

Deithe [*day • thuh*] — dense forest at the top of Crann Na Beatha in Albios

Eagla [*ogg • luh*] — castle in Samhradh

Earrach [*are • rah*] — southeastern worldly realm

Eilean [*eye • lee • an*] — an island to the southwest of Iomlan; in exile following the War for Descendants; one of the seven worldly realms

Farraige [*far • uh • gay*] — castle in Eilean

Fas [*foss*] — castle in Earrach

Fomhar [*fove • err*] — northwestern worldly realm

Fuar [*for*] — capital of Geimhrigh

Geimhrigh [*gev • ree*] — northern most worldly realm

Hallamor [*haul • uh • moor*] — the capital of Albios; home of Eabha and Cion; meeting place of the gods

Hel [*hell*] — the underworld; one of the two otherly realms

Iomlan [*um • lawn*] — the main continent

Oighear [*ire*] — castle in Geimhrigh

Omra [*ome • ruh*] — capital of Samhradh

Orga [*ore • gah*] — castle in Fomhar

Samhradh [*sour • rah*] — southernmost worldly realm

Scamall [*scom • ull*] — capital of Briongloid

Scamhog [*ska • wog*] — capital of Bitu

Speir [*spare*] — midsized city in Briongloid

Spiorad [*spear • id*] — village on Briongloid and Samhradh border

Sruthar [*suh • roo • thar*] — capital of Fomhar

Talam [*tall • um*] — the world that consists of the seven worldly realms and the two otherly realms

Trasnu [*trass • new*] — small coastal city in Briongloid

Tromlui [*trom • ly*] — castle in Briongloid

Tus [*toos*] — forest in Caillte near the northern coast

Tusnua [*toos • new • ah*] — ocean between Eilean and Iomlan

COMING SOON

Don't miss book three in the Crowns of Talam series as Aisla's journey continues in

SHARDS OF WIND

Coming 2025

Acknowledgments

If writing my debut novel was a test, writing its sequel was a trial.

I learned so much from drafting, editing, writing, revising, and finally publishing *Under Cold Moons*. I was eager to dive into the next installment of the story and apply my discoveries. Imposter syndrome reared its ugly head within moments of writing "Prologue" on the page in a new and terrifying way. Through the voices of characters I have come to know and love, I found my feet again, and the journey they took me on was unlike anything else I've ever experienced. I trusted Aisla, Weylin, Rania, Ruairi, Eire, Callum, Muinin, and Taistealai to guide the pages of *Blood of Ember,* and hope you enjoy the end result as much as I enjoyed stumbling into it.

I can confidently say Talam would not exist without the consistent comfort, grace, and encouragement from my loving husband, Eron. Every fear I encountered, all of the anxiety-induced tears and the whispers of self-doubt were diminished in the face of his unwavering belief in me and my world. I appreciate you meeting every moment of jubilant celebration with enough joy to match my own.

Thank you to my mum, who reminds me to listen for the birds and look for the stars and find peace in the simple everyday moments. To my grandparents for their guidance and unconditional love. And to Caeh, for your support and words of affirmation. I am truly blessed to have a family that allowed me to dream, and gave me the confidence to chase those dreams.

Yoshi, Obi, and Luna—my four-legged children who keep me on

my toes and inspire me with their own big personalities and consistent company.

Jade, thank you for being the best friend and being there for me in every step of this journey, helping me work through obstacles and celebrate milestones. I've never had a sister, but the closest I've come is Kat. Thank you for keeping me humble and always being down for a sweet treat. And thank you to Koula, Basile, Zaharoula, and Devon for being my second family.

Ireland, for being the first person to finish *Blood of Ember*. Thank you for your love, friendship, and encouragement that has a way of making me feel so fulfilled. Zoe, I am so grateful you were my first ever writing partner, and I appreciate you standing by Talam since its origin. And to all of my longtime friends who share a passion for the written word: Ricki, Kate, Britton, Faith, Victoria, Sievey, Beasley, Jasmine, and Taylor, thank you for inspiring me. Thank you, Erica, for every motivating pep talk, and every shared laugh.

To the new friends I have made through publishing my debut novel: Therese, Desiree, Kona, Susanna, Grace, Candice, Sarah, Isabel, Kate, Erin, Allison, Samantha, Kristen, Karina, Amanda, Maria, and everyone else who has given *The Crowns of Talam* a chance—please know you gave me the courage to continue. And to my fellow author friends who motivate me in new ways every day, Sarah, Bex, Victoria, and Chelsey Ann, I am endlessly grateful.

Without the wonderfully creative hands of Kelly Guthauser, Becky Wallace, Noah Sky, Alyssa Hurlbert, Veronica O'Neill, Sarah Mori, Dakota, and Drew Flanagan, this novel would have never found it's way into the world. I am so grateful to the voices of the professors that helped me find my own in UNCW's Creative Writing department, Nina de Gramont, Emily Smith, Tim Bass, Bekki Lee, David Gessner, Sayantani Dasgupta, and Michael Ramos.

My 2022 trip to Ireland and Scotland allowed me to bring Talam to life at last, and getting to return in 2024 is something I was so blessed to do. I am thankful for Norse and Gaelic mythology and culture, which inspire the lore and language of the nine realms.

To anyone that has made it this far, thank you for continuing this adventure with me, and I look forward to our next chapter.

Finally, and most importantly, I give praise to my Heavenly Father for the passions he has given me, and the way he has held my hand every step of the way.

About the Author

L.E. Van Veen lives with her husband and three dogs in Coastal North Carolina, although she spends a good deal of time lost in fictional lands. She has enjoyed stories set in different worlds for as long as she can remember, and has long dreamed of building her own. After studying Creative Writing at UNC Wilmington, she began work on her debut novel, *Under Cold Moons*, a YA fantasy novel inspired by years spent dreaming.